Four Children for the Emperor
Four elements at war
An Empire forged of honor
A throne forged of steel

Darkness shall drive them
Storms shall tear them apart
At the Empire's edge they stand
Stop wind, stop hope, stop breath.

Four Children of the Empire
And one by one they fall.
Blood shall bind their fates
And blood shall free them all.

THE FOUR WINDS SAGA

WIND
of
TRUTH

REE SOESBEE

WIND OF TRUTH
©2003 Wizards of the Coast, Inc.

Cover art by Stephen Daniele
First Printing: December 2003
Library of Congress Catalog Card Number: 2003100849

9 8 7 6 5 4 3 2 1

US ISBN: 0-7869-3045-4
UK ISBN: 0-7869-3046-2
620-17997-001-EN

U.S., CANADA,   EUROPEAN HEADQUARTERS
ASIA, PACIFIC, & LATIN AMERICA   Wizards of the Coast, Belgium
Wizards of the Coast, Inc.   T Hofveld 6d
P.O. Box 707   1702 Groot-Bijgaarden
Renton, WA 98057-0707   Belgium
+1-800-324-6496   +322 467 3360

Visit our web site at **www.wizards.com**

PROLOGUE

The Empress's scream echoed through the abandoned hall-ways of the palace; her first and only cry during the difficult birth. For more than three days, she and her handmaidens had been sequestered with a midwife in the her private chambers. Outside, the hallways were empty, kept barren so that none would hear the pained cries of a woman in the throes of birth. Nevertheless, Empress Kaede bore the agony and long, suffering hours without any sound other than soft requests for water or another cool towel for her forehead. She, like her ancestors before her, had a spirit of strength. Her lone cry of pain marked the end of the birth as the child slid forth at last into the midwife's hands.

"The child is here," one of the handmaidens murmured soothingly to Kaede as the Empress fell back onto her pillows. Kaede smiled, half-understanding, then lapsed into uncon-sciousness. The handmaiden watched as the midwife drew the child from its mother and cradled it in a warm cloth.

Other children would already be kicking in the midwife's hands, but this one was silent and still. Moreover, the child was covered, head to foot, in a thick, pale shroud that shielded its form from the outer world.

"A caul," gasped one of Kaede's young handmaidens in awe. "He wears a caul! It is a sign!" She fluttered her hands in an invocation to the spirits and then clung in fear to the hem of the Empress's robe. Several other young women whispered their own prayers, gathering closely around the midwife to stare at the unmoving child.

Shooing the younger women away, the plump midwife placed the baby upon a wooden table where hot water and more cloths awaited. She drew a black-hilted knife from her belt and cut away the embryonic wrapping that swaddled the child like a thick, cloudy veil. "It is a sign that the child cannot yet breathe!" she said in a practical tone as she slid her knife though the tough lining. Gently, she drew the child forth from its shroud. The gauzy covering fell away with a soft sigh of air.

The child lay still on the table, exposed and unmoving as the midwife cut its cord and washed its face with warm towels. The babe was a boy. A perfect boy, with a shock of white hair covering the crown of his head and two perfect hands clenched together as if in prayer. His skin was bluish, tinged with lack of breath, and he did not shiver despite the cold air of the room.

"He's not moving," said one of the wide-eyed maidens behind the midwife. "The child is born dead!"

"Don't say that," the midwife chastised. The midwife clenched her teeth, praying to the kami to save her from such stupidity. White hair. A strange blessing must be upon this child. Few in Rokugan were born with white hair, and those among the Crane Clan considered it to be a special mark of favor from ancient heroes. The Crane even dyed their hair white in hopes of receiving such a blessing, but this child was no Crane. Born of the Emperor and Empress, his lineage hailed from cold Phoenix mountains and rich Lion plains. Such a mark was highly unusual. Great power lay within this child's frail body. The midwife redoubled her efforts to bring the child to life, but it seemed to resist all her attempts. She lifted the child, striking it gently to encourage the first intake of breath, but it did not move. The boy hung from her grasp by one ankle, his other leg crossed at the knee, his hands clasped against his forehead in an attitude of meditation. The midwife struck the child again, hoping to jar it into breathing, but there was no response.

At last, the midwife leaned back upon her knees, looking down with sorrow at the still form of the child. She had tried everything—cleaned its lips and nose, tried to start blood flowing in its tiny limbs through warmth and chafing, struck it to cause an intake of air—everything she could think of. It had been too long without breath. There was no further need to try. The child had already passed into the heavens, without even pausing on the firmament of the world.

"Dead!" the other handmaidens cried. "The child is dead!"

Ignoring the whimpering girl, the midwife placed the babe on the table, cleaning it again as if to try and coerce life into the still form through sheer tenacity. Behind her, one of the handmaidens fled from the room, running out the doorway toward the main halls of the palace. The girl's frantic weeping echoed in the empty corridor, her retreating footfalls like the scattered fall of autumn leaves before a winter wind.

The midwife lifted the boy again and looked with great sorrow at the tiny body. Though her second child, he was the first son of the Empress and, at last, a male heir for the throne. The nation had celebrated for three days in anticipation, praying to the kami that the child might be a boy. Now, the prayers of a nation had been answered, but to no avail.

The babe lay in her arms, still and silent, hands tight together and eyes closed in death beneath that shocking fall of white hair. "I am sorry, little one," the midwife whispered. "You must return, too soon, to the void."

"Let me . . . hold him." The Empress's voice was weak, but the mere sound of it silenced the flurry of whispers from the maidens assembled at her side. Kaede lifted her head from her pillows, once more aware of her surroundings. It was as if something had called her from her sleep, denying her the rest she desperately needed. The mother could always tell when something was wrong with her newborn child, the midwife knew. It was some ancient instinct, perhaps guided by the ancestors of old.

The midwife sighed and wrapped the unbreathing baby in a clean cloth. Carrying him with a gentle hand, she walked from the table to the birthing-cot and knelt beside Kaede's pale form. "He did not make the transition into this world, Empress-sama." The midwife bowed. "Your son is at peace within the Great Void." Although she knew well that all the words in Rokugan could not ease the pain of a stillborn child, the midwife still felt the need to say them. She slid the tiny little form into Kaede's arms, laying the child against its mother's breast for the first—and last—time.

"Nonsense," the Empress said with a small smile as she looked down at the silent babe. "He is not dead."

The midwife's eyebrows raised in surprise. The child was not breathing. His skin was blue. Was the mother experiencing some form of delusion? But . . . this was the Empress, and she was a powerful shugenja and priestess in her own right. It would not be appropriate to contradict—

A whisper of wind flowed restlessly through the room once more, and Kaede looked up. "You are right, sister," she said quietly to the air, "he is not alive, either."

"Who . . . who are you speaking to, Empress-sama?" the midwife ventured fearfully.

"The Oracles. They are here, watching." Kaede smiled, and drew her child closer to her breast. "His birth is auspicious, indeed. They have come . . . to see him live."

The midwife glanced about nervously at this proclamation, but saw nothing more than a handful of weeping handmaidens, the Empress, and an empty room. Still, the room seemed somehow fuller despite the wind that ruffled her hair from some unseen window. It was as if the walls themselves stretched outward to hold more than those who stood upon this world.

"Bring me your knife." Kaede ordered, and the midwife rushed to obey. Around the room, the handmaidens wept and moaned in small piles as another roaming wind blew in through the open doorway. Without pausing to close the thin rice-paper door of the chamber, the midwife picked up her black-hilted blade and placed it in the Empress's hand.

Kaede took it and gently opened the child's mouth. Upon the child's tongue lay a small black stone. Kaede removed the stone and placed upon the still unmoving child's chest as she wiped his lips clean once more. "You cannot awaken this Prince with the blows of a warrior, mama-san," the Empress said gently to the midwife. "He is a little priest in prayer, and from prayer may only be revived with a whisper of the truth."

The midwife stared in amazement as the Empress lowered her lips to her child's mouth, blowing inward gently to share her own breath with the unmoving babe. As she did so, the child kicked once in a sudden spasm, and then lifted its head to draw breath from the Empress's own source. Kaede's handmaidens gasped and lowered their heads reverently in prayer as the child let forth its first sharp cry of life.

Heavy footsteps pounded down the corridor behind the midwife, stopping in shock at the open doorway to the Empress's chambers. Shocked that anyone would dare enter the Empress's private quarters at such a time, the midwife spun around with a sharp chastisement on her lips—but never delivered the assault.

In the doorway stood Toturi, Emperor of all Rokugan. At first his face was concerned, but the lines quickly smoothed into the more appropriate mask of peace and tranquility expected of a samurai. Only his eyes betrayed a deep sense of relief and pride as he gazed down upon his weary wife and their wailing newborn son. Others crowded behind him, obviously responding to the terrible news of the child's death delivered by the handmaiden that had left the room before the miracle.

"Emperor Toturi-sama." The midwife bowed very low, placing her head to the floor in a wave with the rest of the Empress's attendants. "I have the honor of presenting your wife and child—" she glanced back at Kaede expectantly.

"Sezaru," Kaede murmured, looking up at her husband with shining eyes. "His name is Sezaru."

"—Toturi Sezaru," the midwife continued. "May he live long, and may the kami bless you all."

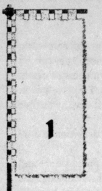

1 THE ASHES OF AN EMPEROR

The funeral pyre stood at the edge of the ocean's shore, beneath the high cliffs that supported the grand city of Otosan Uchi. Thousands of mourners stood upon the seashore, surrounding the wide pyre that had been constructed to bear the emperor's body on his journey to the world beyond. Toturi's soul would be borne by the flames into Tengoku, the Celestial Heavens, and there he would find rest. But for those thousands thronged along the ocean's shore and along the high rocks of Otosan Uchi's cliff face, there would be no rest and no peace. The Emperor had been murdered, and there was no appointed heir.

The skies over Otosan Uchi shone with gold and blue, shimmering in the summer's last heat. They seemed to waver, and those who knew the weather's path could tell that the skies would weep before darkness came tonight. They would weep, and in doing so, would join the rest of the Empire in that task. For the procession that moved beneath the skies of the Imperial City were not blazoned in the banners of festival, nor in the bright flags of ambassadors or of peace. The procession was a bier, carried by monks of the holy temple of Shinsei. They carried a bier that was covered in the dreadful stark whiteness of death, and the body upon the golden platform was the Emperor's own. Covered in white wrappings, it was impossible to see the terrible wounds that covered the Emperor's body.

But that did not mean Sezaru did not know the wounds were there.

Toturi Sezaru stood at the end of the long processional and watched the monks of Shinsei as they made their way through the streets toward the burial pyre. Small pieces of his white hair, the color of an eggshell, fluttered softly in the wind against his scarlet and gold robes. Most of it was bound back in a long braid that snaked across his shoulders, but some always escaped even the most tenacious braid to drift in the wind like clouds. Sezaru's black eyes shone like impassionate stones at the slow march of the monks toward the high pyre, and he turned a small netsuke carving back and forth between his fingers. He had grown into a tall young man, his bearing resembling that of his proud father. His movements, however, were distinctly his mother's, with quick fingers and graceful, flowing shifts. Even among these resemblances, Sezaru's eyes were distinctly his own, resembling neither father, nor mother, nor any of a hundred other relations. Those who looked into his eyes found themselves distinctly disconcerted, as if they had plunged into an abyss from which no light could escape.

Now, those eyes searched each of the others that stood around him, gauging their strength and their purpose upon this foreboding day. His mother, the Empress Kaede, rested upon a small cushion before the bier. She had aged in the last few days and seemed distant, as if her spirit was too long contained upon this world against its will. Her hands seemed so small inside her orange and gold sleeves, the skin pale and touched with faint threads of blue. Kaede was the Empress, yes, but also the Oracle of Void—a powerful shugenja and one whose motives were not always her own. The Oracles were the chosen of the spirits—the dragons who governed each element. Without Toturi to give her purpose upon this world, what would she become? Would she return to the Dragon that shared its spirit with her, or would she remain as Empress? And if she left this world, who would take the throne?

Rokugan was a powerful nation, stretching far from eastern shore to the western mountains, and millions of peasants, nobles, and courtiers lived within its borders. It was a country of honor and purpose, but now spun like a raft on a river's current. Without an Emperor to rule them, the country's connection to the divine kami was severed. Rokugan would be struck by bad fortune; dangerous winds of fate would tear at its fragile stability. The country might well fall into ruin and anarchy.

Toturi, Sezaru's father, had died in battle. Any samurai should wish to die fighting against the demon enemies of the south, but Toturi died without a clear heir, and now Rokugan stood within a hair's breadth of destruction, pivoting on an axis that was rapidly falling to ash. And moreover, who had summoned the demon that took Toturi's life? What malign power moved against the Empire, threatening stability and peace?

There were too many unanswered questions, and not enough truth.

Sezaru's eyes narrowed as his thoughts moved on to those who stood nearest him. To one side stood his older sister, Toturi Tsudao. Tall, strong, her chiseled face like something carved of marble, she did not show the slightest sign of grief—although Sezaru knew her heart was breaking. Tsudao had idolized their father. He epitomized all that she had ever sought to be, and without him to guide her, she would be lost as a child in a forest. Yet she was the eldest of their line, the true heir to the throne by birth. Her black hair cascaded around her shoulders, unbound in mourning. Her brown eyes betrayed only anger.

Sezaru was next in line, standing just a short distance from the orange-robed monks. He watched as the Brotherhood of Shinsei carried the simple wooden platform ever closer to the bier. They passed the waiting throngs of mourners with a rhythmic step, their chanting growing louder as they approached the bier. Their chanting merged with the sound of waves and wind, blending in harmony with the ocean's restless dance. As the monks reached the royal family, they knelt before Kaede and placed Toturi's wrapped body at the Empress's feet. Gently, without disturbing the peaceful fall of her garments, the Empress reached out to place a single chrysanthemum upon the fallen samurai's chest. There was a moment of silence as the orange-robed monks prayed softly over the Empress's kneeling form, and then the monks lifted the bier a final time and carried it toward the pyre.

Sezaru glanced about once more, looking at the distant ocean waves cresting white against the grey of the sea's stormy nature. The sea was active on the surface, but in its depths it held secrets no man could know. So, too, was the soul of Sezaru's youngest brother, Naseru, who stood just beyond Sezaru's right shoulder. He was a thin, sleek man, hands folded within the green sleeves of a finely embroidered robe. Sezaru knew that his younger brother was as crafty and cunning as any courtier, and more dangerous than most. The fact that Naseru's lost eye was covered with a black patch did not mean that he was blind to anything. He made up for his lost eye with a thousand spies, each carrying whispers to their master's ear. Their father had demanded Naseru take the Hantei name, an ancient appellation descended from the first line of Emperors, in order to appease the spirits and stop a terrible war. Nevertheless, Hantei Naseru was Sezaru's brother by blood— and more ambitious than any of the rest.

There was another who should be standing here, Sezaru thought, a fourth. But that one was not a brother by law—only by blood, and even then, only in half. His name was Kaneka, of the Akodo. Kaneka was Toturi's first son, born out of wedlock and the get of a common geisha. Simply thinking of him made Sezaru's eyes narrow. Already, the whispers among the peasants spoke of possible revolt. They would support him, as Toturi's firstborn, if they found fault within the children of Kaede.

How could the Empire become so lost within such a short time?

The chants of the monks drew Sezaru's mind back to the present, and he watched as they placed the bier high upon the wide pile of wooden logs. Empress Kaede did not move at all as the monks sprinkled incense and dust upon the pyre. Her eyes were dry. Her face was passionless. Were these the marks of a stoic Empress, or the signs of a spirit already disconnecting from reality?

The monks placed lit torches against the dry wood and the fire soon spread among the lowest levels of the pyre. Watching the flames dance, a vision of the past flickered in Sezaru's mind. He saw the past, frozen as if in ice, a fragile moment of almost-forgotten time. He was young, standing at his father's side while the announcement of his brother's birth was made public. It was time for Sezaru to go north to the Phoenix lands where his mother had been raised and educated, so that he could learn the way of the shugenja. The flame leaped again, and for a moment Sezaru heard his father's face as clearly as if he had stepped into the past.

"Remember, Sezaru-san," Toturi smiled. *"Nothing is more important to a leader than knowing what to take and what to leave aside."*

His sister's movement toward the pyre awakened Sezaru from his reverie. The flame was fully alight, and mourners trailed past in a long line of white. The assembled nobles of Rokugan pressed their hands together and threw flowers on the fire. With a stiff, martial movement, Tsudao bowed formally to the fire. Her duty done, she turned on her heel and marched through the mourners, back toward Otosan Uchi. Sezaru suspected that tears hung, unshed, in his sister's eyes. As their father's favorite, Toturi's death would hurt her most of all.

Naseru moved as well, bowing toward the pyre with more elegance than their sister. His palms were folded within the brilliant green robe that he wore. Hands hidden like snakes within the grass, thought Sezaru. Would Naseru mourn? Sezaru suspected not, but he also knew that his brother would be the most likely to take revenge for Toturi's death. Thus were the lessons of the Hantei.

The thread of mourners passed and waned into a trickle. From a trickle, it became only a few, their sandaled feet leaving behind marks of their passage in the sand like turtles leaving the shore. Time passed and the pyre blazed, and still Sezaru did not move.

He knew that he should go; leave the pyre behind and enter a new life without his father's presence. It was time for the future to begin and the past to be left behind, yet Sezaru did not turn. He stared at the skeleton of Toturi's pyre as it blazed against the cliff shore. The tide would come soon, and the ocean waves would lap close against that flame, but the water would not consume the blaze. The mourners were gone; the sun going down behind the cliff illuminated the city in a blaze of orange and red. Otosan Uchi's own pyre of sunset, as if the city burned with her Emperor. It would not last. In a moment, event he sunset would be gone, and Sezaru, Kaede, and the monks would be left with only the fire's light to illuminate the empty sands.

And then, moments later, even that would die, and Sezaru would be alone beside a pile of ash and regret.

"A leader knows what to take and what to leave aside." The voice was not Toturi's, but Sezaru's own, mocking his inability to walk away. One by one, the others left them. One by one, until Kaede, Sezaru and the monks were the only ones left beside the Emperor's pyre.

He died in vain. The voice murmured, coiling within Sezaru's mind.

"No." Sezaru whispered. "Emperor Toturi died a hero."

A hero without purpose. In the end, when Rokugan needed him, he failed.

Ignoring the voice's whisper, Sezaru closed his eyes to the fire and spoke his thoughts. "I will avenge you, Father," Sezaru's voice was soft, almost lost within the wind, but his faith was strong. "I will find those who murdered you, and I will see that they pay for their treachery."

Sezaru had never lacked direction or purpose in his life, but the pure truth of this matter sparked aflame within him that was not unlike those burning on his father's pyre. Whatever the circumstances, his father had been murdered. Someone was responsible, and they must pay. He would stay here no longer. There were other tasks that must be tended, other truths that must be sought.

Turning his pale face away from the fire, Sezaru opened his eyes to the road that would lead him up the cliffs and away from the shore. It was time to leave his father's body behind, but Sezaru would never put his father's burden down.

Sezaru walked alone down the road toward the Imperial city, leaving only his mother and the monks at the ashes of the pyre. Kaede would remain until morning, seeing that Toturi's ashes were fully consumed by the funeral pyre and his soul safely passed beyond.

"Sezaru-sama?" The voice interrupted Sezaru's meditation. He looked to his side. A small man, half-smiling, stood there. He wore robes of sun-burned yellow ochre. "Your mother wished me to speak with you."

Sezaru slowed his pace, allowing the strange man to step beside him. The stranger smiled a broad grin, almost unseemly in this time of mourning, and his long hair was thickly touched with the white of years gone by. As Sezaru watched, the man drew a pipe from his sleeve and lit it, puffing slightly on the tail as smoke began to ascend from the cob of the pipe shaft.

"You have the advantage of me, old man," Sezaru murmured with little patience. "You have given me an introduction, but you have not given me your name."

"You know me already," the man's gray-brown eyes curled in mild humor. "See if you don't."

Sezaru was taken aback for but a moment. The man's face was oddly familiar, but there was a quality to him that radiated through his flesh and his spirit. The young shugenja did not have to touch the old man's spirit to know that the creature walking beside him was not a mere mortal. Within the glints of the small fellow's eyes shone a strange and distant light not unlike . . . Sezaru grasped the truth in a brief flash of insight. The strangeness within this man's eyes was not unlike that held within the gaze of Sezaru's own mother.

"Good evening, Oracle," Sezaru said, correctly guessing the old man's nature. Quickly, Sezaru went over the words he had used before. Good. No questions. The Oracles were strange, enigmatic creatures, and mortal man was allowed only one question from each Oracle. If he were not careful, a man could use his sole life's question to inquire about the weather. Sezaru nodded in greeting and bowed with respect to the tiny man.

His greeting gained a larger smile and a faint chuckle from the old man, and he nodded his wrinkled face in assent. "Very astute, Sezaru-sama."

"The Oracles are always welcome in Otosan Uchi," Sezaru continued politely. "But it is rare that one chooses to visit."

The little man nodded, but then shook his head in dissent. "Yes, and no. We always take interest in the world when great events happen. It is our way to watch as the world changes and see each new path arise." The old man looked away, as if avoiding some issue, but Sezaru did not mistake his forced joviality. "But there are other reasons, as well."

"Oracles always have more reasons than they reveal."

"Oh, yes." The Oracle nodded in assent. He paused, his gilded sandals crushing a small shell against the cliff road as he walked slowly by Sezaru's side. "Death is important. So is life. Balance, imbalance. This is a time of greatly balanced imbalance, Sezaru, and you are a part of it."

"You speak in riddles." Sezaru was not surprised.

"Look again, Sezaru. Are you certain that you do not know me better than you think? No, no," he interrupted Sezaru before the young shugenja could gather his energies to pierce the veil. "Look with your eyes, not with your soul."

Sezaru blinked, a sign of uncertainty, and then he stared at the Oracle's face. His eyes pierced through the shifting wrinkles, and the signs of age upon the old man seemed to vanish for a brief moment under Sezaru's studious gaze. The hair darkened to a chocolate brown, and the Oracle's eyes almost gave way to a teacher's stern stare.

"By the kami," Sezaru breathed. "Tonbo Toryu!"

The Oracle chuckled. "Yes, that was my name when I was your teacher. It is no longer my name, of course, but I use it to keep things straight."

"As Oracles often do." Sezaru kept his composure even against this surprising evidence. "You are an Oracle now, and no longer the person you were before."

"I would tell you of it, Sezaru, but not tonight. There is more to the tale than can be told in an evening—particularly this evening—

and it is not so very important." Toryu drew another breath from his pipe, allowing the smoke to drift in small, twisted currents through his teeth.

"I see," Sezaru nodded. Sezaru struggled to see any signs or patterns on Toryu's robes or in his demeanor that would give away his nature and the nature of the Dragon he served. Was it Fire? Water? It could not be Void, for that post was filled by Kaede. "Now you stand with my mother on the threshold of this world."

"Not for long." Toryu saddened a moment, his smile fading. "Oracles were not made to be within both worlds, Sezaru. You are a shugenja, with the powers of the kami at your command. You know the pull of the elements, and you know the burden of the Oracles. It is your nature to understand. Kaede is pulled in two directions. Soon, under such conditions, even the finest silk will tear in two."

"Kaede cannot leave Rokugan." The very idea was anathema. The Empress, abandon Rokugan at its hour of greatest need?

"No. She cannot, can she?" Toryu turned away, as if denying his own words. "We cannot change our paths . . ."

He drew a small black sphere the size of a baby's fist from an inner pocket of his robe, tossing it from hand to hand as he considered the darkening sky. His question seemed as much for himself as for Sezaru. The cold wind rippled against the cliff wall, carrying darkness in its wake. The sun had long ago fallen beneath the wall of stone above, and the shadow of Otosan Uchi stretched against the shore below until it disappeared into the waters of the sea.

"I know the question you long to ask, though you are very careful not to say it." Toryu's eyes curved in amusement. "I will answer it anyway. I am the chosen vessel of the Dragon of Thunder. As all the Oracles, I will serve as best I can until the Dragon moves on." The strange light in Toryu's eyes grew brighter as he spoke of the great being that lived within him, but to Sezaru it seemed only a half-step from enlightenment to madness.

The implications rocked Sezaru, and he forgot all about his mother's situation. His eyes widened slightly, and he ran one hand over his long, white braid. "Thunder." He repeated. "But . . . there is no Oracle of Thunder."

"Fire, Air, Earth, Water, Void . . . and Thunder. There has always been an Oracle of Thunder, Sezaru, but until now, the Dragon of Thunder did not choose to speak with a mortal's voice." Tonbo shrugged. "An imbalance of balance, perhaps, a change in the way things must be done. Small shifts, causing great changes, and here I am. Chosen."

"I do not understand."

"You were not meant to understand, Sezaru. Not now. Not yet. But you will, in time." The ashes of Tonbo's pipe gleamed in the growing darkness as the Oracle drew in another breath of smoke. "We are in an unbalanced state of balance, but that will not last. All things change, Sezaru, and those who cannot find their place will be crushed by the changes. The first change will rock the Empire."

"My father's death." Sezaru's mind turned back to the pyre, and he looked down from the cliff road toward the gleaming flames of the funeral site far below.

"Ha!" Toryu's bark was unsettling. "That, yes, but that is not all. We are not yet undone, but we are unraveling. Who killed your father? Where is the heir? When the celestial heavens shift out of balance, Sezaru-sama, who will put it right again?" Toryu laughed, holding out the fine black pearl. "What is this? All riddles, Sezaru. Everything is a riddle. Life is a riddle."

Sezaru knew better than to ask the Oracle to explain his puzzles. Wisdom could not be handed out; it must be earned. He remained silent, staring down at the gleam of the fire against the dark beach. Kaede still remained there, alone with the monks on the shore. She must be feeling the same cold wind from the ocean that now cut through Sezaru's own robes, but she did not move. On her shoulders lay the future of the Empire, but even she did not know the truth about Toturi's death.

Without responding to Toryu's words, Sezaru turned and began walking toward the top of the cliff again.

"You do not want to know the answers?" Tonbo Toryu drew another breath from his pipe, his eyes reflecting the red glow of the coals against the darkening night.

Sezaru paused in his path up the mountain and turned back to look down upon the Oracle that stood below. "I will always seek answers, Toryu-sama," he said quietly, his strange eyes pools of darkness even in the dusk that surrounded them. "But you cannot give me what you do not have."

"You are correct, Sezaru. But I can give you this. You will need it when the night is darkest."

Toryu laughed and flicked the small sphere toward Sezaru, who reached to catch it, saving it from a long fall. The little orb sank into his fist, feeling cold as ice against his palm. He opened his hand, staring at the black pearl within, and then looked up toward Toryu.

But the Oracle was gone.

As Sezaru walked away toward the gates of Otosan Uchi, he could hear the Oracle's admiring laughter drifting on the cold night wind.

2 | A CHANGE IN THE HEAVENS

The morning dawned in a quiet awakening, gray clouds hovering close to the sun. Over Otosan Uchi, the sky hardly lightened, and a misty fog shivered against the city's walls as if seeking warmth.

The palace of Otosan Uchi seemed too hollow, echoing sorrow like a tightened drum. Every footfall, every movement within the lacquered corridors and *shhh* of the rice-paper doors reverberated through the corridors of the magnificent building, but it was not enough to fill the emptiness of Toturi's death.

In the central chamber of the palace, courtiers whispered and moved around the Steel Throne, their silken robes flowing like waves about the shore. Sezaru walked among them, unconcerned. He had arrived early in order to watch as the others came into the room. Much could be told about a man by the way he entered a room, and Sezaru needed to know the truth—about his brother, his sister, and the woman who had given them life.

REE SOESBEE

The Throne Room was the central hub of Otosan Uchi. Within its powerful presence, Sezaru felt small once more, as the child he had once been. Around him, the elements moved in harmony, and he felt his spirit blend easily with the power of Void that infused the royal chamber.

"Void, blessed strength of darkness and absence," Sezaru whispered to himself, a faint chant to right his mind, and cared not at all that the courtiers scattered before him like petals in the wind. The Void settled about him, bringing with it the gift of open mind and strength of will.

Today, before the dawn, the Empire would have a true heir.

The procession continued, bushi marching into the palace, escorting generals, lords, and noble samurai. Sezaru watched, his eyes distant but taking in everything. Among the marching soldiers, scattered shugenja moved, offering their priestly comforts to all who would listen and praying for the spirits to take Toturi back among them in glory.

To one side of the chamber, Crab and Scorpion and Crane stood side by side, their voices lowered in anticipation and concern.

The one in the shell does not yet know, the one with the stinger suspects, and the one that flies readies itself to stoop.

Sezaru grimaced, quieting the voice. It always seemed stronger when he was in contact with the Void. Now was not the time for idle thoughts or argumentative spirits. All of the great clans—Lion, Phoenix, Unicorn, and Dragon—were gathered, with a plethora of minor clan attendants moving through the room seeking guidance and offering lesser insights. They would claim any opportunity to prove their worth, to serve the Empire.

With his dark, cold eyes, Sezaru scanned them all, seeing the courtier's faces with the sudden sharpness of vision granted by the Void. All of them bowed and looked aside, fearing his gaze, fearing the one perspective that matters—the long view of time and Empire. *The view our mother has avoided.*

The doors opened, and Hantei Naseru entered the chamber. All of the courtiers bowed, and several rushed to his side. Dressed in rich but not ornate robes, as always, Naseru spared hardly a glance for Sezaru. The green silk rustled around his bold stride, shifting in rivers from his waist to the floor. He walked like a samurai, but his eyes were those of a snake. He challenged the room with his gaze and dared those assembled to meet it. None would.

One of the courtiers, however, did not hurl their attentions toward the newcomer, but instead chose this opportunity to make his way to Sezaru's side. The others did not notice; their interest in Naseru's arrival stole their attention.

"I beg your forgiveness, my lord," the unassuming young man bowed before the Emperor's firstborn son. "But you have a grave face."

"As is only appropriate on this grave day." Sezaru was not fond of word games. Turning his face from his brother's commanding presence, he looked up at the courtier by his side. The youth was dressed in light gray fabrics, covered with the brown mon of the Miya family, an Imperial house bound to serve the Empire above all else. The Miya were the heralds, the voice of the Emperor to his people as well as healers and courtiers.

"Good morning, Miya," Sezaru said politely, his appraisal instant and secure.

"Good morning, son of the Emperor." The Miya carefully avoided saying Toturi's name directly. It was told in the ancient scrolls that when death was new, speaking the name of the dead might call the spirit back from its journey into the Celestial Heavens. So this Miya had training as a shugenja, then, thought Sezaru. Good.

"Your brother seems confident."

"As he should. He is a Prince of the Empire, and a well-trained one." Knowing full well that the Miya did not care about Naseru's duties, Sezaru nevertheless avoided the unasked question on the courtier's lips.

"Yes." The Miya nodded. "May I introduce myself, Honored Lord?" When Sezaru nodded, half-amused by the youth's impertinence and well-trained graciousness, he continued. "I am Miya Gensaiken, son of Miya Iutazu. Recently assigned to the Imperial Court."

"And what did you do before you were assigned here?" Sezaru asked, still watching Naseru maneuver through the courtiers.

"I listened."

A laugh escaped Sezaru's lips, and he turned to look fully at the Miya. For a moment, the illusion of untrained youth remained, but then Sezaru's quick eyes took in the facts that he had missed. The Void whispered around this one, speaking of fortune and providence. Sezaru saw that the Miya was older than he had originally assumed, his unlined face hiding the maturity that lay in his eyes and the movements of his hands.

Before he could say anything else, the doors of the Throne Room were drawn open once more. Beyond them stood Tsudao, looking as uncomfortable in her formal robes as Sezaru would have been in her golden armor. Her eyes were somber, and even the pale makeup her handmaidens used to cover the dark circles beneath them was not enough to keep the undying sorrow from her eyes. Long black hair swung in a simple maiden's foxtail, too much like its mistress to be confined in the full regalia of a courtier.

Unlike Sezaru, who waited in the shadows, or Naseru, who moved easily among the flowers of the "Imperial Garden," Tsudao strode into the room like a great cat seeking its prey. Her face turned to the side, catching Sezaru from the corner of her eye, and she stepped toward him with a soldier's gait.

"Sezaru-san," Tsudao said, completely ignoring the Miya at his side, "I am glad to see you here. May I stand with you?"

"Sister," he replied in a quiet tone, "you are always welcome. May I present Miya Gensaiken?"

Toturi Tsudao nodded politely as the Miya bowed.

"My deepest sympathies, daughter of the Emperor," the Miya offered. "I was just speaking to your brother about the court. It seems empty without the great man who once steered its path."

"Thank you." Tsudao did not bother to look down at the Miya, but her voice was sincere. Her golden eyes lingered on the courtiers and bushi that littered the room, and Sezaru could see her hands clench within the black sleeves of her formal attire. "They gather like maggots on dead flesh."

"They come to mourn," Sezaru gently corrected her, then agreed. "And to feed."

"One of us will be the next Emperor."

"Or Empress," Sezaru whispered beneath his breath.

"And they cannot wait to see who it will be. Already, they forget our father and seek to replace him with another warm body. Do they have no sense of mercy?"

"No, Tsudao, they do not." His dark eyes caught hers. "Nor can we, for it is certain that the enemies of Rokugan will have none."

"Rokugan has no enemies," Tsudao said, although her voice was uncertain.

"If that is true, then who killed our father?" The silence hung between them like a burial shroud, and for a moment Sezaru thought his tempestuous sister might forget that she stood in a crowd of onlookers. "Tsudao," he continued when her golden eyes had darkened from their sudden anger, "Rokugan has always had enemies. Or do you forget the reason that the Crab Wall stands in the south?"

"I do not forget," she said, "nor do all those who die there fighting the Shadowlands."

"Then do not be so angry at those who fear for the Empire in these troubled days." Sezaru felt the chill swell of the Void pooling within his soul, guiding his words as surely as the stars made their imprint on the soul of a newborn child. "They only seek to know the future."

"The future is the province of Dragons and Oracles," Tsudao retorted, but there was no sting to her words.

"And generals." The Miya stood, almost unnoticed, at Sezaru's right elbow as he shooed away other courtiers seeking to overhear the sibling's private conversation. Sezaru had nearly forgotten the young man but was suddenly grateful for his assistance.

Tsudao's lips curled slightly in a chuckle, and nodded. "Yes. And generals. But . . ." Whatever words she might have chosen to argue the Miya's point were suddenly lost in the swish of rice-paper doors as once more Imperial servants opened the entrance to the main hallway. For an instant, Sezaru assumed this would be the entrance of their mother, Empress Kaede, but when the figures stepped through they were dirty, tired, and ragged.

Akodo Kaneka, bastard son of the Emperor Toturi, walked up the corridor to the throne room. At his sides were two more men bearing the mon of the Akodo, whom Sezaru quickly recognized. Akodo Ginawa and Akodo Ijiasu. Both honorable men. Both friends of Toturi.

At the same time, unbidden, servants opened the doors to the side chambers of the Throne Room. From the entrance where his father stood so many times before, Kaede now stepped lightly upon the hardwood floor. Her white-stocking feet made only a faint brush of sound across the chamber, but it nearly drowned out the breathing of the courtiers who stood in surprise and amazement.

Kaede took her eyes from the Steel Throne that was her destination for but an instant. Her eyes flickered about, quickly identifying those standing in the chamber. As one, the courtiers bowed. Sezaru felt his own head lower, but within his spirit, the Void itself bowed lower as though recognizing the immense power of her soul. At his side, he felt rather than saw Tsudao's sharp bow, and the Miya's flowing movements of respect.

When he looked up again, his mother's eyes were locked upon Kaneka, taking in the visage of the son she had not borne. Something strange flickered about Kaede's features—not the sorrow or pain that one might have expected from a mother meeting her husband's bastard child, but a dispassionate interest. The Void leaped with a sudden contraction, and Sezaru took in a sharp, pained breath. Only the Miya seemed to notice.

"Your father was going to see you when he died," Kaede's soft voice pierced the veil of silence, and her eyes did not leave Kaneka. She looks straight through him, disregarding all social convention to speak her first words to Toturi's lost son. It is not every day that an imperial bastard walked into the throne room. A subtle charge hung in the air, and Sezaru could sense deeper currents, cold and shifting within the Void.

"I know," Kaneka said, inclining his head and bowing to the small woman that held the attention of a thousand eyes. "I wish I had been at his side."

"He wanted you here," Kaede said softly, "not drowned in blood beside him. He wished for you to take a place alongside our children. The Empire needs all of you." The implication of her words rock the once-silent courtiers. White faces, powdered for the occasion, went pale beneath their carefully painted masks. Turning away, Kaede swept through the throne room, followed now by four rather than three.

Sezaru's steps were long and slow, falling into place behind his sister, but before Naseru. Uncomfortable, the dirty soldier stepped to Naseru's side, keeping his hand instinctively at his belt where a sword should hang, but his side was empty of all but the small wakizashi that is a samurai's honor.

Naseru's eyelid twitched. When the others were not watching, he turned to look at Sezaru. Sezaru, who had been waiting for his glance, whispered to his younger brother with his mind, knowing Naseru's unspoken objection. *Yes, Naseru, this is the way it must be.*

Naseru's eyes narrowed, and he nodded curtly to his brother's unspoken whisper. He took a deep but subtle breath, relaxed, and focused once more upon his mother.

Sezaru turned his attention to the Void, feeling the power even more strongly in the presence of his mother. Hazy, pale, and strange, her face seemed reflected within a mirror, almost surreal above the orange and gold robes she wore.

Hazy, even to me, thought Sezaru. I, who watch the swarm of chances, the twisting requirements of necessary balance and obligatory collapse, cannot read the movement of her spirit. With my mother, the Oracle of Void, everything is different. Unbalanced. Unchosen, like a decision that has yet to be made. Around her, everything is hazy. I can see it in her face, an emerging sense that this is not going to be easy. If there were some way to take this burden from her, some way to help her, to allow her to walk the single path ordained for mortals instead of the forking paths of the future, I would help her if I could. There are too many distractions in Kaede's mirrors, too many futures she has learned to ignore in the face of the single present.

Mirrors. The inner voice mocked. Standing here, so close to Kaede, the voice seemed a roar between Sezaru's ears, and he winced from its raw nature within his soul. What do you know of the mirrors within her, Sezaru? You are not a reflection of Kaede. Kaede is not the type of being who heals. When a crack slashes into her existence, she changes. There is no way to return to the one who existed before the wound. You . . . you are always as you will be. Unchanging. Alone.

Slowly, Kaede moved to take her place upon the throne. She stood, closed her eyes, and prayed, just for a moment. She sat, opened her eyes as she placed her hands upon the jade and emerald armrests. It seemed to suit her, the throne merging easily with the small woman who rested upon its strong foundation. For a moment, she seemed too small, a child resting where its father once sat proudly, then she grew in stature, a woman, an Empress born to rule with compassion and grace. Once more a shift came, and she seemed all at once too large for the throne, her spirit expanding beyond the realm of mortal man and encompassing all the stars within the void. With a stunned gasp of realization, Kaede threw her head back against the steel.

"No!" she cried, her eyes opening.

Sezaru was close enough to see that they were black, empty, with small stars floating among the merged pupil and iris like holes cut through into the heavens themselves.

"I cannot stay here," Kaede whispered, and a wind that none could feel lifted her hair into a black cloud around her porcelain features. "This is wrong. The throne is mine, but I do not belong to myself."

Beyond her, with the second sight of a shugenja, Sezaru could see shadows of Void shifting within her hair and playing beneath the sleeves of her elaborate robe. The courtiers leaped to their feet and backed away. Bushi stood their ground, planting their feet or bowing before the awesome display of power upon the Steel Throne. Kaede turned from one to the other, the force of her gaze causing many to fall to their knees and bury their faces against the cold floor.

"No," Kaede said once more, rising from the throne as though a strong wind blew her to her feet. "No."

Sezaru stepped forward, desperate to assist Kaede in her moment of uncertainty. He felt the Void around them both, joining them in spirit even as it tore her from the throne. Never before had his connection to the powers beyond this world seemed so true, so deep and awesome—and yet he knew that his mother saw more, felt more, *understood* far more than he ever could about what was happening.

Sezaru, no. Kaede did not move, did not whisper, but still he heard her voice as if it were within his own mind. *I must . . .*

But precisely what she must do, Kaede did not say. Instead, her eyes turned toward some vision that only she could see, silencing the voice within her mind.

For a moment, Sezaru considered reaching out to stop her, to keep her upon the throne, but he knew better than to interrupt the call of the Void. He had torn the hearts of demons out through their screams and between their claws, but he was powerless to say a word that would shatter against the barrier between them.

"Keep the throne empty, for now." Kaede said to Toturi's gathered children. "None of you are ready. Not until the Will of Heaven becomes clear, not until you save the Empire from fire . . . from thunder . . . and from itself."

Sezaru's lips moved along with Kaede's, hearing the voice within echo Kaede's unspoken lesson. "You are the four winds of change, and the Fortunes will preserve you and guide your steps."

With a stubborn wrenching of will, Kaede looked down at her children, pulling herself from the call of the Void for one last, fragile moment. "Goodbye," she whispered softly, but Sezaru could only half-recognize the voice. Then somehow Kaede stepped through the boundaries of reality, disappearing in a single, fluid motion past all of them and out of the room.

In a single breath, she was gone.

The courtiers stood in shocked amazement, some backing away, others bowing in deep reverence toward the empty Steel Throne. The children of the Emperor Toturi looked at one another with long stares, uncertain, until at last Naseru turned and strode away. "It seems we are to rule without taking the throne," he snarled in parting.

The others watched him go.

Sezaru whispered, "Four Winds and a void between them." He knew Naseru could still hear, but the words fell on uncaring ears as his brother continued toward the massive doors of the Imperial Throne Room.

"We must search for the Will of Heaven," Tsudao said with certainty.

As if unwilling to seem less resolute than his half-sister, Kaneka echoed, "For the Empire."

Sezaru shook his head, trying to grasp the deeper meaning of what they had just seen. He walked smoothly from the throne, leaving Tsudao and Kaneka alone to glower at one another. Beside him the Miya herald Gensaiken fell quietly into step. At first, Sezaru frowned at the courtier's impertinence, but then he realized that Gensaiken was smoothly managing to steer him through the crowd, avoiding questions and keeping the blustering courtiers from Sezaru. Again, the eldest son of Kaede was grateful. Gensaiken was indeed more than he seemed at a single glance.

When they reached the open hallways of Otosan Uchi, Gensaiken paused. Sensing the young herald's concern, Sezaru turned back to gaze at the Miya.

"Please . . ." said Gensaiken, his question left hanging.

"Yes, Gensaiken-san?"

"The throne is empty. The Empire is without a ruler, and the world will soon cease to be the place we have known and protected for so long. Sezaru-sama . . . a samurai should never admit to fear, but I know that the days ahead will be . . ." Gensaiken shuddered, unable to finish.

Sezaru nodded, understanding. "We will bear it. Rokugan, like its throne, is made of steel."

"The people will not accept that. Someone must lead them—with or without the Emperor's formal resolution."

"Would you have me steal the throne, Gensaiken-san?" Sezaru's voice was more cutting than he had intended, and he saw the young herald look away in embarrassment.

"Someone must take it, Sezaru-sama," he persisted. "And of them all, you are the only one who could possibly understand what has just occurred. We are both learned men. We know the Empire has become unaligned with its place in the heavens. Kaede's ascension, her claim on the throne . . . Void has taken on the role of the Emperor. It will unbalance the heavens. Until these things are resolved . . . we are unprotected. With the Void aligned with the throne, we have no true guardian. Balance has been shifted. You know what that will mean. In such an imbalance, the very spirits of this world will sicken and waste away."

"I will not allow that."

"Will you stop it by taking the throne?"

Sezaru stood silent for a long breath, and then turned away. "No. Not now." He took three more steps down the hallway, and then heard the faintest of whispers come from the Miya behind him.

"What can I do?" The Miya's voice was soft, shaken with unspoken fear. Turning once more to look at the Miya, Sezaru felt a moment of embarrassment and pride for a man so loyal. The Miya's heart shone in his eyes.

"Do what you have done before, Gensaiken-san," Sezaru replied. "Listen."

"And what will you do, Sezaru?"

"I," the Imperial Prince paused for a moment to consider his thoughts, and then smiled. "I will ask questions."

With that, Sezaru left the Miya behind and walked deeper into the recesses of the Imperial Palace. He would ask questions— about his father's death, his mother's disappearance, and most importantly about the Will of Heaven.

"And I know precisely where to begin."

3 THE FIRST STEP

"Even a journey of a thousand miles begins with a single step," Sezaru reminded his companion.

Toturi Koshei winced, drawing yet another thorn from his sandal. "How many single steps have we made so far, Sezaru-sama?" he asked, chuckling. "I feel as if I have started ten thousand journeys!"

The two men sat on rocks in the forest, their horses resting nearby with bags of feed over their noses. Sezaru smiled wryly at his yojimbo's commentary, keeping any further wisdom about the long trip to himself. It had been many weeks since they had set out from Otosan Uchi; many weeks since Kaede's disappearance and the cataclysmic imbalance of the Empire had begun. In that time, war had sprung up once again. The Phoenix and the Dragon rained blood down upon once-sacred peaks, and Sezaru's bold sister struggled to stop what would soon be open warfare. To the south, the Crab and Crane renewed their age-old dance of battle on the Yasuki Plains, possibly guided by the skillful hand of Hantei Naseru. Of Kaneka, the fourth wind, Sezaru did not know or care. Let him dance in the fields with his peasants.

The cold air ruffled Sezaru's white mane, pushing the limbs of the trees around them into rhythmic patterns. Koshei looked up, startled by the sound. "This forest is haunted, Sezaru-sama," he said quietly, without fear.

"Not haunted. Simply filled with spirits."

Toturi Koshei glanced around at the swaying branches, the wind tossing against the legs of his long pants. "The spirits are active."

Sezaru nodded, rising from his seat on the boulder. He brushed a bit of moss from his robe and turned his face into the wind. "They are restless. Something has stirred them."

"We should go." Protectiveness hung in each word of his yojimbo's lips, and the young Toturi vassal stirred restlessly beneath the swaying forest boughs. Green light streamed down from the afternoon sun, blotching shadow and light in ever-moving patterns against the pine-strewn ground. One of the horses blew indignantly, shaking its head and causing its bridle to chatter and clang. Koshei stood and reached to settle the steed, running his calloused hand down the horse's long bay neck with gentle reassurance.

"Soon, Koshei-san," Sezaru whispered, his voice carrying easily even on the rising wind. "But not yet." Koshei knew better than to ask his master why they sat alone in the forest instead of continuing their mission, but Sezaru knew what his friend was thinking. "There were always reasons, Koshei, even if you cannot see them. There were reasons why we visited the Oracle of Earth but did not stay, and there are reasons for this journey as well. Oracles are difficult by nature, and it is best to be certain of one's path before continuing on."

"Sama?" Koshei said quietly, "Why didn't the Oracle of Earth tell us what we wanted to know? Why didn't he know?"

Sezaru's slight smile faded, and an unconscious power trickled around him, wrapping against his skin like another cloak. Their journey to the temples of the Oracles had been, for the most part, fruitless. The Oracle of Wind was too capricious to hold much information; the Oracle of Earth stood too firmly entrenched in his foundation, unable to see or react to changes with any swiftness; even if he could discover the location of the Oracle of Fire, that being's raw fury would destroy any interest it had in restoring the Empire. There was only one last hope, and it rested on the other side of these hills.

A rustle in the brush caught Sezaru's attention a half-instant after his senses told him of her presence. Toturi Koshei moved in a fluid gesture, standing between his master and the intruder before either could react to the sound. His hand rested on the hilt of his katana, but he did not strike. As the woman came forward out of the trees, she smiled to see Koshei so discomforted.

"Koshei-san," she teased, her dark eyes shining behind a thin white mask. It accentuated her beauty rather than truly hiding her features, and her even teeth shone in comparison with its pure, pale sheen. "I have already seen your sword up close. I have no need for you to show it to me again."

Koshei's face reddened at the double entendre, but he did not move until Sezaru spoke.

"Knowledge is a strange thing, Koshei," Sezaru said, his voice quiet and detached. The wind rose around them, keening against the swishing percussion of the boughs. "It cannot waver, and once given, cannot be taken back. Be careful what you offer." Sezaru turned his eyes past his stalwart yojimbo to gaze upon the Scorpion maiden that stood at the edge of the small clearing. "I have been waiting for you, Angai-san." His voice was faintly chiding.

"I am sorry, Sezaru-sama, that you were forced to wait. I hope your journey was not unpleasant." Her bow was as much to show her beauty as her respect, but her eyes did not lower from Sezaru's ice-blue orbs. He did not answer. "White Shore Lake is on the other side of those hills, and I have brought you what you requested." She slowly withdrew a small parcel from her sash and held it out toward the shugenja. "I hope you will accept my present."

Sezaru chuckled. "Carrying out one's orders is no gift, Angai. Do not play that game with me." Rather than continue with the elaborate ceremony of the gift-giving, Sezaru indicated that Koshei should take the package from Angai's white hands.

Koshei reached out and snatched the gift swiftly, stepping back from Soshi Angai with a disdainful grimace. Checking the paper-wrapped package quickly for any deception, Koshei turned and placed it in Sezaru's hand. Sezaru pretended not to notice Koshei's discomfort or Angai's small smile. "Well done, Angai-san." Sezaru nodded. "Now we must move down to the shore."

"She is coming with us to meet the Oracle?" Koshei never let his eyes leave the deceptive Scorpion.

"No. But then again, neither are you." Leaving the horses behind, Sezaru began to walk down the path over the crest of the hill.

Koshei took his eyes off Angai to grip the horses by their reins. Sezaru could tell his yojimbo was struggling to keep silent. Much like the Oracles, Toturi Sezaru was not one to be questioned.

Sezaru strode over the hilltop, his two companions not far behind, and looked down upon the intense view that spread before him like a lady's sash. A tremendous lake, pure and blue, reflected the sky and the distant mountains as if in a mirror. Cliffs sank their roots deep into the glassy waters, vanishing into their own reflections without protest. The center of the lake was deep, deeper than any other in all of Rokugan, and no diver ever claimed to have seen even distant images of the bottom.

Sezaru's eyes could see more than any diver, even from above the rise of the shore. The Void centered upon him, stretching out with ethereal fingers into the silent. There, within the cold and silent depths, a palace rested upon the black bottom of the lake's waters. The palace of an Oracle.

"She is there," he whispered, "but the waters are disturbed." His eyes looked into the distant waves of White Shore Lake, feeling the chill wind that glided across the open waters below. "Koshei, Angai. You will camp here by the lake. I will return before tomorrow's nightfall, or I will not return at all."

"My Lord," Koshei ventured, "you may need my sword."

Sezaru's pale face twisted into a smile, and his eyes retreated from the faraway stare. "Will your sword prove useful to me if you cannot breathe, Koshei? Will your strength be so great when you are a hundred *li* beneath the waves? You remain here.

"And you, Angai, you will stay as well. No—" Sezaru held up a hand before her mouth could open. "I need you both. The palace of the Oracle of Water is a dangerous place. It is said that both the dark and light halves of the Water Dragon live within sight of one another, staring into their own infinity across a plane of watery reflection. If that is so, then I do not simply venture into the unknown, but into the balance between light and dark . . . a balance that has been disrupted."

Disrupted by the Oracle of Void. Kaede. The inner voice was strong, confident, jeering. Sezaru closed his eyes and reached to the sides with extended hands, feeling the wind press against his body, pushing him one step closer to the shore. *Yet again, she has abandoned you. You will die, empty and alone, drowned in the waves of her decision.* The Void called to him, its song stronger at the edge of the silent lake. The presence of the Oracles and of the Dragons themselves always called to his inner nature, reaching into the power that was contained within Sezaru's soul. Without even a thought, he could sense the strength that lay hidden in the darkness at the bottom of White Shore Lake. He could see the moss-covered palace, sense its guardians, and feel the presence of the one who lived within. Yet the voice continued, mocking his resolve. *You will doom them all with your false certainty. Your pride will lead Rokugan into the depths in search of answers, but when you get your answers, you will drown there, with all the rest.*

"No."

"I'm sorry, Sezaru-sama?" Angai bowed, confused. She and Koshei stood a few feet behind him, lashing the horses to nearby trees and preparing camp as he had told them. By the sun, he guessed that had been several hours ago.

Sezaru turned away from the shore, realizing that he stood only inches from the water's edge. Ice-cold ripples lapped below, curling about his feet as if beckoning him into the waves. "I must complete the spell, and then I must go."

Sezaru turned from the lake, walking away to a more private spot on the edge of their campsite. He sat upon one of the flat boulders, allowing the warm sun to touch his face. A deep breath, cleansing his body and easing his mind, and then he sent out his thoughts into the calm depths of his soul. There rested the source of his power, and it was time to draw a bit of that reserve forth.

Sezarua, often called the Wolf, brushed his white hair aside and drew forth Angai's small package. The paper fell away at his touch, drifting out of his hand on the wind. Within lay a golden ball the size of a large man's fist made of fine thread, spun by a master weaver. Sezaru let some unravel in his fingers and felt its texture. It tingled against his skin; finely woven, and spun with magic. This thread would prove as strong as Scorpion steel. "Excellent."

He called, and void answered. As it always did.

The rush of power Sezaru felt when he reached into the darkness was stronger here than at many other places in the world. The presence of an Oracle, so close by, empowered the spirits and made the connections between worlds wider and more open. As his consciousness passed out of the physical world and into the immaterial, Sezaru was struck for a moment by the sound of his own breathing—so unnecessary, so loud and strange, like the roar of a dragon.

He could feel all life around him, every fish and bird on the lake, every animal within the deep forest that surrounded them. Angai and Koshei stood out as blazing lights against the dark background of silence, their bodies frozen in a space between time. Thin rope dangled from Koshei's fingers, hanging upon the air with a thousand shudders of movement—but still, so still, paused in the blackness between breaths. The world slowed to a complete stop, and only the faint sound of Sezaru's own breathing echoed in the emptiness of true Void.

He reached further, sensing the villages beyond the lake and the growing things that sprouted from the earth near the buildings. Sickness, age, happiness, and youth were all one within the void. They were balanced, held together in a tightly spinning circle of spirituality. The world was at peace with itself.

But beyond even that, to the far north—war. The Dragon and the Phoenix spread their wings over a burning land, raining blood down upon samurai and peasant alike. Thousands were dying. Thousands more would soon die upon their blade-like claws as the two clans collided over the farmlands below their mountain passes. All that rage, all that tyranny . . . over grain. Over food. Over life.

To the far south he sensed a blackness that spread from Otosan Uchi like a cancer upon the spirit of Rokugan itself. Sezaru did not have to look into the sickness to know its source. The heart of that writhing, unbalanced mass would be the courts of the Empire. The last spot where Kaede stood before she stepped forever into the void.

Is she here, now, with us? Can she hear you breathing, Sezaru? Do you think that she would care if that breathing suddenly ceased?

Softly, in . . . out. There was an echo, trance-like, reflecting back from within the depths.

In . . . out.

Once more.

Echoes . . .

Sezaru leaned forward. He drew his mind back to the task at hand and looked down into his palm. Sezaru held the ball between his hands and gently breathed upon it, feeling the power of Void sink into each strand, every thread within the tightly wound sphere sinking into his strength and drawing upon his soul. The Wolf sent his senses more deeply into that space between worlds, that primal, primitive yet ancient awakening that lay between the stars. Void heard his call, and whispered between his words as he spoke gently to the spirits around him. He whispered, and the Void echoed once more.

Each string of the skein seemed to gather some of the darkness within it, twisting around the threads themselves and connecting it to his soul. The ball spun in his hand, sinking within the darkness, moving despite the complete absence of time.

This will not avail you.

The voice was always stronger when he was within the Void. It became even more assertive, more combative. Sezaru ignored it as best he could, and concentrated upon the ball in his hand. With a few more words and gentle gestures, he drew out a length of the string and guided it into the Void. It hung there, unsure, and then sparkled with white light. Spirits from the depths joined him, gliding along the string to give it power and a presence in both worlds. Now, no matter where the trip into the Oracle's palace led, he would have this companion. No matter how the Oracle of Water her dark twin disoriented him, he would always be able to find his way back to the surface—as long as he held tight to this slim, golden thread.

Sezaru smiled, lifting the silence of his thoughts and opening his eyes. Around him, the world moved. A bird flew past overhead, and the rope thrown by Koshei finished its revolution, landing with a soft thump on the ground near Angai. The fire cracked once more, and the waves of White Shore Lake rippled against the shore. Far away, the movement of the distance villages receded from Sezaru's mind, although their presence was still stamped against his memory.

"Angai. Koshei." The two samurai turned to obey as he spun a bit of the shining golden thread out between his fingers. "One of you will sit by the lake shore and hold this thread. You must not let it go—not to tie it off, nor to set it down even for a moment. If you do so, then I will be lost within the darkness at the lake's bottom forever. Do you understand?"

"Yes, Sezaru-sama." The answer was immediate, given as one.

"Good. You will take turns, giving the lake your absolute attention. If anything unusual happens—any distortions in the lake's reflection—you will tug the string three times to let me know."

Again, both of the young samurai nodded. Sezaru paused a moment to stare into their eyes but saw no deception there. Most of all, he saw no doubt. Their confidence in his abilities was stronger than his own—and that was in his favor. Doubt was unacceptable. Doubt destroyed all it touched and crumbled the will of even the mightiest mind. Sezaru would not allow it to weaken him or those who followed him.

He stepped away from the rock, handing the end of the slender thread to Koshei first. "If you grow weary or your thoughts begin to wander, you must give this to Angai for a time." Sezaru's eyes swept to Angai with no mercy. "And you must do the same. If you pause for even a moment out of pride, you fail in your duty to me."

"Yes, Sezaru-sama!" Their voices were resolute. Sezaru gazed at them for a moment longer before he turned away and walked once more down to the edge of the lake's lapping waters.

The lake lay cold and still before him, the last light of a dying sun reflecting off the glistening silver waves. It was almost nightfall, the perfect time to enter into the darkness. By the time he reached the Oracle's palace far below, it would be day once more.

Sezaru reached out with his senses, calling this time not upon the power of Void, but on the gentle reassurance of Wind and Water. Feeling their presence fill his body and enter his lungs, he took the first firm step into the lake. He would not rely solely on Water, for this was the Oracle's domain, and she could withdraw her blessings at any time. Instead, he offered his strength to Air, and felt the rush of wind within his lungs. His bargain with them was cemented in a moment, and their payment agreed upon in future offerings. Beneath even the deepest waters of the lake, he would be able to breathe—for one day only. With the golden thread spilling faintly out behind him, he should be able to reach the depths and return in that time.

His form nearly shrouded by the flickering of the last rays of the sun against the waters, Sezaru walked into the water's embrace. In a fragile moment, he was swallowed completely by the waves of White Shore Lake, and the lake was still once more.

4 TO MASTER THE WAVES

Darkness.

A silent thickness, combined with a lack of air, conspired to trick Sezaru's mind into thoughts of death and oblivion. But this was not oblivion. This was not true darkness. This was only water, playing tricks and games to lure the unwary to their doom.

The water swirled around him, clutching against his ornate robes as he stepped deeper into its embrace. The faint light of the world above, so far away, twinkled as ripples swirled across its surface. Like a false sky, the ripples glinted light down to him; a thousand stars fractured by the movement of waves. Was it still day, or had the sun vanished entirely? Were those ripples the reflection of the firelight that now warmed and cheered his companions? Sezaru could not say. In a moment, the light would be gone entirely. There. With that single step it had vanished away.

This, then, would be the first test. He must locate the Oracle without light to steer by and without breath in his lungs. Only his bargain with the spirits of air kept him alive. The golden thread glistening faintly behind him reminded him of the lost light of the world above.

Farther and farther down, through corridors of freshwater coral and banks of kelp that flowed like the wide plains of the Unicorn. Fish swam in schools, their silvery scales glinting in the dull light of the glowing moss. Three of them swept past Sezaru, and he could see that they had no eyes.

The waves ahead of him reached on and ever on, without sign of stopping. White Shore Lake was tremendous, and he had but a day to find the palace of the Oracle of Water. The light grew ever fainter, until at last he was illuminated only by the faint golden glow of the gently trailing cord. He came to the edge of a chasm, a wide empty ravine whose depths were shrouded in darkness even thicker than the waves. It seemed endlessly deep, drowning forever beneath White Shore Lake.

A choice, pondered Sezaru. Do I go down or cross it and continue following the lake bottom?

He reached out to feel the spirits around him. Within a few seconds, he opened his eyes again, pupils dilating strangely in the dark. The spirits were silent—more so, they were absent, refusing to respond to his call. He could feel them, but they were bound not to tell him the way. The powers of the Oracle, no doubt. This was her domain, and he would have to gain entry on his own merits. At least he was certain the spirits would still come to his spells—so long as those spells did not transport him to the Oracle against the boundaries of this test. He would have to reach the palace alone and unguided.

Sezaru knelt by the side of the chasm and reached out to feel the currents flowing though the darkness. They moved swiftly, left to right as if the chasm was a conduit for such motion. Like a river, he thought, within a pond. Although the lake held many smaller currents, this one was immense. He could feel the tug of the waves upon his sleeve as he withdrew his hand from the cold darkness of the ravine.

With only hours to search the bottom of White Shore Lake, this natural "river" of sorts could prove useful. However, if he simply threw himself into the waves, he would have no chance of controlling his movements and might well fall to the bottom of the ravine or be crushed by the current against the sides of the chasm. He would have to find a boat, of sorts, to navigate this hurdle.

Sezaru walked along the side of the chasm. The ravine was nearly as wide as three roads. Attempting to leap or swim over would meet with failure. The current again barred his way, swirling the waters both above and below the chasm into a frenzy. Going over was impossible. Swimming directly into the current, suicide. Sezaru frowned.

Walking along the sharp edge of the ravine, Sezaru squinted into the dark waters ahead in the direction the underwater river was taking, deep into White Shore Lake. As he pondered the river's purpose, Sezaru noted a bank of sharp rock ahead. It reached high above the lake's bottom, standing higher than several houses. Deep within the shoal and rock, Sezaru could make out the outline of a cave mouth facing the river. On the rocks before the cave were bones speared by the current, beasts undoubtedly drowned during the storms of winter. In some places Sezaru could see identifiable bones that could only be human. A skull grinned at him as he approached.

A soft, half-aware moan of sleep came from the depths of the cave. Those speared upon the rocks were fodder for a beast within. Yet Sezaru could not pass along the ravine's edge without passing against the cave opening. Who knew if the monster inside were awake or asleep? If he called to the spirits and the beast was at all sensitive to the movements of magic, he would awaken the creature. Worse, most of his damaging spells were gifts of the spirits of fire, and Sezaru doubted very seriously if there were any fire spirits at the bottom of White Shore Lake.

If you were a warrior, you could simply destroy the beast with a single stroke of your katana.

"If I were a warrior," Sezaru replied, smug in the knowledge that he had the upper hand, "I would be drowning."

He moved slowly toward the cave, readying a small knife in his belt. He slipped along the shadows at the edge of the stone, avoiding the bones while still hiding himself against the cold rock.

When he reached the shadow of the cave mouth, Sezaru slid into a crouch and withdrew a small mirror from his sleeve. He held it in his hand, extending his arm before him until he could see within the dark cave. He could see only a limited distance as silt and sand flowed inside the cave, shielding it from view. But at the edge of the reflection in the mirror, Sezaru saw the shape of a massive tortoise shell, and a tail that resembled a thickened club covered in bloody spikes. If the rest of the creature was that massive, it would stand easily three times as thick as a horse. Armored, with the tail for a weapon and possibly claws . . . very dangerous.

Sezaru watched the beast for a few moments longer, then considered the area around him. Rocky shoal extended above him at a steep angle. Even with the buoyancy of the water, it would be a nearly impossible climb—and in the wrong direction. The other side of the cave was bordered by razor-sharp rocks against the swiftly sweeping chasm of current. The only way to cross was to enter the cave and exit on the other side of the spikes that extended along the front of the aperture.

Sezaru set down the knife and knelt for a moment at the edge of the cave. Tying his over-robe against his lower legs to keep it from flapping, he wrapped the silken fabric close to his calves. Picking up the knife once more, he shifted its balance from hand to hand. The water would prove his enemy in any fight, twisting the knife's motions with current even as he struck. A seasoned warrior might be able to adapt quickly for the pressure of the waves, but Sezaru had not spent his life studying the blade. He would not be able to rely on steel.

Moving softly, Sezaru placed the mirror back into the pocket within his sleeve. He held the knife close to his side and slipped into the cave, one foot delicately paused above the stone as he listened to the beast's ragged breathing. Each step, balanced by the water, had to be absolutely silent—yet the current around him tugged and pulled as if desperate to see him fail. He shifted his weight, step following silent step, moving through the cave and venturing closer to the beast. The light at the other side of the stones grew brighter, and he could see a space between two sharp stalagmites.

The currents began to shift. Sezaru paused for a moment, only a few feet from the opening, and then cautiously stepped forward once more.

His foot rested for a moment on a shard of rock placed just below the tall spiked stalagmites. In the first breath, Sezaru thought it would be stable. Yet as he shifted forward, placing his weight on the protruding stone, it turned beneath his foot. Before he could draw back his weight, the stone slipped out; rattling against its neighbors and sliding noisily down the faint slope back into the heart of the cave.

The heavy breathing stopped, then choked and snorted.

Sezaru spun, knife in one hand and the other already reaching out with arcane posture to draw forth the spirits to his defense. A roar exploded from the darkness within the cavern. The beast rose with a ferocious howl of rage and hunger.

It was massive, even larger than Sezaru theorized. Huge, clawed feet extended from all four apertures in the tortoise's shell, and a head as large as Sezaru's torso snaked out of the front of the beast. The head appeared much as a lion's, but sleeker, with long moustache-like tentacles extending from the beast's muzzle. Teeth like sharpened shards of glass protruded from its massive jaws, and its claws scraped against the rock beneath it with the sound of glass shattering against stone. It lurched to its feet before Sezaru could complete his spell. Its spiked tail slashed through the water toward the shugenja.

Just before the tail could smash against Sezaru's head, he felt the familiar rush of the kami answering his call. The spirits would not guide him to the palace of the Water Oracle, but they would still aid him. The water thickened, hardening into a plane of ice. With a shattering crash, the club slammed into the icy shield, spikes crushing web-like cracks into the thick sheet of ice. The shield cracked but did not break, giving Sezaru another chance to call forth an attack of his own.

As the tremendous beast lurched forward, half-swimming and half charging through the cavern, the shugenja fanned his hands. Ice shards launched forth from his fingers, exploding into spears. Most of Sezaru's attack shattered harmlessly on the beast's thick shell, but some of the shards drove painfully into the creature's fleshy neck and face, digging beneath the surface and freezing the skin where they touched. Greenish blood swelled out around the wounds, clouding the water around them.

The beast roared, opening its terrible mouth to swallow the shugenja in a single chomp. Sezaru spun to the side, using the water's current to speed his moves, and the beast's teeth chewed nothing but empty waves. One sharp talon shredded Sezaru's sleeve, tearing into his flesh. Sezaru hardened his mind against the pain. Pain was a physical reaction, unacceptable to a shugenja whose mind needed to be focused on the spiritual in order to command his spells. His life was already on the line. He could afford no distraction.

Red blood mingled with the green clouds from the beast's own injuries as the creature roared again. The water in the cave churned and swirled, whitening from the activity as the two combatants turned and swirled for better position. The beast moved with incredible speed, using its rear webbed feet to propel it forward against the current toward its enemy.

Sezaru tried another offensive spell, changing the stones at his feet into sharp caltrops of iron and launching them toward the creature. Again, most of them shattered on the beast's shell or stuck harmlessly in its thick, plated armor. Only a few caused damage, falling beneath its tender feet and injuring the webbing between its clawed toes. But it was not enough, and the beast swam upward so that it could avoid the sharp caltrops now scattered on the cave floor.

Sezaru's mind raced as he tried to summon and control the kami despite the lancing pain in his right arm. The spell worked, and bubbles of steaming hot air surrounded the beast. The water turned scalding, bubbles of air both blinding and damaging the creature's sensitive face. It howled in agony, lashing with its tail toward Sezaru, who dodged again, allowing the tail to pass over him. Water rushed past, churning with green and red clouds in the wake of its spikes.

The creature slashed again at Sezaru, its neck serpentine moving and its massive jaws snapping the water into white foam.

Sezaru dodged again, feeling pain lance through his arm. His time was growing short. Despite the cloudy water, the beast had all of the advantages in this fight—armor, movement, and familiarity with the area. Its only vulnerability lay beneath that thick shell, and no spell of Sezaru's could pierce that heavy armor. With his spells so limited, Sezaru had few options. Water wouldn't harm the creature, fire wouldn't burn here, earth spells would only collapse the cave on them both . . . then Sezaru was suddenly inspired.

Murmuring another prayer to the spirits, Sezaru threw his small knife into the swirling currents. The beast hurled itself toward him, clawed paws slashing, eager to dig its steely talons into his flesh. The knife swirled, unsure of its own buoyancy, and then spun toward the oncoming monster. Despite the danger, Sezaru remained perfectly motionless, pressing his will against the spell. If Sezaru moved even an inch, the spell would not be accurate; if he did not move, the beast would tear him to shreds.

Instants slowed to hours. Many times before, Sezaru had placed his life in the kami's hands—but perhaps never before so literally. The monster's teeth glinted, cutting through the cloudy water like iron knives as it raced toward him. Sezaru stood, implacable, dedicating his soul to the Void. Like two samurai in a duel to the death, the world around them simply ceased to be; nothing existed except Sezaru, the beast, death, and victory.

At the last moment, the spirits saw their chance, and the knife flew forward. Slipping easily between the beast's arm and armored shell, the blade of the tiny steel weapon parted the flesh inside the monster's shell. The monster screamed, unable to stop its forward propulsion as the current carried it, and the knife remained firm in place. The beast thrashed as steel slipped swiftly through its flesh, cutting away flesh and tissue until it reached the heart.

Sezaru watched his enemy's face, standing inches from his own death, waiting until he saw the final blow reach its mark. The monster's heart burst as steel tore it open. The beast's jaws slackened, and at last Sezaru stepped aside. The victor in their strange duel, he allowed his already defeated opponent to finish its lunge—and slide to a crushing halt against the spiked stones at the mouth of the cave. With a long, shuddering breath, Sezaru bowed slightly to his defeated opponent. The beast had fought with courage, and such courage deserved recognition.

Sezaru stepped out of the other side of the spiked stones. The dim light from the golden thread glistened against his skin, illuminating thin trails of blood that trickled and clouded the water at his right arm. Reaching down to wrap the silk fabric tightly against his bicep, Sezaru tied his sleeve against his arm. At least it would prevent further blood loss, even if the wound wouldn't heal while he was underwater.

As he stepped out of the cave, Sezaru noticed that one of the spiked stones near the edge of the ravine had broken apart, sending long splinters along the edge of the cave. One of them, very near the edge, was long and flat, curved into an almost canoe-like shape. It was smooth, with a flat surface. Though heavy, it had a good shape. Sezaru smiled. The kami were pleased with him, to have arranged such a gift.

He stood once more, arranging his hands into a pattern that would call forth the spirits of earth. "Lighten," he whispered to them, "lighten and flow."

The stone began to shiver, moving faintly as the spirits heeded his call. The long, canoe-like piece of stone grew lighter and more susceptible to the flow of the water, its consistency becoming more fragile. It was a necessary trade. The stone's stability would be sacrificed so that its weight would be reduced. Now, it would be able to sail along the water's current in the river, but any shock, collision, or even minor impact would shatter it instantly. He pushed against the curved shard. With a strong heave, he slid it into the swift current of the ravine and leaped aboard.

The ravine was cold, and the icy waters chilled him as his roughly-made raft tossed on the current. He traveled swiftly, each rushing wave threatening to throw him from his perch. The rush of speed was encouraging, and the golden thread in Sezaru's hand spun out behind him in golden curls. For a moment, Sezaru smiled, thinking of Angai or Koshei on the other end suddenly seeing the cord spin at a tremendous rate into the water below.

Sezaru stared beneath the raft, looking down into the dark oblivion that lay at the base of the cleft in the earth. Water churned below, just at the edge of his vision, crashing against spiked shards of rock. Beneath that was nothing.

Light broke through the surface of the lake for a moment, shining down in thin shafts through a wonderland of water below. Sezaru looked out over endless beds of kelp, swirling schools of fish, and gigantic creatures swimming in their wake, chasing the scattering flocks before them like a dog herding sheep. There, deep beneath the waves, at the lowest point of the lake's sandy bottom, the golden streams of light illuminated a palace made of coral and shell. The wide swath of the ravine rushed on directly to the palace, making a broken course across the lake bottom. All he had to do now was follow the ravine and hold on.

5 | MEETING WITH THE ORACLE

Sezaru lay against the thin slab of stone, watching as the Oracle's palace grew ever closer. The last few hours, spent avoiding sharp spurs of rock along the ravine sides, had been harrowing. Sezaru's arm throbbed angrily, the wound still sore and clotted with blood. The hours of travel had only exacerbated the pain, making it more and more difficult to steer the wallowing raft. He had followed the current its full course to the bottom of White Shore Lake. Even the noonday sun far above the surface of the lake could not illuminate this dim hideaway. Before him, the Wolf saw a tremendous palace, hidden in the depths of the lake.

The palace was smaller than Otosan Uchi or the great spreading homes of the Crane, but it held a luster that no other could match. Though it was hardly more than a tower with a shingled building beneath, it shimmered with power. The water spirits swam in patterns around the castle's walls, causing the stone and coral to shimmer in rainbows like the scales of an exotic fish.

Sezaru shifted his weight to force the makeshift raft toward the edge of the ravine. The currents caught it and took it to the side of the ravine where it risked smashing against the stone walls of the chasm. Sezaru prepared a simple spell of air, delicately moving his hands in time with the prayer. The water shivered and hummed with the immense strength of the air spirits as they lifted him from his rushing perch on the stone canoe. Sezaru jerked his feet up, watching as his raft spun beneath him and smashed into the wall of the ravine. For a moment, Sezaru felt the strong tug of the chasm's current against his legs, dragging him down into the darkness. The pull wrenched his body downward, nearly tearing him from the hands of the air spirits.

He slid downward into the dark pull of the chasm, but then the spirits redoubled their efforts and lifted him. It was a strange sensation—half-swimming and half-flying through the water—and Sezaru was thankful when the spirits placed him at the side of the chasm, just a few feet from the palace wall.

He stared up at the tall walls surrounding the main spire of the palace and watched the waves playing against the stone. The walls were a faint greenish color, sparkling with coral, underwater phosphorescence, and bright pearl shell. Sezaru walked slowly around the wall, seeking an entryway to the palace inside, his fingers touching the wall with a deliberate reverence. There was no entrance, no breach in the perfectly smooth stone. Sezaru considered scaling the walls, however undignified that might appear, but he changed his mind when he realized that the coral would slice him to pieces. Perhaps a spell to leap over the wall? Even as the thought crossed Sezaru's mind, he saw the swirl of water above, thickening and rushing past just on the other side of the wall. Somehow, he doubted the spirits that protected the palace would be inviting. If he attempted to swim over, the water spirits guarding the palace would tear him apart.

His fingers paused against the stone, feeling a faint crack in the smooth pearl. The crack was thick, but short, like something carved into the stone. Sezaru wished for his knife, which he had left within the creature at the cave. He swept away the kelp and coral with his sleeve. The coral shards sliced into his hand, but he continued, praying for the spirits to guide him as he cleared the growth away from the wall.

One by one, the characters became clear. Stepping back, Sezaru took a long look at the mysterious characters that were carved into the wall. In two long rows, one directly above the other, were carved the images of the animals that made up the Rokugani calendar. Six above, and six below, they marched side-by-side above a small verse carved in elegant calligraphy. Sezaru ran his fingers over the animals, feeling each one shift slightly beneath his hand. Like pieces of a puzzle-box, each animal slid when directed, pushing back into the stone. He looked down at the verse, reading it softly to himself.

> *Into the depths you've come, a hundred li below*
> *One of us will guide you, beyond this coral row.*
> *One will destroy you, two will ignore you,*
> *And one will carry you up and away*
> *Four more will hurl you deep, to the ravine below*
> *And he last three will your breath betray.*
> *Death walks with loyalty, so beware*
> *Lest darkness take you to its lair.*
> *Four seeking the depths walk with the Unicorn*
> *Flight needs wings, on the air to be borne.*
> *Neither sun nor moon completes your quest*
> *Nor will those standing to depth's left.*
> *Choose well, visitor, lest you betray*
> *Your life, your future, and your way.*

Sezaru steepled his fingers and pondered the riddle. Obviously he would need to choose just one of the creatures. The others would end his quest one way or another. He would have to use logic and his knowledge of Rokugani tradition to solve the puzzle. If he failed . . . some of the other options seemed highly unpleasant.

He looked once again at the twelve animals carved into the wall:

| Hare | Dragon | Serpent | Horse | Goat | Monkey |
| Rooster | Dog | Boar | Rat | Ox | Tiger |

The first six lines were explanatory, detailing simply how the puzzle worked. One of the twelve creatures would open a gate into the palace. The others would cause him harm—or death. The most benign of those would do nothing at all, thus ending his quest, and the only one even vaguely beneficial would carry him to the surface of the lake, far from his goal.

Death walks with loyalty. Not much help there. The dog, the goat, and the ox were domestic creatures, and thus could be considered loyal.

Four seeking the depths walk with the Unicorn. That line gave him a bit more to work with. The Unicorn clan traveled the length and breadth of the world, but they did not travel that road on foot. Their horses carried them. What other animals traveled with them? Dogs, perhaps, as companions. Or oxen to help the wandering horse-nomads draw their carts? Perhaps. Still, that was only three, at best.

"Walk with the Unicorn," murmured Sezaru. Perhaps that didn't actually mean to travel with the Shinjo. Perhaps it was far more literal. How did Unicorns walk? Sezaru smiled, identifying another common thread. He found four such creatures on the list—all those with hooves: the goat, ox, horse, and boar. This meant, if he read the line correctly, that their partner animals were not of use to him if he wanted to continue. Very well, then. Cross off the serpent, rat, and the goat and ox pair.

Sezaru read the next line easily, already certain of its answer. *Flight needs wings.* Only one of the animals on the calendar had wings—the Rooster.

Sezaru wished the rest of the poem were as simple. *Neither sun nor moon completes your quest.* There were two possible ways to read this line. First, he could align the Rokugani calendar with the calendar of the Houses. In that case, the month of the Hare would be also the month of the Sun, and the Dragon would align with the Moon. No, Sezaru decided, that wasn't right. Knowledge of that calendar was esoteric, not useful. So far, this poem had been extremely literal. He would continue in that vein. It was more likely that the intent was for Sezaru to excise the first and last animals on the list, the Sun, representing the beginning of the day, and the moon, representing the end. Cross off the hare and tiger, respectively.

Sezaru had narrowed his choices significantly, and he rolled the golden thread in his hand. *Neither sun nor moon completes your quest. Nor will those standing to depth's left.* To depth's left—those to the left of the hoofed animals. That removed the boar, horse, and dragon.

Sezaru's eyes went back to the line he had skipped. *Death walks with loyalty.* Of his original choices, the goat, ox, and dragon had been eliminated by other means, leaving only the loyal dog. Cross off another animal from the list, and that left only one possibility.

After tying the golden cord to his belt, Sezaru rose and placed one hand on the carved icon of the monkey. He pressed his fingers against the stone, feeling it slide inward with his touch. Like a puzzle-box, the bricks slid to the side, opening a thin thread within the pearl wall. As he watched, the bricks slid in order, falling aside like droplets of water to either side of the gate and leaving the center open.

Sezaru stepped gingerly inside the open gate, his hands clenching into fists as he gained his first glimpse of the palace. The gardens were covered with entwined sea-kelp, forming a loose canopy over open areas of luminescent plants. Pearl paths led to an open tower formed of iridescent shells and softly glowing fish. But these wonders did not capture Sezaru's attention. All he could see was the crumpled woman kneeling in pain at the base of the shell-like throne.

The room around her was a ruin. Destroyed chips of shell, burned and twisted, lay across the floor like discarded pieces of pottery. A set of magnificent swords, long ago lost to the sea, rested in a twist of cord beneath their ornamental stand. The stand itself was ruined, the loose splinters of enameled wood floating in the water at strange angles.

The woman knelt by the side of her throne, a single pale hand grasping the clam-shells at the base of the tall chair. Her delicate face was bloodied, her eyes closed, but her body still held a palpable aura of power and strength, as though the Dragon that watched over her was in frenzy and the water kami raced through the palace seeking to destroy whatever had harmed their chosen one. The palace was shifted, its walls cracked by terrible struggle. Columns of cracked ice lay in shattered rivers across the floor, marking the dead like gravestones over the ashes of their sacrifice.

"Oracle!" Sezaru rushed through the twisting paths to her side. He leaped over the small staircase that led up to the dais and knelt beside the small, dark-haired woman.

"Too late, child of Void," the Oracle of Water whispered through her pain. "I could not hold them longer, but by the laws of the Dragon, I could not waive your tests." Despite the bruises, she still retained her *on*, the face that Rokugani nobles showed to the world. Her visage was cool and impassive, unruffled by the combat. The Oracle's calm demeanor was impressive, given the imbalance that surrounded her.

Even though he was concerned for the Oracle, Sezaru phrased his words cautiously. Every mortal received only one question of an Oracle in a lifetime. Incautious phrasing could undo him, denying him the reason he had come in the first place.

"Stand, if you can." He helped her into the throne, easing the Oracle's slender body onto the conch shell. As he did, he felt the power within her small frame quiver and strengthen. Before his eyes, her wounds began to heal. Already, the Dragon moved within her, purifying the Oracle's body with its touch.

The attack must have been recent, but Sezaru did not dare waste his question on such an obvious matter. The wounds on the Oracle's body closed slowly, but the wounds to the palace would not be healed as easily. Whatever had broken in had managed to evade the spirits of water and defy a Dragon. There were few in Rokugan that could possibly face an Oracle within her palace.

She opened her eyes, and for a moment, rage crossed her serene features. Sezaru stood his ground as she raised her countenance. "There is little time to delay," she whispered. "Those who have caused this damage are moving toward their goal, while you stand here waiting for truth to find you. There is no time, Imperial Wolf." The way the Oracle spoke seemed halfway between mocking and compassion. "Already, you are too late to stop what has occurred here. And soon, you will be too late to stop the next attack."

"You were attacked." Sezaru murmured, agreeing. Oracles were not known for their forthcoming natures, but in this case, he felt understanding pass between himself and the frail woman on the throne.

"Yes, Sezaru-san," the Oracle said. Would his mother's eyes, once so compassionate and so filled with joy, now look on him with that draconic detachment? "I had prepared your answer for you, but it was stolen by those who came before you, taken by your greatest enemy."

His greatest enemy? An answer . . . stolen? Sezaru's brow furrowed, and he ran his fingers through his hair. "The Oracles are the soul of wisdom, yet you were surprised by this enemy, surprised enough that he defeated your guardians without alerting you to his entry." Sezaru carefully kept his tone neutral, phrasing statements and not questions. "You knew I was coming, though you could not foresee his entry."

The Oracle nodded, her long dark hair flowing in the water's waves. "This intruder knew how to conceal himself from the spirits of water, even in their own haven. He used powerful magic. *Dark* magic. There are only two things of water that I cannot read, Sezaru-san. The first is the flow of rain, which cascades too fast for even my eyes to see its passing. The second . . . the second is the flow of blood. I do not believe I need to tell you why my powers abhor its nature."

Blood. The darkest of all magic came from blood and flesh. "Maho," Sezaru whispered. "Magic used by the unclean servants of the Shadowlands—and by their masters, the great Oni."

"One thought defeated will rise again, his face hidden behind another's mask," the Water Oracle whispered beneath Sezaru's words. Her voice was as light and soft as the whisper of the waves outside his father's palace; but it held an icy finality that chilled Sezaru to the bone.

He raised his eyes, stepping toward her. "You know why my mother left the Imperial throne open without an heir to protect it. Without an heir, the Empire is strewn like wheat chaff on the wind."

"Worse," the Oracle murmured. "It is an egg balanced on one end—and soon the world will turn, and the egg will fall to the ground. Cracked, it cannot continue."

Sezaru's eyes grew wide. "The heavens are out of balance."

"Void cannot also be the sun, Sezaru."

The Water Oracle held up first one hand and then the other. In one lay a black pearl, shimmering in darkness so great that Sezaru could almost see stars in its reflection. In the other, she held a small copy of the Imperial Throne, brilliant in a ray of light. The Oracle drew her hands together slowly, as if some great unseen force pressed against the movement. When her hands touched, there was a flash and a sharp cracking noise, and Sezaru felt his stomach twist. She opened her palms once more, and in them was only dust.

Her voice an echo of the past, the Oracle spoke, "When the celestial heavens shift out of balance, Sezaru-sama, who will put it right again?"

The Wolf's keen senses gripped the question. This was the second time an Oracle had asked it of him, and now it meant even more now than when Tonbo had posed it. "Mortal hands made this imbalance when they forced Kaede to take the throne by causing my father's death. The one who killed my father is also moving to destroy Rokugan."

The Oracle raised an eyebrow at Sezaru's quick assessment. "Very good, shugenja, but time is running short. Already, the sun is approaching the horizon in those lands far above. Your cord weakens, and your spell will soon fail. You must leave this realm. But first . . . I believe you had a question for me?"

Sezaru could feel the Oracle's intense gaze on him. He had considered his question carefully, yet the information the Oracle knew—her attacker, those directly behind the cataclysmic changes facing Rokugan—could he truly ignore the implications of that, or leave unasked the opportunity to discover their identities?

The golden cord in his grasp twisted between his fingers, and Sezaru's eyes narrowed in realization.

"What was my answer?" He bowed slightly as he posed his question, both as a sign of respect and to hide the triumph in his eyes.

The Oracle paused, lacing her fingers before a slightly bowed mouth. "You are as clever as your mother," she whispered with the sound of rain tinkling on glass. She rose from her throne, her torn kimono fanning out behind her. She walked across the room to a broken table that had rested within an alcove of the wall.

"Here, in this place, lay your gift," she moved aside a torn silk cloth that had once covered the table, revealing a strange, upright holder. For a moment, Sezaru thought it might have been a sword-holder, but he realized that it was much too wide to hold even the largest Crab no-dachi. The broken wood was U-shaped, wider at the bottom than at the ends, as if designed to hold something circular.

"This was where the Dragon's Talon lay, Sezaru—a gift that would have allowed you to find and best your father's killer. But now it is gone, and there is nothing in the world that can replace it. This artifact was a talon of the Celestial Dragon, broken when he tried—long ago—to tread upon the earth. The land rejected him, casting him back into the stars, but his talon remained in the mountainside. It still bears shards of the Dragon's power—the only dragon with no Oracle, no eyes upon the earth. It is his sole conduit, his only link to mortality, and it holds more power within it than even an Oracle. However, such power does not come without dangers. The Celestial Dragon is also attuned with all those of his kind. The talon can locate any Dragon—or any Oracle. We cannot hide from it, nor can our magic affect the talon's bearer. With this, you could find Kaede, if that is truly your will."

Sezaru cursed silently as the voice in his mind echoed with mocking laughter. Such a treasure . . . lost. His last hope of finding Kaede and solving the riddle of the throne she left behind, and now it was in the hands of his enemies.

The Water Oracle continued. "The power of the talon is of the land of the Dragons, of the kami and the spirits of the Celestial

Heavens. As such, it is a power that stands as their equal. It can harm them or even kill them. The Sun has died and been reborn—the Moon as well—but Dragons? They are eternal creatures, Sezaru, separated from the cycle of this mortal world except through us, their Oracles. If one is destroyed . . . it will not return." Her eyes were bright and strange, like pools of water sparkling with light. "That is why the talon was stolen before you could take it, Sezaru. That is your enemy's plan."

Sezaru's world rocked. He sank to his knees to consider the implications. If one of the Dragons died the element would fail and fall to ash. The world would end, consumed in imbalance and ravaged by the anger of the Celestial Kami. One by one, each of the Dragons—ancient guardians of fire, air, water, void, and earth—would die forever.

"Blissful Kami," Sezaru slowly rocked back upon his heels. Inside, the voice's laughter redoubled, reverberating painfully into the depths of his soul. "That cannot be allowed to happen." No wonder the Water Oracle was so forthcoming with her information. Surely her Dragon must know the implications of this theft. By helping Sezaru, the Dragon of Water was protecting its own existence.

"I must go," Sezaru pushed back to his feet, steely determination in his eyes.

"I have lost your gift, shugenja, and tradition demands that I replace what has been lost. Although I have little beyond the talon and my own wisdom, I do have something—an item once kept secret within palaces and locked doors, but lost into the ocean. And thus, it came into my care."

She moved back to her throne, her hand rising into the water around her as the lake swirled at her command. The great conch shell of the throne swiveled, turning on its edge to reveal a small alcove beyond. Though the room was dark, Sezaru could see an object hung upon the wall. It was as round as a man's torso and carved from a single sheet of obsidian. Circular, it glimmered faintly with reflected light, revealing the distorted image of Sezaru and the Oracle within its mirrored surface. Though the images were true, they had glassiness to them, a depth to the image that shone far beneath the surface of the glass and into a void of darkness.

"The Obsidian Mirror," Sezaru breathed, stepping into the chamber and standing a foot from the black stone circle. "It was thought lost at the Day of Thunder. How did you come to have it?"

Although she did not have to answer, the Oracle smiled. "When Bayushi Kachiko returned from the Burning Sands, she sent away her servants and walked by the sea." The Oracle of Water placed her hands on the frame of the mirror, drawing it down from its place upon the alcove's wall. "She knew then that her days were numbered, that the Empire did not favor the heroes of its past. She cast aside the mirror then, swearing that no lesser samurai should know its secrets, and it sank into the depths of the ocean below. She died, much later, her body swallowed by the dark waters of a secret lake, but the mirror . . . the mirror, the waters brought to me."

The Oracle drew a silken kimono over the mirror, wrapping it tightly in soft folds of delicately woven silk. "It has lost much of its power now, I fear, as the Moon that created it has changed and is no more." As the kimono covered the reflection, Sezaru felt the voice within him lessen, its laughter and its taunts fading into silence once more. "But it still has magic within it. Magic—and an intelligence that even I cannot understand. Do not come to rely on it, Wolf, or it will possess you. Remember that—" she gazed into his eyes as she passed the mirror into his hands— "no matter what lands you tread, or what visions you may see, do not trust the mirror fully, or all will be lost."

"I swear it on my honor." Sezaru bowed. "I will not forget."

6 PUZZLES AND ANSWERS

Water pooled around Sezaru's silken robes as he stepped out of White Shore Lake, the golden thread wound into a ball in his fist. Beneath the other arm he carried a thin package as round as a serving-platter. The sun was setting, its dim glow illuminating silver ripples across the wide lake. He had escaped drowning by mere minutes.

Soshi Angai drew the ribbon of golden cord to her as Sezaru moved, a silent smile illuminating her beautiful features. Angai bowed again and lifted a folded robe from the rocky shore. As Koshei approached from the campsite, she held the robe out with a deep bow.

"Sezaru-sama—" Angai's eyes twinkled behind her frail white mask— "I regret to say that nothing of interest occurred here while you were away. The sun rose and set, the wind came and left again, and four flocks of birds have passed overhead without even so much as a song. However, there is one great battle that has occurred in your absence, but it is not my duty to tell you of its hero." Her tone was sober, but held much mockery behind its smooth and gentle tones.

"Oh?" Sezaru raised a white eyebrow as he took the dry robe from Koshei's hands.

Koshei, too, seemed pleased to see him. "Your share of the victory, Master, and may it please you." Smiling, Koshei bowed as he handed him a platter of rice balls, rolled around sweet pieces of raw fish.

After Sezaru changed into the dry robe, he sat beside the small campfire in the gathering dusk and listened to his two companions talk quietly about the world. He ate in silence, and the others did not ask about his journey. Some knowledge was only for the seeker and not for his yojimbo, no matter how trusted they were. Yet his eyes traveled past their gentle faces toward the bundle of silk resting by the packs near the river. It called to him in a way he could not understand, with the half-familiar echo of dreams long forgotten.

"We leave this place tomorrow," Sezaru replied to a half-heard question spoken by Toturi Koshei." There is even more to do than we thought—and very little time.

"Time, sama?" Angai asked respectfully, her soft voice catching the Wolf's attention. He tore his gaze from the bundle long enough to meet her eyes and nod.

"Someone is sabotaging the Empire from within. The Oracle confirmed that my father's death, my mother's disappearance— all of these events and all those leading up to them—were carefully arranged." Sezaru saw their eyes widen.

"Can we find them?" Koshei's hand skipped idly toward the sword by his side. As if without knowing his own movements, his fingers clenched near its handle. "Is there enough time?"

Angai lowered sooty lashes over her dark eyes, considering Sezaru's words. "If you know their faces, there are those among the Scorpion who can discover if those who would attack the Empire in this way are known to us. If they are not, then there is only one other solution." She and Sezaru exchanged long stares as Koshei blinked in confusion.

"Your suspicions, and those of your clan, would be correct," Sezaru agreed. "Those who would harm the Empire are almost certainly allied with the Shadowlands. But that does not mean their power is limited to that dark land."

Koshei's eyes hardened. "The samurai of Rokugan have always known that there is darkness among us. In the time of He-who-must-not-be-named—"

"Fu Leng," Sezaru interrupted. His voice was sharp. "Always call him by his name. To hide his name is to inspire fear. Though he may be dead, we must not allow him even that faint power."

Abashed, Koshei nodded. "Yes, Sezaru-sama." Still, he huddled closer to the fire before continuing. "When Fu Leng possessed the last of the Hantei Emperors, there were those even among the great clans who turned traitor to the Jade Throne—warlords, generals, courtiers, and even members of the Imperial house who swore allegiance to the Shadowlands and were tainted by its power."

"If there were such individuals among the clans now, using their influence in the courts to persuade Toturi to travel on that day, down that road—" Angai pushed a lock of dark hair from its fallen rest across her white mask— "they could also have persuaded Kaede to abandon her throne, found a way to influence her decisions, to call her attention to facts that only supported her concerns, and none that alleviated them." Her face was sober. "There are words that can be spoken, thoughts which can be brought to the forefront of a ruler's mind without ever raising their suspicions."

"You know much of such things?' Koshei asked wryly.

Angai did not look at the samurai beside her, instead raising her cup of tea in a sip that conveniently hid her expression. "I learned a great deal from the Crane during my time among them," she said.

The double-entendre was not lost to Sezaru, and he smiled. "Angai is correct. No matter who our enemy may be, it is clear that he has spread his icy touch throughout the Empire. My sisters and my brothers are too involved to see what is before them. They have not my clarity of vision. Yet even if I told them what I know, I can guess their responses. Tsudao would hunt the Empire with sword and battle-cry, destroying all those who stood before her—and she would miss the very heart of the treachery she sought to root out. Naseru would seek to ally with the darkness just long enough to uncover its secrets and destroy them in a great betrayal—but in so doing, he would risk his own soul. And Kaneka . . . well, who knows what he would do? He is a die to be rolled by a powerful hand, and more likely to become a stone on the board than an Emperor placing them."

"Then, what do we do?" Koshei asked. His hazel eyes were serious and quiet.

"We seek answers wherever we can find them—and we find a way to reach the Empress wherever she has gone."

Angai's mouth opened into a silent O, and Koshei's hand clenched into a fist. Sezaru placed his bowl of rice upon the ground near the fire. "It is a puzzle," he continued, "that has been placed before us. It must be solved."

He rose from the fire, wringing the last of the moisture from his unbound hair. With a sweeping movement, Sezaru walked toward the lakeshore again, staring down into the reflection of the stars upon the water. The lake was without ripples, like a long glassy sheet of obsidian spotted with the faint brightness of stars. It seemed like an unbroken window into the void. Behind him, Sezaru could still feel the soft tug of the Obsidian Mirror, its surface shielded from his eyes by a sheath of silk and shadow.

"Sezaru-sama," Angai said softly, but her voice carried clearly against the water. "Do you think this puzzle has a solution?"

All puzzles have solutions, Sezaru thought, but he did not answer aloud. Instead, he turned away from the lake and reached to pick up the bundle that lay by their packs. "Keep the fire burning, Angai-san," he murmured. "Soon, very soon, I will need the warmth." He felt the heaviness of it, the smoothness sliding beneath fabric. Despite the chill night air, the bundle was warm in his hands.

Sezaru turned away, his steps echoing faintly against the rocky lakeshore. Angai and Koshei did not follow. For an instant, he imagined how the scene must appear; his loose white hair the only shining light against a background of black stars above and black stars below. How strange, he thought, to be trapped as they were in only one world. Two worlds were open to him—two worlds and more, and all threatened by the imbalance in the heavens.

When he reached a point where their fire seemed only slightly brighter than the other sparkling lights, Sezaru placed his burden down upon a large stone. He paused to listen, but the voice that mocked him so often from the depths of his soul was silent. Only soft sounds whispered in the night—the distant crackle of fire and the ripple of water softly touching rocks. The voice's silence disturbed him more than any words it could have murmured in his mind. Sezaru shook his head, focusing his will for the task ahead, and began to unwrap the Oracle's gift.

The silk flowed away beneath each pass of his hands, uncurling like soft petals. It fell away, revealing the smooth obsidian within. When the mirror was fully uncovered, it lay heavily against the silken pool upon the stone. The obsidian faintly reflected a thousand stars above in the heavens, opening up a new world within the world.

The Obsidian Mirror, formed of the blood of the moon god Onnotangu. The blood fell eons ago, when the founders of the clans fell from heaven, before Rokugan was conceived. Sezaru touched the glass, feeling its infinite smoothness. Although the Obsidian Mirror had a place in many Rokugani myths, its most famous owner was—

An image flitted against the black glass—a woman beautiful beyond comprehension, her black lace mask delicate against perfect features. She stood in the golden gardens of Otosan Uchi, throwing open its massive gates as a band of weary samurai gathered against the storm.

Sezaru shook his head, lifting his questing hands from the mirror's surface. The impression had been powerful, almost overwhelming. Her name was Bayushi Kachiko, once Empress of Rokugan and a member of the Scorpion Clan. During the War of the Thunders, she sat by the bedside of a dying Emperor, poisoning him slowly. And all the while, she watched the Mirror, taking in the changes in Rokugan and using that knowledge for her own ends.

In the end, her plans turned against her, and the Empire was saved only because she chose to work with the other Thunders against the powers of a dark god—Fu Leng, child of Lord Moon, Master of the Shadowlands.

The mirror's surface rippled, and for a moment, Sezaru heard the voice in his mind whisper, *Caution.*

He jerked his hands away, realizing that they had moved toward the mirror of their own. The mirror showed him an image of Bayushi Kachiko on the Day of Thunder. What might it do if he held it while considering the power of Fu Leng? The implication chilled Sezaru, and he took a step away from the stone. This mirror was powerful, but like all things, it was a tool—an item of dark spirit, of Void and of the Moon. Sezaru stared into the starry sky. Where was she, the moon goddess, the one who had taken on the burdens of the moon when Onnotangu died? But she was not in the heavens tonight. This was the time of the dark moon, the empty sky, and the river of stars was Sezaru's only companion against the darkness.

Sobered, Sezaru took the mirror from its bed of silk and placed it against the stone. He padded the silk into a cushion and knelt before the Obsidian Mirror. Steeling his mind, Sezaru pressed his fingers together and whispered a prayer to the kami. Only with their guidance would he be able to step into this puzzle and find his next move. Like a *go* board, the pieces around him were already being placed, and he must make his move soon or not at all.

Sezaru steeled his mind into sharp focus. Anger, loss, impatience . . . these things offended the kami and would surely lead him to destruction. He must leave them behind. There were greater matters at hand.

He opened his eyes.

The stars in the mirror glittered faintly, and Sezaru reached out to brush them away. A sweep of his hand across the obsidian surface, and the stars fell away from the smooth glass like pebbles. The way cleared, Sezaru reached out with his consciousness to find the cold glass before him. Then, releasing his intuition, he swam into the glassy, unfamiliar darkness and left the world behind.

It felt as if he was floating in emptiness, suddenly bereft of wind, air, and breath. The elements still existed around him, outside the glass of the Obsidian Mirror, but in this place he could not feel them. He spread his hands, reaching out to the utter blackness that encompassed him.

"Show me," he whispered.

Sluggish at first, the Mirror shifted around him in long, slow patterns. He felt it questioning, testing, like a child in the darkness reaching for a guiding hand. Yet beneath that delicate innocence, Sezaru could sense something greater, something dark, horrible, and lingering—waiting to be set free. It did not fight against him nor struggle to control or condemn him. It only watched from the infinite blackness. Its very passivity was threatening, forcing Sezaru to keep his guard aware.

The darkness hovered around him, eager and curious, touching his face with bleak fingers. He turned, seeking in the darkness for the portal though which he had come, but found nothing. Only blackness surrounded him, unlit by even a grain of star.

"Show me," his voice was louder this time, echoing in the emptiness that surrounded him. Disconnected from his body, it seemed as if the world of the elements was a vast distance away, and the darkness was the only reality he had ever known.

He could see madness before him, staring him in the face with yellowed eyes.

"Show me!" Sezaru's command was that of an emperor, a ruler used to giving orders and having them followed. He called on every memory of his father that he possessed and shouted once more, "Show me my mother! Show me Toturi Kaede!"

The darkness gathered around him, moving with the press of Sezaru's will. He reached out with his hands, gathered it, and felt it gathering him into its embrace. He suddenly realized that if he chose, he could step through it into the Void. A path of shining lights coalesced before him, inviting him to walk forward. This was not the time—nor was he interested in the emptiness of the Void. He was interested only in Kaede. Sezaru steeled his thoughts and forced the mirror to listen to his command.

And then, the world changed once more.

Around him there was no longer darkness but instead a thousand brilliant points of light. He stood on a shelf of stars, staring down at a cavern of moonlight and brilliance that burned into Sezaru's eyes.

"Can we not stop it?" Kaede's voice, his mother's voice, soft and sweet. Sezaru peered past the veil of stars and saw her, kneeling beside a dragon. The dragon's scales shone with an inky blackness, and its eyes glowed with purest starlight. Its coils looped around Kaede, holding her protectively as she wept over its blind eyes. Beneath one clawed foot, Sezaru could see blood spreading like a thousand crawling spiders, seeping out from a wound within the dragon's heart.

"Kaede-sama!" Sezaru called, but as he did so the image rippled. They were nothing more than an image shown in the mirror. Quickly, he controlled his anger and need and pressed his feelings into nothingness. She could not hear him, could not see him. In fact, he had no reason to believe that this was a scene of the present. It could just as easily have been the future—or the past.

"There is nothing we can do." Another voice. This time, male. Even as Sezaru recognized it, the speaker stepped into the vision's view. Tonbo Toryu knelt beside the Void Dragon with a look of infinite sorrow. "Only a complete convergence of the elements can undo what the shard has done. Death is inevitable." Tonbo knelt beside Kaede. "I tried to stop, Kaede-sama, stop us all from walking this path. The darkness lies within imperial blood. I know that now. But now it is too late. I am so sorry."

"No," Kaede raised her head from the noble creature, tears sparkling upon her face. Looking down once more at the dragon whose tremendous head rested in her lap, Kaede shivered. "This blood, Toryu, this death and all those to follow, is on my hands."

"Behold! The end of Rokugan!" Tonbo Toryu whispered, his voice empty and hollow. He turned away, his aged face etched with sorrow, etched with regret. "Because of our weakness, we reach the end—the end of the elements and the end of the world."

As he spoke, the stars began to tremble, falling one by one from the black cloak of the heavens as the dragon died. Far below, in Rokugan, the oceans turned to blood, washing over the land in terrible swells as the earth itself broke open like a heart betrayed.

"It will be the end—" Kaede's voice carried an unimaginable pain as the dragon's glorious eyes dimmed and closed— "of us all!"

Sezaru's eyes fluttered open. The world around him shifted into painfully sharp focus—rocks, trees, lake, and the soft murmur of Koshei and Angai speaking over the crackle of the fire. Everything seemed deeply clear—the rushing of the elements around him, the murmur of the water kami within White Shore Lake, even the distant song of wind kami far above.

He could see tiny images in the Obsidian Mirror, growing fainter as the reflection of the stars began to encroach on the blackness within the mirror's depths. Within a few seconds, the shimmering likenesses of Kaede, Tonbo, and the Void Dragon vanished into nothingness.

Chilled, Sezaru stood and placed the silken bands once more around the mirror's surface. As he wrapped the Obsidian Mirror, Sezaru considered the implications of what he had just seen. The Void Dragon, dying. Kaede, with blood on her hands. The elements, shattered and falling into dust. Well, obviously, because the world around him wasn't ending, this vision had been of the future.

But could the future be altered before it could occur? He could use the mirror again, seek for an earlier reflection, follow it back to . . .

No.

Sezaru stood in shock, amazed at how swiftly his thoughts had turned to the Obsidian Mirror to solve his problems. It was addictive, demanding, a possessive spirit set free within him. Without noticing it, his hands had already begun to unwrap its binding, releasing its shimmering surface so that he could take another glimpse within. And once within it, he could watch as the future happened, see the world as it unfolded. He would never need to move or act. He would simply watch and be entranced by the images revealed deep within its mysterious surface.

No. Sezaru shook his head, clearing it of the Obsidian Mirror's siren call.

The Oracle of Water's words floated back to him as he stood on the lakeshore. *Do not come to rely on it, Wolf, or it will possess you.*

Now Sezaru fully understood her warning. If he sought too often for the future within the mirror, he would become its pawn and lose any free will of his own. In effect, by asking it for answers, he would lose his ability to change the images he found within its glassy core.

"I must find answers another way," he said, tucking the mirror back within its deep wrappings. "Tonbo Toryu . . . in the vision, Toryu said he sought to warn Kaede before this could happen. He must know something that can aid me, if I can reach him in time. Perhaps he has answers that he does not know—or perhaps, with the theft of the Dragon's Talon, the world has changed for him as well."

As Sezaru strode smoothly back toward his companions in the camp, a dark shadow hiding near the stone twisted and moved. With the silent movement of water flowing toward an inevitable sea, it slipped into the night.

7 | TWO WINDS IN DARKNESS

Toturi Koshei ran through the woods, his katana thumping against his back with each step. He had secured it between his shoulders with a thin cord. The run was long, and he breathed in quiet pants as he jogged through the autumn woods. Sunlight drifted down through the oak and ash trees, illuminating the wide path. Koshei smiled, enjoying the activity.

He passed over a hill, feeling the sun warm on his back, and leaped over a branch that had fallen into the road. Only a short time now, and he would be at his destination. The woods were busy today, filled with squirrels rushing to fill their larders before winter came. Birds swooped in patterns above the forest, crows cawing in victory as they drove the hawks away. In a few weeks, it would be winter, but for now, the rays of the autumn sun warmed the world around him, turning it to gold.

As he crested a hill, the treeline opened, and he could see the road widen ahead. He jogged through the edge of the forest, smiling as he looked down on the palace that spread its golden gates upon the plain. Kyuden Seppun, the palace on the hill, smiled down upon the forest below from the center of a wide wall. Green-robed magistrates on sturdy ponies rode between the massive gates, carrying missives, new codes of law, and records of justice from across the Empire. Somewhere below, amid the palatial walls, the Imperial Magistrates were meeting with the master of the lists, Hantei Naseru, Sezaru's brother, who made judgment based on the Emperor's word.

Toturi Koshei smiled and then took up his jogging once more. It was his duty to inform Naseru-sama that he would soon be having guests.

* * * * *

Sezaru and Angai walked solemnly through the Seppun forest, following the road to Kyuden Seppun at a leisurely pace. Sezaru's mind was taken up by the puzzle of the Obsidian Mirror. Angai watched the sides of the road, searching for any disturbance within the peaceful woods. All the while, she followed him demurely, covering her concern behind a mask of a handmaiden's duty.

The rumble of hooves broke through the peaceful sounds of the forest, and Sezaru looked up to see two horsemen coming toward them. Angai drew her fan from her belt, turning it so that the metal blades were concealed in the pretty patterns of the fan. Sezaru reached for no weapon, but simply raised his eyes from the road to meet the horsemen.

They were dressed in green, carrying shining pikes with the symbol of a golden laurel on a green flag at the end. They reined in their steeds before Sezaru and lifted their pikes in a salute to the Emperor's son. "In the name of Hantei Naseru," the captain said, "Imperial Prince of the Empire and servant to the Emperor's word, we greet you."

Sezaru smiled. "As usual, my brother's ability to plan for all occasions never ceases to amaze me."

Watching the guard's faint flush, Sezaru smiled. As he had expected, Naseru was caught completely unprepared for his older brother's visit. How fortunate that Sezaru's foresight had saved Naseru a bit of face. No doubt, Naseru had every movement of the armies of Rokugan marked on a map; he knew the movements of every spy in Otosan Uchi, and could accurately predict internal clan coups from the largest uprising to a simple conflict between the sons of the minor families. He was the center of Rokugani justice, and the spider within a web as large as the nation. But when it came to understanding Sezaru, Naseru never could—and never would—be able to predict his actions. It was the one flaw in Naseru's web—and oh, how Sezaru loved to remind him.

They followed Naseru's samurai down to Kyuden Seppun, taking their time and enjoying the afternoon sunshine. By the time they arrived, the gates of the palace had four men on each side, dressed in their finest attire and holding aloft keenly honed naginatas. They stood erect and saluted as the horsemen rode between them. Sezaru and Angai followed at a more leisurely pace, the Wolf's robes shimmering in the warm autumn glow.

At the end of the row, the doors to the palace were open, allowing fresh winds and warm air to circulate through the massive building. Inside, Sezaru could see many samurai buzzing about a central chamber, carrying papers to and fro as if the truth could be found in them by pacing out each word. At their center sat a man upon a steel and bamboo stool, stroking his narrow beard with a steady hand while he listened to three arguing justices at once. The man nodded to one, shaking his fingers negatively to the second. As he stood, the third bowed and backed away, still reading his case aloud. Four steps later, Naseru turned to him, barked a short command, and then continued on.

His black eye, the one not covered by a silken patch, was fixed on Sezaru. He crossed the pine floor of the room with powerful strides, and the samurai scattered before him like cawing crows. Naseru reached the edge of the palace at the same time Sezaru passed the fourth guard. They stood in silence, a few paces from each other. At precisely the same moment, and with precisely the same hint of resignation in their eyes, the two brothers bowed acutely equal bows, and then snapped once more to attention.

"Sezaru-san," Naseru greeted him. His voice was clipped and precise. Naseru's face was stern, his nose cutting a hawk like silhouette. "You are welcome in this place, my brother."

"I thank you, Naseru-san." Sezaru smiled, watching the play of shadow against his brother's features.

"What is the purpose of this visit, Sezaru? Have the kami sent you to divulge wisdom? In this time of trouble, the Empire could use wisdom to shield it against the dangers it must face."

"There is wisdom in all things, my brother, and all paths lead through danger before they reach peace." Sezaru baited him, knowing full well his brother's true question. "Have the kami come to you, brother, whispering riddles in the wind? Or are you simply concerned for the future, that you seek their guidance?"

Naseru's brow furrowed in minor annoyance. "You have traveled far, my brother. And after our father's death, none heard from you. You were closer to Kaede-san than any of us, and her actions must have been particularly surprising to you." Naseru gestured, and Sezaru fell in step with him easily. "I thought that perhaps if any of us had heard from her . . ."

It was likely that hearing from Kaede was the last thing Naseru truly wanted. His brother was never that transparent, and Naseru always had more than one plan in motion. "No, Naseru-san, I have not heard from her." That much, at least, was true. "Has the Empire been well?"

Sezaru followed his brother through the winding paths of the gardens around Kyuden Seppun. The sand crunched softly beneath their feet, and Sezaru could hear the soft echo of Angai's footfalls some small distance behind them.

"The laws are broken no more and no less than they were before, yet the courts are frightened, Sezaru. They chatter like birds, backing first one candidate and then the next." Naseru folded his hands into his sleeves, tucking his fingers out of sight. "Without a powerful leader, they flail."

"As any army would do, without their general."

"Come, now, Sezaru-san," Naseru replied smoothly. "Do you truly think that a general could bring these severed parts together? Look about the Empire. Even with the Void in your eyes, you must surely see the obvious. Rokugan's generals are too busy leading their armies against one another to lead the Empire. The Dragon, Lion, and Phoenix clans are at war. The Crab and

Crane renew old rivalries, and the Unicorn attack any who threaten the peace. Which of course—" he sighed in disparagement— "in itself breaks the peace."

"Rokugan's peace has always been fragile."

"But its throne has been strong. Yes, yes, even in the hands of those who did not truly deserve to possess it."

"And where is the weakness in the throne?" Sezaru's white hair fluttered in the soft breeze as he paused to look out over the raked sand of the gardens. Five black rocks jutted out from the white sand, marking their place within the garden in shallow, concentric rings of ranked sand around their bases. Like the elements, thought Sezaru, like the dragons that bear their weight, pressing against the earth and causing ripples. Are we merely reflections of those ripples, our lives moved by their mere presence?

"It lies in us, Sezaru, in our accordance to Kaede's will. The Empire must be guided into the future, or it will fall into the horrors of its past. Do you not agree that an heir must step forward and protect the Empire from itself?"

So that was Naseru's intent. If Sezaru agreed with him that Rokugan needed a clear heir, he would be breaking Kaede's will—and because his magic was as respected as Kaede's, his agreement would lend significant credence if Naseru chose to break her command and seize the throne. Yet, if Sezaru disagreed and said that Rokugan did not need a leader, it would be tantamount to stating he did not seek the throne.

Clever. Very clever.

Walk carefully, for this way lies more dangers that you can imagine. Poor Sezaru, so used to solving riddles and puzzles set forth by the kami, yet so helpless when it comes to the working of mortal man. Sezaru pushed aside the mocking words and smiled.

"Do you see the rocks in the sand, Naseru?" he asked. "Like them, we stand amid shifting terrain. They are surrounded by ripples created by their mere presence. Given time, the ripples will return, and swell, and flow—and one will overwhelm the others. But does that truly matter? When the rain comes, the sand will be smoothed and flattened by its passage, and the ripples will exist no longer."

REE SOESBEE

After a moment spent contemplating Sezaru's words, Naseru whispered, "Have you seen the storm on the horizon, brother?"

"It is the reason I walk the breadth of the Empire in search of the Temple of Thunder. When I find it, I will know the truth."

"The Temple of Thunder." His brother frowned. "My . . . servants . . . know of it. It exists in the Shadowlands, deep within those Dark Lands. You walk into great danger, Sezaru. But, if you tell me why you seek it, I will endeavor to have my servants provide you with a map that will aid you in your quest."

So eager to be rid of me, Naseru? Sezaru wondered. Perhaps my brother thinks I will walk into the Shadowlands and become tainted, unable to return. One less contender for his precious throne.

Still, a map would provide Sezaru with a starting point—and if anyone possessed a map of the Shadowlands, he was not surprised that it was his brother.

"I seek it because it holds the answers to danger." Sezaru turned away from the garden and looked once more into Naseru's eyes. "Kaede's danger. Right now she stands on the edge of a precipice that will swallow all the Empire. I have seen the threat that stands against her." He flicked one hand against his silken sleeve. "It is real. I feel the storm coming, Naseru. And it brings with it the destruction of us all."

His brother's eyes widened as he tried to assess the nuances of Sezaru's words. "But you said you had not heard from Kaede-sama . . ."

Koshei trotted up to them, kneeling instantly as he reached his master's side. Naseru's voice died, and the brothers fell into silence.

"Your rooms are prepared, sama," Koshei said. "You asked me to tell you when all was ready."

"Very good, Koshei-san. I am certain that our host will not mind weary travelers resting before dinner?" Half a question, half a demand, Sezaru raised his eyes to meet Naseru's piercing gaze.

"Of course not, Sezaru-san," Naseru stared at him for a long moment, then turned and prowled back into the throng of magistrates waiting for his attentions. Naseru would stand by his word, Sezaru knew. Before the Wolf and his companions left with the dawn, the map would be delivered to their chambers.

Sezaru kept his face very straight while he followed Koshei to their rooms. He would have to remember to commend his yojimbo after they had left Naseru's palace. Koshei had performed his duties exactly as he had been asked.

* * * * *

Rokugan spread out before them in rolling hills and thick forests, and the three companions traveled ever southward through its wide glades. After six days of travel, they were deep in the Lion lands, heading toward Beiden Pass and the roads south toward the distant Shadowlands. The late afternoon sun slanted downward over fields of thick grain, and the peasants in the field carried burdens of rice and wheat in wicker baskets on deeply stooped backs.

The roads were hard-packed earth here, well-traveled by traders and armies for centuries. Beiden Pass was the only true trade route across the mountains that divided Rokugan like a belt across its waist, and the Lion, Crane, and Scorpion clans argued heatedly over its possession. Troops marched through the area often, but as soon as they came and left once more, bandits would return to plague the lands like locusts. The stench of their activities hung upon the ground like a low fog, testing Sezaru's senses. He could feel the lingering horror of their actions—the murdered peasants, the thievery, the anger and the brutality. To Sezaru, these things fouled the land like a plague, and he covered his face with an ancient mask to avoid their stench.

Angai led the way, her familiarity with these lands bred into her with her Scorpion blood. Her family had fought and died for Beiden Pass, and like all Scorpions, she was deeply connected to it. If they were to make their journey with speed, they would need her guidance.

When she paused, holding her hand in the air, they responded in an instant. "We camp here," she said, staring at the tracks on the ground with concern. "There is too much movement on this road recently. It is better if we continue when the light is better."

They made camp by the edge of the road in a little flatland where signs of old fires broke the smooth consistency of rich soil. The sun set with a golden shimmer across the fields as the Lion peasants carried their heavy burdens home again.

The night was cold and clear, with a touch of winter's breath on the wind. In the distance, owls made their hunting cries, and the occasional sound of movement through the rice fields kept Sezaru and his companions on edge. When the moon rose slowly, pregnant with winter's first frost, Sezaru awoke to the presence of others moving nearby.

Angai was already awake, drawing her mask down over her features in a swift movement. Koshei's eyes were blurring open as Sezaru moved to his feet, the faint sound of sandals against earth echoing in the night air. As Angai lifted her steel-bladed fan to her breast, her dark eyes tried to capture any movement outside the ring of firelight.

"Hold your ground!" a gruff voice commanded as Sezaru caught a glint of light across bare steel. "In the Emperor's name!"

Slowly, four armed samurai approached the camp. Their movements had been stealthy, their steps almost silent against the hard-packed earth. Steel katana gleamed in their hands, catching glints of firelight as they moved to point at each of the three.

Sezaru's lip curled slightly in a smile as Koshei jumped to stand between them. His yojimbo took a defensive stand, sword down, chest bare from sleep. There had been no time to replace his vest, but he held his katana in a ready fist, prepared to meet whatever assault dared attempt to harm Sezaru.

"Bandits," Koshei snarled.

"Worse," Angai countered. "Lion Clan."

Four orange-garbed warriors stepped into the light, their weapons bared and ready for combat. They glared at the companions with muddy faces, their clothing patched and torn. The solders—if that was indeed what they were—seemed competent, if ragged, and held their weapons in steady hands. "You stand on Lion lands," the leader said with a glare. "Do you have writs of passage from your daimyo?"

"We need none." Sezaru replied. "We travel on no clan's business."

The samurai glowered, raising his weapon. "Ronin? Or bandits?" His gaze took in their garments, clean and whole, as well as Sezaru's priestly bearing. "If you're bandits, you seem to be profiting from your work." One of the other Lion chuckled with a sinister bearing, but a glare from his leader silenced him. "Well, whoever you are. I am Fujitze Yoshito, son of Fujitze Sumero, daimyo within the Akodo House of the Lion. You travel on the lands of house Fujitze, loyal samurai of the Lion Clan. We have had more than our share of trouble with bandits since the Emperor's death. If we should find that you are working with these ronin that plague us . . ." The threat was apparent in the young Lion's tone, but Sezaru could hear the uncertainty and concern in the samurai's voice.

Fujitze. A very small house within the Akodo family, raised only a few years ago from peasantry into the nobility through marriage to an Akodo. The Akodo had spent nearly a generation as ronin samurai, abandoned and cast out by the Empire. When they were given back their name, many of them rejoined the Lion Clan, bringing with them their peasant allies, wives, and retainers. For a moment, Sezaru paused, deciding whether he should school this ignorant half-peasant or laugh at his presumption. Luckily, he did not have to make that choice.

A rough voice came from the shadows outside the campfire, and the sounds of several more samurai marching closer echoed in the night. Angai traded concerned glances with Koshei, but the mask that came over Sezaru's features at the sound stilled them both. "Bah, leave them be, Yoshito-san!" the voice shouted brusquely. "They're no harm to you or to the Lion. This one only does as the spirits will him. We should bow and thank the kami that he deigns to walk on the earth at all."

Koshei took a step forward, a growl erupting form his normally shy throat. He lifted his sword slightly, and the Lion around them responded with a steely rustle of blades. Sezaru placed his hand on his yojimbo's shoulder and stared at the figure that approached them from outside the light.

He was tall, dressed in Lion Clan orange with a long katana handing at his side. His features were arrogant, his body chiseled by hard labor and long hours of combat. The men around him were a strange blend of peasantry and samurai, their class distinction showing only through the weapons in their hands. His features struck a painful chord deep within Sezaru's soul, for they looked so much like his father. His father and also Sezaru's father—Toturi.

"A pleasant evening to find you, Kaneka," Sezaru dropped the honorific, causing the samurai around them to bristle. "And you are where you truly belong, I see. So close to the ruts in the earth."

At that, one of the Lion leaped forward, sword bared. His weapon sheared from Koshei's raised blade, dancing along the steel. Angai's fan swirled out, blazingly fast as Koshei disarmed the Lion in a single vicious thrust. The sword flew to one side, its tip thrusting deep within the ground as Angai's blow struck at the base of the samurai's neck. He cried out and then sank to his knees, falling to the ground and pressing his face into the dirt. Angai and Koshei readied their weapons once more, standing like a wall between Sezaru and those who dared threaten him.

A gruff laugh came from Kaneka, and he commanded the other Lion to stand down. They obeyed reluctantly until he grabbed one by the scruff of his neck and shook him soundly. "Defend Lion lands!" Kaneka roared. "Defend her people! But for the sake of all that's holy, don't defend them against their rightful Prince!" The words were another jab at Sezaru's honor, but the Wolf gritted his teeth and ignored it.

Around them, the Lion looked appalled, their swords lowering in confusion as Kaneka stepped against Koshei's blade and stared ice into the yojimbo's eyes. Unsure, Koshei remained stalwart until Sezaru placed a hand on his shoulder. Only then did the yojimbo step aside. Realizing what their master meant, the Lion samurai around them slowly lowered their blades, one or two falling to their knees in humble obeisance to the Imperial Prince. Some of them seemed ashamed that they did not know enough of the Imperial Court to recognize Sezaru. Others seemed angry that their friend had been so easily bested.

"Toturi Sezaru. Sama." The pause was just long enough to clearly show Kaneka's resentment. He was Toturi's bastard son, born not of the Empress Kaede but of a common geisha. The Fourth Wind, and one that stank of dirt and peasantry—shouting from the ruts in the earth that he would one day rule the heavens in Toturi's name. Sezaru despised him, reviled his arrogance and his ignorance, but he could not doubt the protection that Kaneka and his men gave to the peasants of Rokugan. Hunting bandits? Likely, they had already caught them all.

"Kaneka-san," Sezaru responded, stressing the lesser honorific. "Akodo, I believe?" He feigned indifference. "How good of you to remember the face of Empress Kaede's eldest son." Sezaru's gaze did not waver from Kaneka's, their eyes locked in a competitive stare. "Your men are eager for battle, Akodo-san. It would do them well to remember that not every traveler is a threat to Rokugan's peace."

"It is good that Rokugan's nobility is so concerned for her people."

"Rokugan's people must be kept safe from those who would lead them into danger."

A faint growl rose from Kaneka's men, but Sezaru ignored it

"The lands are sickening, Prince. The crops are dying. What danger do you mean? Spiritual? Military?" Kaneka snorted. "The true danger is starvation, but I don't see the courtiers arguing about that in the palaces of Otosan Uchi." Kaneka reached down and pulled up a withered patty of rice, its grains blackened and sick. "Are the nobility concerned for this, shugenja? Or have they even noticed?"

Sezaru stared at the plant in Kaneka's hands, feeling the earth spirits within the bundle. They were cold, mournful, blocked from the sun by some terrible imbalance. Reaching out with his spirit, he could feel many others like them—fields where the crops would never grow, rivers whose waters were fouled and choked by the broken flow of the spirit world. Kaede's imbalance was growing. Her decision to leave the Steel Throne empty was already affecting the world.

"Have no fear, Akodo-san. We will be safely out of Lion lands tomorrow, and therefore you can commend yourself on your guardianship."

"Headed south, Prince?" Kaneka's smile was predatory. "I'm sure you will be safe in Scorpion lands. Bandits are never heard of there, though they have been having problems with the occasional oni." The demons of the Shadowlands traveled throughout the Shadowlands, but it was an oni within the Scorpion lands that had claimed their father's life.

"When we return, I shall be certain to send you word of our triumphs."

"I shall look forward to receiving those small tidings of joy." His emphasis on the word "small" was not lost on Sezaru. "Farewell, Wolf. May your journey be swift."

Kaneka turned away, signaling his men to regroup and move on. With a quick kick to the ribs, he awakened the samurai on the ground and rolled him over, calling to the others to drag their groggy companion back onto his feet.

Sezaru watched the Lion samurai retreat into the darkness, catching a glint of Kaneka's icy eyes as the son of Toturi led his ragged brigade into the night. Four Winds for Rokugan, but only one would, in the end, claim the throne and guide Rokugan into the future. If there was to be a future at all.

"May the kami preserve us from ill fortune," Sezaru murmured to himself, and silently turned away.

8 | JOURNEY INTO DARKNESS

In the south of Rokugan lay the lands of the Crab, marking the Empire's southernmost border—and the only territory that jutted up against the dangers of the Shadowlands. When the Crab Clan first formed, they took these dangerous lands for their own, raising a wall between themselves and their enemies and swearing to stand upon it until the last Crab died spitting into their enemy's blighted face. These were not prosperous lands, nor beautiful ones.

Gray-blue, like the Crab clan's banners, the sky above rumbled with the sound of distant thunder. Drops of chill rain struck the ground from time to time, marking the earth with large dark circles of water that would bring no growth. Early snow melted from those mountains in great rivers, flooding the ground that would, in a few weeks, once again turn to ice.

Yet, as forbidding as the Crab lands were, they seemed a paradise compared to what lay beyond the Wall. From his vantage point on the parapets of Kyuden Hida, Sezaru could see where the wall divided the two territories—gray, fruitless, stone-covered mountains of the Crab to the north; the blackened, boiling, vicious plains of the Shadowlands to the south. Only the Wall, towering in a colossal vein of stone from the eastern ocean to the distant western cliffs, kept the border clear.

In the distance, beyond the wall, figures moved in shambling packs through the tainted land, their shuffling steps marking them as undead or lesser beasts cowering from some greater hunter. Occasionally, a massive oni would make its presence known near the wall. Less often, one would dare to attack or attempt to make its way past the Wall. When that occurred, the Hida would marshal upon the wall, destroying their enemies with relentless ferocity.

The spirits of that land had been corrupted long ago, and they sang to Sezaru. Their call was twisted, tainted by the Shadowlands, vicious and cruel. And yet something in their call, some dark harmony hidden within their movements, was a faint imitation of the sickness he could feel even now, moving through Rokugan.

Kaede, Kaede, thought Sezaru, is this what Rokugan will become because of you? Is this the doom to which your decision will condemn us?

Or worse, there may be no Rokugan left at all. . . .

Sezaru shook his head with a grimace, no longer able to tell if the words came from him or from the voice haunting his thoughts.

"What's wrong, Sezaru-sama?" The voice came from behind him. "Not fond of Crab hospitality?"

Sezaru looked away from the darkness of the Shadowlands to meet the Crab's gaze.

"It is fine, thank you, Hida-san," Sezaru greeted the son of the Crab Clan Champion with polite courtesy—but not too much. Crabs were a rough sort, unused to and unappreciative of the finer points of society. Too much courtesy could seem like obeisance. Not enough, and they would claim insult. Crabs were hard and cold like their lands, but they were honorable men. One simply had to walk with caution. "Have the snows melted sufficiently to allow travel, Durogai?"

"Oh, almost." The burly Crab broke into a smile that was little more than a crack in the granite of his rugged face. "You seem eager to leave. You spend more time on this wall than in the gathering halls below. Best be careful, or you'll be recruited as a Crab!" His laughter rumbled, echoing against the wall as he pounded one fist into the rock with amusement. "Plenty of spirits here to keep you busy, shugenja, if you'll stay—but they aren't kami. They're spirits of the dead, still trying to stand upon the Wall!"

Sezaru smiled. "The early snows may have lengthened our stay in your palace, Hida, but they have not caused me to forget my purpose."

"Too bad. We could use more shugenja. Ours tend to break."

"Only because you run out of catapult fodder and use them."

"They don't fly well, either. Pity." The Hida grinned. "We tried to use my brother once, but he was too heavy. Broke the catapult before it could fire."

"I'm surprised his weight didn't crack the Wall."

Hida Kuron, Durogai's cousin, was one of the largest men in the Empire—and had a ferocity that matched his weight. Durogai chuckled at Sezaru's comment, and once more drove his fist playfully into the stone. "I don't know why you want to go into that wretched land, shugenja," he said with a sobering shake of his head, "but it will surely be a shame if you do not come back."

"My purpose calls me there, Durogai. Fear not. It will call me home again."

Durogai stared at Sezaru with a long, hard gaze. "If you are tainted by the Shadowlands when you return, your position will not help you. Your kami will not help you. You will be destroyed. You know our purpose."

"Then I will be careful."

"Heh." Durogai looked at Sezaru with an unreadable expression. Leaning on the wall, he continued, "Sometimes, careful isn't enough". They stared at the plagued lands beyond for several moments in silence before Durogai spoke again. "You search for Oracles in that dark land?"

"One Oracle. The Oracle of Thunder. He lives in the broken city of Volturnum."

Durogai considered that. "Is he a Dark Oracle, shugenja? Born of a dark dragon?" Crabs were not known for their understanding of religion—or any spiritual matters.

"Dark Oracles technically have no dragon patrons, Durogai, though their power comes from the Dragon. But the Dragon does not choose them. It does not tell them what to do. They draw their power directly from the corruption of the element they represent and exist as sort of a cosmic insult toward the dragons—existing both because of them and despite them."

"A cosmic insult?" The Crab laughed. "Like the Crane?"

Sezaru choked slightly at the Crab's rude jest but managed to keep his composure.

"Do you see that range of mountains there, framed in the branches of that twisted tree?" Sezaru nodded, and Durogai continued. "There, in a bowl formed by a dead volcano, you will find the lost city of Volturnum. Good luck making it that far, with winter so near."

Sezaru knew that Durogai spoke the truth; Naseru's map implied much the same, but with detailed depictions of the lost city. "Are there any samurai among the Crab who know the road there, any who could lead me?"

Durogai chuckled. "Yes, but you can't have them."

Sezaru's brow furrowed. "You would deny me—?"

"I would deny nothing to the son of the Emperor," Durogai cut him off, "save that which is not his to command. My troops are all commissioned, sent to defend our land from the Crane. They're not here, so you can't have them! Even if I wanted to, I could not call them away from the war just to babysit a prince who wants to poke about in the Shadowlands. No, Sezaru-sama, not even with your 'good cause.'"

Durogai laughed, but to Sezaru it sounded darker this time. "As for my Hida . . . well, those who stand the Wall cannot leave it undefended. With the war, our defense is already overlight. One strong oni could snap us like a drum if we loosen our guard even a little. The only other samurai here are the Crab who take their orders from the Imperial Army and serve the Empire directly. Can you command the Imperial Army, Prince?"

"No." Sezaru felt the blood rising in his veins. "Even a prince cannot countermand the orders of the Imperial Guard. Not without the permission of the Emperor or one of the Imperial Generals."

"Hm." Durogai frowned. "That's what the Magistrates said. They had quite a deal to say about the matter. Too bad I had to listen." He rolled his eyes.

Of course the Magistrates "mentioned" his limitations. Naseru didn't want Sezaru to journey into the Shadowlands. He would consider it too much of a risk. He wanted to eliminate Sezaru as a threat, not watch his younger brother die of Shadowlands taint. It would be in Naseru's best interest to keep Sezaru pinned here on the Wall, unable to complete his quest for another season.

"So much trouble." Durogai faked a sigh. "Too bad, then. Looks like you stay with us a little longer." The burly Crab pushed away from the wall and began to walk back into the palace. Sezaru stared in anger out at the dark southern lands, fists clenched upon the parapet.

"Hm . . ." Durogai said. "Ah, Prince, it seems I almost forgot something." He pulled a crumpled piece of paper from his shirt and attempted to smooth out the worst of its wrinkles with one hand. "A letter came for you. I trust it bears good news. I hope you don't mind that I mentioned to the Imperial Guard that Tsudao-sama might wish to know where you were."

Sezaru took it curiously, staring down at the character drawn upon the parchment. It bore the name of Toturi Tsudao, his elder sister. Quickly, he broke the seal and unfolded the letter.

My brother,

It is a pity I could not leave the war in the Dragon lands long enough to visit you, but Naseru mentioned your journey in his last set of missives. A lucky turn of fate that my men recovered them after Naseru's magistrates were destroyed, or I might never have known.

I hereby turn over command of five samurai from the Imperial Guard into your hands.

Bring them back safely.

Toturi Tsudao, General of the Imperial Guard

Sezaru laughed, and beneath him in the corridor he could swear he heard Durogai's rumbling echo in answer.

* * * * *

The gates of Hida palace cried out sharply as they opened, the rusted metal grinding against a chain with links half as large as a man. The portcullis, iron and thick stone, ground open just high enough for the small band and their horses to pass beneath, and then it slammed down into the hard-packed earth beneath the wall.

Sezaru was escorted by five Imperial Guardsmen, all Crab, stationed at the Hida wall to carry out the Emperor's orders and act as his eyes and ears. Together with them and his two constant companions Koshei and Angai, Sezaru took his first few steps into the Shadowlands. The Hida had provided them with ponies—rugged, hardy beasts designed to keep low to the ground and put on tremendous bursts of speed for short periods. They were also, Sezaru assumed, designed to be abandoned as fodder should an oni approach too close—in hopes that the monster would pause to eat the ponies, and the samurai could escape. Another example of straightforward, pragmatic Crab thinking.

"Sezaru-sama," Koshei asked in a low voice, riding his pony close beside his master's. "Are you well?"

Sezaru's face was as pale as his white hair, his hands clenched tightly within the thick silk robe he wore to keep warm. "No, Koshei. But it will not get better. This land . . . is sick. The spirits here are dark and corrupted. They pull at me. But I can resist them."

"Is there anything I can do?"

"Yes, Koshei. You can pray and keep watch."

"As I always do, Sezaru-sama. As I always do."

* * * * *

The journey took over a week through marshes and thick, muddy land that chilled their feet through thick woolen socks. With each step deeper into the Shadowlands, Sezaru felt the draw of darkness weighing heavy on his shoulders. The land was dangerous in the extreme. Twice their group had to take wide-sweeping routes to avoid patches of heavy quicksand, and once the samurai were forced into battle against small creatures with mouths the size of a man's head. The Crab handled them effectively, butchering them without sympathy. There were no war cries, no tales of honor or shouts of victory. The battle was silent in the hopes that they would not draw the attention of other, more dangerous creatures.

Each day was torturous, the sun creeping across a foul-smelling sky. Minutes stretched into hours in this fetid land, each day blending into the next mercilessly. Sezaru felt the heartbeat of Rokugan fading away, dying, and submerged by the cruel environment of the Shadowlands. With each moment, he moved farther away from home and safety, farther from the spirits he knew, and into a land of corruption.

Listen to them, Sezaru. Hear how they call you. . . .

Sezaru squeezed his eyes closed, wrapping himself in prayer. His beads cut into the flesh of his hand, smudging them with blood. The voice was right. In his mind, he could hear the twisted kami of the Shadowlands as they called out in rapture and delight. They felt his presence, longed for his touch. How did the Crab live, day to day, with this agony so near them? Sezaru watched as the Crab samurai made camp cleanly and efficiently in the growing dark. Dusk was coming, and with it danger.

Where are the spirits that shelter you, Sezaru? Whisper your prayers to a faithless wind. They will not be heard. This is a land of bartered faith, purchased honor, and forgotten purity. There is nothing for you here except darkness . . . and failure.

"Be silent!" Sezaru hissed. He stepped away from the others and paced the border of the camp, engrossed in prayer and meditation.

"Sezaru-sama?" Angai asked, her voice betraying actual concern. For a Scorpion, she almost seemed worried. How foolish. Angai was a Scorpion; she had been taught better. Sezaru tore his sleeve out of her grasp and stepped away with a disdainful motion.

"Return to your work, Angai."

She stepped back, eyes dilating but no other sign of her surprise showing in her features. She bowed and returned to the heart of the camp, kneeling to prepare the sod where a campfire would be lit when the night grew too cold to bear. The camp would create as little light as possible to avoid the attention of those who wandered in these haunted lands.

The Shadowlands shifted around Sezaru, and he felt the hungry eyes of the spirits watching, even from afar. The lack of light would not save them from notice. It was already far too late for that.

You are submitting to fear. The stink of it clings to you like Taint. You must be stronger than this.

The voice seemed so strong, so powerful. Its tone was unwavering, relentless. Sezaru shook his head ferociously, ignoring the strange glances. "No," the Wolf snarled, tucking his hands into his sleeves and turning away from the camp. He would walk in meditation, pondering the riddle that the Oracles set before him, and he would drive out this specter that haunted his soul.

A thousand men marched to Volturnum to fight for Rokugan. Their blood still stains the city. Why do you think these few more will make any difference? You should have come alone, Sezaru. You have damned them all with your weakness.

Sezaru stared out into the gathering darkness, forcing his will to fight against the voice. It was an old battle, one he had fought since childhood, but for the first time in many years, Sezaru felt a sudden chill. He had always taken it for granted that he would win, that he would master the dissenter that mocked him from within his own mind. He would make its strength serve his needs. But in this place, the darkness weakened his resolve and added ballast to his paranoia. He clenched his fist once more around the prayer beads, no longer feeling their smoothness, only feeling their pain.

"Sezaru-sama!" The shout seemed distant, irrelevant. Sezaru stood beneath a blackened tree, feeling the pitted shadows beneath it as they slid across his flesh. The first light of the moon shone through the tree limbs, illuminating the ground in curls of black and white. Across the plain, the mountains of Volturnum stood out in stark relief against the moonlight, like blackened cutouts against a bitter yellow-black sky.

Turn your back on them, Sezaru. Their danger is not your own. Leave them to suffer, as you brought them here to die. They are only fulfilling the destiny you have set before them—and you are fulfilling yours.

"I . . . will not . . . be yours to command." Sezaru forced his feet to move, his head to turn, his body to spin about so that he could see the camp. It lay some distance behind him. The voice had done its work well, drawing him farther away than he had guessed.

There, in the small ring of firelight, he saw unsheathed steel. Like ghostly images, the Crab samurai leaped forward. Like sparks flying from the coals, the Crab flew over the fire, swords reflecting the flickering light in burning shards. Angai's fan swirled in a delicate kada, becoming a shield against the darkness, shining rays of light out toward her enemy. Koshei shouted again for Sezaru, falling back and seeking his master's silhouette in the darkness. Their eyes met for an instant that seemed like an eternity.

Is this a vision or reality? Are they in pain, or is this just another dream, another vision born of madness?

The Wolf did not know, and he did not care. He raised his hands and began to chant, summoning power and vigilance and calling on his reserves of arcane wisdom.

Are they even in danger? The voice mocked him. *And if they are, why are you so willing to save them? You brought them here, after all. You brought them to the Shadowlands to die.*

"The Shadowlands cannot have them—and you cannot have me." Power exploded from Sezaru's hands in a blaze of fiery light. The inferno roared ten-thousand-fold, taking the shape of a massive steed with hooves and eyes of white fire among its hide of flame. It raced like a spectral defender toward the campsite, and at last Sezaru could see the beast that stood on the other side of the defenders' line.

It was massive, standing almost the height of three men above the ground at its tarry apex. Its jaws opened large enough to swallow two men whole, and four slimy arms writhed in tandem, two to either side. Its skin was like a slug's, mottled and covered in thick black slime. As it moved, sliding across the ground in snake-like fashion, it reached for one of the Crab.

"Tsuburu no Oni!" The Hida screamed, warning his companions even as the beast tore him asunder. With some last strength, he plunged his naginata deep into the creature's tongue as it stuffed him into its dripping maw. "Its weakness . . . eyes!" The Hida died, still screaming to his companions over the final crunch of his bones. He died a Crab.

The oni roared, swinging its arms into the Crab who tried to tear apart its hide with their pole-arms. Sharp-bladed spears twirled in patterns of death, but their blades bounced off the oni's thick skin, sticking like captive flies on the sticky tar that covered the beast. Within a second, another Crab was dead, his body hanging from the oni's mouth. The third Crab lunged forward with a long knife, plunging it deep into the oni's belly. The creature did not bother to howl—it might have lost its still-kicking meal—and instead reached down to slap the Crab against its flesh, trapping him in the gooey tar with a massive whack. The Hida flailed desperately for a few moments, plunging his knife into the demon as deeply as he was able despite the sticky ooze. Grunting and sweeping away the attacks of the last two Crab, the oni pinned its captive beneath the thick layer of ooze that covered its body. The samurai flailed for a minute, face pinned beneath the oni's hand; then the struggling stopped.

Sezaru's horse of flame reared, plunging its hooves into the Tsuburu's jutting belly. The oni roared, sweeping the horse with two tarry arms, the sticky substance hissing as it made contact with Sezaru's guardian. The flame steed neighed in agony, striking out once more and leaving burning brands seared into the oni's skin. Its attack drew the oni's attention from the Crab, allowing them to regroup while the demon battled with the creature of fire. The respite would last only a few more seconds, and Sezaru lifted his hands to begin another spell.

There was a second flash, this time not as bright as the flame. As Sezaru pointed with one outstretched hand, lightning cracked down from the heavens. The bolt arced harmlessly past the Crab and scattered throughout the field, shattering into a hundred arcs that swelled and surrounded the oni. A terrible flash of light erupted from its center, causing the Crab to step back in confusion as the brilliance passed between them and the oni. There was a brief sizzling sound, like meat over a campfire, and then the oni screaming.

"It will not destroy the oni—only hold him!" Sezaru called to Koshei. Instantly, his yojimbo understood.

Toturi Koshei raced past the blinded Crab, keeping his eyes closed and his katana before him. After three steps, he leaped, praying that he would clear the lightning. When his feet struck something sticky and sank through to the hard flesh below, he grinned. Right on target.

By the fire, Angai called to the Crab, directing them backward and out of the line of fire. She stepped in front of them as they rubbed their eyes and struck defensive stances. Angai held out her fan like a shield, spinning it between agile hands as she listened ardently beyond the blaze of mystic light, protected by Sezaru's magic.

Beyond the lightning, the oni growled, shaking its massive head back and forth as it tried to clear its vision. It swatted ineffectively at Koshei as the yojimbo hurled his body up the oni's belly. Koshei avoided the flailing arms by sound, stepping swiftly on the exposed rolls of flesh like a jiggling stairway. He found the Oni's head and crawled through sticky tar to reach its neck. The black gook clung to him, making it difficult to move, but Koshei wrapped his arms around the oni's tremendous, fleshy neck and plunged his sword into its gelatinous eye.

"Sezaru-sama!" Koshei called, the oni's claws rending his jacket to shreds. If those claws so much as drew a faint line of blood, they would spread the Taint to his yojimbo's soul—and Koshei would never make it out of the Shadowlands alive.

Sezaru prepared another spell, feeling dark spirits surround him. With a soft curse, he lowered his hands. The spirits that had followed him from Rokugan were expended. His spells now would call only upon the darkness of this land, tainting his very soul and forcing him to bargain with the Shadowlands. He could not do that—not even if it meant the difference between his yojimbo's life and a terrible demise.

Sezaru caught Angai's questioning stare and nodded, folding clenched fists into the sleeves of his robes. If he cast a spell, he would doom himself. If he did not, Koshei might fall to the Shadowlands. He could do nothing more than pray—for both their souls.

As the beast reached up with clawed fingers to tear Koshei away, Angai released her fan. Steel blades whirled through the air, steel hissing as the fan swung toward the oni, its upper arms raised to tear at Koshei, claws dripping with taint and tarry residue. Angai's fan struck, true to the mark and sharp as any samurai's katana, slicing through one arm with a sound of snapping bone. The monster roared, rearing back and opening its other arms in a gesture of pure hatred, ignoring the man who clung to its back as the lightning faded away.

Dying, the oni lunged forward for Angai, determined to wreak as much damage as possible before its now inevitable death. Angai's hand flashed up, catching her fan in midflight and spinning to block two of the oni's grasping hands with the fan's blades. It was a mockery of a geisha's dance, darting from side to side, hiding her body behind the whirling arcs of the steel battle-fan. Meanwhile, Koshei dug ever deeper with his sword, desperate to reach the oni's brain before it could harm his companions.

With a shout, the two Crab leaped to either side, each engaging one of the creature's arms with practiced efficiency. To either side of Angai's whirling shield, they darted back and forth, slashing with their pole-arms and allowing Angai to put up a defense against the beast's claws. Working together, they slashed the beast mercilessly.

At last, with a great shudder, the Tsuburu howled and faltered. Koshei's blade sank an inch further into the empty socket of the creature's eye. The beast sighed once—a terrible, stench-ridden wind—and then collapsed on the brackish ground.

Koshei slid from the oni's back, the Crab helping him pull away from the sticky mass. The panting yojimbo fell to his knees outside the campfire, pouring water over his body to cleanse it as much as possible of the residue. Moving to his feet again, Toturi Koshei walked toward his master with his sword drawn.

Sezaru watched him come, listening as the voice hissed deep within his mind.

You failed him. Your lack of judgment brought him here—for what? A riddle that cannot be answered! A waste of time. He trusts you with his life, and you were willing to throw it away. When the time came, you could do nothing for him. This is the master that rules a samurai heart? This is the Emperor you would be? Better that he cut out your treacherous heart with his blade and leave you both in this dead land forever.

Toturi Koshei walked forward to face his master, standing before him with bruised body and weary soul. Sezaru searched his yojimbo's face for some sign of his feeling, but the samurai's mask was complete, his face emotionless and compassionless, like all those who learned Rokugan's lessons well. Koshei paused, body dripping with sweat and panting from exertion, and then laid his darkened blade on the ground at Sezaru's feet.

"My life is yours," he said without pride, "as it has always been."

Sezaru looked down at Koshei's lowered head, letting the silence speak for him. With each breath he listened for the voices within his soul, waiting for them to corrupt this moment of sacrifice and victory.

Their silence disturbed him, almost as much as the hesitation within his yojimbo's eyes.

9 | THE TEMPLE OF THUNDER

Five weary horsemen rode into the fallen city of Volturnum, their ponies staggering under the demands of distance and speed. Their legs shook, and their gasping breaths echoed hollowly throughout the massive ruins. Yet, save for that sound and the ricochet of hooves against stone, the tall walls and fallen pagoda roves seemed eerily silent and desolate.

Volturnum.

The city stood deep within the Shadowlands, refusing to fall to either taint or shadow, but its crumbling walls could not forever withstand the endless march of time. Long ago, the Shadowlands had corrupted the lands around it, turning them to black waste and mountains of chipped bone. Yet Volturnum remained, untainted by the nearness of Fu Leng's plague. Its high walls were formed of obsidian and granite, deeply inlaid with shafts of jade. One road lay open to the world, yet by some means that none could understand, the creatures of the Shadowlands could not pass.

Sezaru felt a great weight lift as he rode beneath the archway that parted Volturnum's high walls. Despite the broken roves and fallen buildings, the city felt alive somewhere deep beneath the surface. There were spirits here—terrible, strong, and vigilant—and they were pure. He breathed a long draft of air, blessing the wind that bore it from the north. It smelled faintly of jasmine and of home.

"My Lord?" The Crab guardsman turned back, his narrow face filled with concern. "It grows dark soon. How will we find your destination within this broken place?"

"I will seek it out, Yenobu." Sezaru replied with the first small smile in over two weeks of travel. Closing his eyes, he spread out his senses to encompass the city. If the Temple of Thunder was here, he would find it.

Sezaru felt his mind rush, besieged instantly by terrible energies that battled within the city's aura. Two massive forces fought for dominance, shaking the energies of the city far beyond the balance. If he did not move soon, they would notice him—and at this range, he was like a leaf upon the water, with no stable ground to hold his stance.

Sezaru gasped, his mind slamming back into his body. He knew instantly where the Temple of Thunder stood and forced his pony's head toward the center of the spiritual contest.

"We must hurry! There is a battle, and we can shift the tide!"

The others kicked their horses behind him, the weary beasts giving one more run before they collapsed from exhaustion. The ponies staggered, throwing their bodies forward down curving streets, over fallen walls, and through a maze of rubble and debris. As they turned the corner into the city's central plaza, Sezaru's animal could bear no more. It skidded to a halt, head down and body shaking, falling to its knees as the shugenja threw himself from its back.

There, at the center of the broken city, stood a temple with walls that shone in hues of gold and black. From its open doors flame roared in gouts, controlled by some powerful hand deep within the Temple's holy gardens. Immediately, a swirl of air put out the billowing flames, the spirits wrestling in a massive burst of elemental power. Spirits of water flowed out from the temple as Sezaru hastened up the stairs.

"Remain outside!" Sezaru cried as he turned at the doorway, forced to shout to be heard over the swells of energy that illuminated the temple. "I will call for you when I know what is occurring!"

Angai and Koshei climbed to the top of the steps, as far as they were allowed by Sezaru's orders. There, they drew their weapons and bowed almost as one. Sezaru turned, his robe swirling in the winds that whipped the air, and strode into the temple's heart.

Through the brilliant light, Sezaru could make out five figures. Beyond them, four more stood in a billowing darkness. In the center, Tonbo Toryu walked a narrow path, calling to the others with a voice as loud as thunder. Despite his ardent words, the darkness coiled and struck at the light, and Sezaru could sense a massive imbalance between the two sides, as if their very presence was causing the rift that shook Volturnum to its very core.

"My brothers and sisters," Toryu continued as if he had not seen Sezaru standing in the temple's hall, though the Wolf was certain their eyes had met. "Cease your fighting! This battle can only destroy the very world you are sworn to guard!"

"Ours is not the fault, Thunder," one of the spirits in the darkness cried. "Blame the one who split the balance. Kaede should stand where you do, in the apex of our spirits, but now she has taken a side."

"I have taken nothing—only followed the path of my husband!" The voice, from one of the light spirits, was Kaede's. Sezaru's heart leaped. She was here! Perhaps he could see her, speak with her . . .

"You took the throne—even for a moment—and the union you forged between the Void with the Celestial Heavens has doomed us all!" The voice from the darkness was distinctly female this time, a hissing accusation that struck out like a slap. "You have condemned the Void to light!"

Now Sezaru understood. It was indeed a battle he had stumbled upon—but a spiritual one, a battle of the Oracles, dark against light, struggling for supremacy. Was this Kaede's doing?

"Void holds no place, dark or light." A soft, whispering voice spoke from the illuminated area on Tonbo's right. The other

Oracles were only manifested within this place in a spiritual manner. Their bodies were translucent, shining with the spirits of the Dragon they served. The Oracle of Wind, for it was she that spoke, appeared as a woman's form, and filled with swirling winds and the bluish aura of a bright summer's sky.

The earth shook, and Sezaru was thrown down. He gripped one of the support beams of the Temple, clinging to its enameled wood as he tried to hear the conversation shaking the world. On the porch, he could hear the rattle of steel, and looking back he signaled to his companions to hold their places.

The Dark Oracle of Earth spoke with a rumbling voice. "It is too late to argue the cause—"

"—what is needed now is to find the balance." The Light Oracle of Earth finished his brother's sentence. Despite the philosophical differences between the light of a Dragon's soul and the dark shadows it cast, the Oracles were in many ways the same. A cosmic joke, Sezaru had called the Dark Oracles—a cosmic joke in the manner of a shadow that hides beneath the sun. Without the Dragons and their Oracles, the Dark Oracles did not exist— shadow without light. Yet to be rid of them, one would have to destroy the very Dragon whose light could not help but create darkness, and that was unthinkable.

Blue-white tendrils of wind swirled at the border between the two sides, wrestling against an explosion of fire that sought to keep it away.

"There is only one answer!" roared a being of black flame, his eyes white and unholy in their destructive joy. "Kaede must be destroyed!"

A ball of fire exploded around the speaker, tendrils of ebony fire reaching out to singe and burn the Light Oracles. Even as it began, wind stirred the pools of water in the garden around them, extinguishing the flames before they could cause any damage.

"No," Toryu spoke again, his voice shaking with effort. "That will not seal what has been broken."

"Thunder should not be here. It should have no voice. You are not one of the elements, Tonbo Toryu. Your Dragon is a Celestial being, not an Elemental one." Scorn laced every syllable of the

Dark Oracle of Fire's words. "You are not one of us. Do you seek to break the balance even more, by betraying your own Dragon as Kaede has betrayed hers?"

A murmur of assent rumbled through the darkness.

"Kaede aligned the Dragon of Void with the Celestial Heavens," said Tonbo Toryu. "A Dragon's very nature is changed. As the keeper of a Dragon's soul, I am equally involved."

A dark rumble echoed up from the depths of the earth. "Thunder cannot align itself. You are not the answer to this puzzle. Only Void can right what Void has ripped asunder. Kaede must die." The cold stone rumble within the speaker's soul chilled Sezaru, making him grasp the pillar beside him with numbed fingers.

"Even that will not solve our problem," Kaede's voice was pained, weary. The sound if it nearly broke Sezaru's heart. "If my death could heal this rift, do you not think I would have offered it gladly?"

"There is another way." The pause was pregnant with strain, and Sezaru struggled to hear the Oracle's next words. "The balance has been shifted. It can be returned." Unlike the soft, wise voice of her lighter counterpart, the Dark Oracle of Wind's voice was sensual, breathy, and coy. "The Side of Light has five who stand upon it, but we of the Dark have only four."

Sezaru ignored the pain that lanced through his mind and struggled to comprehend what the Dark Oracle of Wind was suggesting. Void had placed itself upon the side of light—without meaning to, but it had been done. Of the elements, it was the only one that had no dark counterpart. . . .

. . . until now.

"The Dragon of Void stands before the light. Therefore, it must now cast a shadow. A Dark Oracle of Void is the only option. Someone must take that post and carry out its burden upon the world—with all the evil it implies."

Toryu's words sank into Sezaru's mind, drowning out the howls and laughter that plagued the shugenja's soul. A Dark Oracle of the Void? The creation of such a post would balance the elements, but it would also bring a great evil into the world. Void was one of the strongest of the elements, and divided into

Light and Darkness, it would add a great power to the darker side of creation. But if it were not done, the world would pay an even greater price.

"Toryu-san, no—" Sezaru began, but his words were echoed and overwhelmed by Kaede's cry before anyone could hear him.

"Toryu!" she screamed. "You must not!"

As the wind around them rose into a fury, Sezaru felt a great heat press against him. For a moment, the world hung in fragile balance. Sezaru began to step forward, summoned from his shadowed watch by a force greater than his own formidable will. Something called to him, drawing his perspective down to a single focus, like narrowing the stars down into a single point of light.

Sezaru looked up to meet Tonbo Toryu's eyes as the world changed once more.

"I abdicate my post as Oracle of Thunder and leave my place at the side of the Celestial balance." Thunder rocked the temple, and lightning raced through the heavens as if the doors to Jigoku themselves had been opened. The earth shook as Toryu's voice grew stronger, and Sezaru saw the quiet resolve in the little man's eyes grow into iron.

"I hereby take up the mantle," Toryu said softly, "of the Dark Oracle of Void."

With that, the tempest struck.

"No, Toryu! You must not!" Kaede's voice rose with the wind, nearly drowned out by the thunder and the explosions of rain sweeping through the temple. She stepped out of the light, and for a moment Sezaru could see her, dark hair unbound and flowing in the wind, her eyes like starlight with the power of the Void.

"Listen to me, Kaede." Toryu took her hand as the heavens opened around them. The temple shook, the earth wavered in its stance, and the wind and rain pounded against the stone like demons raging in the night. "There is great danger here. Though I take this mantle, I am not an evil man. If I do not take it, the power unleashed by your decisions will give the darkness a great strength. Until we can find a way to reverse the damage you have done, I must bear this burden."

"There *is* no way, Toryu."

"Sacrifice caused this strife, Kaede. Sacrifice can heal it."

The power that surrounded them grew stronger, and in its wake Sezaru could see soft motions of a massive being coiled like a serpent in the mist. Yellow eyes burned like suns in the starlight, and ivory claws shredded illusion, leaving only the harsh reality of Toryu's choice. "If the Dark Oracle of Void is chosen, it will be someone of great strength. Someone with power. Someone with the potential to bring an awesome new evil into the world." Sezaru saw Toryu's eyes flicker for an instant toward him, then pull away. "That cannot be allowed, Kaede. I will take the post, and when this balance is healed, I will step away from it, so that it can be disbanded and Void can be one power again. If another took that post, evil would not give up power so easily."

"The Dragon of Thunder—" she began.

"Has other disciples. He will survive without me, but Rokugan may not. Not unless I take this step and place myself between the Empire and destruction." Toryu dropped Kaede's hand as the coils of the Void Dragon began to close about him. A shadow grew, long and deep, across the ground beneath the dragon's terrible claws.

Around them, the other Oracles were becoming faint, their light extinguished by the powerful influx of Void. Sezaru swore that he could hear mocking, rejoicing laugher from the darkness as the Dark Oracles prepared to welcome their new brother into the fold.

Sezaru felt power rushing through him, pressing him to his knees with its awesome presence. He struggled to keep his mind clear, to retain his focus despite the presence of the Dragon incarnate. He could no longer hear the wind or feel the pounding rain. The temple seemed like an empty shield, standing between the Wolf and the world beyond.

Toryu's voice continued, despite the roar and fury of the elements encompassing them. "What I have done will not seal the rift, Kaede. The balance will not accept a good man in a position of great evil. Either I will become corrupted, or I will be destroyed—and replaced with a true Dark Oracle."

"No, Toryu . . ." Kaede protested, tears flowing down her face.

"There is little time, Kaede!" The little man held her elbow, forcing himself against the wind that drew him into the Void Dragon's coils. "The Talon of the Dragon is awakened. We are all standing on the razor's edge. Whoever has taken it plans to destroy us all. Only the mortal world can change the future. As Oracles, we must watch—and wait. Our duty constrains us. Listen to me, Kaede! This is critical! We cannot act. We cannot change the future. We can only hold the present together . . . and pray."

"There must be something," she said, raising her head as starlight encompassed her. "We must do something. I cannot remain still when the entire world is at stake!" Kaede's cry was born of frustration, torment, and anguish.

"No, Kaede! If you take this into your hands, you will kill us all." As Toryu spoke, the starlight swelled against them, and the coils of the Dragon wrapped around Kaede in tight circles. The Dragon glowed like a thousand suns, sending rays of light past the walls of the temple, racing through the streets of Volturnum. Beneath that brilliant starlight, the shadow that lay beneath the dragon's feet fell away into utter blackness. Sezaru felt rather than saw the samurai at the doorway falling to their knees, covering their eyes from the burst of celestial light. Those who stared into it would be blinded, their eyes forever burned by the radiance.

There was a bone-chilling shriek as the shadow reached out to engulf Tonbo Toryu. Stars in his eyes, his hands still outstretched toward Kaede, the little man slowly sank into the blackness. The last impression Sezaru saw of his face was one of torment, swallowed whole by an unfathomable evil too dark to hold a name.

When the light faded and died and the shadow melted away, Sezaru was alone.

* * * * *

"Master!" After the echoes of the Oracles faded, Angai's voice seemed pale and shallow. "Sezaru-sama!"

Koshei stood at the very edge of the stairway, just between the twin posts of the Temple doors. His face was red from the searing light, one sleeve cast before his eyes as his fist lay against his temple. His other hand gripped the hilt of his katana, his body poised to leap inside if Sezaru called his name.

Angai called out again, "Sezaru-sama, did you discover what you were looking for?"

"Yes, Angai-san." Sezaru's voice resounded hollowly through the now-empty temple. He stood, feeling his legs shake slightly with the reverberations of power around him. "We sleep here tonight. Tomorrow, we head back to Rokugan. I found what I was looking for . . . or perhaps it found me. There is only one place that will help us understand what we have seen here, for they have chronicled such attacks before." Sezaru swept past his retainers, lost in deep thought. "The libraries of the Miya."

10 THE FIRST STEP TO TRUTH

I do not understand." Angai rode her pony next to Sezaru's, keeping his voice low so that the flat imprint of hooves into snow covered his words. "Why did Toryu take the post, if he knew it would corrupt him?"

"He has given us time." Sezaru stared out at the snow-covered road, his eyes cold with long thought. "The post of Dark Oracle of Void is immensely powerful. If an evil man accepted that duty, he could again use that power to unbalance the world. We live in dark times, Angai-san. Those who stole the Dragon's Talon may have somehow manipulated Kaede into seizing the throne, abdicating it, and opening this position."

They rode in silence for a while, Sezaru lost in thought. Finally, he spoke again. "There may already be someone who seeks to take over the position. Toryu may know who that is, and he might have chosen this position to keep them from becoming the Dark Oracle of Void. If that individual is already powerful—a shugenja or an evil maho-user—they might be able to use the Dark Oracle's power to become infinitely more so. The other Dark Oracles would take the opportunity to make war on the light. With Kaede in her weakened state, there is a good chance that they would win. If that happened, the elements would align with the darkness . . . forever."

"And the Empire would become like the Shadowlands?"

"Worse. The Empire would become a *force* of evil, not simply a land corrupted by it. The Shadowlands would be a paradise in comparison."

Soshi Angai paused for a moment, trying to take in the scope of that image. "But only if the post of the Dark Oracle was taken over by a powerful shugenja, someone with complete knowledge of the Void. Someone unafraid to wield that power, who could be corrupted by the dark side of the Void Dragon's personality."

Angai was Sezaru's companion, a trusted retainer, but she was till a Scorpion. He listened to her words and found the question beneath them. "Yes, Angai-san. Someone who could be corrupted." He caught her eyes and held them, showing the young Scorpion a fraction of his true power. She gulped once, staring like a rabbit in a wolf's path, and then he released her.

"Do not fear, Angai. Even the greatest power cannot corrupt the truly faithful." As he spoke, he could hear the mocking laughter of the voices in his soul. They did not believe his words—what were words, after all, but empty air? Sezaru shook his head, clearing his mind before the whispers could taunt him further.

"You understand, Sezaru-sama, the Scorpion have given much for the sake of the Empire. We would not be unwilling to give more." Her eyes were cold beneath her mask.

More? More than honor, more than life . . . what else could the Scorpion give? Sezaru did not ask. He already knew the answer. It was an implied threat, a warning, should he ever consider . . .

But no. He would not even look down that path.

"What of the Dragon's Talon?" The snowy road crunched beneath her pony's hooves, and he drew his robe more tightly against his body. "How does that figure into this?"

"That I do not yet know, Angai-san. But I am hoping the libraries of the Miya will hold that answer—and more."

"The Miya?"

"Historians of the Empire, among other things. Their libraries are as large as those of the Phoenix—and contain more information on history, ethics, and the Shadowlands, whereas the Phoenix libraries specialize in magic. If the Dragon's Talon has figured anywhere in history, the Miya will know of it. If such an imbalance of the elements has ever occurred before, we will find records of it there." And, at worst, he added to himself, while there I can gain a grasp of the Empire's stability—or lack thereof.

Sezaru placed a hand to his temple, feeling a sharp throb of pain. Although the imbalance in the elements had lessened with Toryu's sacrifice, Sezaru could still feel the darkness pressing against the world. The elements still struggled against one another beneath the surface of reality, shifting the flow and ebb of currents dangerously into flux.

"Master?" Angai said, her wide brown eyes filled with concern behind her white mask. "You are weary. The Miya palaces are not far away, but if you wish to camp . . ."

They had been nearly twenty days on the road from the Crab lands, avoiding the battles between Crane and Crab as much as possible as they drove toward their goal. The land around them was frozen, patched here and there with unmelted snow.

"No, Angai. It is not safe to rest on these roads any more. Already the world becomes unstable, its very soul struggling for balance. We cannot rest until we reach our goal."

Angai half bowed from her saddle, her eyes still resting on Sezaru's pale face.

A few pony-lengths ahead of them, Koshei stopped, raising his fist into the air to signal a halt. Sezaru watched as Koshei moved forward on the road to identify a horse-trail only a few hours old. When Koshei looked back to signal the all-clear, he did not look into Sezaru's eyes.

How long had they been like this? Sezaru wondered. Koshei had been silent most of the way home, but the pressure in the air—the unbalancing of the elements—had kept Sezaru's full attention. Perhaps for too long. The needs of the world were great, but a lord's first duty was to those who served him.

Motioning to Angai to remain behind, Sezaru rode forward to pace beside Koshei's sturdy pony. The snow flew up from his steed's furry legs and white plumes snorted out from the small beast's nostrils as he saluted the other pony. Koshei made no such greeting, maintaining his silence and keeping his eyes locked on the road before them.

"Are we far from the Miya Palaces?"

"No, Sezaru-sama. An hour at most."

Sezaru looked at his yojimbo with placid eyes. "You are troubled, Koshei-san." When the other man did not answer, he continued. "Does your duty cause you difficulty?"

"No, Sezaru-sama!" The answer was emphatic. "I am yours to command."

"As befits your post, and your honor." Sezaru flicked a bit of snow from his pony's reins. "Water that is pure has no fish, Koshei, yet there is something swimming in your thoughts."

Koshei looked away for a moment. "My Lord, it is not my place—"

"I am making it your place. I am not only your lord, Koshei, I am also your priest and shugenja. Speak to me of the burdens of your soul."

Koshei took his time beginning, pausing to consider his words. When he did speak, his words were simple and to the point. "You have told us—and I have seen—that the elements are unbalanced. You are a part of the elements, my lord. More so than any man I have ever known. Thus I fear for you, Sezaru-sama, that the imbalance you feel could too easily become part of your soul."

Sezaru's eyebrows raised. "You fear for me?"

"When I became your yojimbo, I turned my back on my family and my past. They meant nothing to me. I could not allow them to interfere with my duty to my lord. Since then, I have fought for you, saved your life, and prayed each night to the kami to be allowed to live and die in your service." Koshei's eyes slanted back toward Angai then darted forward once more. "I left my past behind—as I try to leave each day's actions behind me. If they cannot teach me to serve you, then they have no purpose. If you die, my duty—my entire life—will be in vain. And more than that . . . I believe the Empire will fall."

"I carry a heavy burden on my shoulders, yojimbo."

"I carry a heavier one, Sezaru-san, for I carry you."

Sezaru looked down at his yojimbo's dark eyes, hearing the wisdom in his words. "In each breath we take, Koshei, there is a piece of the great truth. All things are one. Together, yojimbo, we will both carry Rokugan out of danger." Sezaru moved his hand through the air, stirring the wind spirits with a simple touch. "Do not let fear blind you. Rokugan has been saved by treachery before. It may be that it will be saved once again by such methods."

Glancing back at Angai once more, Koshei said, "I will continue to watch your back, Master. No matter how softly they speak, Scorpions never lose their sting."

"Of course, Koshei-san. I would accept nothing less."

* * * * *

The guards at Miya palace greeted Sezaru and his companions with quiet reverence, raising green and gold flags with the Imperial chrysanthemum upon them to mark the coming of an Imperial Prince. The Miya palaces were often the home of the Imperial family during winter. Sezaru remembered many days in these corridors, hiding from his sister's childhood bursts of wrath or studying joyfully in the massive libraries. The Miya often bred into the Imperial line, making more than half of them cousins to Sezaru and his family through one long, complicated genealogical trail or another.

But for now, he was most grateful simply for their tea.

"I thank you, Miya-sama."

"Gensaiken, my lord, surely you remember me?" The young courtier smiled as he helped Sezaru from the pony's back, pressing a warm cup of chai into the Wolf's hands. Other members of the Miya family tended to Sezaru's companions, bowing and smiling as they led the weary travelers between the thick oak doors of the outer castle. Inside, warm air scented with mint welcomed them, and ladies with fresh robes over their arms led the three to separate chambers.

"We were concerned for you, my lord," said Gensaiken. "With all the troubles in the world, the Steel Throne has been sorely grieved for its lost son."

Sezaru sipped his tea, settling into the cushions within a private chamber. He recognized the room. Furnished in rich golds and harvest colors, it had been his father's room while his mother was pregnant or away. The rooms they shared together were only used when both the Emperor and the Empress were together at Miya Palace, their private retreat together from the world.

"I have been traveling, Gensaiken-san. I have come to see the Miya libraries, so I might learn from their wisdom. Nothing more." Sezaru glanced around to see the maidservants pretending not to listen. Even here, his enemies had eyes.

"The Empress will be pleased to hear that, no doubt." Now Gensaiken had Sezaru's full attention. "She will not be able to see you immediately, of course, as her duties require her complete attention."

Sezaru hid his confusion, keeping his lips behind the rim of the steaming chai cup. "Busy?"

"Always," Gensaiken said placidly, keeping his eyes focused where he could see the maid in his periphery. "With her husband gone, she buries herself in her work. Most times, she will not even exit her chambers to make the day's formal announcements. We, the Miya, must make due and carry out those duties for her. I can only hope that our diligent service grants her some peace."

"Peace?" Sezaru choked. "But the Empress . . . the day of her coronation . . ." The Wolf's mind flashed back to Kaede's enigmatic statements, her refusal of the throne, and her disappearance before the entire court. How could Gensaiken possibly have kept that a secret?

"The court is well aware," Gensaiken said, "that Kaede returned shortly after her episode. The Dragon itself sent her back, to ensure the Empire was cared for until the Heir could be legally chosen. Still, she keeps herself private, obeying the commands of her Dragon, and we carry to her only those issues most critical to the Empire's safety. Until the Heir is placed upon the Steel Throne, the Empress reigns."

So, that was how the Miya kept the Empire stable. The scope of the lie was immense—so bold-faced and loudly trumpeted that none dared challenge its veracity. No doubt, courtiers were paid to mention that they had "seen" Kaede, or that she had kept her appointments with them. Those less trustworthy—or less in need of money—were simply turned away, and the Miya could cite the Empress's bereavement.

"I see." Sezaru could sense Gensaiken's hesitance. Sezaru could, no doubt, explode this situation wide open by telling the assembled courtiers what he knew of Kaede's disappearance, or he could simply play along with the ruse and allow the Miya to continue their charade. "Do my siblings attend the Empress often?"

"Only Naseru-sama, my Prince. His Emerald Magistrates guard the Miya who bear the Empress's messages to the far corners of the Empire."

So his devious brother was aware of the ruse. It would have been a surprise if Naseru hadn't been fully informed, whether the Miya told him or not. Someone in his network of spies might have even thought of the idea, but the Miya implemented it first. Thank the Celestial Heavens for that. Naseru walked too close to the throne as it was, and his ambition was far too obvious for Sezaru's comfort.

"And my sister?"

"She leads the Imperial Troops in the north, keeping the Dragon-Lion conflict from spreading across the Empire. It is rare that her messengers visit here, rarer still if she comes herself. Tsudao protects us all from the fires of war, Sezaru-sama."

And none of them could put aside their burdens long enough to see the dangerous road that stretched before Rokugan. Sezaru sighed, watching the wisps of steam rising from his tea part and vanish before the exhalation.

"You are troubled, Prince?" Miya Gensaiken's young face bore faint lines of stress, and Sezaru could see that bearing the secret of the Empress was taking a quiet toll on his family.

"My mother was ever cautious of placing her decisions in the hands of others," Sezaru murmured. "I cannot believe she would be pleased to know that her messengers travel without her blessings."

Gensaiken understood immediately, but his face hardened instead of filling with fear as Sezaru thought. "Her blessings reach all the Empire—from the pits of the Crab, where the Hiruma labor, to the mountains of the Dragon, where peasants pray for food. They steer the Crane and Lion from danger, and they keep the courtiers from poisoning one another in the night. Because your mother watches us all, the Empire is safe. I fear that were her eyes averted, the Empire might know darkness such as it has never known. And, I humbly beg your pardon, the number of contenders for the throne would rise a thousand-fold, borne aloft on the pikes and swords of their families.

"We are blessed to have your mother among us, Sezaru-sama. We are honored to bear her messages to the hundreds of thousands of weeping families, devastated monasteries, and broken lands of the Empire, helping them find peace and prosperity once more. It is our honor, our deepest duty, to do as she would wish." Gensaiken's voice was level, neither seeking approval nor carrying a threat.

"And do the Miya pray each day for her return to the public eye?"

"A hundred voices at a hundred shrines make that prayer." Gensaiken did not blink or move, his face as somber and discrete as a statue.

Slowly, delicately, Sezaru placed his cup upon the porcelain saucer. His hands moved with the grace of sparrows, brushing long strands of pale white hair back away from his sleeves. And through it all, Sezaru's eyes were locked with Gensaiken's, trying to take in the measure of the man across the low table. Silence filled the room for a long whisper of time, and only the sound of the snow falling against ebony windowsills broke the perfect illusion of calm.

"What is best for the Empire," Sezaru said at last, his voice hardly louder than the whisper of snow, "is stability. While you can provide that, Gensaiken, I wish you luck. I am sure that few others could . . . *care* for my mother with such dedication."

"I thank you—"

Sezaru raised his hand to interrupt the Miya. "But do not test me, Gensaiken. My love for my mother is equaled only for my love of Rokugan. Both are very dear to me, and I keep a close watch on those who serve them. Serve them well and see to their safety, or your soul will bear the burden of your . . . errors."

"Serve them, my lord? Oh, no, Sezaru-sama," Gensaiken said with half a bow, his head elegantly lowering above the table. "The Miya, and all their retainers and prayers, they serve the Empress. But I, my lord—" Gensaiken kept his eyes lowered— "I serve only you."

This one, Sezaru though as he returned the man's graceful bow, would bear careful study.

"If you are refreshed, Sezaru-sama—" Gensaiken stood with a gentle swish of his brown and gold robes— "I will show you to the library so that you may begin your studies."

* * * * *

The libraries of the Miya were brightly lit, warm, and well-attended, with thousands of scrolls organized in careful order throughout the long corridors of wood and stone. The scholars bowed when they saw Sezaru and Gensaiken enter the chambers, lowering their heads so that the Wolf could clearly see the balding pates of elderly men whose hands shook from thousands of hours of holding scrolls. Many of them barely hid smiles, whispering behind raised sleeves when Sezaru turned away to walk down another lantern-lit corridor.

"They do not seem surprised to see me." Sezaru watched as two scholars whispered in fierce tones, jabbing fingers at an unrolled chronicle spread open on the table before them. They hardly noticed the Imperial Prince or his guide walking past, so involved were they in their disagreement. One of them reminded Sezaru of a red hen, flapping his sleeves like wings without ever actually achieving flight. The other rolled on his cushion like a wallowing cow, his mouth opening and closing as he chewed the cud of esoteric thoughts. The imagery made Sezaru smile.

"Why should they be? They know that I keep you aware of everything that occurs." Of course, it was a lie.

"You are very diligent. And very discreet."

"I thank you, Sezaru-sama." Gensaiken chuckled. "It would not do to allow them to think your spiritual quests took your attention fully away from the Empire. Were that true, they might turn to Naseru, Tsudao, or others to hear their issues. Their souls would be without the respite that only you can provide."

"When did you become my firmest ally, Gensaiken?" Sezaru asked half in jest.

Gensaiken turned toward Sezaru, pausing in his trek through the ancient stacks. "You once asked me what I did in the Imperial Court. I told you that I listened. Perhaps I listened even more deeply than you could have imagined, Wolf."

"And what have you heard?"

"I have heard enough to know that Rokugan does not need a general to command her. The Empire does not need a farmer to plow her with rough hands, nor a politician to hide her face behind a steel mask." Gensaiken's eyes were earnest, and beneath the young shugenja's polished demeanor, Sezaru could sense the uncertainty and fear. "Her soul is bleeding, Sezaru, and I believe that only you can heal her. For as long as we can, I and others like me will hold the Empire together. But when the time comes, Rokugan will not be saved by the desperate reflections of peace. Those are only illusions, mirrors that the Miya hold up to blind those who cannot bear the truth. The Empire will be saved by the light you bear, the one we are reflecting, Sezaru. Your soul, the wisdom of *your* light and no other must lead us out of darkness."

Mirrors, Sezaru. Do you remember? We are all mirrors of one another. You cannot control where your reflection lands . . . or where the mirror ends. Perhaps in the end, Gensaiken is no more than an image of you. When your light turns to darkness, what will he become?

"My lord, are you all right?" For a moment, Sezaru thought Gensaiken might have heard the voice. The young Miya shugenja lowered the lantern, his dark eyes reflecting the flame within the glass. But no, the voices were his own. Even Kaede, with her great awareness, had not been able to hear their whispers. It must be the strain showing on his features, Sezaru thought, only that.

"I am fine, Gensaiken-san. More than fine." Quietly, Sezaru reached out and placed his hand on the Miya's shoulder in an intimate gesture of trust. He thought of Angai and Koshei, of the Crab samurai that had died in the Shadowlands without even a kind word from the man they protected. The Empire needed a leader, it was true, but Gensaiken was right. It was also in need of someone who would care for its soul. "I am fortunate to have those such as you on my side."

Gensaiken bowed with great dignity, his mild face flushing with pride. "Thank you, Sezaru-sama. Come this way, please. The scrolls you wished to see are not far."

A ladder allowed Gensaiken to climb to the top of a long pillar of scrolls, carefully placing his hands in the carved cupolas to withdraw two simply-carved wooden tubes. "You mentioned that you were interested in the lives of Oracles before they were chosen, Sezaru-sama. I have spoken—discretely—with the Master Librarians. They assure me that this is the best place for you to begin. These were written seventy years ago by a Miya historian who spent his life going through the scrolls and chronicling each Oracle, the time that the post changed over, and to whom it was given. If nothing else, they will give you a chronicle to follow in your research. They are a bit dusty—" Gensaiken sneezed as he slid back down the ladder with his burden— "but they are quite complete, I'm told."

* * * * *

Snow fell thickly about the Miya palaces, biting into the corridors of the library. Though the fires were stoked, they cast humble shadows of warmth that did not reach into the depths of the shadowy chamber. Many of the less dedicated scholars left, replacing their scrolls in dark cupolas and scurrying out to the warmer, well-lit rooms above.

Somewhere in the upper levels of Kyuden Miya, ladies laughed and blazing fires lit council and private chamber alike. Courtiers and nobility were entertained by dancing, stories of the Empire, and the common gossip of the court. But here, beneath the cold and solid earth, their revels did not lighten hearts or warm souls. The cold tables and dry, whispering texts revealed their secrets only to the most dedicated; the most stalwart.

For sixteen days, Sezaru studied the scrolls of the Miya, finding snippets and hints—but no answers. He left the libraries only to eat and to sleep in a tiny monk's chamber beside the library that was warmed with a small fire. He slept on a brown futon laid against the stone floor, taking his meals in a small black bowl without question. Each morning, his food would be brought by Koshei—other times by Angai or Gensaiken, but still Sezaru refused to climb the long, curling stairs back above the ground.

The answers came slowly, like seeds buried in frigid earth. They sprouted, driving aside the voices that whispered, but their growth was too slow—and they were far too slender a thread to hold an Empire.

When Gensaiken came to check on Sezaru at sunset of the sixteenth day, he found the Wolf kneeling on the futon beside the fire, all scrolls put away. His hands were cold and pale, folded upon his lap in silent thought as he stared into the flames.

"Master, are you well?" the Miya ventured.

"Bring Angai and Koshei to me." Sezaru would say no more until they were all gathered in the small room. Once all three of his trusted servants were there, he turned his gaze from the fire, allowing his eyes to flicker across their countenances before he began.

"The scrolls of the Miya record all history as it passes, keeping record of every birth, death, and major occurrence within the Empire's history. They speak volumes to those who can decipher their spider web of coincidence.

"Each Oracle is human before being chosen. Their mortal lives shape them, perhaps drawing the Dragons' attention, or perhaps they are guided by the Dragon to their inevitable fate. Whatever the cause, there have always been Dark and Light Oracles, controlled by the Dragons, but their mortal life still guides their choices. They do not lose their soul, even though they may lose their humanity.

"Furthermore, the Oracles upon arising to their position finds their souls intimately connected to the Dragons through a . . . focus point, if you will." Sezaru saw Gensaiken's brow furrow as the younger shugenja began to realize the implications of this information. "The chronicles detail the journey of each Oracle-to-be, visiting the shrine of their Dragon in order to be joined. Each time an Oracle is chosen, this journey is taken, and the histories record it. But history does not detail the similar journeys of those who would be Dark Oracles. For obvious reasons, those dark shrines are not as well-known as the sacred places of their opposites.

"History tells me much of the Dark Oracles, of their actions in the past. They are all very powerful—more so when they are first created. Devastations are chronicled in the scrolls—cataclysms and natural disasters brought about by a newly-born Dark Oracle in the full flush of his power. Each time one takes his position, within a year, his power is felt across the Empire.

"I fear that, as this is the first Dark Oracle of Void, his expression of ascension will be immense." The weariness that Sezaru felt crept softly into his voice. "However, as I noted, the Oracles of Light have foci to merge their souls with that of their Dragons.

"It can therefore be assumed, though it is not within the histories of the Empire, that the Dark Oracles have similar tokens of their immortality. If I can find the foci of the Oracle of Void, I may be able to use them to balance the element and restore what Kaede has set wrong—to remove the shadow; to take away the light."

Angai nodded. "By merging the foci?"

"Or something similar." Gensaiken provided the answer. "Depending on how the magic works."

"Precisely," said Sezaru. "But that is information I cannot find in a library. I must travel to the Phoenix lands and seek permission to use their archives."

"The Phoenix?" Koshei scowled. "Between the weather and the war, we will be hard pressed to reach Kyuden Isawa before spring."

"Yet we must."

"My lord—" Gensaiken bowed as Sezaru shifted his attention to the young shugenja— "I must concur with your yojimbo. The trip you suggest, even in spring, is nearly impossible due to the war. The Phoenix use their magic to ward against intruders and bring the wrath of the kami on all those who invade their lands. With the Dragon and the Lion at their door, their efforts will be redoubled.

"That aside, Kyuden Isawa rests on the highest cliffs in the Phoenix lands, far above an ocean that will have long since turned to ice. It cannot be reached by boat while the snow holds, and it cannot be reached by land in case the ice melts. To ride through the mountains would be risking your life.

"I do not ask you to stay for my own sake, Sezaru-sama, but for the sake of the Empire." Gensaiken passed his brown sleeve before him, drawing out a fan to lightly stir the air in the small chamber. "The longer you are here, the more I can maintain the illusion that the Empress is asking your council. The courtiers must see you in the palace. They must be assured that the Empire is in safe hands, or they will return to their wars after the winter's peace. The longer you are seen in Kyuden Seppun, the more the clans will become accustomed to your leadership."

"The Steel Throne cannot have a master," said Angai. "Kaede proclaimed it. Have you forgotten your place?" Her tongue was waspish, bitter. "You sound like one of Naseru's cronies."

"Better that I sound like one," Gensaiken said placidly, never taking his eyes off Sezaru, "than say nothing. Besides, Naseru's cronies whisper the throne into his hands. Or what of Tsudao, taking power with a military coup? Though you are not concerned for the throne, I must be."

"Scorpions know that thrones can be bought and sold if need be."

"But at what price to the Empire?" Gensaiken replied acidly. "Have you truly done all you can, Gensaiken? Have you used the secrets at your disposal? Do you know how to twist their pride and chain their spirit in order to secure their loyalty to Sezaru?"

"I see you know much of such things."

"More than you will ever understand," Angai said in a low, dark voice.

"I may not understand the tricks of the Scorpion, but I know how to serve the Empire." Gensaiken turned toward Sezaru, spreading his empty hands in supplication. "Do not forget the Empire, Sezaru-sama. I beg you, do not lose sight of Rokugan, or you will only save us from one dark fate to deliver us into another. Stay in the court—at least through the winter."

"Angai-san, Gensaiken-san," Sezaru said quietly. "Do not forget your manners."

Both blushed and lowered their heads in humble bows. Sezaru considered both their words before he spoke, his eyes glinting back and forth between them.

"Three days," Sezaru said at last. "Gensaiken-san, I will remain in the court for three days to make appearances and keep your authority—and your ruse—intact. After that time, I travel to the lands of the Phoenix. No, I will brook no argument. It may be dangerous to go, but it is more dangerous, by far, to remain. But I will not leave you to this task alone, Gensaiken. As you can see, Angai-san knows much of courts and how to manipulate them. She will remain with you through the winter and come to me in the Isawa lands when summer comes. With her aid, I am certain you will be able to solidify the court and ensure peace within the Empire." Angai glowered, but remained silent, bowing her head at Sezaru's word. "But I will not remain until the spring. Three days, Gensaiken, and no more."

11 LOOKING INTO THE ABYSS

The winter storms railed around Kyuden Miya as if determined to make Sezaru regret his decision. Yet after three days of frigid cold and blustery winds, the fourth day dawned with clear skies that shone over glistening acres of white snow. Although the roads were covered in three inches of thick white powder, it made no difference to Koshei or his master. The way to the Phoenix palaces lay directly north, and nothing short of a cataclysm could change that route. Roads or no roads, they would find a way.

As Gensaiken bade them farewell at Kyuden Miya's front gates, Koshei could see the regret and quiet plea in the young shugenja's eyes. The Miya spoke no word, only bowed in respect as he offered Sezaru the reins of a sturdy mountain pony. Koshei did not expect that Sezaru would change his mind. The three days spent in the grand courts of the Miya had both solidified Gensaiken's position and given great credibility to the Miya ruse. It was all the Wolf could offer without sacrificing his true goal.

Koshei mounted his shaggy pony without preamble, thanking the Fortunes silently for the beast's shaggy fur and even stride. Those were the gifts he and his master would need to help the Empire, not idle words and courtly banter. The court would go on for another turn of the seasons without notice. Koshei understood enough of such tings to know that by loaning the illusionary Empress credence, Sezaru ensured that his allies at court could keep civil war at bay for a while longer. That would have to be enough.

Sezaru met Gensaiken's eyes once more with calm assurance, then mounted his pony and turned away. Kicking his horse until the tromp of its hooves kept time with Sezaru's, Koshei maintained a steady pace just behind Sezaru until they were well away from the palace.

The pair headed due north, through the forests of the Miya and toward a section of Crane lands that bordered the ocean. Beyond the snow-covered plains were the distant pinewoods of the Asako family; the gatekeepers of the Phoenix. Past that, high into the mountains where the icy winds blew, the treacherous mountain roads would take them deep into the cold plains of the Isawa family. The trip would take nearly three weeks under the best conditions, and closer to five if the snow returned.

Koshei rode ahead just far enough to scout the terrain, never letting Sezaru out of his sight. When the forests began to close in again and the hospitable Crane lands slipped away behind them, he ceased riding ahead altogether.

Their camps were sparse, with small fires and little warmth. But that was not the great worry for Koshei. Too often, his master seemed lost in thought, paralyzed by the troubles on his shoulders. He ate little, allowing Koshei to preserve their rations but encouraging the yojimbo's silent worries.

Koshei watched Sezaru pray each dawn and dusk, falling back into their usual routines. As for Koshei, he never prayed. The Wolf did enough for both of them. Let the spirits remember Sezaru's name. Steel held all the memory Koshei would ever need.

They traveled through many small villages, stopping at shrines along the way to revere the ancients. At each shrine, Sezaru would enter and make reverence, bowing to the statues of the ancestors and lighting incense to the kami. Koshei remained outside, watching the peasants who struggled against the chill wind and skittered to and fro from their homes. Their bodies were fragile, weakened by a meager harvest and early frost, and they stared at Koshei's thick traveling robes with awe.

In the Crane village of Aiseki, Sezaru stumbled while exiting the shrine. Immediately, the nearby peasants fell to their knees, pressing their faces into the snow and lamenting their ill fortune. Koshei rushed to his master's side, helping him to stand on unsteady legs. Sezaru frowned, closing his eyes for a moment and leaning slightly on his yojimbo's arm.

"Master, are you well?" Koshei asked solemnly.

"The elements are shifting, Koshei-san." Sezaru's voice was soft, almost uncertain. "The change ripples through the land like stones in water."

As he regained his feet, Koshei stepped before him and shouted to the peasants. "Go back to your homes! You have seen nothing here."

The poor folk scattered before him, clutching their clothing, the women weeping at a samurai's wrath. In other times, their village would have been burned to prevent them from talking about what they had seen, but Toturi had been a kind ruler and his children followed in his lead. There would be no fire, no devastation to cover Sezaru's misstep. For that, the peasants would be grateful. However, it was likely that the shrine would be destroyed. Ill luck had befallen an Imperial Prince. Ill luck, therefore, would infect the village.

"My lord," Koshei said as he walked beside Sezaru, "can you ride?"

"Yes. It has been this way since we left Kyuden Miya, but it grows worse with each passing day. Ill fortune follows us, seeking our trail. The imbalance in the elements has not been healed. It has only been clotted. Until Toryu is corrupted by the power of the Dark Oracle, it will continue to pressure him. And the imbalance will still exist. It infects the elements like a sickness."

Koshei listened to his master, watching as Sezaru's normally even features twisted in pain. "Come, let us get away from this village. It is plagued with misfortune, forgotten by the kami."

"There may be those who have forgotten the kami, yojimbo—" his master's touch upon his sleeve was like ice— "but I assure you, they are quite incapable of forgetting us."

Sezaru's words may have been meant to ease Koshei's mind, but instead they sent a chill shiver down the dark haired samurai's spine. He helped his lord mount, and they set out upon the road once more in silence.

* * * * *

The nights afterward were cold and bitter. Fires would not burn for long, and the snow whirled around them in wild drifts. Sezaru visited no more shrines, praying from dawn to dusk each day even as his horse fought its way through the storms. Koshei tied his master's reins to his belt, guiding both horses through the snow.

Sezaru spoke less and less, his mind twisting around the imbalance of the elements. From time to time, Koshei could hear him speaking as though engaged in a battle of wits. His voice echoed through the slowly falling snow from time to time, answering some unasked question. For a while, Koshei tried to make sense of Sezaru's words. In time he ignored them, unable to understand the deep meaning behind his prayers and whispered arguments.

"Master," Koshei said at last, turning in his saddle and drawing Sezaru's pony near. "Look. There. We have reached the pine forests of the Phoenix."

Above them, in a dark line against the white mountains, the trees stretched like a wave against the sand of the snowy shore. The trees were the only color in the mountain passes—the only color, that is, that was not waving above broad tents and on emblazoned banners.

"The Lion and the Dragon Clans." Koshei lowered his hand from his eyes.

"They are busy with their war. I believe it would be impolite to disturb them."

"Hai, master," Koshei agreed, glad to hear Sezaru speaking plainly once more.

"Then—" Sezaru nodded, a faint smile breaking his lips apart— "we must go around."

For the next four days, the two traveled through the low mountains of the Phoenix, avoiding the scouting parties of the warring clans. The constantly falling snow served in their favor and hid their tracks.

"The spirits aid us," Koshei ventured, but Sezaru shook his head and passed his hand between them as if he were drawing a knife from its sheath.

"The kami are busy with their own misfortunes. They have no time for ours." Koshei brushed snow-covered hair out of his eyes and turned away, but Sezaru continued. "Look at my hands, yojimbo."

Koshei looked. Sezaru's pale white fingers were outstretched, shaking with cold—and with something else. As before, they touched and wove the strands of energy together, but the pale links of power were strained and wan.

"The kami have no need to watch our wars. Soon . . . soon the kami will have a war of their own." Sezaru lingered a moment longer then dropped his hand back into his sleeve. "Toryu is weakening. It is a struggle to resist the power that the Dark Oracle position offers him. With each passing day, he loses a bit of himself. And the kami feel each weakening moment. Soon, all of the shugenja in Rokugan will feel it—not just me."

"The magic is changing?"

"More than that. Something dark is congregating, waiting for Toryu to fall. It follows us, even now, waiting for the opportunity to strike."

After that, Sezaru went silent again, and Koshei trudged on in the gathering darkness, keeping a careful watch behind them as they marched onward.

* * * * *

They camped at the edge of the pine forest, well into the lands of the Asako. Koshei hid their campfire in a low ravine beneath the wide boughs of the pine trees. It was the first decent fire in a fortnight. Koshei fed it small twigs and branches to keep its hunger raw while he cooked rice in a clay pot within the hot coals beneath the pyre.

Sezaru sat on a stone nearby. His white hair hung loosely around his shoulders, blending with the snow that fell from the heavens.

Koshei placed a bowl of rice in Sezaru's hands, rocking back on his heels afterward to warm himself by the fire.

"There is danger this night," Sezaru hissed suddenly, lifting his face above the bowl. In the steam rising from the rice, Koshei thought that Sezaru's face bore the visage of a demon. A strange redness gleamed in his eyes. "Danger has been stalking us, and tonight it will find us."

The dark-haired yojimbo let his hand drift toward the hilt of his ever-present katana. He darted glances across the fire, into the swaying branches of the pine trees that surrounded them. These ravings could be more of Sezaru's recent internal arguments, or they could be genuine prophecy. Above them, the stars scattered themselves against a black silk canvas, twinkling silently in the night. The woods were quiet, punctuated by the occasional fall of snow released from a burdened branch. The night was empty.

"Do not sleep tonight, yojimbo," Sezaru placed his empty bowl of rice on the ground and stood to look up at the night sky. "The moon will not rise tonight. Her face is hidden in the heavens, ashamed to look down on the world below. We are falling, Koshei, falling into the Void."

A rustle shook the distant branches of the forest. Koshei spun on his toes, feeling the numbness in his fingers and feet fading into a chill hum of readiness. A samurai must always be prepared to give his life for his lord.

There. A movement in the forest that was neither man nor beast. Their horses shuddered, pricking furred ears against the wind to catch another hint of sound. Their breath steamed against the wind, twin jets of wasted warmth against the uncaring winter cold.

"They will try to stop us." Sezaru moved cautiously around the fire to stand by his tense yojimbo. "They cannot allow us to gain the knowledge hidden in the Isawa libraries. I foresaw this but hoped that traveling in winter's snow would hide our passage."

"They?" Koshei whispered, still uncertain if the threat was real or imagined. He kept his hand on his sword-hilt, standing in a lion stance and prepared for attack from any angle.

"There are forces at work against us. We have seen them maneuvering, even if we do not know their faces. Those forces pressured my mother into accepting the throne, knowing what it would do to the Empire. They twisted fate to create a Dark Oracle of Void." Sezaru's demeanor was calm, but his body was as taut as a bow. "They murdered my father. And now . . . they are here."

A sickening howl rose above the sound of wind and snow, crying its lonesome ache into the night even as it spoke of death and devastation. It was the sound of decay, magnified a thousand-fold as if taint and corruption were given a voice. Little feet scampered through the darkness, scouting for their scent.

As Koshei watched, scrabbling creatures emerged from the forest. Tree branches waved as though shaking off snow, but their burdens were far darker and more horrible. Some had green claws, extending from knobbed fingers like thin steel needles. Others hissed through snakelike mouths, their venomed fangs dripping black acid against the melting snow. As they came through the thick forest, the trees waved and swayed with their presence—and the presence of something much larger, following the smaller beasts with a single-minded determination.

Koshei leaped forward to intercept one of the slavering creatures, his sword swirling in a flash of steel to slice the lizard-like creature in half. Its body fell in even pieces on either side, sinking into the snow at his feet. Koshei heard Sezaru begin a soft chanting behind him, and he looked back to see his master's fingers pressed together in quiet prayer.

In the bushes nearby, other creatures snarled at the death of their companion. The severed lumps at Koshei's feet shivered and writhed, still dripping poisonous blood. Its unloving eyes continued to roll in the sockets, and its teeth gnashed in impotent rage. Koshei kicked it aside, keeping his woolen socks away from the wet, sticky blood. "Master," he ventured, seeing many more eyes opening within the brush around them, "they are undead!"

Three more hurled themselves out of the brush, racing on all fours across the snow toward them. Koshei slanted his sword downward, racing to intercept them. His sword whirled in the icy air, slicing through first one creature's upraised leg and then another's exposed neck, but the third dodged the rapid flurry of blows and lunged past the yojimbo. Spearing the injured beast on the tip of his sword as he spun in a circle, Koshei drew a thin throwing knife from his belt and hurled it at the creature. The knife bit deep into the beast's neck, severing its spine at the junction of the shoulder-blades and sending the beast rolling on the ground in a tumble.

Sezaru's chanting grew louder, and he lifted his hands to trace mystic symbols in the icy air. As he did, many more of the small beasts rushed forward to take advantage of the opening. Koshei moved like a blur, circling first one side of Sezaru and then the other to destroy each of the beasts as they came. One cut disemboweled a screaming, viper-headed lizard, another took two blows to the midsection before its torso rolled free upon the ground in a spatter of blood. Still, eyes continued to open in the shifting forest, and the branches of the trees grew ever more laden with writhing bodies.

Koshei's steel sliced through the face of another beast, sealing its yellow eyes with blood. As he did, Sezaru spread his fingers once more and reached out toward the swaying trees. Koshei felt a strange, spiritual tug, followed by a ripple in the air that seared through the snow like a melting ripple. Around him, the branches of the trees burst into light flame. The small creatures howled, their skin blistering and rippling with the extreme heat. The wave of scorching air rushed outward, marking the forest with a ripple of flame that burst into life and then hissed into nothingness. Water poured down from the melt-off of the upper branches, pouring to the ground like buckets dropped by a forgetful eta.

The water was steaming from the effect of Sezaru's spell, made boiling hot by the power of air and fire.

Tens of the little beasts shrieked in mortal pain, flesh searing from raw muscle and bone. Koshei intercepted those maddened enough by the pain to rush forward into the circle, watching as Sezaru's fire spirits used the small campfire to send out flickering lances of flame. As the creatures came too close, they were sliced by Koshei's swift steel, or burst into howling balls of flame. Sezaru stood in the midst of the chaos, his fingers still folded in an attitude of prayer. The smell of seared flesh and rotting carapaces filled the air.

Sezaru chanted again, his eyes flashing as another wave of the lizard-things rushed forward. The flame roared, but this time, it leaped from creature to creature like skipping lightning. Each time it struck one of the small beasts, it hurled them back into the trees, their flaming bodies igniting more of the creatures still hiding in the forest. The fire was bluish, as cold as the snow, ignoring the tree limbs and fallen branches in a rabid hunt for flesh. Koshei watched in awe as it leaped through the clustered creatures. They clawed at one another and howled as the fire burned away their flesh.

Two more leaped at Koshei, their claws digging into his thick clothing. They scrabbled for the flesh beneath as Koshei drew his sword across their backs. Howling, screaming, the two beasts would not release him, and to cut deeper might mean to cut open his own chest with his katana. Instead, Koshei threw himself forward into the fire. The heat of the flames set the beasts aflame, burning his open cloak and thick woolen garments. But the two beasts, blazing like stars against Koshei's chest, released their grip and were crushed against the flaming logs.

Koshei rolled out of the fire, gasping for breath and choking against the smoke. The two creatures clawed at the logs of the fire, scattering the flame and coals as they desperately tried to escape. The dark haired samurai struck out at them with his katana, gripping a flaming log in the other hand to press it against the beast's eyes. The creatures screamed, lashing out one final time with dripping claws, and died in the flame.

"Koshei-san," Sezaru's voice held earnest warning, "Stop amusing yourself with the small ones. It is time."

Koshei rolled to his feet, his sword in one hand and the lit branch on the other. From his vantage point, he could see that the Wolf's eyes were fixed on a single point, out beyond the trees.

Something horrible moved beyond the edge of the firelight, and those few small beasts that remained fled from its presence. It staggered toward them with heavy, uneven steps, brushing aside the ancient pine trees with a sweeping, powerful hand.

Huge, jowled chins lowered beneath sharp ivory fangs. Three eyes, each glimmering with yellow hatred, glowed in the dim light of the scattered fire. It stood easily twice as tall as a man, with powerful arms and long-knuckled fingers that scraped the ground before it. Its face held a vaguely ape-like appearance, and its back boiled with more of the small, lizard-beings. The monster's skin was blue, dappled with graying, patchy fur above scabrous legions and rotting flesh. Its presence was so hideous that Koshei felt his soul pressed toward the ground, one knee forced to bend, slamming into the earth with heavy resistance. Koshei gritted his teeth, struggling to force himself to his feet once more, but the oni's presence held him despite his struggles. It was all that he could do not to kneel before the hideous creature.

The beast spoke, with slurred syllables and rough, bass tones. "Wolf of Rokugan," it jeered, and the little creatures at its feet yipped and hissed in kind. "Prepare yourself to meet the kami you command. On this night, you die."

Koshei was proud to see that his master neither bent nor bowed despite the beast's awesome presence. Sezaru's brow was slightly furrowed, but that was the only sign of his intense concentration. As the shugenja's robes swirled around him in the wind, he pressed his fingers against his shoulders in the signs of the kami. The oni sneered at Sezaru's defiance and rolled forward on his backward-bending knees to swipe with iron claws at the shugenja. His fist sheered away just before reaching Sezaru's billowing silk robes, the claws sending out sparks as they dragged across a hardened shield of air.

"Who sent you?" asked Sezaru. "Who summoned you?"

The oni did not answer, reaching with both hands to encircle the shugenja in its claws. Although it could not reach him directly, it could crush against the shield of air and possibly cause him indirect damage. Sezaru twisted, lowering his hands in a shove and extending his palms with a violent motion. Fire roared from his palms in a violet shower of sparks, but the oni only grunted and tightened its grasp.

Koshei renewed his efforts, roaring in agony as he ripped his knee from the hard-packed earth. Bowed into a horse stance, the yojimbo fought to move forward, to place himself between the oni and his master. Each step brought a tearing, hideous pain, but he endured it.

Sezaru extended his hands and raised them above his shoulders with a shout, and the sky answered. A bolt of lightning tore down from above, slamming into the oni with a blaze of light. Roaring, the creature fell back, and Koshei felt its concentration drop.

The yojimbo lunged three great steps forward and half-crouched by his master's side with his sword before him. As the oni reached again to claw at Sezaru, Koshei was ready. His sword sang loudly from the oni's claws, showering them both with flakes of iron broken from the beast's natural weaponry. The creature snarled, drawing back its hand before the furious onslaught, and focused its concentration once more on the yojimbo and his Prince.

Koshei felt his body being crushed, but he slammed the blade of his sword against the ground, using the weapon to help him remain standing. "Better that my blade bear dishonor," he gasped, "than that I bow in any way to you!"

Sezaru chanted again, snarling the words in uncustomary anger. The spell raced along the Wolf's fingers, jumping in a wide arch into the oni's eyes. The beast roared, green ichor spilling from its face as it clawed at the blue-white crackling energy. The pressure continued, and Koshei saw Sezaru stumble once beneath the awesome force of the oni's power.

"Who sent you?" Sezaru repeated.

"The master of all things dark and foul," the oni retorted with a swing of its claws. The yellow eyes widened with anger. Smaller creatures skittered beneath its feet, crunching when they did not get out of the way swiftly enough. "He who will control you. He who will command you. He who will be your salvation. I come from the darkness, Wolf—a darkness that you already know but do not yet understand. You are well acquainted with my master. Oh yes, far more than you know."

Sezaru drew forth a blade of spiritual energy, launching it toward the oni at awesome speeds. The beast dodged but not swiftly enough, and the sparkling blade dug into its flesh. With a twisting motion, Sezaru thrust the blade further into the beast, hearing it roar in agony. "Your master will fail," he said simply.

As he redoubled his efforts, drawing out the spiritual blade and sinking it back into the oni's flesh, the beast reached to claw at Sezaru once more. Although his iron claws could not pierce the wind-barrier surrounding the shugenja, Koshei saw a flood of the smaller lizards careening from the oni's back and plunging toward his master. Even as the beast died, they would overwhelm Sezaru, poisoning and destroying him.

Koshei forced himself to his feet, honor overwhelming the power of the oni's magic. His sword whirled before him, trying to cleave each of the smaller beasts before they reached Sezaru. He kicked the remains of the ruined fire toward them, seeing his prayers rewarded as the flames licked and caught against the broken branches scattered on the ground.

Sezaru raised his hand, and a second sword of starlight appeared. A third, fourth, and fifth surrounded it, glittering with flecks of light. Sezaru had the oni screaming in pain, roaring its fury and hatred as Sezaru's magic tore it apart.

But the smaller beasts were far too fast and too prolific for one samurai to stop them all. They swarmed over Koshei, claws cutting into his arms and legs even as he ended their foul half-lives. He screamed Sezaru's name, placing himself between the shugenja and the smaller beasts, taking as much of the assault as possible. Given time, he would be able to destroy them all.

Given time . . . but time was not his ally.

The oni screamed again as the blades sliced its flesh apart, and slowly its body dissolved into mist. Koshei did not know if the beast was dead or simply banished—and he did not care. All he saw was a lizard-beast on the far side of the circle slipping past Sezaru's barrier of wind and steel and sinking its venomous teeth deep into the shugenja's chest. Sezaru drew a knife and cut the beast away even as his yojimbo slaughtered four more of the undead creatures.

Koshei howled in fury and cut down the smaller beasts as he made his way to his master's side. Several more died before his blade. Others, frightened by their master's banishment, raced into the woods to be lost in the darkness.

Koshei knelt before Sezaru and stared up into the Wolf's eyes in pain and horror. Sezaru withdrew his hand from his chest. Blood had turned his white robes scarlet. The beast's bite had cut deeply, placing the poison near the heart and slicing open the pale white skin of his chest. Sezaru fell to his knees before Koshei, brushing away his yojimbo's arms as Koshei tried to catch him.

"Sezaru-sama!" Koshei cried in anguish. "Take my life, if it will save you!"

"No, Koshei." Sezaru's voice was soft but still strong. "You fought with the strength of ten men. No other could have given me the time I needed to defeat the greater threat."

"I failed you! You are poisoned! I must get you to a healer!"

"Someone knew our path, Koshei. We are not safe here." Sezaru was calm. "I may not make it to a healer. Already, the poison works its way into my heart.

"You cannot die. The Empire relies on you. You are its only hope." Tears fell down the yojimbo's cheeks, and Sezaru smiled.

"If I am, Koshei, then you are, as well." With that, Sezaru slumped forward into his yojimbo's arms, the snow falling white and cold against his porcelain cheek.

Koshei's scream of rage and denial echoed through the forest, unheeded by a silent sky.

12   THE CROSSING

The blistering darkness crushed him so tightly that he could not move, could not breathe, and could not speak. It charred his bones and shattered each breath that he forced himself to draw. He could feel his skin charring, singing away from his body in ashen drifts. The pain of it pulsed in every vein like hot lead.

Sezaru opened his eyes and saw nothing.

It stretched, empty and alone, falling beyond the range of mortal understanding. He reached out tentatively with his spirit and touched nothing save the dark fires of Void and starlight. An old koan leapt into his memory. *Things are exactly what they appear to be. Behind them . . . there is nothing.*

The eons stretched on endlessly. Sezaru floated in the Void, lingering.

Pain lanced through his chest once more, and he looked down to see the wound bleeding. The scarlet of his blood washed over his pale skin, sending jeweled droplets into the emptiness.

Sezaru.

Go away! he wanted to shout, but the lack of wind in his lungs made it impossible. He struggled against the burning darkness, pushing out with all his strength, but to no avail.

Sezaru.

The voice sounded different—deeper, stronger, less mocking. Perhaps in death, the demons that haunted his soul finally understood mercy. Nevertheless, he steeled his mind against them with the resolve he had learned as a child. It was this strength that had made him a powerful shugenja, rallying his spirit against distraction and emotions that would cloud his mind. He called upon it now, trying to force back the burning grip that held him hovering among the stars, but still his world did not change.

Sezaru, open your eyes.

The sound was overwhelming, filling the darkness around him, and suddenly Sezaru understood that this whisper was not of his own making. It came from a distant point outside his soul, not from the depths of his being. This was not the voice that had plagued him since childhood. This was something far more powerful—and not of the mortal world.

He opened his eyes and stared into the darkness.

The constellations around him began to take shape, igniting one by one in the glossy blackness. He watched as the stars of the ancient heroes surrounded him, their stories fresh in his mind as their bodies blazed into life. *These are your ancestors. They surround you. You follow in their footsteps like a child seeking wisdom, wishing to learn for yourself what they already know.*

"No. I seek . . ." What had he been searching for? It had seemed so desperately important only a moment ago. Why could he not recall now? Think. Logic would remind him. If he could only remember what he had been doing before . . . before the emptiness that was *here*.

You sought to repair the damage done to the throne, the voice whispered curiously.

The throne. The throne should fall to the first son. Yes, of course, that made sense. Except . . . if the throne were empty, that would mean Toturi was—

Dead. Gone to honor.

Memories flooded Sezaru. A grand pyre by the side of the ocean. Toturi's courtiers, his generals, his friends, lined up along the road from Otosan Uchi as they walked in the incense trail left by the priests who led them to the shore. Blood upon a steel blade. Kaede's proclamation. Her disappearance. The elements . . .

"The Empire is in danger." Sezaru's mind sharpened. He gripped the pain that came with his flood of memories, narrowing the imaged into a single bright point. With sheer determination, he forced his emotions of loss and betrayal back into a single pinprick, allowing it to burn him like the wound that bled down his side.

And you are here. The voice was not mocking, but neither was it entirely . . . mortal. It seemed curious, mildly concerned, and almost distant. *Brought to me by a strength of will beyond any other I have ever known. You would not release your goal, even as you lay dying.*

"Dying." He suddenly realized the truth. "Koshei! The forest!"

I know no Koshei. He is not with you. It seemed almost regretful.

"No. He is still in the forest. He was wounded only by the claws of the beasts, not by their poison." Sezaru's mind raced. Dying, the voice said. Dying, not dead. Not yet dead. The Wolf clung to that distinction. "I must return to him. To the Empire. If I am not already there. Is this reality, demon, or is it a dream?"

Can it not be both?

Sezaru had no answer.

The voice continued softly, *You are with me. You have come seeking.*

The starry darkness around him seemed to shift and twist, and for a moment Sezaru felt his stomach churn with motion sickness. The universe fluctuated and slid, coiling about him as he shook his head to clear his mind.

"I seek truth. If you can give it to me, then say as much. I have no time for games, spirit."

Impatient. You have all the time in the world. Soon you will be dead, and there will be no rush at all.

Sezaru gritted his teeth. Whatever this was, wherever the oni's poison had trapped him, the creature seemed to know just enough of humanity to taunt him. "So, you know the truth? About who killed my father, where my mother has gone and how to save her? How to keep the Void Dragon from dying, as I have foreseen?"

Seeing the future is dangerous. Walking the path you have chosen, even more so.

"I have no choice."

You are wrong. Of all the creatures of the Celestial Heavens, and of the earth below, Man is the only one that has any choice at all. The voice mused for a moment; several constellations shifted and others were born. *If you continue in this, you risk your own life— what little of it you have left before you.*

"Then it shouldn't hurt anything for you to tell me what you know."

The voice chuckled faintly, and the starry heavens rolled in a gentle wave. *I know you are in greater danger than any other being within your Empire. Hunted by foe and friend alike, you search for truth in a land of lies and risk your life for answers that will not avail you. Look at your search, Sezaru. To find your father's killer? What use? In the end, the throne will still be empty, the Empire at war, and your father will still be dead.*

"He will be avenged." Sezaru clenched his fists at his side, wishing that he could escape this place, yet the barriers of his prison seemed endless, and despite his constant attempts to summon enough will to defend himself against the burning sensation that held him frozen among the stars, he could not move.

Avenged? How can you be satisfied with that, while all the Empire crumbles?

"What would you have me do?" Sezaru snarled. "Ignore my family honor and the death of my father?"

If by doing so, you saved the Empire he loved more than his life, how have you done wrong? And if you ignored that duty simply for your personal vengeance, would he be proud of your decision?

The words, so casually spoken, were like an icy slap in Sezaru's face. He considered them, feeling cold chills against his spine. Would Toturi believe in his journey? What would he have said about Sezaru's quest? No. Toturi *was* the Empire. He was the Emperor. The throne was more than a symbol. It was the heart of Rokugan. "I cannot turn back. There is more to my quest than vengeance."

Is there? Truly? For vengeance is the deepest wish of your heart. I see it, waiting there, like a tiger preparing to be released, a drive to kill those who harmed you by taking away your father. And your mother.

Deep within his heart, Sezaru knew that it was partly true. If he had been with Toturi on the day the Emperor was attacked, he would have rained fire from the heavens, scorching the land raw before he allowed his father to be harmed. He would have easily sacrificed the land, the samurai around him, and all those who stood near simply to save his father's life. But was it out of devotion to the Empire or to his family?

For a samurai, the distinction was crucial. A samurai had to be willing to give his life for his lord, but on rare occasion, when his lord's orders countermanded what the samurai knew to be best for the Empire or when they offended the kami, a samurai had the right to refuse. Sezaru remembered a vivid image from his childhood: the wide plains of the Unicorn Clan, the manes of their steeds bound with white ribbons of mourning. A samurai knelt on a wide white sheet, reading his final haiku to the spirits of the wind. His lord had ordered him to butcher an innocent village. This was his refusal. Blood spattered the white sheet as he opened his belly; he made no sound during the cut. Within a moment, his second's blade swung down over the back of his throat, and the Unicorn died as he had lived—with honor. Such refusal meant he sacrificed his life in ritual seppuku, but to a samurai, his honor—and the Empire—must mean more than one man's life. Sometimes the Empire must come first.

His father or the Empire? Were those truly his only choices?

And if they were, did that not disprove the belief that the Emperor *was* the embodiment of the Empire? Sezaru struggled to separate his vengeance, still his emotions, and utilize only logic and intelligence. Emotion was the enemy of a samurai. If he allowed it to conquer his will, it would lead him into darkness.

Your riddle is complex. To save the Empire, you must give up your drive to save the Empire. To find your father's killer, you must stop seeking and turn aside to rediscover the true sickness in Rokugan's heart. There, if you also have good fortune, you will find two answers: one for yourself and one for the Empire.

"I know who you are now." Sezaru looked out into the shifting stars. They shone and moved like torches carried by peasants on festival nights; like the scales of a great serpent, encircling the world.

I have always been with you—not that you would know. In all of the motions of the sprits, in the call of your soul to the void . . . The stars gathered, their luminance reflecting down on Sezaru and tinting his skin with a golden glow. The burning fire around him slowly solidified into claws, and the smoke that rose from the Dragon's breath became the mist of the heavens around him.

"The Dragon of the Void." Even as Sezaru said it, the celestial being came into focus. What Sezaru had taken for stars were the reflections of the heavens within the Dragon's scales. "So. This is a dream."

You might term it such, but it is also reality. The Dragon moved, and the universe shifted around Sezaru. With the movement of each coil, the constellations were rewritten. *Our time grows short. The cold comes to claim you. You must remember this, Sezaru. Remember what I tell you now, for our paths will not cross again.*

If you continue, you will die a traitor to your deepest desire, Sezaru. There is always a price for knowledge. If you turn back now, you will succeed. If you do not, then you will lose your destiny and never know the true path laid for you. Choose wisely, Sezaru. The Empire . . . or the man.

The chill that had touched Sezaru's spine was growing, encompassing his torso and trickling like ice water through his veins. "What is happening? Is this death?"

Sezaru's mind hung on a fragile balance, trying to understand the Dragon's prophecies and keep his fear and anger in check. Deep in the back of his mind, the voice—his voice—whispered a mocking refrain.

The cold grew so bitter that it ached through Sezaru's muscles, cramping his legs and arms. It raced through his veins, turning his pale skin blue, and tore a scream from even the disciplined shugenja's lips. The Dragon of Void watched impassively as Sezaru lifted frozen hands before his eyes, staring down at them as the fingers began to fall away into flakes of broken snow.

"What is happening?" He choked, pain searing though every inch of his body with cold blue flame.

The end—the Dragon whispered as Sezaru's body melted into ice and snow—*is only the beginning, beneath another mask. Look for your future in the stars, Sezaru, and then decide if you can turn your back on it. Forever.*

In the end, as the cold took him, Sezaru's last thoughts were of ice, pain, and destiny.

13 | SECRETS OF THE PHOENIX

I'm astounded by people who wish to know everything when the world is as uncertain as the wind." The voice was female, young and soothing. A damp coolness pressed against Sezaru's eyes, shielding them from the light.

"Tell me." Hoarse, aching with weariness, this was unmistakably the voice of Koshei.

"He will live," replied the woman, "but there will be pain."

Sinking back into the darkness, Sezaru felt the chill racing through his veins again, searing into his skull with hideous, relentless hatred. The poison, still in his body, fought to destroy his mind.

He struggled, fighting against it, and the cold cloth fell from his eyes for a brief, flashing moment. Although he could sense that the only light in the room was a distant candle, the brightness nearly blinded him. Sezaru felt a strong hand grip his own, and he clenched it with single-minded agony.

Darkness, sweet oblivion, swallowed him before he could scream.

* * * * *

". . . the path is long, the way unknown."

Sezaru struggled to consciousness, his mind grasping the sound of the voice. It was an anchor to him in the darkness, the sound of a woman's whisper in an empty room. As he organized his fractured thoughts, he became aware of other sounds—a fire crackling in the fireplace, the sweet chime of a distant temple bell.

"Where—?" His throat was dry from long disuse. Coughing, he tried once more. "Where am I?"

The girl's voice stopped, and he heard the soft slide of a silk sleeve against the floor. Cool hands pressed against his cheek, holding still the wet cloth that covered his eyes. "Good evening, Sezaru-sama," she whispered. "Please, do not move." Brushing her fingers lightly against his face, she drew aside the cloth. "Tell me, Lord, can you open your eyes? Is there pain?"

He blinked crusted, dry eyes. Panic gripped him, but he banished it with the iron of his will. "There is no pain. But I see only darkness."

"No pain. That is good. I am not surprised that you cannot yet see—" her words held a smile— "as I have my hand before your eyes." A soft, delicate chuckle—not a maiden's idle giggle, but instead the wise, pleasing murmur of an educated woman. "I am going to remove my hand. If there is any pain, or if your headache returns, you must tell me immediately."

"Yes," Sezaru agreed, smiling. "As you say, Lady Healer."

"My name," said the softly smiling voice, "is Sayuri."

Slowly, the light returned. The blurred image of a delicate hand slid away from his line of vision, hovering just below his cheek as if to leap back in protection should he cry out in pain. A distant fire softly lit the world, but as he peered through the haze and dimness, he could just make out a modest stone bedchamber dressed in silver and mauve. The room seemed over-bright, as if the fire gave off more light than a hundred torches.

"Where am I?" he asked again, leaning forward slightly and trying to sit up. The motion made him dizzy, and he fell back onto his elbows.

"Isawa Palace," she replied. "The lands of the Phoenix."

Sezaru sighed, lying back again on the futon. "Koshei?"

"Ah, yes. The faithful yojimbo." Sayuri laid the soft cloth over his eyes once more, damp now with fresh water from a bowl by the bed. The water trickled into his eyes, cool and soothing against the itchy ache of his retinas. "He was nearly as close to death as you were when first he arrived at our gates. But with rest and a good healer he will be fine in a matter of weeks."

"Asako . . . ?" Sezaru asked weakly. The Asako were the gate-keepers of the Phoenix, their palaces many *li* closer to the south. Why so far under such difficult circumstances?

As if reading the question from his mind, the woman at his bedside continued, "The Asako palaces are besieged by the Dragon-Lion war. Taking you there would have been suicide—for you and for your yojimbo. Though the Isawa were farther, it was his only hope of survival. Astounding, really. He must have walked over a hundred *li* with you on his back. Had I not tended him myself, I would have thought it impossible. His feet were bloody stumps, and his wounds . . . well, Sezaru, let us simply say that I thought the kami would reward his duty to you with a favored place among their number. It took the direct order of the Phoenix Champion to remove him from your side." Gently, she laid another damp piece of silk over his eyes. "Your injuries were far worse than his. He was not infected by the poison that ran through your blood. And good that he wasn't; we did not have enough antidote to heal two."

Sezaru sighed heavily, closing his eyes beneath the cool darkness of the wet cloth. "The poison?"

"Difficult and dangerous, but I guess you already assumed that."

"An oni?" He knew the answer but asked anyway.

"Of course." Sayuri turned away, and he listened to the sound of her silks sliding, hushed, across the cool stone floor. The liquid rippled as she changed it, pouring fresh mountain water from a pitcher into the bowl.

"Why are you here, then, shugenja? And do not tell me your injuries alone brought you into Phoenix lands. We know who you are. We know your purposes. But the thread of your life is muddled, difficult to fathom." A soft note crept into her voice. "I alone have tended you since your yojimbo brought you here. Your sleep was troubled. You often cried out as in pain."

"Did I speak?" Coldness gripped Sezaru, and he pushed the cloth from his forehead. What secrets had escaped him in the darkness?

A long moment passed before she answered. Sayuri took the cloth from Sezaru, dipping it once more in the water. Her hands remained there, feeling the brush of ripples as they crossed her skin. "You spoke of many things. Among them, an attack upon the Oracle of Water." The Isawa's long dark hair swept the floor where she was kneeling, stirred only slightly by a breeze from the open window. He could not see her face clearly, as it was obscured by the long fall of unbound dark hair and by the weakness of his eyes. Yet he could tell that she was beautiful, her even features framing two large, dark eyes. "It was determined that someone would need to tend you. I volunteered. When you have recovered fully, I will commit seppuku to keep your secrets safe."

The implications staggered Sezaru. "You volunteered?"

"The moment you spoke of the Oracle of Water, I knew I could not leave your side. Better I tend you and then die than that I be denied even the small peace you could give me." As she spoke, she leaned close to Sezaru once more, offering the cloth for his eyes.

Now, he could see her face. Catching her delicate white wrist in his strong grip, he stared into her eyes. So familiar, so ethereal, and yet somehow incorrect. She froze in his grasp, and he lifted the other hand to brush her hair away from her face.

"Oracle . . . ?" he whispered, but as soon as he spoke the words, he knew they were wrong. This woman had power, yes, but not that of an Oracle. The strength of her aura was softer, kinder, and untouched by the inhumanity of a Dragon's soul. Though she was the mirror image of the Oracle of Water, this was not she.

"My name is Isawa Sayuri, as I have said, Imperial Prince. The Oracle of Water was my sister, Mitako." Slowly, he released her. Her white skin slid against his fingers as she leaned away, and her black hair fell once more to obscure her features. "They told me to forget her when the Dragon took her away. I knew she would not return. But every summer, I walk the beaches of White Shore Lake and float cherry blossoms on its surface. She always loved the cherry blossoms. I know she cannot see them beneath the waves, so I bring them to her." Sayuri lowered her eyes. "When you spoke of her, I knew I had to be the one to listen."

Instinctively, he knew her pain. To be separated from one's twin, to have that kindred soul stripped from you by circumstance. As he wished to know Kaede's fate, so too did this woman seek to understand her sister's. "Seppuku will not be necessary," he said quietly. Her dark eyes turned to meet his in surprise. "I only require your oath."

"You have it, and more, my Prince."

"Do you know why I am here?"

She nodded. "To seek the foci of the Oracle of the Void." She pushed the cool compress upon him again, shielding his sore eyes from the light. "A fortuitous circumstance. I recently had the privilege of aiding Isawa Riake, the Elemental Master of Water, with his most recent task: to discover if the Dark Oracles had foci of their own."

"What did he discover?"

"I will tell you a secret, Imperial Prince—the very secret that you have come to Isawa Palace to learn. In exchange for your benevolence and my life, I will tell you of the Dark Covenants of the Oracles, the foci gathered and protected by the Dark Oracles and their servants. These are items of foul power, formed by the shadow of the Dragons. And a new one has been born recently, though we know not where."

"Tell me more," he commanded, his weak voice still holding the dictum of his Imperial birth.

"I have already gathered the information for you, Sezaru-sama. When your eyes are better, you may peruse the documents at your leisure."

"My eyes may be weak, but not my mind. Get them. Bring them. Read them to me now, Sayuri."

He heard the soft rustle of silk, echoed by the swish of her long hair as she stood and bowed. "As you wish, my lord."

The days passed quickly in the Isawa palaces as Sezaru's wounds healed. Though still weak, he insisted that Sayuri continue to read to him of the Oracles and their magics. The Dark Covenants were more powerful than he imagined; their strength bolstered by imbalances in the elements.

Koshei recovered more swiftly than his master and soon spent the majority of his time kneeling outside Sezaru's room. Inside, Sezaru and Sayuri bowed their heads, one black and one white, over long and ancient scrolls.

The Dark Covenants. The images described in the texts inflamed Sezaru's mind. Like the foci of the Light Oracles, these items could control and demand the Dark Oracles to do their owner's bidding. Yet they were immensely dangerous, difficult to control, and like asking questions of the Light Oracles, each item only worked once for its bearer. After that, the Dark Oracle was no longer constrained, and woe to the one who had dared to command them.

There was more—much more—in the libraries of the Isawa. Descriptions of the various Dark Covenants, from a lantern that burned with green, sickly flame (belonging to the Dark Oracle of Fire) to a bowl that turned any liquid placed within it to a deadly poison (the Dark Oracle of Water). Yet there was no information at all on the Dark Covenant of the Oracle of Void. Not entirely surprising, considering it would only recently have been formed by Tonbo's acceptance of the position.

Yet Toryu *had* accepted the post. Therefore it *must* exist.

Sayuri proved an excellent helper. She was intelligent, trustworthy, and capable of astounding intuitive leaps. From time to time, Sezaru found himself simply listening to her voice as she read the scrolls aloud. Occasionally, he was forced to ask her to read parts again, furious with himself for listening to the sound and not the information contained within her words.

They studied on the wide balcony of his rooms when it was pleasant outside. Well-bundled in woolen robes and kept warm with hot tea, Sezaru enjoyed the cold wintry days with the sun brilliant in an ice-blue sky. Even Koshei was persuaded to join them from time to time, though he did not understand the scrolls.

At last, Sezaru slammed his fist into the table with frustration. "Spring is nearly here, the roads are clearing to the south, and I am no farther to finding the Dark Covenant of the Oracle of the Void than I was when I lay dying from the oni's poison."

"Do not despair, sire," Sayuri murmured, her dark eyes looking up from the text that engrossed her. "We already know far more about the Dark Oracles and their Covenants than before. We have scoured the Phoenix libraries. The answer must be here . . . somewhere."

"No, Sayuri." Sezaru shuffled through the papers idly, his hand restlessly passing over passage after passage. "The Dark Covenants are powerful items; they are our only hope. Unless we can find the Dark Oracle's foci—his Covenant—and bring it to Kaede, I have no chance to save my mother. Already, the power of the Dark Oracles grows stronger. I know that you can feel it, Sayuri. Is there nothing we can do?"

Sayuri poured another steaming glass of the tea, watching as the steam rose into the clear winter sky. Her beautiful face seemed distant as she regarded the scattered texts, eyes lingering on first one and then another. "Is there no pattern to it? No thing we can predict from the locations of the other Dark Covenants?"

Sezaru shook his head, running a hand through his white hair in frustration. "Nothing at all." He rose from the cushion and walked to the edge of the balcony. Far below them, the gardens of the Phoenix lay brushed by white snow, the twisting paths through oak and aspen trees no more than wandering black lines. They seemed like the wandering trails of a dreaming calligrapher, criss-crossing the white paper of the garden.

The balcony offered a view of the tall, broad walls of Isawa palace, dotted by flowing banners of mauve silk. On the tallest of them, the image of a flaming Phoenix rose and fell with the wind. Sezaru stared into the silken flames, trying to piece together the knowledge they had gained into a useful picture. "The future . . . Koshei-san," he said. "Bring me my satchel—and a map of Rokugan."

"Yes, Sezaru-sama!" Koshei rose, bowed, and strode into the other room.

"What are you going to do?" asked Sayuri.

"The Dark Oracle of the Void was but newly created. His story is not yet told; it has only started. Though the Phoenix are masters of magic, even they cannot read the future."

Koshei returned with a long tubular scroll and Sezaru's carrying bag. As the yojimbo pushed aside the other texts and laid the map on the table, Sezaru opened his bag and reached inside.

Gently, slowly, Sezaru withdrew a silk-wrapped bundle and laid it upon his lap. The bundle felt warm to him, despite the chill temperature and its glassy composition. One of the folds fell aside as he touched its surface gently, and Sayuri drew in her breath with a gasp of surprise.

"Fortunes keep us safe! Sezaru, that can't be—"

"It is, Sayuri." The rest of the fabric fell away from the Obsidian Mirror, and the black glass seemed to ripple in the sunlight. No reflection shone on its surface—not Sezaru, nor Koshei, nor Sayuri's pale and frightened face.

"You must not. Even I have heard the ancient legends of that artifact. Though I am no Void scholar, Shiba Ningen tells tales that frighten the children. It is a thing of evil, Sezaru." Her eyes hardened. "It will bring misfortune upon you. Upon us all."

"We have no choice. What have the libraries of the Miya and the Phoenix given me? Only hints, guesses . . . and no answers." Sezaru's face hardened. "There is no other means at our disposal."

"We could research more. Study more. The answers—"

"And risk my mother's life? No, Sayuri, such talk is foolishness."

"Please, Sezaru," without thinking, Sayuri reached out and touched Sezaru's hand. The unexpected contact reminded Sezaru of the burning heat within the Void of his dream; blazing through his veins with sudden fire. "I fear for you."

Quickly, too quickly, Sezaru drew his hand away from hers, stilling the rush of emotion at her touch. Emotions were dangerous to a samurai, and they were a shugenja's worst enemy. Should he allow them to affect his actions, he would fail. He turned his back on Sayuri. "Leave me."

"Imperial Prince, I cannot." The Isawa shugenja fell to her knees. Behind her, Koshei lifted his hand to the hilt of his sword, a dark look crossing his features at the woman's rejection of Sezaru's order. Sezaru raised his hand and signaled Koshei to stand his ground. "If you choose to do this, if you truly deny its danger, then I must be here. In case something goes wrong. Each time you use such an object, it carves a deeper niche into your soul. I can see from your face you have used it before. The call of the mirror grows stronger each time you listen. If it tries to control you, then there must be someone to bring you home."

Her defiance was also unexpected, and Sezaru half-turned to gaze on her with a mixture of anger and gratitude. "You think that you have the ability to defeat the mirror, if I cannot?"

"No." Her voice was as cold as the winter wind. "But I believe that I can try."

He nodded and turned his back on her again. He did not look back as he walked to the end of the balcony and knelt with the mirror in his hands. The glass was smooth and cool beneath his fingertips, reflecting no light from the noonday sun above. Though he knew that Koshei and Sayuri were still behind him, the mirror did not show their faces.

But now, as if just beginning to realize its purpose, it showed a reflection. Pale against the mirror's surface, Sezaru looked into his image. His white hair flowed like a river of snow against the obsidian sheen, and his face seemed to be chiseled out of the same stone. His eyes were bright stars with dark centers, and without meaning to, Sezaru fell into their gaze.

The voice within his mind, so long silent, whispered, *Lost . . .* and the shadows took him.

The stars were lost this time, flowing like silk against the mirror's cold sheen. He ignored them, ignored their glitter and their luster, knowing them to be as false as an oni's lies. The mirror lost its innocence and shed its false premises like silken shrouds, drifting one by one into the darkness as Sezaru passed through them. He knew the mirror's name; he did not believe its whispers any more.

"Show me." Sezaru understood that the mirror knew why he had come. Some part of its innate ability allowed it to read the mind of its user and know his purposes. Perhaps that was another reason why the mirror was so dangerous. Those purposes were now part of the artifact, drifting forever in its glassy shimmer like a man who stands between two mirrors, losing his mind in the infinite reflections of himself. Sezaru found his mind returning to Bayushi Kachiko, the mirror's former owner. Was some small part of her trapped here, forever lingering in the darkness?

An image shuddered in the dark reality—a white hand moving across a man's face. The scene was of a luxurious bedroom dressed in black silks. Kachiko's memory? The man had white hair, his face hidden in shadows as the woman moved over him. Her kimono fell away, drifting to join the darkness pooling on the floor. Her white back, arched delicately, moved with a vitality he had never known. She stepped into the man's arms with a long, soft laugh. Kachiko and an unnamed Crane lover, no doubt. The man's arms wrapped around her, his fingers twining into the long black waterfall of her hair. He loved her. He controlled her. And yet, she owned him utterly and fully, with all the unimaginable depth of their love. Her laugh rippled once more, and for a moment, the voice was not Kachiko's—it was Sayuri's.

In that moment, the man's face beneath the white hair was Sezaru's own.

"No! Kachiko's shadow, with a cruel twist. This mockery is not what I have come for!" Sezaru shook away the image, denying what he had seen.

"Show me." he repeated, this time pooling his energy into the demand as he had done once before. The mirror shifted angrily; it enjoyed its small distractions, and was unwilling to give them up. Yet it bowed, defeated by Sezaru's will, and the scene shifted once more.

This time, the darkness was natural, like that of an earthen cave deep beneath confines of stone. Within the room, a pillar, and on that black pillar lay a box made of a stone so black that it seemed to absorb the darkness around it. No gloss, no sheen lay on the box's surface—only a thick darkness more potent than the night.

"The Dark Covenant." Sezaru reached out with an intangible hand to caressed it, drawn inexorably to its dark power. Touching it, he knew. He understood. The cave would be easy to find, simple to locate, and the Dark Covenant would be his . . . as it was meant to be.

"No, Sezaru." The voice was not his. It belonged to Tonbo Toryu. *"Do not do this thing. If you choose this path, your mother is already dead."* With that, it faded and was lost in the reflections of the Obsidian Mirror.

But was that truly Toryu or another trick of the mirror? The future or some forgotten voice from Sezaru's past? If it was the future, did that mean that Sezaru would be the true cause of Kaede's death? Or, if he denied the call of the Dark Covenant, would that be the factor that destroyed her?

The possibilities were as endless as stars within the Void.

He must leave this place, find the peace outside the Void, and meditate upon the meaning of this vision. *Yet the mirror held him, possessing his mind. He had touched the darkness at its heart, passed his hand through the covenant that held the Void in place, and now, the Void held him.*

Not so bad, the voice chided. This is not a bad place to be. We are surrounded by the Void that has always been our shelter.

"This is not the Void." Sezaru struggled. *"This is the Mirror."*

But the difference was not so great, was it?

Again the image of Kachiko, waiting for her Crane lover, surrounded him. This time he was not just an observer. He was a participant. He stood within her private sanctum, his white hair reflecting the faint light of the moon outside her open windows. The chamber held the faint scent of her perfume, and the roll of her laughter raised goosebumps on his arms. She rested within her dressing area, behind silk draperies that hung fro the high mahogany beams of the ceiling. Her naked body cast its silhouette upon the silken curtain, moving in a soft dance of lover's reverie. She waited there for her lover, her soft sighs drifting in the warmth of a hot summer night. Sezaru stepped slowly toward the curtains, unable to resist the siren call beyond. His shaking hand reached up to draw back the drape, to look beyond.

Kachiko, awaiting her lover . . .

Kachiko . . .

Sayuri . . .

Sezaru's hand pulled the drape back, no longer caring about the Dark Covenant, the Obsidian Mirror, or any purpose beyond what lay before him. This was the place he was meant to be; surrounded by darkness, drawn in by the laughter of a woman in love.

Here, he would be content to stay. Forever.

The woman turned, reaching for his hand, her face obscured by the flow of her long, jet-black hair. . . .

And the mirror shattered.

Gasping, choking, his lungs burning with the scent of that lost chamber, Sezaru reeled. The wood beneath his hands was the cold flooring of the Phoenix balcony, covered with shards of obsidian. Koshei knelt by the side of the chamber wall, clutching his throat as a spell of choking gas began to clear. Sayuri stood over Sezaru, Koshei's katana in her hand. Tears flowed down her face, but otherwise her face was emotionless. The setting sun shone behind her like the phoenix of her clan, its red light like blood upon the black fields of her hair.

Sezaru drew in a long, shuddering breath, trying to clear his mind of the mirror's deceptions. Everything seemed lost and empty. The cold air chilled his lungs as he struggled to rise.

Above him, Sayuri cast aside the katana and fell to one knee to help him.

"What happened?" he asked, anger rising in his soul.

"You fell into the mirror. It was not going to let you go. And you . . . you . . ."

Denied. He had been denied that perfect moment, that peace. Now there was only a world of pain around him, a world of imbalance and corruption. That perfection he had grasped between his fingers; lost forever in a jumble of shards. Sezaru drew a handful of he obsidian pieces into his hands, not caring where they drew blood from his white palms, and fought back tears of rage and loss.

"You gave yourself up to its power."

"What have you done?" He struggled to control the fury of his voice. He rose to his feet, fingers dripping with blood and shards of perfect black glass.

"I have destroyed it, as it would have destroyed you." Unabashed, unafraid, the Phoenix maiden stood before his anger.

"You have lost our only hope of victory." His mind raced, coming up with thousands of reasons to destroy her. Her impertinence had cost him the Obsidian Mirror, and all that it contained. Rage turned to hatred in a minute's fury.

His vision still clouded by the mirror's power, Sezaru saw himself striking her. As clear as any memory of his childhood or lesson of his past, the sound of his blow shaking the balcony with its unrestrained furor. She crumpled beneath it, her head snapping brusquely to the side as his fist landed. Small shards of obsidian impaled themselves upon her perfect cheek, their black blades staining her perfect features with blood.

In his mind, he struck her again and again and again until the softness of her face was unrecognizable—the white porcelain of her cheek brittle and broken, stained red with blood. Over and over the vision played, stealing his sanity, his control, his very soul.

No.

Rage. Sezaru choked back his emotion, realizing that the mirror's hold on him had been even greater than he could believe. Already, he mourned its death more than his father's, more than any other tragedy in his life, including the impending fall of the Empire. Sayuri was right. The mirror grasped his soul within its black glass and would never have let him go.

The most chilling part of it all: he would never have wanted to leave.

"Sayuri . . ." Sezaru began, struggling to control his emotions. Sayuri did not cry out, nor whisper a complaint. She simply knelt before him in silence, tears staining her cheeks, as he stood before her in rage. A true samurai, she waited in peace for her Prince's judgment.

She saved my life, Sezaru thought.

She destroyed our only hope. It is your right—your duty—to kill her.

Shaking in rage, Sezaru found that his hand had already leaped above his shoulder, poised for a brutal strike. With intense effort, he forced it down. The vision of the mirror would not come true. Not today. Not ever. Closing his eyes, he fought the darkness to a standstill and made his mind walk away from the mirror's still-hovering grasp. Sayuri . . .

Emotions are a shugenja's worst enemy. The voice whispered the old adage into his ear, mocking him with his failure to control the mirror. To control himself.

Koshei stood beside him, the katana back in his hand. The usually-controlled yojimbo was shaking, his sword raised in an aggressive stance. "Her life is yours, Master," Koshei whispered with barely controlled anger. "I request the honor of taking it for you."

Kneeling before him on the balcony, her hair a banner in the soft northern winds, was Sayuri. Her shugenja abilities told her what was happening. The yojimbo would not have known that Sezaru stood on the brink of the mirror's power. He must have fought to protect his master from Sayuri's "attack." It was only Fortune's providence that Sayuri was able to destroy the mirror.

But she had done it by stealing Koshei's sword. The yojimbo would never forgive that offense.

Sezaru's irrational rage hovered just beneath the surface, threatening once again to overwhelm him. Regardless of rational thought, the wounds were still too fresh to be ignored. The images of the mirror haunted him, and so long as he remained on Phoenix territory, he would never be free of them. Her face, behind silken shadows . . .

"No, Koshei-san. We leave tonight to acquire the Dark Covenant of Void. There is nothing more for us here." Sezaru spared one last look at Sayuri's resolute visage, then turned and walked away.

Even if they did not believe it, the lie would not be questioned.

14 | OLD FRIENDS

The cave was as dark and cold as Sezaru had envisioned it in the Obsidian Mirror. The stone mountains that surrounded it reached up as if to cut the heavens with their chiseled teeth. Only the Dragon Clan lived in these mountains—alone with the rugged stone and the empty sky.

Koshei tethered their horses outside the cave. The yojimbo had been silent since the Phoenix lands, his anger slowly seeping away as they moved farther and farther from the Isawa territories. He took his katana from the saddle and pushed it through his belt, straightening it purposefully as he strode after Sezaru.

The Wolf stood at the entrance to the cave, a soft white light gleaming in his hand. The kami were kind here, unused to finding those who could speak to them, and were more than willing to offer their counsel and spiritual gifts. Sezaru half-smiled. Wind spirits tended to talk a great deal and say nothing at all. The light would be enough.

"This is the location?" Koshei peered into the gloom before them.

"So the spirits say." Raising the light to look at the cave walls, Sezaru frowned. "These walls are of worked stone, but very old. If I were to guess, I would say they were older than Rokugan. The inscriptions on the stone are . . . extraordinary. A very primitive version of the Rokugani tongue. Likely, this cave was once inhabited by the first men and women of myth, those who bowed down before the fallen children of Lady Sun and Lord Moon. Those were the people who formed the first clans, who built the Empire. This cave might have been here since that time, Koshei-san."

"Then I shall try to treat her with the dignity due the aged and . . . hopefully not infirmed." Koshei poked at the walls with his hand as if to see whether or not they would shake.

Sezaru laughed, striding into the cave with steady resolution. "As the Dragon say, 'The mountain does not move.' "

This time, Koshei joined his smile, following his master into the darkness beneath the stone.

The cave was strangely made, twisting through natural corridors and then turning with a sharpness that was clearly formed by human hands. The carvings on the wall were almost illegible, rubbed into the stone by the passage of time. Small alcoves were carved horizontally into the stone, placed like ladder-rungs that climbed to the ceiling. They were filled with dust and debris— and the occasional abandoned animal nest.

At the end of the long, sloping corridor, the passage widened. They were deep beneath the surface of the earth now. The small white light nestled in Sezaru's hand lit the walls with a bare, cold glow. The air was musty and smelled of stale urine and stagnant water. Koshei wrinkled his nose. "Some animal must have lived here."

"I am glad it did not die here." Sezaru studied the wall closely. "This cannot be the end of the cave. The chamber I foresaw in the Mirror—" his voice still shook subtly when he thought of its obsidian lure— "was smaller than this. It had a pillar in the center—just here." Sezaru walked through the cave once more, examining the walls with a closer eye. "Either there is a passage we have missed or this chamber has a false wall."

"Or both," Koshei said morosely. "My father once told me to keep my bones from the earth, though I don't think this was what he meant. He was speaking about dying on the battlefield."

"By the Fortunes!" Sezaru breathed, brushing dirt away from the carvings around one of the alcoves. "This is a grave!"

Koshei leaped away from the wall as if Sezaru had found a demon living there. "G-grave?" he stammered, "There are no graves in Rokugan. Not since the time of the Necromancer Iuchiban. No one would be foolish enough to leave their ancestor's bones where they could become . . . servants."

"Beasts, you mean. Undead blasphemies."

"That, too."

Sezaru sighed. "As I mentioned, these caves likely pre-date the Empire. Iuchiban was hardly more than a twinkle in the fabric of the universe, much less born, raised, and attempting to conquer Rokugan. Necromancy was unknown in those primitive times."

"Then I suppose they had one advantage over us."

Running his fingers along the edge of the alcove, the Wolf studied the alcoves nearest the end of the corridor. Hundreds of them rested between the deep cave and the surface, each marking the dusty grave of a forgotten samurai.

Slowly, Sezaru closed his eyes and focused his will on the shifts of elemental power within the cave. The earth spirits, stubborn and sleepy, resisted his attempts to communicate with them. Yet even without their assistance he could sense the strong power of Void nearby. But the power was not as he usually sensed it. This was strong and slow-moving, as though the stars had been poured through with sap.

The source was down, even farther beneath the surface of the mountain, hidden in a darkness that had never known light. In such a place, the shadows were long, indeed, untouched by the faintest hint of forgiving light. Thick and cloying, it clung to the walls of that deep place with strength beyond mortal measure. But how to reach it?

Only through darkness, whispered the voice within his soul. Its mockery seemed bittersweet, almost reassuring in its familiarity. *Darkness will call to it, and it will rise to meet its destiny.*

Instead of fighting against the voice, for once Sezaru listened. The Dark Covenant was a malevolent thing, indeed—and evil knows evil. Perhaps the darkness that tormented Sezaru could be harnessed to locate the Dark Covenant?

Sezaru placed the small white ball of light in his friend's hand. "Koshei, leave me."

His yojimbo bowed and obeyed. When the sound of his echoing steps faded into nothingness, Sezaru sat in the darkness and considered. Magic required a balance. Shugenja attempted to make deals with the kami when possible, and to shift the balance the elements when the kami could aid no further. Sezaru felt the drift of power throughout the mountain, locating the small pulses of Void that lingered in the darkest, most hidden places. For the first time in his life, Sezaru tapped into the darkness that plagued him, allowing it to guide his fingers and shape his spell. A rush went though him, the feeling of a caged beast released to roam, and suddenly Sezaru felt his power grow. He fought it, forbidding it to control his actions. It struggled, eager to overwhelm him, but Sezaru clenched his fingers into mystic symbols and chanted words long forgotten to the Rokugani tongue. The need filled him, driving his will and supplanting his power. He thought of Kaede's face, covered in tears as the Void Dragon died. The Wolf's power surged against the influence of the darkness, commanding it to obey his will, and suddenly the evil within the heart of the world opened before him.

He could sense Koshei's soft concern, his dislike for the Phoenix girl, the pride resting in the yojimbo's soul. Koshei was a dedicated person, one with immense strength within his quiet spirit. Very little darkness resided within him; he was free of ill intentions and dark desires.

Then on to the others. Woodsmen on the mountain, stealing from their lords. Samurai many *li* away, indulging in pride, rage, and cowardice on the front lines of the Dragon-Lion war. In everything, from tree to beast to man, there was a hint of darkness. One by one, Sezaru began to gather those strands, drawing on them to fuel his spell.

Past them, into the heart of the Empire, corruption reigned in every heart. Courtiers pulling strings to destroy families, lives brutally ended in a single moment of passion or hatred. Lies, secrets, the darkness of the soul clung to the Empire's robes like maggots on a decaying corpse. Sezaru saw them all, understood them, and wove them into the net he forged of will and magic.

You have always known that you could do this, the voice said in triumph.

"Yes," Sezaru realized, "but I never had a reason—and I never will again." Drawing the net of power between his fingers, Sezaru spread it upon the mountain's heart. He coiled it around the source of power deep beneath his feet, letting the shadows of other people's souls wrap themselves around the Dark Covenant. With a surety that surprised him, he pulled the net closed.

Void is the spirit that guides us, that drives us, the heart that beats upon the soul. Its shadow is not the mere absence of that drive, but a corruption of it, a darkness that does not conquer the light but absorbs it. Controls it. Destroys it utterly.

Was that the future that Tonbo Toryu feared?

Sezaru allowed the ethereal ropes to slide through his fingers, drawing the Covenant nearer. He felt the spirits contained within the net struggle, unsure of their purpose, but he pulled again, and once more the Covenant moved. Sezaru felt the secrets within the strands twist and pull, unwilling to serve another, but he forced them back into place with his will and drew upon the net once more.

At last, lying within his fingers, lay the small black box of his dream. As he touched the ebony surface with hesitant fingers, the net of secrets and lies dissipated. He no longer needed their service. Let them return to the hearts they blackened; those who had perhaps known an instant's peace while they were stolen away. It absorbed the darkness of the cave, somehow casting a faint glow that was not its own. The luminescence was strange, ethereal, and disturbing—but by its light Sezaru could at last see the Dark Covenant of the Void within his hands.

Justify it all you want, Sezaru. The power lies within you. Now that you have surrendered yourself to it, even for an instant, it will never lay dormant again.

Sezaru gritted his teeth, forcing the voice and its black taunts into silence. Sacrifices had to be made. That was the nature of magic.

The box in his hands felt cold and strange, its surface unmarred by ornament or jewel. Where it rested, the light seemed to bend to avoid it, hovering in a dark aura that swelled with each breath Sezaru drew. His fingers caressed its surface without thinking, adoring the delicate lines and perfect dimensions. What lay inside the box? How did it glow without casting light? The strange magic contained within the Dark Covenant could engage a thousand Phoenix scholars for a hundred lifetimes, trying to unlock the secrets of a Dragon's shadow. For a moment, Sezaru considered opening the ebony latch and lifting the lid. Before his fingers could move, he placed the box on the floor before him, denying it further access to his soul.

"It is a dangerous path you hold before you, young man. Would that I knew the words that would turn you away."

The Wolf looked up in the strange half-darkness. A figure stood against the wall on the other side of the cave, casting no shadow into the gloom. Its weary stance showed pain in every muscle, and each movement of the wizened arms was filled with agony. It took Sezaru three breaths to recognize his old teacher, and another whispered gasp of shock before the Wolf could speak. "Toryu."

Tonbo Toryu shrugged, his shoulders thin and frail beneath black and gold silk robes. His thin, waving beard was darker than Sezaru remembered, flecked with black and shot through by strands of iron. The soft gray-brown eyes were no more. Instead, twin orbs of amber glittered golden behind Toryu's brushy eyebrows. No pipe hung reassuringly from Toryu's hand, but smoke flowed softly from his nostrils as if mocking the Dragon whose shadow now gave him purpose. Though his face was still kind, it seemed more haggard. The price of his decision weighed heavily on Toryu's shoulders as if it would soon break him.

"Sezaru-san. You have come farther than I could have expected." Even his voice sounded different, as if it echoed through a thousand chambers. The ringing sound of it reminded

Sezaru of Kaede in some faint manner. "If I were human, I would be proud of you."

"I'm here to free you." Sezaru glanced down at the Dark Covenant, keeping it always at the corner of his vision.

"Your vision is narrowed by your grief," Toryu replied. "You have gained my Covenant, and with it you can unite the Oracle of Void once more into one entity. I knew you would understand."

"You knew that I was there . . . in Volturnum?"

"Of course." The Dark Oracle of the Void moved from wall to wall like a shadow beneath a swaying light. "And you understood even more than I hoped." Toryu's weary smile was like a low, flickering candle. "But merging the two Covenants—even if you can find the Covenant of the Light Oracle—may be an answer too late to solve the question."

"The Dragon's Talon."

Toryu nodded wearily. "It moves, and I can sense it. Whoever stole it means to destroy us all—the Dark and Light Oracles, the Void Dragon, and Rokugan. The only question we have to ask is: 'How will they get the Talon close enough to a Dragon to destroy it?' There is little power in this Empire that can blind a Dragon's senses, if it chooses to seek someone—or something." Toryu ran a shaking hand through his thin, black hair.

"You seem ill." Careful as always, Sezaru did not phrase his concern as a question.

Toryu shuddered, passing a hand before his eyes. "The darkness . . . is greater than I could have known. Sometimes I feel as though I am but a passenger in my own body, the rider of a horse no longer beneath my control."

Sezaru watched him, sensing the immense power within Tonbo Toryu's soul even as he watched the pathetic frailty of the Dark Oracle's body. "The power of the Dragon's Shadow rides you."

"Yes. Yes." Toryu squinted, scuttling closer. "I would give my soul for Rokugan, Sezaru. My very soul. Whatever the cost, there must be no imbalance. But if I step away, if I leave . . . something worse will happen. I feel it in my bones now. The position calls to others. Already I have fought three who wished to take the post from me and left them in charred ashes." His voice dropped to a whisper, and haunted eyes sought out Sezaru's. "Have I truly become the monster that I feared?"

"No, Toryu-sama." If the Dark Oracle's resolve weakened, all would be lost. "So long as you can still remember why you took the position, then the post has not yet converted you."

"Of course," the fragile little man agreed. "Of course." His eyes flickered again to the ebony box lying before Sezaru. "If you cannot find the Light Oracle's foci, if you cannot merge the two . . . then this position will destroy me. Another will take the post. Everything I have done, Sezaru, will be for nothing."

Sezaru shook his head. "Your sacrifice will not be in vain."

"I cannot change the world. I cannot change this, Sezaru. Only mortal man has that capacity. I know that! Kaede knows that." The Dark Oracle was ranting, his voice elevating into a rumble that echoed in the cavern. By the shadowed light he seemed a specter clinging to the darkened wall. "But we cannot act!" The warning in his voice was as much for Sezaru as a reminder to himself. Tortured eyes darted again to the box, to Sezaru, and to something in the darkness that Sezaru could not see.

"I will act for you."

"You must. But to do so, you may risk the Empire. By the immortal kami, Sezaru. What have we done? What have we done, indeed? In the end, the throne will still be empty, the Empire at war, and your father will still be dead. No matter what you do for us, Sezaru. Even if the Void is balanced at last, the Empire may yet crumble." Toryu's slippered feet slid, hushed, against the stone. His robes swayed behind him as he paced back and forth. "Kaede. Kaede is in danger."

Madness hovered in Toryu's voice, accenting his words with menace. They chilled Sezaru, and the Wolf heard an eerie echo of the past. Pushing it away, he answered the Dark Oracle with confidence. "I believe those who imbalanced the elements—who set up Kaede's fall—are the same powers that killed my father. By fighting them here, Toryu-sama, I may gain a hint of their identity. I have not forgotten my father's death, nor the Empire's plight. I never will."

"Then hurry, Sezaru. Hurry. Find your mother's Covenant, and merge the two before everything . . . everything gets dark. I do not know what to do. There is madness before me, Wolf, and it consumes me. But . . . what if you are wrong? What if we are all wrong? I must seek . . . I must do something."

"You can, Toryu."

The Dark Oracle's eyes lifted to Sezaru's with rabid eagerness. "Ask. Ask anything of me, Sezaru, and I will do it."

Wishing only to ease the old man's mind, Sezaru said, "Find the Dragon's Talon, Toryu. Once the foci are merged, I must be ready to prevent them from taking that final step. If I am successful, then those who killed my father and attacked the Oracle of Water will have no choice but to use the Dragon's Talon to attack and destroy the Dragon of Void."

"I will find it," Toryu promised. "But you must find the Light Covenant. Find it, Sezaru, or there will be nothing left of the Empire for the Steel Throne to rule. And I will not allow that. I will not. I will not." With that, the Dark Oracle of the Void sank backwards into the shadow and was gone.

Sezaru looked down at the box, realizing that he now held it in his hand. When had he picked it up, he wondered, gazing at its ebony sheen. Had he been holding it when he asked Toryu to seek out the Talon?

Mortal man may have one question for an Oracle of Light, one demand from those of Darkness. The Light Oracles give theirs freely, while the Dark obey only those who hold their Covenant . . .

. . . and only once, for any man.

Sezaru plunged the Dark Covenant into his sleeve, extinguishing its faint, strange light. Such things were better considered in the day, when the shadows were less long and far less capable of betrayal. As for the Wolf, his steps were hurried as he walked toward the surface, driven by a dark understanding of irrevocable time.

15 IN THE MOTHER'S EMBRACE

Six months
later . . .

Turmoil wracked the Empire, spreading destruction and famine in their wake. As Sezaru studied the Dark Covenenat for some sign of its power, the armies of the Shadowlands marched upon the Imperial City, tearing down its fabulous walls and turning its streets to ash.

In the days after Otosan Uchi burned, the Empire fell to depression and chaos. Most peasants—indeed, even many of the lesser houses of the Empire—did not understand why the great city fell. Even Sezaru and his magics could only discover that a force from the Shadowlands came into the Empire when it was at its least defended, burning the citadel to the ground and scattering the city's ashes to the winds. The leader of that assault wore a strange silver mask and hid his form beneath a cloak the color of fire. Sezaru had heard of such a man—Daigotsu, self-proclaimed master of the Shadowlands. But why attack Otosan Uchi, and why now?

Sezaru mourned, as the Empire mourned, when the city of the Emperor was no more than a black corpse burning above a raging ocean. On the beach below Otosan Uchi, his father had been sent to the Celestial Heavens for his final rest. So, too, did the city's ashes float on the white waves of the sea.

Sezaru traveled the long road between the far northern mountains down to the forests of Kyuden Miya, hearing darker tales with each day. The wars to the north raged on, thousands of samurai dying with each assault. To the south, the Crane and Crab butchered themselves over treaties seven hundred years old and treacheries both old and new. Blood covered the swords of even the most loyal servants of the Empire. Truly, the devastation that Sezaru had foreseen in the elements was coming to pass.

And it was growing worse with each passing day. As he slept, Sezaru dreamed of more cities burning. He saw the Shadowlands rising, led by a figure of fire and of darkness. The form and feature was unknown to him, but the laughter was achingly familiar. The Wolf awoke from his dreams in a panicked sweat, instinctively drawing the power of the Void to him in order to defend himself against the assault. But the night was empty, and the dream quickly faded like campfire smoke in the wind.

Miya Palace stood on the edge of stony cliffs, the green banners conspicuously missing from high walls. Where once Sezaru had seen it in all of fall's glory, now it awaited spring with a bitter emptiness. The trees of its forest that surrounded it were barren and black, twisted against a graying spring sky. Constant rains flooded the gardens, washing out any hope of color. The guards at its iron gates held aloft their halberds with iron resolve, fading into the stone walls as though they were an extension of Kyuden Miya's grim demeanor.

The courtiers no longer walked in the gardens, whispering their politics to the winter snows. Instead, they hid from the spring rains within thick walls, huddled against the stone of the palace as though seeking some shelter from the ash that colored the sky and the ashen ground. It was impossible to tell when the sun sank beneath the horizon, for the dark storm clouds hid the bright orb deep beneath their woolen sleeves.

As he was unexpected, no one came to meet Sezaru at the wide Kyuden gates. The guards did not salute, unable to recognize the Wolf's face beneath the cover of twilight and the darkening night. Koshei introduced them simply as noble travelers from the Dragon lands—true enough—and the guards allowed them entry beyond the palace walls. There were enough noble refugees leaving their houses, abandoning family lands now bloodied by war.

They handed the reins of their ponies to the servants before the oak doors of the main palace. Inside, Sezaru could hear loud voices giving political speeches to an assembly. Pushing open the wide doors with a pale hand, the shugenja and his yojimbo paused on the doorway to look inside. A long hallway of mahogany led to a pair of sliding rice-paper doors four times the breadth of a man. They were elaborately pained with scenes of water birds, high mountains, and lonely willows—the work of a master artist. The two stepped inside, Koshei pulling the wide doorway closed behind them.

Down the huge foyer, through the ornate rice-paper doors, an argument held the imagination of the court. It echoed down the corridors to the Wolf's ears, burning them red with anger.

"The Empress asks—no, she *demands*—that the Sezu and Mariashi Houses come to an agreement over the disputed lands. If necessary, every member of the Mariashi house will be brought before an Imperial Magistrate. And I assure you, councilor, that the Empress is not feeling generous on this eve. As you have seen in the past, those who rely on her mercy will quickly find themselves on their knees." Gensaiken's voice was as hard as a weapon's steel, folded within layers of silken etiquette.

Another voice, filled with quiet fear, "Your honor, the Mariashi markets are filled with goods. If you begin to question every member of their House, the trade routes will stall. Food will mold and be lost. Peasants will starve—"

"But your wasteful feuding will stop!" Gensaiken snarled.

Sezaru and Koshei walked stealthily down the long mahogany corridor, Koshei's hand never leaving its grip on the hilt of his sheathed sword. They shouldn't have bothered trying to hide their footsteps. The murmurs and dark rumble within the council chamber covered any sound from outside.

"It is the Empress's will," said Gensaiken.

The tall Mariashi samurai snarled and said, just beneath his breath, "The Empress has not been seen in months. How are we to know her will?" His whispered statement shocked the court into silence—a moment of stillness filled with ice.

Gensaiken smiled, a long slow smile in the stillness. "If you wish me to disturb the Empress's mourning, I will send a guard to break her meditation and bring her to you. I am certain she will find this petty argument far more important than the peace of the Celestial Heavens."

The ice froze the air in the room, and the Mariashi samurai's face grew wan and pale. "N-no . . ."

Miya Gensaiken continued, enjoying the man's fear. "I have heard you whisper before, Mariashi Tsanaou. I have heard your tales of the Empress's vanishing. I am quite certain you have been assured that all is well in the palace, have you not?" When the Mariashi nodded in open fear and bowed, Gensaiken continued. "Empress Kaede grows weary of your bad manners, Tsanaou-san. The last samurai to question her return—and therefore her strength and the stability of the Empire—committed seppuku on the lawn of the palace. Tell me, Tsanaou, have you brought your sword with you, this day?"

"My humble apologies, Miya-sama," the Mariashi bowed again, his lips thin.

Sezaru watched as the ambassador of the Mariashi backed away, allowing his family to continue their discussion before the dais as he exited the room. Sezaru's heart grew cold as the samurai left for his inevitable demise. Gensaiken ruled through fear and deception. It was clear that the Empire saw through his ruse, but for the stability of Rokugan, none could be allowed to question it. A dangerous balance, and one that would eventually give way to panic and chaos.

"The Mariashi will not give up their claim on those lands," one of the other samurai took the place of his errant companion. "They belong to us, and the Mariashi are both proud and loyal to the Empire. We have always cared for the lands. We will not abandon them now."

Another voice, this one female and filled with arrogance. "The Mariashi lost all title to those lands when they fell into debt. They have no right to make promises they cannot fulfill."

"Promises made more than twenty years ago!" The Mariashi roared, and the council room erupted into angry mutters. Shadows cast against the rice-paper doors showed figures in motion, raising their fists to one another with barely controlled hatred.

"Hold your blows, Mariashi -sama!" Gensaiken's voice quieted the crowd instantly.

Sezaru slid the rice-paper doors open only a fraction and peered inside. Gensaiken rested on a silver pillow at the foot of the Steel Throne, his brown robes made of the finest silk weave. He waved a golden fan lightly in the air, staring down at the assembled courtiers before him with a stony gaze while guards behind him gripped their thick-bladed pole arms.

Those kneeling about the dais were dressed in brown or deep green—the colors of the Sezu and the Mariashi—and separated themselves on the smooth floor with a thick line of empty floor space. Eyes filled with anger glared across the invisible divider, barely restrained by Gensaiken's command.

Sezaru sensed the aura of the room and found things very out of place. The spirits in the room were agitated, tainted by dark emotions and almost gleeful with wicked purpose. They flitted from person to person, tugging at old memories or drawing up feelings of resentment and anger. All of them whispered in Gensaiken's ear as they passed, telling the young shugenja on the dais all the secrets that they stole.

A subtle taint pervaded the room, inciting those within to unnatural anger and disturbed focus. It was as if Gensaiken twisted the emotions of the room around his fingers, snarling the web into hopeless knots.

"The Empress has already made the determination. Those of the Mariashi lineage will bring before her all records of their debts, so that the Miya historians may seek the truth of this matter. Until then, the Mariashi trade routes will be shut down, their produce and merchandise seized, and their lands guarded by Imperial troops."

The order would snarl paperwork for months, allowing valuable food to rot and thousands of peasants to starve. Further, from the looks on the faces of the Mariashi and Sezu courtiers, the feud would only grow more bitter from these Imperial demands. One more word, one wrong motion, and the courtiers would draw swords here, in the Imperial Throne room itself. Yet Gensaiken sat upon the dais behind his waving fan, every motion subtly revealing his pleasure in the discomfort of those around him.

And all of it done in the Empress's name.

"Gensaiken." Sezaru's voice was cold and ringing as he stepped out from behind the sliding rice-paper doors. Without further preamble, the Wolf strode across the council chamber floor, scattering the Mariashi and Sezu courtiers before him. They stared up at him, the anger fading into shock. Koshei kept pace one step behind him, guarding his master's movements though the fire-eyed crowd.

"Sezaru-sama." Gensaiken bowed from the waist, his demeanor showing nothing of the panic Sezaru hoped the Miya felt. "Her Imperial Majesty did not inform me of your visit. I apologize." He bowed again, the golden fan sweeping the dais.

"No doubt she did not."

"I will have the guards arrange—"

"No." Sezaru cut him off, not caring when the courtiers whispered in disbelief.

"No?" The Miya guards took a step forward as Gensaiken's eyes grew wide, but he gestured them to cease. Better for them, as Koshei's sword was already an inch out of its scabbard, his thumb readying the blade. The two men stared at one another, Sezaru livid and Gensaiken coolly casual. "You seem upset, Sezaru-sama," Gensaiken murmured. Even though is voice was quiet, it reverberated like a clap of thunder though the silent room.

The spirits sense you. Release your fury, Sezaru, and all here will know fear. The throne can be yours that easily. That simply.

Sezaru tried to steady his will, to seize control of the feelings that disrupted his harmony. "Rise, Gensaiken-san," he said between clenched teeth, "and speak with me privately."

"I am sorry, Sezaru-sama, but I cannot." After a pause so thick with silence that a ship could have sailed on it, Gensaiken continued, "Your mother has ordered me to stay with the courtiers until this situation is resolved."

Of course, no such command could have been issued. Gensaiken was hiding behind the lies and deceptions he had built around the illusion of Kaede's return—an illusion that Sezaru had fostered. The Wolf felt his body shake with suppressed anger as the voice within his head reached a fever pitch.

Betrayed. Sense the thoughts of the courtiers around you, Sezaru. Look within Gensaiken's plans. The secrets that the spirits were carrying to Gensaiken's ear swirled around Sezaru. He saw executions, laws passed to constrict and choke Rokugan's army, strange movements of courtiers though channels of blackmail . . . all forming a grand whole that he could not understand. The information was too new, too rushed, too hurried into his mind by wind spirits overeager to please—dark spirits, whose touch upon his mind made him think of whorehouse perfume and the thick, cloying smoke of a funeral fire. Within their whispers, he could see the pattern of Gensaiken's betrayal.

He must be punished! The last word rang in Sezaru's mind, echoing through his anger.

Gensaiken closed his fan with a snap upon his wrist, and four of the Miya guards moved forward. "Allow my guards to escort you to your room, Sezaru-sama, and I will come to you in time."

Echoing Gensaiken's own words, Sezaru said, "I am sorry, Gensaiken-san, but I cannot. My mother is expecting me." With that, he spun on one heel and began to stride toward the rear door of the chamber behind the Steel Throne. Through those doors led a passageway to the Imperial Chambers, which, they both knew, were completely empty.

Miya Gensaiken's eyes narrowed in a brief instant before his sunny smile returned. "Forgive me, Sezaru-sama, but your mother has left explicit orders not to be disturbed."

The guards stepped forward again, blocking Sezaru's path.

Koshei stepped between his master and the other samurai. Silent and stoic, he stood in a tiger stance, watching the four men with motionless eyes. Sezaru never moved, standing quietly before Gensaiken with a cold and calculating smile. He could feel his eyes burning with anger, his body tense and stiff beneath his soft silken robes.

"I think you will find she is expecting me." He risked a glance at the assembly, noting with amusement how the courtiers struggled to memorize every word. This was a battlefield with an audience, and Sezaru was determined not to lose. Though his brother, Naseru, was more proficient in these matters, Sezaru was not entirely without wits in the public arena.

Sezaru had knowledge, but Gensaiken was a master of the game. He made a subtle motion to the rest of his guards, and suddenly all of the were blocked. "I sincerely regret, Sezaru, that should you go up those stairs and disturb the Empress's serenity, I will be forced to ask each one of these courtiers assembled to commit seppuku with me, as punishment for allowing you to break the orders that Empress Kaede-sama has given us. The blame will not simply be on my head, but on the heads of all those who know of her commands and do not attempt to fulfill them. As the Empress commands, so shall the Empire serve."

Gensaiken bowed once more, laying his fan before him and clapping his hands in command. The guards stepped away from the door to the Imperial Chamber, maintaining their stance at the other entrances.

The reality of Gensaiken's threat forced Sezaru to restrain the impulse to call upon his magic and blow open the Imperial Chamber door. If Sezaru called the Miya's bluff and opened the Imperial Chambers, proving that Kaede wasn't there, Gensaiken would close the door behind him and slaughter every courtier in the room.

Koshei growled, the choking sound of his final restraints. Whispering so that only Sezaru could hear him, he said, "They insult my Master's name, his honor, and his power. They lie about an Empress's word. And now, they threaten . . ." He choked back the rest of his words, hand drawing the sword another half-inch from its sheath. "I beg you . . . let me take his head before he proves that he has no honor at all."

Sezaru simply stood, silent and foreboding, holding back his own anger.

"It is clear that you are upset, my Lord Prince," Gensaiken said. "Please, allow my guards to escort you. No, I insist. Your mother would never forgive me if I allowed her eldest son to do himself harm."

So it was to be imprisonment, however politely phrased.

You could destroy Gensaiken with but a thought. You could kill everyone in this room with a single spell and seize the Steel Throne with a motion. No one would question you. Gensaiken has laid the groundwork for your ascendancy. Showing your power now would only seal your throne. Emperor, firstborn son of Toturi, your destiny . . .

Is it? Sezaru thought bitterly. The words of the Void Dragon rang once more in his mind. Of all the creatures of the Celestial Heavens and of the earth below, Man is the only one that has any choice at all.

There would be no slaughter. He would do as Gensaiken asked and claim his vengeance later. "Send my retainer, Angai, to me at once. I will hear the tales of the court while I take my rest."

"That will be quite impossible, Lord Sezaru." Gensaiken's demeanor betrayed no hint of the glee that Sezaru sensed within the Miya shugenja. "She was executed yesterday for crimes against the Empire. Those were the orders of the Empress, and none dared contradict."

The words struck Sezaru like a blow to his stomach.

Beside him, Sezaru felt more than heard Koshei's hands clench on the hilt of his katana, drawing it before sensibility could stop him. Moments slowed, and the firelight shone from Koshei's katana, ripples on the water of an irrevocable act.

Emotion is the enemy of a samurai. If he allows it to conquer his will, it will lead him into darkness.

Four guards lunged forward to block Koshei's blow. It had no hope of reaching Gensaiken. Koshei ducked beneath one halberd, blocked another, and leaped a third. Sword still in his hand, the yojimbo lashed out with a strong kick, catching his opponent in the midsection. He was rewarded with a guttural yelp as the man had the wind knocked from his lungs.

The Miya were swift, whirling their pole-arms in a blazing wall of defense. One struck low toward Koshei's knees, but he muped up, stepped on the halberd, and snapped the hilt before spinning to kick the guard. His sword landed on the man's leg, cutting it in two as the Miya screamed.

The third and fourth guards rushed forward. Sezaru yelled, "Koshei-san, cease . . . this . . . *now!*"

Sezaru saw Koshei struggling to restrain his lunge, unable to obey his master's wish due to the rush of his assault. He slowed, twisting to remove his sword from the battle. The slice cut open a Miya's shirt, baring the flesh beneath but not raising even a single drop of blood.

Pulling the strike cost him. As he stepped away, unbalancing his stance, the remaining Miya thrust his halberd into Koshei's side. The yojimbo gasped, falling to his knees as the guardsman twisted the spike of his weapon in the wound.

"Stop!" Sezaru's command shook the room, causing the dark spirits of air to flee into nothingness at the sound of his wrath. The courtiers fell on their faces, sleeves covering their eyes in a gesture of complete supplication.

On the dais, Miya Gensaiken turned to Sezaru and looked at him with sternness and sorrow. "Do you wish to surrender peaceably?" Gensaiken spread the wings of his golden fan. As he did, the guardsman twisted the halberd again, forcing Koshei to arch his back in agony. Though the yojimbo still held his katana in a steady hand, Koshei did not struggle nor fight back. His lord had commanded him. He would obey.

Sezaru ground his teeth and folded his fists into the long black sleeves of his silk robe. "On behalf of my yojimbo, I offer a most sincere apology to the Miya family. This assault was shameful. If you wish, I will order his seppuku immediately."

Even as he said the words, Sezaru knew that Gensaiken would not order such a thing. Koshei's wound was to his belly. He would die far more painfully and for a far longer time on his own.

"I have no choice in this, Sezaru," Gensaiken whispered, for Sezaru's ears alone. "There are greater powers at work here than my own. Go peacefully, and we will speak soon." Then, Gensaiken called out, "No, Sezaru-sama. The court of Empress Kaede is a court of peace. The Fortunes will judge your servant. Let them decide if he should live or die. It is within their hands."

With a gesture, Gensaiken ordered the guardsman to remove his spear from the yojimbo's side. To Koshei's credit, he did not cry out when the long spike was removed, nor did he collapse. He simply wiped his sword on his own vest in a shaking, forced motion and then sheathed the ancient katana in the scabbard by his side. Blood stained his clothing, pouring from the wound in slow eddies. He could not go to his master's side, so he simply knelt where he was, clenching a fist in the wound to try and still the bleeding.

Two guardsmen stepped forward to drag Koshei to his feet, but Sezaru stopped them with a fiery glance. He moved to his yojimbo's side, offering his own shoulder for the yojimbo to lean upon as he rose.

"Master, you should not . . ." Koshei whispered weakly.

Sezaru ignored him, lifting Koshei and placing one arm around the yojimbo's waist to help him steady himself.

"Angai . . . I could not let her death go unavenged. I have shamed you."

"No, Koshei. You have saved me." Sezaru's voice was faint, meant only for his yojimbo's ears. "If you had not attacked them, I surely would have, and I doubt Gensaiken would be willing to let my life be placed in the Fortune's hands."

Surrounded by Miya guardsmen, they left the throne room, Koshei leaning heavily on the Imperial Prince's arm as he walked. They walked through the corridors of Kyuden Miya in silence, faces grim and foreboding. The guardsmen around them were no real threat, but the knowledge that Gensaiken remained in the courtroom with the courtiers would keep Sezaru and Koshei from attempting any escape. Gensaiken played his tricks like an expert, placing each stone upon the board in perfect concert until Sezaru was completely surrounded. And only now, the sound of their footsteps echoing from deep stone walls, did Sezaru see through the illusion and into the light.

There would be no royal chamber, no private suites. They were headed to the dungeons—and to darkness.

16 | TRUTH BEHIND MASKS

Deep beneath Kyuden Miya, under the cold libraries and twisting corridors of ancient stone, the dungeon of an ancient Emperor lay buried deep within the earth. The chambers had been built hundreds of years ago, in the reign of a Hantei remembered only as the Master of the Stone Horse. They were carved by thousands of eta, working their fingers bloody against the sea-cliff. Many of those eta died where they fell, ruined by exhaustion and poor food. Their bodies were thrown off the cliffs into the sea, their bones becoming twisted rocks at the bottom of the mountainside, covered with gnarled roots and broken vines.

Through the wall of his chamber, Sezaru could hear the drums of Kyuden Miya. He could not tell if it was night or day. He judged the time only by the condition of Koshei's wound. Had two days passed? Three? The smooth stone walls held no hint of warmth, no window by which to gauge the light. Outside Sezaru's cell, the darkness did not waver from hour to hour, becoming brighter only when the guard opened the upper doors to check on Sezaru or bring more water—both at seemingly random intervals, impossible to predict. Only a faint, distant light illuminated the cell at all, leaking around the large oak door at the top of a long flight of stairs outside the corridor.

The castle had not originally been built by its gentle Miya inhabitants. Long ago, another family—one wiped from the Imperial records—had lived here. Even the reason for their destruction was not recorded, though some peasants still whispered that evil magic and necromancy was the cause for the ancient nobility's fall. The castle remained uninhabited for generations, its lands fallow, until the Miya were raised to noble status and granted both title and the keep. Gentle samurai and diplomats, the Miya blocked off the passages that led down to the dungeons, having no need for their dank cells. Some entries remained, hidden within the palace, but few remained who knew where to find them or even knew of the dungeon deep in the earth below. Now the only remnant of those more brutal inhabitants were the dungeons far beneath the castle walls, forgotten and left to dust and empty stone.

These dungeons now held Imperial Prince Toturi Sezaru, and his last loyal friend. The cell was warded, shielded against all magic. Such prohibitive spells were exceptionally dangerous, most likely placed here by some ancient Elemental Master at the behest of long-dead Emperors and Empresses who ruled ancient Rokugan. Ironic, Sezaru thought, that their spells would serve to imprison an Imperial Prince.

In the depths of his sleeve, the Dark Covenant lay, cold against the soft silk of his robe. Sezaru kept it hidden, using slight-of-hand tricks to keep it from searches and discovery. Not that it mattered; the cell's power would keep him from drawing on its magics in any way.

Koshei made a soft noise, tossing beneath the thin, worn wool blanket spread upon the stone floor. Though Sezaru had used their ration of water to cleanse his yojimbo's wounds, still he feared the worst. Without his healing magic, there was little he could do to improve Koshei's chances of survival. Internally, Sezaru cursed his own blindness once more. Perhaps if he had stayed the winter, remained at Kyuden Miya, he could have seen what was occurring. Stopped it. Discovered Gensaiken's treachery before it became imbedded in the court.

Saved Angai . . .

Sezaru pounded one fist against the stone wall of his cell, awakening himself from his delusions and self-pity. Gensaiken was a master, practiced at being underestimated. If Sezaru remained, he would only have placed himself more fully in Gensaiken's grasp. Sezaru knelt beside Koshei's sleeping form, checking the sodden bandage once more and trying to flush out the wound.

Koshei murmured in his fevered sleep. "Sezaru! No! I cannot let you . . . ! Death lies there." His words were blurred, but Sezaru understood the weight that burdened his yojimbo's heart. Koshei had attacked when he heard of Angai's death, thus preventing Sezaru from loosing a magical torrent that threatened to overwhelm them all.

You could have destroyed all who dared oppose you. The voice was contemptuous. *A true Emperor would not have been so merciful. It is best that you are here, buried alive beneath your shame. You are not suited for a throne.*

"That is not my way." Sezaru frowned "That way lies darkness."

A darkness that has always lived within you. You have already opened the door to it, Sezaru.

Soft footsteps intruded on Sezaru's thoughts. The wide door at the top of the stairs opened, and brilliant orange torchlight cut deeply into the gloom. Sezaru could see the light growing closer through the thick portcullis of bars that divided the cell from the passage outside.

Soft murmurs were exchanged somewhere down the hall, and then Gensaiken came into view, walking down the long stone corridor and flanked by two burly Miya guards. The soldiers knelt to either side of the barred opening to Sezaru's cell, staring downward with their swords half-drawn from their scabbards. One of the guards held a torch aloft in his other hand, lighting the corridor so that the two men could talk despite the latticework of iron. As Gensaiken bowed faintly in respect to Sezaru's Imperial blood, the Wolf's eyes narrowed with hatred. Ignoring

Gensaiken, he rinsed the scrap of silk once more and applied it to Koshei's side.

"Greetings, Sezaru-sama." Even under such conditions, Gensaiken still kept his formality. He stood outside the warded room, safe from Sezaru's magic.

"Gensaiken." Sezaru would play no such games.

"Now, now. Your madness must truly have affected you deeply, to forget your manners."

"What is it that you want, Gensaiken? This smug mockery seems beneath you." Sezaru was unruffled by the other man's prideful tone, refusing to allow his temper to rise. That had occurred in the throne room. Sezaru would not allow it to happen again.

"I want to speak reason." One of Gensaiken's guards placed a gold silk cushion on the floor, and the councilor knelt. "Your mind has become unbalanced. I seek to show you the way to clarity, Sezaru-sama—a new manner of thought; a strength you have yet to tap that will bring you power and a future that could be brighter than the stars."

Sezaru snorted. "This, from a man holding the Imperial Court hostage. Really, Gensaiken. Try again, and perhaps you'll have better luck."

Unruffled, the courtier smiled. "Have my words in the past been so unpalatable? Have I not struggled to see that you had everything you needed for your quest? Your quest has led you to dark places, Sezaru. Any shugenja can sense it within your aura. You are not the man that left Kyuden Miya four months ago. Come, now, listen to me."

"I still seek my father's killer," Sezaru retorted. "I still carry the burden of my mother's abandonment. I stand beside the Empire. How is that so different?"

Solemnly, Gensaiken murmured, "The Sezaru that I knew would never consider slaughtering a room filled with innocents simply to avenge a traitor."

"This has nothing to do with my retainer, Gensaiken." Respectful of the dead, Sezaru did not speak her name. "Her death was not yours to command."

Gensaiken flicked an invisible speck of dust from his immaculate silk sleeve. "She was a traitor. I discovered her breaking into the Imperial Chambers, collecting proof to overthrow Kaede's illusory presence. Three of her own clan testified that she became obsessed with entering the Empress's chambers. When the Imperial Guard found her there, like a common thief, they put her within this very cell. Thereafter, I had no choice but to order her execution. She had entered the Empress's personal chambers, sought to defame Kaede's name and presence within the court, and refused to comply with the Imperial Guard when they attempted to take her into custody.

"I did not wish to kill her, despite this treachery. You must believe me." Regardless of Gensaiken's earnest words, Sezaru did not. "One of the Imperial Guards who took her into custody confirmed that she bore the Taint."

Sezaru shook his head, refusing to believe it. "My servant? Tainted?"

"Possibly from your trip to the Shadowlands. I warned you against it, but you insisted, and Angai bore the price." Disdaining honor and tradition, Gensaiken spoke her name scornfully. "Though her Taint was not yet strong, it was irrevocable. Nothing could be done except to order her death."

"Am I meant to believe this fantastic tale?"

"Believe what you wish. I can only tell you what occurred. Angai said many things—many horrible things—before she was destroyed. The guards refused to listen, but I was forced through duty to try to understand. She said that if you returned from your journey to the Phoenix lands, your soul would be tainted. She was correct.

"The Dark Oracles control you, Sezaru. You have made bargains with them, and it leaves black streaks in your spirit. Any shugenja could detect it. Would you truly want those bargains to be known? There are many who do not know the difference between the Dark Oracles and the simple Taint of the Shadowlands. You would be suspect. The court would no longer trust you. At best, they would turn you away from the Empire in exile. Until the touch of those dark powers can be cleansed, you must be my guest in this cell."

The torch in the guard's hands flickered, light casting strange shadows across the corridor. The black lattice of iron bars seemed like a vertical maze, illuminated by the shifting torchlight.

"I made no such bargains." Sezaru's mind shifted uneasily to Tonbo Toryu, but he pushed the images away.

"Listen to me, Sezaru. I am asking you to stop this quest before it destroys you. You are no longer serving the Empire. You are only serving yourself. What have you accomplished save for darkening your soul? How has your quest served Rokugan? The throne is still empty, the Empire teetering. You saw how difficult it was to persuade the Crab and Crane—"

"Into starving their peasants? Yes, Gensaiken, I would imagine that is a difficult task. It is not my soul that has darkened, Gensaiken. It is your own."

The Miya shugenja smiled. "My soul is no more dark than it has ever been, Sezaru. I know what must be done, and I do it. If the Crane and Crab are struggling to feed their peasants, then they will not be spending their time butchering each other."

Although the explanation made sense, Sezaru could feel Gensaiken's lies. His words were too smooth, too practiced, and ultimately hollow. Sezaru took advantage of the long silence to stare deep into Gensaiken's eyes. Without his magic, he could not truly measure the young Miya's soul, but a man's purposes could also be read by more mundane means. Gensaiken's black eyes darted quickly to Koshei's unconscious form, his tongue flicking to moisten thin, dry lips.

"Sezaru-sama, I know you struggle with this darkness. I understand how difficult it must be. Your grief has blinded you. You spend all your time hunting down the Dark Oracles, but what of the Dragon's Talon? Who knows to what sinister purposes it has been turned?"

"I am fully aware that the Talon is in evil hands, Gensaiken. It was more important to—"

"To bargain with the Dark Oracle of Void?" Gensaiken said scornfully. "Better to simply use the Talon to destroy him."

Sezaru's hands clenched. "That will not ease the balance."

"Will it not? If the Dragon's Talon can destroy the Dragons

themselves, surely it can destroy one of their Oracles."

"The Oracle will simply be reborn."

"We cannot prove that. It has never been tried. Now, it likely never will be. The Dragon's Talon is lost to us. It is in the hands of the Shadowlands."

For a moment, Sezaru thought that Gensaiken was only provoking a response, trying to force Sezaru to show his emotions. Then, realization slowly sank in.

"How do you know that?"

"I have agents in places best not turned to the light. While you spend your time in frivolous occult research, I tracked those who assaulted the Oracle of Water. They used blood-magic, and evil spirits are not known for their loyalty. With a little effort, I was able to force the spirits to show me their trail, and my agents followed it." Gensaiken smirked with pride, glancing to either side as if to be certain that his guards could be trusted.

"Gensaiken, if you know where it is, you must tell me. The Empire could hinge on that information." Despite his situation, Sezaru felt a faint hope twist in his heart, igniting his imagination. Perhaps all was not lost. . . .

"I can lead you to it, but we will have to go back to the Shadowlands." Gensaiken's fan flicked back and forth like the tail of a disturbed cat. "Those who have stolen it traveled deep into those Tainted lands."

"Return to the Shadowlands?" Sezaru frowned. "You know what a risk that would be, Gensaiken. Those lands are dangerous, and more so to shugenja. Did you not counsel me not to go when I first sought them out?"

"Yes, but the Dragon's Talon—"

"Is important. I am already aware of its purposes, Gensaiken," Sezaru's voice was filled with acid. "And I am beginning to become aware of yours."

Gensaiken's eyebrow rose slightly. "Ah," he said in a smooth, calm tone, "but I am not implying that you should risk yourself in that black land. Once you are Emperor, you can command the Crab to bring you the Talon. A hundred men would scour the Shadowlands until they brought it out once more."

Sezaru stood, turning his body gracefully to rise like a pale pillar of ice. His pale under-robes glinted silver in the torchlight from the hallway, dark overcoat shed to make a rough blanket for his yojimbo's wounded body. Long white hair flowed over his shoulders, outlining the anger that darkened his blue eyes. He did not answer Gensaiken immediately, instead walking the length of the cell to place his hand against the outer wall. Distantly, on the far side of the ensorcelled stone, he could feel the wind crashing against the mountain. The angry storm's power was awesome, sweeping dust and tree before its wrath. Day after day, the wind tore at the stone around Kyuden Miya. One day, it would break the rocks apart. Perhaps, many generations from now, the wind would carve the stone to grains of sand.

But not today.

"You ask me to seize the throne." Not a question. A resigned statement of fact.

"Once you are Emperor, all of Rokugan will bow to you. If your will is to find the Dragon's Talon, to save the Oracles of Light and end this imbalance, then all shugenja of all the Greater Clans will turn their efforts to that purpose. Don't you see? You cannot do this alone. Your purpose is not your own, Sezaru. It must belong to all of us, if we are to save the Empire."

Sezaru heard the insistence in Gensaiken's voice and saw it for what it was. "No, Gensaiken. I will not betray my mother's will."

"Your mother was never meant to be Empress. She is an Oracle, not a ruler. She broke the celestial balance, and you trust the Empire's future to her?" Faint anger and frustration sank into Gensaiken's tones, and Sezaru closed his eyes to listen more cautiously to the sound. "The throne is yours. It has been bought and paid for."

"Bought, yes. But I will not pay its price."

"You have no choice. If you will not listen to me, you will listen to those I serve. We are not alone in this world, and neither is the Empire. I can no longer put aside their wrath. They will come for you, Sezaru, and they will break your spirit. Do not be a fool. This is your only opportunity. Listen to me, before they arrive. Become Emperor. Your only other choice is to rot in this cell until the

Shadowlands come for you. And they come on swift steeds, indeed. That will surely end your hesitation—and his life." Gensaiken's fan flicked briefly toward Koshei. "You say that you wish to save the Empire, yet you turn your back on it at every opportunity. I am offering you hope, power, and a throne."

"I am a samurai," Sezaru said coldly. "I will give the Empire my body and my mind." In his mind, the Unicorn samurai knelt once more on his wide white sheet, reading his final haiku to the spirits of the wind. Blood spattered the white sheet and the blade of his second removed his head from his shoulders in final deference to his lord. Sezaru turned to face Gensaiken, certain now of his choice—and of the nature of the man who knelt on the other side of the prison door. "But the Empire cannot have my soul."

"Show me your true face, Gensaiken," Sezaru commanded.

Gensaiken flushed, his fan stumbling in its patterned wave. "Sezaru-sama, I do not know—"

"Liar." The Wolf's hatred was palpable. "Even without my magic, I can tell what you are. Your insistence that I break my word, your bloodthirsty actions at the court, and now, you have proven that you do not truly understand the concept of honor. Of duty. Yet you walk among the courtiers with a practiced air, as if you have been among us forever. Perhaps you have, Gensaiken, but not with this name. I have been to the Shadowlands, and I know well the feeling of Taint upon another person's soul. Yet I never felt yours, Gensaiken. How is that?"

Sezaru walked slowly toward the cell door, his footsteps slow and resolute, in time with the distant swell of ocean waves.

"Your madness has come on you again, Sezaru-sama," Gensaiken choked. "You do not know what you are saying."

"I know what I am saying, and I know what you have done. Your treachery is complete, Gensaiken. You have the Empire beneath your fingertips, swayed by the illusion of a fictional Empress. I will accept my share of blame for not seeing through your guise long ago, but as you said when first we met: you listened. Perhaps too well, and I spoke too loudly into your willing ears. The Taint of the Shadowlands is powerful, but it can be subtle, as well. Subtle enough to hide beneath robes of silk and satin."

"Madness . . ." Gensaiken's face paled, and he leaned back upon the cushion as Sezaru stepped ever closer. "You have truly gone insane."

Sezaru reached the edge of the cell, moving quickly into the opening and lifting his hands as if to cast his magic. He roared an incantation, and Gensaiken jumped to his feet. To either side, the guards dropped their torches and drew their swords. Torches fell from their hands with a smoky clatter. One struck Gensaiken's golden fan, flames dancing swiftly along the thin paper and onto the Miya shugenja's hand. Sezaru stepped back, out of the reach of the guard's swords as the two guardsmen stepped between their master and the barred doorway to the cell.

"Idiots! The cell is warded! He cannot use his magic!" Gensaiken's cry was drowned out by Sezaru's parallel snarl.

"His hand! Look at his hand!"

Sezaru pointed, staring, as the Miya shugenja tried to hide the fingers that had once held a golden fan. The false flesh was burned away by the brief touch of flame, hanging in limp shreds from strange, purplish fingers. Beneath it, Gensaiken's hand was a vulgar, scaled thing, twisted by Taint. Short, iron nails clawed at the air, seeking to hide beneath the quickly raised sleeve of Gensaiken's robe. Even as Sezaru stared in horror, he felt something in his belt-pocket grow hot as fire. Before he had a chance to reach for it—or indeed do anything at all—Gensaiken leaped away from the cell.

The Miya guards stared in shock and horror at their master's hand, realizing the Taint that touched him. The one who dropped the torch reacted first, raising his sword for a swift strike to Gensaiken's midsection. With supernatural speed, Gensaiken darted aside, clinging to the wall like a spider and dropping down a few feet behind the samurai's guard. His jaw opened widely, revealing long fangs that slid down from behind porcelain teeth. Like a shark's, the fangs gleamed and glittered in rows, slicing into the samurai's neck as Gensaiken attacked him from behind. The man screamed, reaching back to grip Gensaiken's shoulders as the shugenja wrenched the powerful samurai's neck to the side as if it were made of balsa wood. There was a hideous snapping sound, and the guardsman fell limp at Gensaiken's feet.

The second Miya wasted no time, unsheathing his sword and attacking as his companion fell. "No!" shouted Sezaru. "Leave him! Tell the guards above!"

But his words were of no use. The Miya's sword plunged into Gensaiken's robes, piercing the shugenja's flesh. The samurai continued his thrust, sliding the blade of his weapon through Gensaiken's chest and out the other side.

Gensaiken laughed, even as the katana stabbed through the silken robes at his back. He brought down his disfigured hand upon the steel before him, snapping the blade in two with a single stroke. His arm struck outward, palm connecting with the samurai's chin. The guard flew backward and landed badly against the wall. Sezaru saw several of the Miya's ribs snap with the force of his fall. Still fighting, the guard pushed up on the wall, regaining his footing just as Gensaiken stood above him.

The samurai attempted a foot-sweep, shouting a *ki* scream. Gensaiken shot upward, his robes swirling outward as he flipped forward. He spun over the samurai's extended leg and slammed down on the guard's kneecap with both feet. The guard made no sound, refusing to scream even in his defeat, and drew a knife from within his patterned vest. He swung at Gensaiken, but the other man was quicker. Slapping he knife away with his iron claws, Gensaiken lifted the samurai from the ground by his neck and held the battered man aloft to stare into his eyes.

"Tell me, Sezaru," the beast that was Gensaiken wondered acerbically. "If I promised to spare his life, would you take the throne?"

Sezaru glared from behind the sorcerous iron bars. "I would never insult his ancestors with such a foul bargain."

"A pity." Gensaiken twisted his hand, sinking the iron claws into the Miya guardsman's throat. The skin tore apart in a spatter of blood as he released his grip, allowing the guard to sink to his knees as blood poured down his chest. "That was exactly what I thought you would say."

Gensaiken turned, lifting his robes from the stone floor to avoid smearing them in the fresh blood that coated the ground. He stepped delicately through the carnage, his face reverting again to that of the pleasant young man with whom Sezaru was familiar.

"Their deaths will be attributed to your magic going out of control, of course. The wounds will be covered up by cremation fires, and no one will be the wiser." Gensaiken smiled peacefully, pulling his sleeve down to cover his clawed hand.

"You sound practiced," Sezaru covered his disgust in sarcasm.

"I am," Gensaiken replied. His eyes flickered to Sezaru's. "I would have made you Emperor."

"Of a Tainted land. No, Gensaiken. When I get out of this cell, I will destroy you—and then, may the Heavens will it, I will become Emperor on my own."

"You have so much arrogance, mortal. It seeps through your eyes and poisons those around you. Though you may revile my offer, look what your own means have accomplished. The Dark Oracle of the Void is going mad, your yojimbo has fallen, and all those who are loyal to you are either dead or dying."

Gensaiken stood on the stairs leading up toward Kyuden Miya, the deep slash in his brown robes barely touched with stains of black blood. "By Empress Kaede's order, you will remain in this cell until the end of your days, Sezaru. There will be no mercy for you."

"The only mercy I need, Gensaiken, is that of the Celestial Heavens. You cannot offer me anything. Be gone."

"I will, Sezaru. And the next time you see me, I will hold the Dragon's Talon in my hand and drive it into your heart." Ignoring Sezaru's level stare, Gensaiken spun on his heels and walked up the stairs into the light above.

Sezaru reached into his belt pocket and drew forth a small black orb, the size of a child's fist. It seemed almost to hum in his palm, the warmth fading and receding as Gensaiken grew farther away.

"Toryu," Sezaru whispered, "you told me to save this for the last midnight. It has come. The Shadowlands are coming for my soul, and I have no more answers. Is there nothing left of truth, of hope?" Sezaru allowed his hand to fall, gripping the pearl loosely between slack fingers. "Tell me, Toryu. Tell me . . . anything."

Suddenly, his attention was drawn to the last guard outside the cell, a Miya struggling to live but a few seconds more, fighting against the pain of his death-wound. Gulping blood, the second guardsman turned to Sezaru.

"You must fight them," he choked on his own blood, "as the Empire fights them. Until the last of our will is dead." Defiant, the Miya reached to grip the broken sword that lay upon the floor, plunging it into his own heart before he could die of Gensaiken's wound.

Gensaiken's footsteps receded into the distance as the door to the lower caverns was closed. The light shrank behind it, and soon Sezaru was in darkness again.

17 FREEDOM

It should have been you."

The low moan woke Sezaru from a troubled sleep. He reeled for a moment in the cell's darkness, struggling to realize his location. It came to him in a flash, as did the speaker's identity.

Tonbo Toryu.

The little man was curled up in the corner of Sezaru's cell, holding his knees to his chin in the manner of a child. His robes, once soft oranges and yellows, were now as black and thick as a storm cloud. Silver tracings illuminated the edges of his clothing, shimmering without giving off light. His face was pale and wan, his cheeks sunken and his thin beard ebony against the whiteness. The gray-brown eyes that once looked upon the world with humor and reverence were now jet black, their color drained away into deep pools of the abyss.

Toryu whispered to himself, the words too faint for Sezaru to understand. His eyes darted about the room as if seeking for something. Twin birds, they hovered uncertainly over Koshei's body before lighting on Sezaru's face. Toryu moaned again, gnashing his teeth in anger. "You, Sezaru. Where were you, when the Empire needed you most?"

Sezaru struggled to snap his mind into focus, lifting his upper body from the stone floor to face the Dark Oracle. He could still feel the room's wards against magic, keeping his own power from any activity; but mortal magic could not restrain the awesome force of an Oracle's will. Toryu was truly there before him—no dream, no vision, no trick of isolation and regret. "I don't understand what you mean, Oracle."

"No questions, Sezaru. No questions. The time for questions is over. You've had yours. You've had your chances. So many chances, Wolf. But they weren't enough."

"Toryu, come to yourself. You are not well." Despite the magic suppression of the cell, Sezaru could feel the power of the Void growing stronger, twisting the shadows on the walls into strange, screaming faces. The air was colder now than when he'd first awoke, the chill sinking deep into the rock face.

"You are right, Sezaru. I am not well." Tonbo rocked forward, kneeling in a puddle of black robes and extending blood-covered hands. "I have bathed my honor in blood and drowned all purpose."

Sezaru recoiled from the nightmarish sight. No shugenja would willingly touch blood. It was unclean, filled with evil, and could taint the soul as well as the body. Tonbo continued, ignoring the look of horror on Sezaru's features.

"They were in the Shadowlands. I thought they were creatures of the Taint—dark beings, corrupted and twisted. No longer samurai."

"Who . . . ?" Sezaru paused, trying to conceive of the madness within Tonbo Toryu's eyes.

"They carried it with them. I thought they were messengers of the Lord of the Shadowlands, the Son of Fu Leng," Toryu wrapped his black robes more tightly around him at the mention of the god of the Shadowlands "They come to me, now, seeking my advice. Why should I give it to him? He has no throne. He has no magic. He has only purpose." Toryu's black eyes flashed dangerously. "But he has more purpose than anyone in the world, Sezaru, and it is best you fear him."

Sezaru tried to understand Toryu's rant, turning the old man back to the original issue. "The blood, Toryu-sama. Where did the blood come from?"

"It came from death, of course." Toryu laughed—a high-pitched shriek that raised the hairs on the back of Sezaru's neck. "Ten men. With my hands. My hands, Sezaru, because I did not want to risk myself by calling on the magic of the Dark Oracle. It was the only way to free them from the Taint. The only way to fulfill the command I had been given. They died, one by one, in the marshes of the Shadowlands. I left their bodies there to rot. Only after the last one fell and I had the prize did I notice the mon on their sword-hilts. The chrysanthemum. The symbol of the Imperial House. Didn't you trust our bargain, Sezaru? I said I would bring it to you, and I have."

With bloody hands, Toryu reached into black sleeves and withdrew a long white knife. It was carved, hilt to post, from a single piece of bone. The hilt was ornate, carved into the form of a weeping woman with long, white hair. The blade was incredibly sharp, gouging a thin line in the stone at Toryu's feet as he let it dangle from a slackened hand.

"The Dragon's Talon." Sezaru breathed softly, feeling the resonant power within the knife. It sang with a distinctive tone, unmarked by any element Sezaru understood. Something within the knife seemed almost alive, sorrowing as if it knew the pains of the world. Sezaru's hand moved toward it without thought, seeking to lend solace to its unquenchable grief.

"Not for you." Toryu snatched the knife back with a vicious snarl. "You didn't trust me, Sezaru. You sent the guards to find the knife, and I killed them. Killed them all. With my hands, bloodying myself for your arrogance. This was your doing, Sezaru."

Trying to reach the Dark Oracle with reason, Sezaru replied, "I didn't send the guards, but I know who did. There is a traitor in the palace, a minion of the Shadowlands. He tricked all of us. Those men were sent by his command, not mine."

"When I killed them," Toryu continued, ignoring Sezaru's words, "their blood ran between my fingers, and I knew that you had betrayed me, Sezaru. After all I did for you, for the Empire.

After the struggle, the sacrifice . . . you never trusted me. All you saw was the title. Dark Oracle. And now, son of the Emperor, that is all I have become." Toryu's anger sparked from the shadows, causing them to twist and grab at Sezaru's robes. Strangely shaped arms with tapered fingers plucked at Sezaru's silk sleeves, frosting the patterns of his shirt with overlays of ice. "I no longer need you, Sezaru. Your way will not save the Empire. I know what I must do."

"Toryu, you must think rationally."

"Toryu died with those samurai, Imperial Prince. He died with the blood that covers my hands." The Dark Oracle of the Void shifted to his feet, his thick robes sliding with a thousand dark whispers against the stone of the cell floor. "I never wanted this position, Sezaru. But better me than the other choices. Better a man with morals. Well, the Void has burned my morals from me—the Void and the blood of ten samurai. Who knew a man could be bought so cheaply?"

"What are you going to do, Toryu?"

"I told you. You will have no answers from me, Wolf."

"We have no time for games. The imbalance—"

"Is complete. Not all the Covenants and quests in the world can save us. Void has hopelessly lost its equilibrium. And I have lost my soul." Toryu shook his head vigorously. "There is only one way to balance the elements. To free my soul."

"If you step down, a true evil will take your place," Sezaru protested.

The Dark Oracle's howl ricocheted through the dungeon corridors. "I will no longer be slave to this foul power! If you cannot help me, Sezaru, I swear by the Fortunes that I will save myself!"

The shadows within the cell went crazy, wrapping about Sezaru, Koshei, and the dull iron bars. The cold and bitter touch of the Void sank through Sezaru's skin, awakening the voice within his spirit.

Toryu is mad, it whispered. *His twisted mind snapped under the pressure of the Dark Oracle's power. Coupled with his contact with the Son of Fu Leng—whoever that may be—Toryu is a danger.*

But what is he planning? His freedom? Sezaru considered, watching as the Dark Oracle of the Void shaped his power through the warded room, darkening the hallway and the corridors beyond. He could sense the deepening gloom as though thick clouds of velvet night coalesced around Kyuden Miya. Even the sound of waves against the cliff, once the only soothing sound of time's passage, seemed labored and choked beneath the stone.

A freedom that can only be attained through death.

Toryu is too far gone for seppuku. His hands shake, his eyes are as black as the power he commands. The shadow of the Dragon is fully within him. Power like that strangles a man's soul. Once it gains his measure, it will never let him go.

Perhaps it is not his own death he seeks.

Sezaru's eyes widened, and he pushed to his feet in a sudden movement. "Toryu!"

"That name is dead to me!" Thunder shook the kyuden above, trembling even the stone of Sezaru's deep cell.

"You cannot take things into your own hands. You told Kaede as much. Only mortals can change the world. Oracles are forbidden to act."

"Forbidden by the laws of the Fortunes, yes, but the Celestial Heavens have already abandoned me." The dagger shone in the gloom, a soft vision of sorrow against the rising terror that filled the cell. Toryu gouged the air with its sharp blade as he spoke. "I know the boundaries. I realize the dangers. There is no choice."

"There is always a choice."

"Only for you, Sezaru." Toryu's eyes glittered in his wan, white face. "Only for mortal man. For me, all choice was lost the moment I took up this mantle, the moment this blade—" he held aloft the ivory talon— "fell into my hands. Ten men, Sezaru, with choice, and I took that choice away. Now it is my turn to change the world. I tried to save the world your way, but you failed. I failed." His voice dropped to a hushed whisper. "This is the only way. I tried to stop Kaede from seizing the Imperial Throne, but she clung to her dead husband's will as if it would keep her from losing him entirely. How I pleaded with her. But she insisted. She feared losing her husband utterly, and now she has lost the Empire and driven me to this."

The ice-pale knife glittered in his hand, absorbing the last of the room's light into its tearful blade.

The image trapped within the Obsidian Mirror flashed once more before Sezaru's eyes. Again, he saw Kaede kneeling beside the dying Void Dragon. Again, he heard the ethereal echo of Toryu's words.

"Only a complete convergence of the elements can undo what the shard has done. Death is inevitable." Tonbo knelt beside Kaede, *"I tried to stop, Kaede-sama, stop you from walking this path. But the Imperial blood would not listen. And now . . . now it is too late for both of us. I am so sorry."*

"Do not do this," said Sezaru, slowly walking toward his insane visitor. "Look inside your soul. I know there is some part of you that still resists the darkness. Turn against it, Toryu! Fight it for but a few moments more."

"No, Sezaru." Toryu met his eyes with a black gaze. For a moment, Sezaru thought that the Oracle would end him with the ivory dagger. Then the Dark Oracle's eyes softened, and he lowered the blade with a shaking hand. "It was supposed to be you, Sezaru. I see that now."

The Dark Oracle growled, and the stone of the castle trembled once more with his power. His madness shuddered the kyuden and stormed the ocean into foam.

"I'll make things right. No one will ever be cursed with this burden. The Dark Oracle of the Void should never have existed. I will erase it from the heavens. Never should have been . . . never meant to be . . . a blasphemy against existence itself." Sliding the knife and his bloodied hands into his sleeves, Toryu whispered, "No matter what the cost."

The shadows darkened, dragging Toryu down into their abyssal blackness. Toryu's black eyes melded into the shadows, echoing them with the Void in his soul. Sezaru could only watch as Toryu was enveloped by the shadows he controlled. Within seconds, the Dark Oracle of the Void was gone, taking the Dragon's Talon and Sezaru's hopes into the darkness with him. The Wolf leaped at the shadows but found nothing there except the hard, stone wall. He reached for his magic in a desperate attempt to follow Toryu into the darkness, but the cell's wards still held, and the spirits could not answer his call.

Sezaru slid his palm against the stone, trying to sense any trace of the Dark Oracle's passage. Nothing answered his call. There was only silence and the lingering sense of lost spirits and fractured minds. "Damn," he whispered, closing his eyes and struggling against defeat.

"Master." The feeble voice was Koshei's. "That was the Dark Oracle of the Void?"

Frustrated by Toryu's sudden exit but glad to see his yojimbo awake at last, Sezaru moved back to Koshei's side. "Yes, it was," he answered. "How long have you been listening?"

"Not long. I thought it would be worse if I said anything. Most of it . . . made little sense, Sezaru-sama. He has gone mad."

"Indeed."

18 | A SANE VOICE IN MADNESS

Koshei struggled to rise, but Sezaru placed his hands on the man's shoulders and pushed him back to the ground. "You will reopen your wound," he warned.

"We must get out of this cell," Koshei said.

"I agree. And as soon as Kyuden Miya falls, I am certain we will." Sezaru's wry humor was stained. "You have little strength. You are of no use to me if you die. I command you to remain at rest until we have determined a way to escape."

Obediently, Koshei ceased his attempts to stand. "Where has Toryu gone?"

"Most likely, he will seek out Kaede, trick her into leading him to the Dragon of Void, and then use the Dragon's Talon to destroy it."

"By the Fortunes," Koshei breathed. "Can he do it?"

"Yes, Koshei. He can."

"We have to get you out of this cell. Your magic could stop him." Seeing the cynical look on his Master's face, Koshei continued, "At least, you could try."

"Not alone, Koshei. My magic is powerful in this world, but I have no way to step into the Celestial Heavens. No portal exists within this castle, and I am no Oracle with the ability to walk between worlds. It would be weeks of travel to find a location that would allow me entry, and by then it will be over." Frustration surged through Sezaru's system, forcing him to suppress his anger and distress.

"There must be some way," said Koshei, "some item of power."

"There was, but that path was lost to us in the Phoenix lands." Sezaru's tone was final, inviting no further discussion of portals, the Phoenix lands, or Isawa Sayuri.

Respectfully, Koshei fell silent.

"This is our place. May the Fortunes watch over us and grant us luck."

A soft voice from outside the cell whispered into the gloom, "They have, Toturi Sezaru-sama. And they will."

Sezaru turned, surprised. The upper doors were still barred. No sound of marching sandals echoed upon the stairs, yet there was a figure against the darkness on the other side of the iron bars, barely distinguishable from the shadow in which it stood. Two shadows, crumpled against the doorway, gave evidence of the perfect silence of the attack. The guards slept in unconscious humps on the floor, red-brown lumps already forming on their temples as the intruder stepped through the shadows toward the stair.

Koshei reached for his sword that was no longer there, and Sezaru stepped forward. "Identify yourself," he commanded.

"I am sorry, my lord, but I cannot," the figure said as it came down the narrow staircase, allowing the hood to fall from its shoulders.. "It is foul luck to say my name."

She was dressed in the uniform of the Miya guards, a common katana by her side in a brown, battered sheath. For all appearances, she was nothing more than one of a hundred lesser guards, fixtures in the palace hardly noticed by those who lived within. The woman's face was silhouetted for a moment as she lifted a lantern from her cloak, opening the door of the lantern so that a faint light shone out. In the instant that the light bathed her features, Sezaru saw her face.

"You see, Sezaru-sama, I am dead." Her smile was secretive, no longer hidden by the white lace of a familiar mask.

It took Sezaru a moment to place the delicate features and impish smile, but when he did, the realization stole the breath from his lungs.

"Angai!" His gasp was echoed by Koshei's glad cry, the yojimbo completely forgetting his wound and sitting up with another sharp exclamation of pain. "Gensaiken said you were executed."

Angai's face fell slightly as sorrow touched her delicate features. "When you kill a woman with a mask, you know her only by the shape of lace and porcelain covering her face. All a Scorpion has to do is take off her mask—or allow another to wear it."

"Someone died for you," Koshei said, hushed, his hand grasping the iron bars between them.

"No," Angai said somberly, her unusually somber gaze locking with Sezaru's. "She did it for you, Sezaru. She died so that you could reign."

* * * * *

A short while later, Angai, Sezaru and Koshei whispered against the wall within the cell. The iron door opened only too easily to Angai's cleverness, allowing her passage in and out as she wished. The secret passage that led down to the dungeon opened deep within Kyuden Miya. Sezaru could not sneak out without being recognized, nor could Koshei make the journey in his condition. There were few options.

The tale Angai told of her time in Kyuden Miya only confirmed Sezaru's suspicions. At first, Angai and Gensaiken worked together, using her ability to manipulate intrigue and his charisma in order to keep the court in order. But within weeks, Angai grew more and more aware of Gensaiken's deceptions. Meetings were scheduled without her, notes were passed that did not include her notice, and other movements of the court began to occur at Gensaiken's bidding alone.

With her Scorpion allies and a good deal of blackmail over various court officials Angai began to piece together the puzzle.

While putting up a generous front of courtesy and concern, Gensaiken was in fact sabotaging the Empire. He supported the wars and even encouraged their continuance at the expense of the people. He maneuvered the Crab into a position so that they would have to keep light watch on the Wall between Rokugan and the Shadowlands. After much investigation, Angai became convinced that Gensaiken was receiving messages from the south, but their origin and their contents she could not ascertain.

She described days of watching Gensaiken from a distance, of tracing his family line and his travels in order to determine who this southern contact could be. The notes were passed through the Crane clan, from somewhere near the distant Yasuki lands—the very ones that the Crab and Crane were in conflict to control. But Angai was certain that the origin of the notes wasn't from either clan. Instead, they came from farther south. The Shadowlands.

Angai, hoping to discover some of these letters and find out their contents, tried to enter Gensaiken's chambers one night when his meetings ran late. She was discovered there by the guards—either a piece of bad luck, or (as she believed), dark spirits watching over the room warned Gensaiken. Shortly after she was thrown in the dungeon, awaiting Gensaiken to formulate the story of her treachery and sign the papers for her execution, other members of the Scorpion clan within the castle came to her. They were supporters of Sezaru's candidacy for the throne, and some of them also suspected Gensaiken's Shadowlands connections, but with no proof. They offered her an opportunity, though not without a price.

"The girl who died was a handmaiden to one of the Scorpion courtiers. She bore a certain similarity to me, and because of her sacrifice, one of the noble family in the Scorpion lands will marry her sister and take care of her family for three generations. They lose a daughter and gain noble lineage, as well as money for their sacrifice." Angai seemed sobered by the choice, but then her smile returned. "She died with honor, and Gensaiken is none the wiser. Three of the members of my clan 'testified' against me, to further confuse the issue and convince Gensaiken that they had their own reasons for wanting me dead. It worked perfectly."

"Masquerading as a member of the Miya guard, I've watched Gensaiken since my funeral. Tonight, there was some commotion—some astrological imbalance or something. All the shugenja in the palace are gathering to make sense of it. I used the opportunity to come down and find you. It was the first chance I've had since you were brought here."

"There are secret corridors under Kyuden Miya." Koshei lay on his back, listening, still pondering the implications of Angai's speech.

"There are corridors under almost all of the major kyuden in Rokugan, Koshei-san." Angai winked. "You'd be amazed how many members of the Scorpion clan are architects. It is a family tradition."

Koshei muttered, "And most of those architects don't claim Scorpion blood, I'll bet."

"Enough." Despite his somber attitude, Sezaru smiled. The banter of his two most faithful retainers reminded him of happier times. Those times would return. He would see to it. "Angai, you must go back to the upper chambers of Kyuden Miya and break in once more. Not to Gensaiken's rooms this time, but to my mother's."

"The Imperial Chambers?" Angai blanched. "You're asking a lot. I'm good, but the security of those rooms is three times that of any other chamber. And Gensaiken's spirits may be watching."

"I can step outside this chamber and place a spell on you that will prevent those spirits from seeing you. I cannot do as much for mortal eyes, but your skills should serve you there."

Koshei looked uncomfortable but said nothing. Angai's face was resolute. "Am I seeking proof that Kaede-sama is not there?"

"No. Though I want revenge on Gensaiken, now is not the time. The Empire is in grave danger."

"I understand." She bowed in agreement. "What am I searching for?"

"My mother's Covenant. The Light Covenant of the Void."

Angai raised a delicate eyebrow. "I am no shugenja, Sezaru-sama. How will I know it when I find it? I need more than that."

"No matter what form it takes," he said, "it will be filled with the starry night of the Void. Its power will be such that even an untutored spirit can sense its power."

"How can I be certain it is within Kaede's chambers?"

"Kaede always kept it close, but she could not have taken it with her when she left. The Covenants must remain on this plane unless carried elsewhere by mortal hands. So Kaede couldn't carry it to the Dragon's plane, nor could Gensaiken—a creature of the Shadowlands—carry it elsewhere. The power of the Covenant would protect itself from Gensaiken's blood-magic, and he couldn't risk sending it away with anyone else. It would be too much of a risk. So he locks it up in her chambers, along with the secret of Kaede's disappearance." Sezaru focused all of his attention on Angai. "You must find it and bring it to me. With that and the Dark Covenant—" he gestured toward the secret pocket within his sleeve— "I may be able to stop Toryu. Somehow."

"It will be in your hands before sunrise." Angai rose and bowed again.

"Take this," Sezaru said, pressing the black pearl into Angai's hand. "It was given to me by an Oracle and contains mysteries of its own. Use it against Gensaiken. It has some power I do not yet understand. It may aid you."

The Scorpion maiden nodded solemnly and placed the pearl in her belt-pocket.

Angai then paused, reaching into the folds of the wide Miya belt that she wore over her guardsman's uniform. "I nearly forgot. This package came for you, shortly before you arrived in the palace. I stole it before Gensaiken was told of its arrival. He would certainly have opened it and had it destroyed." Angai handed him the brown-wrapped parcel, her delicate white hand small against the flat, wide surface. "It came with a messenger from the Phoenix lands."

Slowly, Sezaru unwrapped the dark coverings, allowing the string to fall away between his fingers. The paper crackled, weathered by travel, and broke apart. Beneath lay a silver mirror, slightly wider than the span of a large man's hand. Sezaru cradled it for a moment, staring in wonder at the obsidian reflection of the mirror's face. It shimmered a moment with remembered power then faded into the image of a thousand stars.

"The last shard of the Obsidian Mirror," Sezaru breathed. "It must be the largest of the broken pieces. It still holds some of the power of its parent, cradled by Phoenix magic within the silver of its casing."

"But who . . . ?" whispered Angai.

Koshei took her hand, and she fell silent.

Sezaru turned the mirror over, marveling at its craftsmanship. The image of a cherry blossom floating on still waters was engraved into the silver of the mirror's shell.

19 | THE DRAGON'S COILS

The long corridor, scarcely lit by hints of light escaping from Angai's tiny lantern, wove its way beneath the deep chambers of Kyuden Miya. The soft moss that grew within the cave-like twists and turns muffled her footfalls. The corridor was dark and damp, the walls trickling soft rivulets of cold water that shaped the rock. These caves existed long before the kyuden on the cliff above, hidden away in the stone; worn by the gentle trickling of mountain streams. Legend said that during the castle's construction slaves had used them to try to escape. Many of the luckless died deep beneath the mountain, far from the gentle sunlight in the forests. Their bodies had never been found.

None of them held so great a responsibility as the burden that rested on Angai's shoulders. The Scorpion maiden considered, her steps swift and sure even though her mind was elsewhere. The task she must complete was like a knife in her mind—sharp and clear but deadly. One misstep would expose her, and she would face a traitor's death. Worse, her failure would condemn Sezaru and Koshei. Without her aid, they would never escape the dungeon.

"This is the way the world works," she whispered to herself. "Big deeds come down to little actions. By removing a single stone, the entire building falls."

She could repeat her father's wisdom a hundred times, and her chances wouldn't get any better. Kyuden Miya was a three-story castle with more than two hundred guards in residence. They patrolled the corridors in military fashion, punctuated by pairs of roaming sentinels on no schedule at all. Many of the hardwood floors on the upper levels—particularly near the sleeping chambers where nobility rested—were "nightingale floors" that would make soft squealing noises if weight rested on them. The sound meant very little during the day, but at night it would alert any guard on that level. Kaede's chambers were guarded at all times, and even if Sezaru's spell would keep Gensaiken's dark spirits from noticing her, it would do very little against magical traps set by untainted shugenja.

There were only three entries into the Empress's chamber. One was the main door on the third floor of the castle. The second was in the Imperial throne room, leading directly from the first floor to the third in order to provide the ruling family with a safe passage to their personal areas. The third was an open balcony that overlooked the formal gardens of Kyuden Miya and the forest far below—a long climb on cold stone, pulled hand over hand up the steep mountain cliffs. Though it was the most private of the three, it was also the most dangerous and physically difficult.

It was likely that if she chose the first course, directly though the palace, she would be able to enter the room with some efficient fighting, but the guards would be aware of her presence fairly swiftly. If she knew what she was looking for within the room, it would be no issue. However, Sezaru's knowledge did not extend to the form of the Light Covenant, so Angai was on her own to find it within the Empress's suite of rooms. She would need time. Entering through the upper hall wasn't the right choice.

The cliffs would be difficult to climb tonight, slick from the recent rain and covered in winter moss. She'd had no time to scout them and find an acceptable route—even if she could compile rock-climbing gear in such a short time. Magic could propel her up the sheer rock face, but such a spell—even if guided by one of the Scorpion shugenja she controlled—would certainly be noticed by Gensaiken. Even with the awesome thunderstorm above the palace (the mark of the Oracle's passage, Sezaru informed her), Gensaiken was on a razor's edge. He kept close guard over the Empress's chambers, and each of the guards patrolling the outer walls had opportunity to look up and see the Empress's balcony and the cliffs overhead. It could be a death sentence. Angai shook her head, hurrying up the sloping passage. She didn't mind dying for her lord (she'd done it once), but to do so without accomplishing her purpose was unacceptable.

As she reached the opening into the palace itself, Angai slowed. The door ahead was slightly ajar, just as she had left it. Through the slit in the stone, she could see a faint light. Covering her lantern and drawing up her hood, Angai peered into the corridor. Though the corridor was empty, a faint scent of incense lingered in the air. She slipped out of the secret passage, covering signs of the aperture behind the painted screen. It slid easily against the wall, decorating what seemed to be only another corridor in the palace's maze of lower rooms.

Incense. Trails of it fluttered through the corridor as if a paintbrush colored the air. The stunning thunderstorm outside turned night to day, frightening the superstitious into believing that the Fortunes were angry with Rokugan, so the priests walked the corridors, expunging any evil that lingered there. Angai walked through the halls of Kyuden Miya, pausing to watch the procession of orange-robed Brothers of Shinsei in an upper corridor. Through the slats of the balcony, she could see them fingering their beads, chanting softly as the monks in front swung a bronze censer to purify the house.

An idea flitted through Angai's mind. The priests strode in slow progression, chanting prayers to the Fortunes as Angai raced to her rooms.

* * * * *

"I'm sorry, Gensaiken-sama." The humble monks stood before the Throne Room door. "All areas of the palace must be cleansed, lest the storm outside bring ill luck upon us all." The monk's eyes were earnest, his hand shaking with age as he held the censer of sweet-smelling smoke. "If the evils of ill-fortune were to hide within the throne room, we would surely condemn the Empire to their whims.

Six priests and three guards entered the throne room, followed closely by Gensaiken and his eagle eye. Alone within the massive chamber, the small number seemed almost inconsequential, small beside the grand but darkened backdrop of so many political wars. The priests spread out through the darkened throne room, their chanting lit only by the glowing coals of the brazier and a faint lantern light held by one of Gensaiken's guards. The room seemed dark and hollow, its walls distant and hidden from the light. At a signal from Gensaiken, the guards spread out among the priests, following them and keeping watch over their movements through the massive chamber.

Gensaiken stood, resolute. "Her Imperial Highness is ill and must not be disturbed."

The monk nodded sympathetically. "The poor fortune of this storm must be affecting her inner chi. I am not surprised that she feels the sickness of this bad omen. Yet we must cleanse the entire palace, Gensaiken-sama, or the darkness that envelops Kyuden Miya will not be lifted."

Gensaiken clenched his teeth. "The Empress is not accepting visitors."

"Then we will not visit her, Miya-sama—" the old priest bowed, his brotherhood bowing in respect as he moved at their lead— "but we must visit her chambers, and the chamber of the Throne."

The glowing coals rose and fell with the chants of the monks, and the footfalls echoed with the sound of clacking prayer beads. "Is this the door to the Empress's chambers, Miya-sama?" The old priest asked as he stood before the door behind the throne.

Gensaiken cleared his throat. "Her Imperial Majesty is in the gardens on her evening walk. The ill temperament of the spirits has caused her to be unsettled. We must move swiftly through her rooms and finish before she returns."

"Ah," the ancient priest said, his bow deep and respectful. "We would not wish to disrupt the Empress's meditations. We will be as quick as spirits and leave her rooms clear of all disruptive energies. I pray that the fortunes offer her peace. The madness that afflicts her son must weight heavy on her mind." The old man's withered lips smacked softly in admonishment. "The Imperial Prince Sezaru is powerful—too powerful! I fear this darkness comes over Kyuden Miya in punishment for the arrogance that led him to his fall."

The priest gestured as he opened the door to the Imperial Chambers. As the six priests filed through in tandem, Gensaiken turned to the guard by his side. "Watch them. Very closely. Count them both before and after they enter the chambers of the Empress. There must be no mistake."

The four guards followed Gensaiken and the priests up the twisting stairwell, clutching the hilts of their swords. Each step took forever, the nightingale stairs singing in soft harmony beneath the repetitive steps of so many visitors. Through a long, ornately painted corridor they walked, the priests chanting and touching their prayer beads to the walls, the floor, and the paintings as they passed.

Gensaiken watched the priests performing their absolutions, his dark eyes flinching away from their sacred prayers. The smell of the incense seemed to make him uncomfortable, and he stayed a distance behind the pack of Shinsei monks. His guardsmen shadowed them down the hall, watching their every movement and striding ahead to keep all of the monks within their vision. They never left the gaze of the guardsmen, every movement watched, every monk counted as they moved through the chamber. When they reached the sliding paper doors of the Empress's personal chambers, all of the monks knelt upon the hardwood floors of Kyuden Miya, touching their heads to the floor in respect before they traveled into the private sanctuary.

The inner rooms were ornate, each piece of furnishing carefully created by a master's hands. Delicate seascapes covered the walls, painted onto the rice paper with inks so real and vibrant they seemed to bring the ocean close enough to touch. The futon was unrolled, lying warmed and spread upon the floor in anticipation of the Empress's arrival, and a fire was burning brightly in the fireplace as if it had been but recently tended. The balcony windows were slightly opened, allowing the fresh breeze of the ocean to waft the scent of salt and sand into the palace.

One of the monks made his way to the balcony, opening the doors to gaze down at the jagged cliffs below. Quickly, a guard went to him, closing the doors before the monk could step out of sight. "Forgive me." The guard bowed with a guttural half-smile. "But the spirits outside are dangerous."

Indeed, the storm that threatened Kyuden Miya took that moment to shake the walls with a massive clap of thunder. The last glimpse of black storm was safely shut behind sliding wooden doors, the sweet scent of ocean waves clipped from the air.

The monk bowed, drawing his prayer beads through his hands and smiling. "Blessings on you, son of Miya," he said to the guard.

The guard grunted and pushed the monk away from the window and back into the room.

The monks moved gingerly through the room, their hands obsessed with beads and their every move watched by Gensaiken and his men. Each time a monk went behind one of the Empress's screens, a guard walked beside him to ensure he did not harm any of the priceless items that lay throughout the delicate chamber.

"Are you quite finished?" Gensaiken snarled, trying to maintain a patient attitude but foiled by the obvious headache that creased his brow.

"We are, Miya-sama." The old priest smiled, finishing his prayers and absolutions beneath the watchful gaze of the guard. One by one the monks filed out, each of the six carefully counted as they passed Gensaiken at the doorway.

"Search the room," ordered Gensaiken.

The guards did so, but none of the monks remained. Gensaiken nodded, tossed his robes before him, and exited the room. Three guards followed, their footsteps sure and capable.

Angai smiled as she stood silent and alone in the Empress's chambers. Gensaiken never even noticed the ruse.

* * * * *

The Empress's chambers were cold, lit now only by the small fire created as a ruse before the monks entered the chamber. The room showed only a few small signs of occupancy—the kimono over the chair, likely changed each day, and the rustling of the futon sheets before the maids came in the morning. Gensaiken would return in a short period, Angai knew, in order to put out the fire and arrange the room for the morning. She had little time and no clear plan how to get out of the room now that she had gotten in.

But that wasn't the point.

Deftly, her fingers searched every cupola, alcove, drawer and private cubby in a swift search of the Empress's chambers. As she had expected, there was nothing of use to her. Kaede kept a sparse room, filled with few private memoirs or personal touches. Only a small jewelry box, with a few carved ivory netsuke in the various shapes of phoenix, lions, and other mythical figures. The walls of the room were thick paper and tall mahogany beams, the ceiling soft wood and carved balsa. There were screens sheltering dressing areas from the main room, and a wide bath whose waters were heated by a separate fire. Some of the children's toys, memoirs from their youth in Otosan Uchi, were placed on redwood shelves here. Angai's eyes roamed over them, lingering first on a soft frog doll, then on the small, battered wooden sword that must have belonged to Toturi Tsudao. There was a small, round globe containing water and flecks of shining mica to symbolize snow; a worn book of stories which must have belonged to her Master as a child; and a go board made of ebony and ivory, the stones gathered in a soft silk bag embroidered with the character that marked Naseru's name.

Angai shed her guard's cap, letting her black hair tumble down her back as she pondered the room. There were few places to hide anything in the room, particularly anything of power. She considered what Sezaru told her about the Covenants. They were highly magical, usually small, and often concealed as normal items. Their form and function often reflected their true purpose—a lantern for fire or a bowl for water. But Void? What represented Void?

She searched the wardrobes, sliding back the articulated balsawood doors to run he hands through the Empress's magnificent kimonos. Nothing. Shoe-boxes held Kaede's slippers, never to be reclaimed by an Empress who would not walk upon Rokugan's ground again. At her makeup table, it was much the same—jeweled combs, elegant ornaments, and white paste to pale her face for formal court. Nothing of use. Nothing that struck Angai as the kind of item a Dragon would give to his Oracle.

Soshi Angai closed her eyes, visualizing the ebony box that represented the Dark Covenant. It was darker than anything around it, flecked somehow with light that did not exist, and within its black lid lay only complete darkness. Void, empty inside—but unopened and unopenable, inside completely without form.

How could the light replicate such a thing? Kaede's Covenant was the symbol of her tie to the Dragon of the Void. Its nature was linking, to establish the communion between the soul of the Dragon and the individual soul that once belonged solely to Kaede. It would need to be small enough that Kaede could carry it and keep it close.

The Scorpion maiden paced the room, checking every wall for secret chambers or false paneling. If she had been born a shugenja, she could have simply commanded the spirits to show her where the Covenant rested—or better yet, follow the lines of power until they led her to it. Neither option was available, and she was running out of time.

She swung the balcony doors open, staring out at the darkness and the lightning that danced across the sky. Even through the clouds hid the stars, some few flashes of light burst out between the strikes of lighting, showing the night sky—the Void in all its glory. How could one hold the Void? Angai looked at her own hand, imagining it filled with stars. Stars between her fingers, falling out into space . . .

Suddenly, her eyes widened.

Stars not snow.

Angai walked back into the room, staring at the shelf on which the children's toys lay. She reached for the snow-globe. Lifting it from its ornate three-pronged holder, Angai spun it in her hand as a child might do, to see the whirling action of the snow trapped within the water inside the globe.

The water darkened, shifting like oil in the bubble of glass. As the chips of "snow" fell through it, they sparkled like mica, reflecting light that did not shine from the outside—and transforming the small globe into a perfect reflection of a starry night.

"Gotcha." Angai smiled to herself, cradling the fist-sized globe between her hands.

"And I have you," Gensaiken replied from the doorway, his golden fan pausing only long enough to order the guard by his side to draw his sword.

Angai's hand darted to her small ninja-to, the shorter sword of a thief she had hidden within the arm of her guard's tabard. It darted out like a serpent's flashing tongue, ready for the oncoming assault.

With a bellow, the guard spun toward Angai, his longer sword having the advantage of reach. As his samurai retainer charged, Gensaiken raised his hands and chanted.

Angai waited until the tip of her opponent's sword raced past her hand, then slapped the blade aside. Darting underneath his thrust, she cut downward at the samurai's legs. He was too quick for her, leaping up even as his weapon missed and landing to face her once more with his sword drawn tight against his shoulder. All the while, Gensaiken motioned to the spirits with his hands, commanding them to follow his bidding. Angai could only guess how they would respond.

"They've blessed the rooms, Gensaiken." Angai grinned. "Your dark spirits will take some time to arrive."

"You should have kept your mask on, Scorpion." Gensaiken replied acidly. "It suited you. Now we'll just have to rectify that by carving away your face." His chanting ended, and Angai felt a powerful tug on her sword. Before she could grasp it more securely, the spirits of air launched the short blade across the room, stabbing it deeply into the mahogany beams of the far wall.

The Miya warrior struck again, this time twisting his sword blow above Angai's reach and coming down in an angled slice at her shoulders. Moving with the flow of the assault, Angai placed her hand on his elbow, rolled beneath the strike, and ducked to the floor to avoid the blow. She responded with a vicious cut of her own, piercing through the folds of the Miya's sleeve, but no blood followed in the wake of the sword. The samurai darted aside, following her rolling movements as she flung herself from left to right. The Miya thrust across, hoping to cut Angai in half.

Angai pulled herself into a sitting position, feeling the wind of his sword pass over her back. She punched viciously, catching him between the legs, and then slid forward behind him. Like a cat, Angai flipped to her feet, regaining her ninja-to as she waited for her opponent to spin around.

The Miya did exactly as Angai expected—spinning in an iai-jutsu strike designed to drive the length of his katana into her belly. So she wasn't where he expected her to be. The pivoting movement of his body, hurling his weight against the sword designed to sever Angai's torso, made his legs vulnerable. Dropping to the ground once more in a sacrifice move, she kicked at his knees. One shattered, crushed by her heavy strike, and the other spun outward with a dislocating crack. The samurai fell to the ground, screaming in pain.

He never reached the floor. Beneath him, Angai grabbed the Miya's belt and guided his fall right onto the blade of her waiting ninja-to. The blade sank into the Miya's chest, bursting from his back like a swiftly growing tree.

Angai shoved the dead body aside as Gensaiken finished his second spell. Fire roared out of the hearth, extinguishing the wood but swelling in a wave toward her. Her hair singed in the conflagration, and her clothes burst into flame. With no nearby source of water, Angai would be engulfed in seconds. The pain was agonizing, blistering her hands and arms as she shielded her face and upper body from the blaze.

Not hesitating, she rolled herself in the Empress's blankets to extinguish the fire. Gensaiken's chants grew louder, more eager, encouraging the fire-spirit to destroy his enemy and leave nothing but a pile of ash. She twisted in the blankets, spinning them out like a cloak from her singed body. Hurling the whirling fabrics over Gensaiken's head, she tugged the blanket tight like a net. It would only last a second, but that would be enough time to put out the flame.

A ripping sound came from the blankets as Gensaiken tore at the restraining material with a knife. The blade sawed through the golden fabric easily, shredding it as the shugenja fought to escape.

Hurling herself at her sword, Angai fought to free it from the fallen samurai's chest. It moved slowly, uneasily, sliding out with an audible crack of bone.

"Who is your master, Gensaiken?" Angai bantered, trying to ignore the peeling skin on her burned hands.

Gensaiken freed himself from the wrappings as Angai knelt and slid her sword into her shaking hands. "I serve powers greater than you could ever understand, girl."

"I don't think I'd want to understand them. I intend to destroy them." She leaped at Gensaiken, her sword cutting through the air for the Miya's throat. Gensaiken sidestepped, and her blade missed his larynx by only a hair's breadth, tearing a large wound into his shoulder instead. Gensaiken did not even flinch. Catching her balance, Angai slammed her elbow into his throat as she drew back the sword, using her positioning to catch a quick advantage on the slower spellcaster.

"No more spells, Gensaiken," Angai snarled. "You don't have time for them. Tell me what I want to know."

"Or you'll kill me?" Gensaiken choked, coughing up a black mucus-filled liquid from his lungs. He clutched his throat, hissing breath between clenched teeth.

"I'll kill you anyway, and we both know it." The two paired off once more, Angai's feet moving silently on the floor as they circled one another. The pain from the burning was beginning to numb, but that had its dangers, as well. She could feel her balance slightly off, her motions slowed from pain and reaction to the numbness. Gensaiken tossed his knife back and forth, hand to hand, preparing to take advantage of any perceived weakness.

Angai darted forward, using the strength gained by the brief respite to fuel her attack. Her blade rang from Gensaiken's shorter knife, pinning it to his chest. She landed a solid punch on Gensaiken's pale cheek, avoiding his return kick by leaping away.

The Miya followed, not allowing Angai to go outside the range of his knife. He swung, the anger and hatred in his eyes showing clearly. In that instant he changed, his eyes turning red with Taint as his blade sliced the flesh of her forearm. As Gensaiken cut her, he grasped the blade of her sword in his other fist. Ignoring the thick black blood that slid from his fingers as the sword cut into his inhuman flesh, he snarled and snapped the small sword in half. In a fluid motion, he hurled away the upper blade.

"If you will not die to human means," he growled, "then you will die to the Shadowlands."

Beneath the mask of humanity, Gensaiken's features twisted and flowed, shifting to a blackish purple. His claws extended around the broken haft of her sword

"Who is it, Gensaiken?" Angai choked, still pressing the advantage of her speed against him. The wounded arm hung limply at her side, blood streaming down through her fingers.

Gensaiken did not reply but swung again, coupling his blow with a fierce kick. It connected, and Angai fell to the floor beside the hearth, rolling away to keep her wounded ankle from more blows.

"Die, damn you!" Gensaiken shrieked, his knife plunging once more into Angai's flesh. She flinched, grinding her teeth to prevent the scream from giving him any satisfaction. He attacked again and again, two more thrusts of his blade entering her body as she crawled toward the hearth.

Reaching in and grasping a handful of the still-burning wood beneath the logs, Angai spun onto her back and thrust the white-hot coals into his face. Her hand didn't matter, the burning of her own flesh didn't matter—only that Gensaiken's eyes would be scorched away, his face mutilated by the fire. The man screamed, dropping his knife and clawing at his eyes. He lunged away from her, digging iron fingernails into ruined eye sockets as he tried to rid himself of the cursed coals. Angai desperately sought something to use against Gensaiken. Her fingers clawed at the hearth, seeking a loose stone, a broken piece of glass, anything . . . and then she remembered the pearl.

To distract him so that she could get closer, Angai snarled, "Who is your master? Who are you bringing to steal Sezaru's soul?"

"Tried to convince him," Gensaiken rasped. "He . . . must turn. My purpose . . . to bring the son of Toturi into the arms of the Shadowlands. Even though I could not bring Sezaru into the darkness . . . *they* will . . . when . . ." The blackened body of the chancellor seemed completely inhuman, iron claws clawing through her borrowed guard's tabard. ". . . when he comes to reclaim my soul."

Angai seized her chance and grabbed for the pearl, drawing the stone from her belt in a swift motion. The surface of the pearl felt hot against her skin, yet it did not burn her. She only hoped it would be her salvation. Despite the blisters on her fingers sending agonizing pain through her one good arm, she gripped the pearl in the flat of her hand and thrust it into Gensaiken's wounded shoulder.

He fell back, screaming, black blood staining the perfect floor of the Empress's chambers. Where the pearl sank into his flesh, Gensaiken's body rippled, the very bones beneath his skin shuddering with its power. Gensaiken tried to reach up to the wound, his hand shaking and fighting against his will.

"*What have you done?*" His voice rose to a howl.

Angai rolled backward, watching as Gensaiken's flesh bled darkness, the stain of it seeping out every pore, trickling like ebony tears down his cheeks. The dagger fell from his hand, unnoticed, as another scream tore from his throat.

"*What . . . have . . . you—?*"

She could only watch as the pearl disintegrated into his bloodstream, scouring the Taint from Gensaiken's veins. He shrieked again, twisted talons clawing at his own skin, but it was too late. The demon within him was fighting a battle it could not win. The power of the Oracle's pearl was driving out the midnight stain, purifying his soul and freeing him of the Shadowlands's control.

Miya Gensaiken collapsed to the ground before the Empress's hearth, the mahogany wood around him steaming and sizzling from the rivulets of Taint. Angai grabbed his dagger, readying herself for the final blow. Yet as she swept the knife up above Gensaiken, planning to bury it in the kneeling man's throat, his eyes met hers.

Instead of rage, darkness, or hatred, they were filled with regret—and innocence.

Angai held her blow, confusion making her take a step back.

"No!" Gensaiken whispered. "Please . . . kill me. You don't know what it made me do. You can't imagine the horrors I've seen, the pain that was set upon me. Please, for honor's sake, end my life now . . . while I am free of it. Before it can take me again."

Cold and numbed, Angai lowered her knife. "I cannot kill an innocent man."

"Am I?" Tears, real tears, as bright and clear as chips of ice, flowed down Gensaiken's cheeks. "Am I innocent?"

"The sins of our past will haunt us forever, Gensaiken. But you, unlike those you have wronged, will not move beyond them until you have repaired them."

"The Shadowlands took me. It . . . changed me. Against my will, I . . . I—"

"I know." Angai looked at the knife in her hand and then threw it away. "I curse you to live, Gensaiken. Live with the things you've done—pure and free of Taint. The Oracles have cleansed you. Consider this a second chance at life." Her smile was sardonic. "You gave me death. I give you life."

She turned away. The wounds in her body ached, and she clenched one fist over them to stop the bleeding. The cuts that Gensaiken had inflicted were bleeding, but he had been so blinded by rage and hatred that they were not serious. She limped back to the shelf, taking the Light Covenant into her blistered hand. She had no time to consider. Right now, she was going to take this ball of glass back into the dungeons so that Sezaru could save the world. Somehow.

She didn't know much about magic, and from what she'd seen of Gensaiken's hideous transformation, she would leave the Shadowlands to the Crab. Angai was a thief, and a good one. The snow-globe faintly lit in her hand, a thousand stars sparkling within its glass bubble. Sezaru had given her a task, and she'd be damned if she wasn't going to finish what she started.

Kneeling in an ashen pile upon the hearth behind her, Gensaiken wept. When the tears were finished, he would begin the long path back to honor, back to truth. But for now, for both of them, all that mattered was pain.

20 BLOOD BETWEEN THE STARS

Sezaru knelt in another empty cell beneath Kyuden Miya. This one was not warded against his magic. Though the spirits within the palace were frightened, they obeyed Sezaru's call, healing Angai and Koshei with their touch.

Angai's face would always bear the scar of the fire Gensaiken unleashed upon her, but it did not seem to impede Koshei's smile. He helped the maiden dress in the kimono of a peasant servant within the palace, changing his own clothing for that of a gardener. Though bruised and sore, the two would be able to blend into the frightened masses above and make their way out of the palace.

"You're not going with us, Sezaru-sama." It was a statement, not a question.

Sezaru smiled at Angai's boldness. "No. Not that way. You will see me again, Angai, if I am successful. But I am needed elsewhere, and this—" he held up the glass bubble of starry night— "will help me in that task. Now, go, and do not ask questions that I cannot answer."

Angai and Koshei bowed as one, their faces twinned in the dim light of the stone cell. Sezaru watched as they left, each supporting the other. It would be a difficult journey for them, through the heavily guarded palace and out into the forests that surrounded Kyuden Miya on three sides. Once outside, they could change their clothing for standard peasant wear and make their way north to the Phoenix lands.

Sezaru pushed the thought away as the cell door closed on the corridor above. He could leave this place any time he wished, calling on the spirits to carry his body beyond the borders of Kyuden Miya. He could not offer the same to them, but his prayers fell upon their footsteps with the whispers of the spirits that could understand.

And perhaps this time, your prayers will be enough, the inner voice whispered. *But prayers will not save you on your next journey, Sezaru, nor will all of their good wishes and proud fortune. You must go once more into the darkness you have rejected and force it to show you the way.*

Sezaru placed the shard of the Obsidian mirror before him, angling it to capture the faint, irregular glow of the lightning outside. The stone cell had a small window near the ceiling, through which he could hear the ocean's roar and witness the storm that raged above. The Oracle's anger shook the foundations of the elements around Kyuden Miya, and they would not be assuaged by mere incense and chants over prayer beads. They required sacrifice, and their balance would not be regained until Tonbo Toryu's mad plan was stopped.

Again he heard Toryu's last words, whispered in the darkness of his soul, *I will erase it from the heavens. No matter what the cost.*

Light flickered over the shard, illuminating the silver tracings that held it together. Within the darkness of the obsidian, flecks of starlight danced just beyond Sezaru's vision, drawing his attention ever nearer to the world within.

He held the Dark Covenant in one hand, feeling the cold darkness of its ebony form. In the other, the Light Covenant shone, reflecting starlight that did not exist and shining traceries of light across Sezaru's pale white hair. Between them sat the Wolf, his soul, and his hope for the Empire.

The mirror's surface rippled. Though not as powerful as its predecessor, this shard still held a wealth of power—enough, Sezaru hoped, to punch a hole in reality and escort him into the darkness of the Void.

Thus will be the way of things, when a man comes asking, and the world must answer.

Sezaru gazed into the mirror, letting his mind empty. Troubles and cares washed away, unneeded. He could carry no burdens into the lands beyond. Only truth and the Covenants could walk with him.

Death and pain shall surround you, and the Void will follow.

The Wolf stared, unafraid, into the mirror and let his mind fall into the darkness.

He opened his eyes. Once again, he was floating in emptiness, bereft of wind, air, and breath. The Obsidian Mirror was much as he remembered it, but its spirit was broken. Pieces of memory floated around him, lost within the mirror's embrace. There was no lifeline, no sense of purpose to it, only a dark, thick blackness that threatened to swallow him.

The mirror twisted, and memories floated past—his own, those of Kachiko, of a thousand other owners now forgotten by time and history. It would be only too easy to become lost here, to let go and become one within the memories, forgetting about life, the future, the Empire . . .

Somewhere in its depths, the broken mirror laughed.

Sezaru reached out with his consciousness, seeking a means through the mirror to the Void at its depth. The stars were glassy reflections with no life, no will of their own, only copied intelligence fused within shattered glass. It was too dangerous. The mirror had gone mad.

Releasing his intuition and calling upon the Covenants, Sezaru cried out in silence to the mirror's heart, praying that she would hear him.

Even afterward, Sezaru could not be sure whose name he called—his mother's or that of a Phoenix maiden in far away, snow-covered lands. But the sound stirred the mirror's icy heart, and the utter blackness encompassed him once more. The images around him shifted and stirred, their maze unfolding before him. The effort involved in deciphering their messages was awesome. Sezaru could feel the mirror tugging at his subconscious, drawing him in forever. He had almost lost his soul to the Obsidian Mirror in the Phoenix lands. Though the mirror was weaker from the shattering, it was even more complex—twisted and broken, its madness convulsing through thousands of lost memories. Sezaru felt the Covenants in his hands pulsing with life. Only their power kept the mirror's insanity at bay, kept the memories from overwhelming him.

One mistake, and he would be lost.

Sezaru's mind grasped a flash of thought passing before him—the image of Kaede's gentle face. She slept on a bower of stars, all concern and worry swept from her forehead. Sezaru stepped toward her, feeling the Obsidian Mirror buckle and resist, but he continued on.

Within the image, Sezaru saw a shadow approaching, extinguishing the stars one by one. Even through the slowly moving picture he could feel the shadow's cold chill disturbing the heavens. Sezaru fought to reach it, lending his will to his motion as if placing a sail before the wind, but the image moved on without him.

Kaede's eyes fluttered, her lips parting in a sweet sigh. For a moment, a hand reached from the darkness as if to brush away her dreams, but then it stopped, paused, and slid away again. Her eyes opened, disturbed by the question hidden in the Void, and in the reflection of Kaede's dark pupils Sezaru could see Toryu.

"Where is he, Kaede?" the voice was low, soft, but enveloped by Toryu's madness.

"I do not understand." She rose from her bower, long black hair swaying in a non-existent breeze. Sezaru pounded upon the glass, forcing himself to move more swiftly. If only he could be there . . .

"Where is the Dragon of the Void?" Toryu asked softly.

"He is all around us," Kaede replied, spreading her hands in trust and friendship. "He is always with me, Toryu-sama. But he does not choose to take form unless there are dire circumstances."

Toryu nodded. "Dire circumstances, such as an attack upon your person?"

"Exactly. Unless there is some need, he sees no reason—"

Toryu's hand rose in a swift motion, bringing the Dragon's Talon down into Kaede's shoulder. She screamed, reaching to grip the wound as shock and betrayal rippled through her eyes. With one hand, she struck Toryu, knocking him away with the force of an exploding star.

A roar echoed through the Void.

Kaede's anger was palatable, her hands glowing with white fire. Toryu did not even bother to stand as he unleashed a volley of dark spheres from his kneeling position. Kaede turned from side to side, her hands striking each obsidian ball before they could reach her. Once the darkness met with the light, it vanished into smoke and was no more.

Toryu snarled, his body arching with power. Raising his hand, he drew upon the darkness between the stars. It came, shrouding the area like a black cloak, breathing with the terror of a child's dream in the depths of the night. Kaede clapped her hands together and sparks flew before her, their brightness blazing too hot to gaze upon for long. Where the shooting stars met with the cloying darkness, they burst into flame. The creature of shadow moved toward Kaede, but before its claws could tear into her white flesh, the flames burst into light and the creature was consumed.

"Toryu, what are you doing?"

He made no reply, instead summoning flickering tendrils of shadow to wrap Kaede's arms and pull her to her knees. The Oracle of the Void struggled against the tentacles of darkness, tearing her unwounded arm from their grasp. Sezaru could see blood trickling down his mother's shoulder. The stars around her moved in a serpentine pattern, disturbed by the conflict below. As she screamed, Toryu clenched his fist and hurled Kaede against the wall of stars. She landed with a gasp, still enmeshed by the dark slivers. Kaede was weak from the imbalance in the Void, her spiritual nature torn by her drive to see her children and the Empire protected. She would be no match for Toryu's insane anger and hatred.

Their conflict shook the heavens, wrapping the mirror's reality in a sheen of blood and anger. Two Oracles of the same cause, one Light and one Dark, vying with their powers. It was a blasphemy, a bitterness caused by madness and whispered threats.

Sezaru knew he had to arrive immediately, lest Toryu win the battle and all become lost. He raced through the intermediary stars, ignoring the visions that flitted between him and the battling pair. Too much time had passed already!

"It must be undone!" Toryu screamed. "What you have caused, I must destroy!" His hands moved in an intricate pattern, the swell of pure magic rippling the stars around them both. Ignoring the subtleties of sorcery, he spread his fingers and brought down the power like a hammer, tearing his own soul to bring the weight of his will down upon Kaede.

As she fell forward, Sezaru stepped from the mirror's grasp.

Toryu raised the Talon once more, but Sezaru stood between him and his prey. Already the Dragon's form twisted around them, angered and pained. The stars of the heavens rippled, denying their stations in the night sky.

"Toryu, you must not!"

"I will, and I must!" Toryu's words ripped out, slashing like a knife through the silence. "It is better this way, Sezaru. She will not feel the pain of the Dragon's death. Let it be done, and soon it will be over."

Sezaru twisted his hands into the motions of a spell. Magic was thick here, filled with living spirits as the ocean overflowed with water, and they came easily to his call. Wisps of smoke wrapped around his fingers, reaching out toward Toryu in entrancing, beckoning fingers. "Listen to me, Toryu-sama," Sezaru said, allowing the magic to work its wiles. "Hear my words. Leave this madness and this place. Walk with me in the corridors of the Empire. Your place is not here."

Toryu shook his head. For a moment, Sezaru thought the Dark Oracle would listen, that he would give in to the impulses Sezaru placed within his soul. But then, with the shattering sound of chain unbound, Toryu cast away Sezaru's attempts.

"There is no redemption for me. No Empire. Only misery and

cursed blight. Look at me! See what I have become!" Madness swelled in his eyes, and he raised the knife. "I tried to make this easy, Wolf! I would have given her a quick and merciful death, but you have prevented even that last hope!"

Toryu's insanity drove his voice into a shriek as the knife passed close to Sezaru's face.

"She is weak, Sezaru, unbound! Her actions have unsettled the Empire and caused the blasphemy that has imprisoned me. I tried! I tried to tell her this would happen." Black tears flowed down Toryu's cheeks as he lunged forward in another attempt to pass Sezaru.

"Toryu, no!"

Sezaru leaped to the side, trying to block the vicious curve of the dagger's swing, but he was too late. The Wolf hurled himself before Kaede, throwing his body between her and Toryu's sudden attack. He failed because of his love for her. Toryu's strike was not aimed at Kaede but at the heart of the stars behind her—the chest of the Void Dragon, called by the heavens to protect the one that held its soul.

As the dagger sank into the dragon's chest, the stars began to fall.

"Toryu, why?" Kaede's voice was soft, broken, her hands reaching out as the bonds that bound her began to fall away. The Dark Oracle stepped back, staggered once, and fell to his knees. His eyes stared at the hole in the heavens, watching as the Dragon's tremendous head lifted in a silent scream of agony and regret. Sezaru felt the wrenching agony slice through the Void only a moment before Kaede screamed. The Dragon's wound bled starlight, pure and rich against the tapestry of night. The Dragon's Talon fell from Toryu's hand, and he stared in awe and horror at the wound.

"What have I done?" he whispered. Some fraction of his sanity jarred to the surface, and Toryu huddled in agony, unable to tear his eyes from the wound. "The whispers . . . the voices . . . I heard them. I knew the truth. Only it does not seem so true now that the deed is done." Toryu's eyes sought Sezaru's, begging for some stability in his rapidly shattering world. "I was not strong enough, and I think some of the voices . . . I think at least one of them was real."

Sezaru's jaw tightened. "Gensaiken's master, no doubt, using his powers to influence you. You were a pawn, Toryu, as was I." Leaving Toryu to huddle in his doubt and agony, Sezaru turned to his mother. "Kaede-sama, we must stop the bleeding. The wound must be cleansed and closed. Can you do that?"

Sezaru pressed his hands to the wound. The Dragon lowered its head to place its cheek gently against Kaede's tears.

"There is nothing we can do." Tonbo Toryu crawled forward and knelt beside the Void Dragon. "Only a complete convergence of the elements can undo what the shard has done. Death is inevitable." Tonbo looked to Kaede. "I tried to stop, Kaede-sama, stop us all from walking this path. The darkness lies within imperial blood. I know that now. But now it is too late for both of us. I am so sorry. . . ."

His words spilled over themselves, unable to assuage the guilt within his soul. Toryu's eyes still held madness, but now it was coupled with complete self-condemnation.

"I was weak," he whispered, kneeling in the shadow of the dying dragon.

"No." Kaede raised her head from the Dragon, tears sparkling on her face, and shivered. "This blood, Toryu, this death and all those to follow, is on my hands. You would not have fallen if I had not placed my love for my husband above my duty to the Empire. If I had not taken the throne, there would be no Dark Oracle and the Dragon would still be whole. We all bear this burden." Kaede took Toryu's hand. "We must bear it together, for we cannot change the world."

"Behold! The end of Rokugan!" Tonbo Toryu whispered, his voice empty and hollow. He turned away, his aged face etched with sorrow, madness warring with regret. "Because of our weakness, we reach the end. The end of the elements, and the end of the world." As he spoke, the stars in the sky around them trembled, falling one by one from the black cloak of the heavens.

"It will be the end—" Kaede's voice carried an unimaginable pain as the Dragon's glorious eyes dimmed and closed— "of us all."

"No," said Sezaru. "You may be of the heavens, but I am not. There must be a way to change this, and mortal man is the only one that can do so."

Both Kaede and Toryu stared at Sezaru in amazement as he drew himself to his full height, his white hair flowing behind him.

Sezaru strode to the fallen Dragon's Talon, its ivory blade covered in sticky starlight. He reached to pick it up, fingers sliding against the woman's form upon the hilt, and the Void shifted beneath him.

Fool, the voice within his soul hissed. *You do not know what you have done!*

As Sezaru touched the knife, he felt his soul invaded by a great burden. The sorrow of the Dragon's Talon laid itself upon his shoulders in an instant, revealing every broken promise and each stain upon his soul. Though he had lived an honorable life, the unknown tears wept on his account were many, and they burned him to the core.

The Wolf's eyes flew open in shock and amazement at the power flowing through his veins. Sorrow, suffering, darkness . . . all these things flooded from the Dragon's Talon, coursing through him like ice. For a moment, he knew the Dragon's pain, felt its suffering like the finest taste of rice-wine. It invigorated him, fueled his power, and he felt the knife warm in his hand.

Toryu was frightened, his body shaking as he stared at the Wolf. Sezaru could see himself reflected within the wizened man's dark eyes. He was an avenging kami, white hair flowing about him like a veil of purity, his hands outspread with the Dragon's Talon to bring justice to a suffering world.

Sezaru realized that the knife was raised above his head, pointed down at Toryu's bare throat. This man caused sorrow, caused pain, and defiled the celestial heavens. His crimes were great, and had to be punished.

If you do so, you will give up all you have fought for.

All his life, Sezaru had fought the voice's urgings, resisting the words that twisted his soul. Even now, he struggled to ignore them, to drop his hand and cover the Dragon's Talon with Toryu's blood.

If you kill him, you will become him. The voice sounded eager, hungry, and images flashed in quick succession before Sezaru's eyes. Visions of a dark future, the Wolf seated upon a throne of bone and darkness. The knife shuddered in his hands, begging to be released. Distantly, Sezaru could hear Kaede begging him not to strike, but her voice was faint and pale. Toryu did not move, did not blink or flinch, but knelt at Sezaru's feet as if waiting for the bliss of release that the Dragon's Talon would bring.

"It will not be this way!" Sezaru shouted, forcing himself to hurl the dagger from him. All of his strength combined with the power of the darkness in his soul thrust the dagger against the solidity of Void and starry night. It tumbled through the air for less than a breath, twisting light against darkness, cold ivory against the warmth of night. When the Dragon's Talon struck the solidity beneath Sezaru's feet, it shattered into a thousand bright pieces.

21   ETERNAL SOULS

Across Rokugan, the elements reeled, their very natures shifting as the Dragon of Void grew fainter. In the Shadowlands, a massive army readied their blades, preparing to take on the Empire in their weakness and drive all of Rokugan to destruction. Shugenja and priests fell to their knees across the Empire, clutching their prayer beads and lending their strength and prayer to the imbalance in a desperate attempt to right the universal wrong. Though they did not know the source, they felt the shift and understood the danger.

Within the Celestial Heavens, the Dragons of Fire, Water, Earth, and Air stood ready, prepared for the outcome that hung in the balance. When the Dragon of Void met his eternal ending, they would weep for the world as it was engulfed in darkness. The other Oracles, both dark and light, listened for the final breath of the Void Dragon to arrive and then fall silent forever.

The light within the Dragon's eyes flickered like pale reflections of dying stars. Sezaru knelt before the incredible beast, the

Void within his own soul reaching out instinctively to the immortal creature.

"Can the wound be healed?" Sezaru whispered.

A whisper echoed in Sezaru's mind, a voice born half of the dragon's breath and half the sound of Sezaru's darkness. *What are wounds, but a tear in the equilibrium of the soul? How best to heal them, if not with balance and with care?*

Uncertain, Sezaru considered. The voice was his enemy, a darkness that tugged at his soul, but the Void Dragon was a being of light. Could this be a sign of shifting in the balance of his soul?

As Sezaru pondered, his hands found their way to the Covenants of the Oracles, still safely hidden within his sleeves. The items felt almost too hot to touch, their spiritual presence burning with the Dragon's closeness. Carefully, he drew them out and placed them near the Dragon of the Void. The globe of starlight seemed a pure bubble of void, the stars within shining in a mini-universe, unconcerned with the death of the one outside the sphere of glass. The black box flowed, curving into the dragon's shadow as if a part of it. Gently, Sezaru placed the sphere beside the box, watching as the darkness flowed around the sphere, shifting into a shadow of the universe.

The blood of the Void Dragon slowed, but the presence of the Covenants was not enough to ease the wound. Sezaru stared into the Dragon's eyes. "Kaede, what do I do?" he asked in desperation.

"I do not know."

"And even if she did, Sezaru-sama," Toryu whimpered. "She could not tell you without further unbalancing the elements and risking the Void Dragon's life."

Sezaru cursed, clenching his fist and struggling to control his anger. "So I must do it myself?"

Tonbo Toryu nodded, power flowing from stability to insanity. Sezaru could see the struggle within the old man's eyes as he fought to maintain his tenuous grip on reality.

Sezaru looked down at the Covenants, his fingers hovering over them. A mystic presence hummed between the two items, tingling against Sezaru's fingers. There was an unusual magical affinity between them, something that was not explained by their proximity to the Void or to each other. The two items somehow created a third presence, an intangible effect that held solidity but not form. His fingers felt the illusion of solidity, rough edges hidden within magical eddies, but he could not grasp it.

He closed his eyes, allowing his will to seek out the form between the Covenants. Magic swayed in rivulets, trickling from the Dragon's wound, the scattered shards of the Talon. It flowed between the Covenants as if they were prisms of light, breaking apart the magic and shifting it into rainbows of form and shape.

"I cannot do it," Sezaru whispered, feeling his will flow into the prism and shatter into a thousand motes of light.

You can because you must. Softly it whispered in the spaced between his thoughts. *You fear what you are, Sezaru. You do not understand what you can be.* It sounded half-defeated, still struggling to invent the fight that it knew was lost.

I will not be what you wish of me. I will never be your servant.

Sezaru felt the magic between his fingers pulse and change.

You will never be free of me.

Nor you, of me.

Sezaru knew it to be true. Though he had defeated the darkness to come here, still it lived. In those times when the voice within his soul caused him to take action, it still was not a victory. Both good and evil lived within him, and though others tried to force him to choose one side or the other, he could stand between them and deny the forces that tried to shape him. Life was not about good or evil, but about the balance between them both. That was what it meant to be mortal man; that was the core of his being. Not an Oracle, not a dark power, but somewhere in between. A man.

And, perhaps, an Emperor.

With that realization, reality shifted. All his life, he had been asked to choose between the two—and Sezaru had at last made the choice. He would stand upon the line, keeping himself neither to the dark or the light, and remain mortal. Sezaru slipped his hand within the twined energies of the two Covenants and felt the power consolidate. He clutched at it and drew it forth. It radiated power, sending showers of star-like sparks in all directions as it came into being, and Sezaru felt the pressure of something weighty placed within his hand. He clenched his fist deep within the bounds of the spell and grasped the offering of the twinned Covenants. It took all of his strength to draw it forth, but Sezaru focused his will and pulled back his hand.

He drew it into being, his breath stopping as he realized what he held.

"The Dragon's Talon."

Indeed, within his hand he held the ivory blade once more, its carved hilt resting against his palm. Now unbroken, the blade had been reforged by the spells of mortal man and lay in Sezaru's hand like a talisman of the future. Where before it had been the color of melted amber, its white blade touched by the pain and agony of ages. The blade now seemed paler—white this time and clear as icy glass. Nor did the artifact radiate sorrow, but instead a serene peace that flowed through all of the energy in the room, uplifting Sezaru's spirit. The woman carved into the hilt had a peaceful, serene smile on her almost translucent face, her white hair flowing down the handle in an imitation of Sezaru's own.

"I do not understand," Toryu whimpered at the dragon's feet.

"I do." Kaede, this time, her hand stilled in its motion. "Choice, Sezaru-chan." Her soft use of his childhood appellation recalled a time that seemed a hundred years past. "The Dragon's Talon is not a talon at all, is it?" This time, her question was meant for the celestial creature that lay wounded by her side.

My Oracle is correct, the Dragon replied, and its terrible, echoing voice seemed to fill the blackness within the stars and reflect the ultimate emptiness of all things. *The Dragon's Talon is a manifestation of mortal choice, created by the Celestial Dragons. In a way, it is our talon, for through it we place our spirits and our lives in mortal hands. The choice of life or death must belong to you, Sezaru, and others like you—not to us. That choice must exist in the world, even for those who do not choose to make it. You have given it rebirth, renewal, and in doing so have restored the balance. Its sorrows are gone. In time, it will gather more, as choices are made and mortal man continues in his existence. Place it to my wound, Sezaru, that it may know its first pain.*

Sezaru pressed the ice-white blade of the Dragon's Talon against the wound in the Void Dragon's heart. The knife shuddered, unwilling. The Void Dragon roared in pain, lifting its head and bugling as the wound closed. The starlight pouring from its breast slowed to a trickle, then ceased, and Sezaru drew the knife away. He could swear its blade was darker, the white softly christened with a faint hint of ivory, and as Sezaru lifted it away from the Dragon, he felt the knife's weight increase.

"The wound is sealed." Kaede's face radiated joy, and she bowed to the Void Dragon in great reverence. "My Master, you are well!"

Toryu moaned as if in pain. Ignoring Kaede's joy, he whispered, "Destroy me, Sezaru. Destroy me before I fall back into the darkness."

Sezaru clenched Toryu's shoulder, lending the fallen man strength. "This darkness was not entirely of your choosing, was it, Toryu?"

Toryu shook his head, unable to answer, but Sezaru saw the truth in the broken man's eyes. Tonbo Toryu clutched his head, black tears streaming from his eyes. His tenuous sanity whispered through his words of grief and self-hatred, coloring his words with futile remorse. "I cannot tell you more, Sezaru. He came to me and told me the only way to save myself—to save you, Kaede, Koshei, Angai, the Empire . . ."

"Who, Toryu?

The mad Oracle shook his head, black eyes flashing. "His name is pain."

"Toryu," Kaede said, a hint of command in her voice. "Speak."

Toryu balled his fists against his head, digging into his flesh with shards. Blood ran down his cheeks, the scarlet mingling amid the black stains upon his cheeks. "Daigotsu . . ." he whispered, wrenching his hair as though the very word caused him pain. "Daigotsu!" he repeated, this time a shriek. "Heir of Fu Leng, bringer of the Empire's ruin! Nothing! All things! Curse you that you drove me to the darkness!"

Kaede placed her hand upon Toryu's sleeve, using her power to calm him once more. "Is this name familiar to you, my son?" she asked.

Before Sezaru could answer, Toryu hissed beneath his tears. "I sought the Dragon's Talon with my last hope, as you bid me, Sezaru. It lay on Daigotsu's right hand, deep in the heart of the Shadowlands. He did not expect me. His traps were laid for you. But I bested them, I who am the Darkness of the Void." Toryu's face lit up with eagerness as he told the story. "Daigotsu stole the knife from the Oracle of Water, guided by a secret whisper within Kyuden Miya itself!"

"Gensaiken," Sezaru murmured.

"He is obsessed with you, Sezaru. Of all your brethren, you are the one he fears most. He planned to offer you power, stillness, a new destiny . . . but me? None of this. So I took the Dragon's Talon from him. But his words . . . his words still haunt me. I fought against them, but they seemed so reasonable. Kill the Dragon, free Kaede, free myself, the Empire . . . in time, they made more sense than the madness in my mind, and I clung to them. And look, now, what I have done.

"I was wrong." Toryu shuddered beneath the weight of the deception. "If you had not been able to heal the Dragon, my madness would have consumed the Empire." The little man stared up at Sezaru and clutched his black and gold robes close to his body. "Soon I will break, Wolf, and even this wretched half-sanity will be broken. When that occurs, all those things I could not do will come rushing back, and I will be the terror we feared I would become. You must destroy me, Sezaru-sama. You and Kaede-sama must not allow this to happen."

Kaede breathed softly, resisting his insistent demand. "No."

"Kaede-sama is correct, Toryu. If you were to die, then Daigotsu will have his wish. Someone truly worthy of the post will accept its burden, and the Empire will face a worse threat.

"Worse than my madness?" Toryu howled.

"Indeed." The Wolf's pale eyes were cold and stern. "For your replacement, Toryu . . . would be me."

Kaede gasped and turned to stare at Sezaru. "You are certain?"

Sezaru nodded. "It was my place to take the post of Dark Oracle of the Void, to be corrupted by its power. All my life, I have known this. But my destiny has . . . altered."

"Mortal man," Toryu whispered, "can change the world. You were there. You were prepared to be accepted by the Oracles that day in Volturnum. But you did not move, and I was able to take the burden for you." He choked slightly at the memory. "I only wish I were able to hold it longer than I have. I would give anything, Sezaru, to spare both you and the Empire that fate. If only I could live forever...."

Toryu and Sezaru locked eyes, their minds magnetized by a single, impossible thought. "The mirror!" Sezaru drew the silvered shard from his belt. He turned the black and silver glass over and over in his hands. "The Obsidian Mirror, gift of the Oracle of Water. Three times I have braved its power, and three times walked its corridors."

"You are stronger than I." Toryu reached as if to touch the mirror's surface then jerked his hand back with a hiss. "Eternity within black chambers, given life only by memories that are not my own. It is a kind of Jigoku, Sezaru—a hell. But for me it holds more hope than this world."

Toryu stood, straightening his back and limping to stand before Sezaru. His face seemed to have aged a hundred years in that slow moment, revealing the pain and suffering that tore at the essence of his soul. "Show me, Sezaru-sama."

"Toryu, no!" Kaede rose, standing between the two men. "Toryu, there is another way. This cannot be allowed. You will be trapped within that . . . thing—" her voice was filled with revulsion— "for eternity."

"That is rather the point, my dear." Toryu gazed at her. "Ah, Kaede, my dear. Our world is past, and I am an old man. Let me rest, Kaede. Let my last action be one of honor."

Tears streamed down Kaede's face, but she held her body with the regal bearing of an Empress. "You may not. I forbid it."

"You are no longer Empress, gentle Kaede. There is nothing for you to forbid."

"Toryu," she broke, her voice shaking although her body was rigid and proud. "I . . . beg you."

Toryu brushed a long wave of black hair from her shoulder, pausing to stare at her face once more. "Do not, Kaede. Where you once gave yourself for your husband, let me now give myself for your child . . . and for the Empire's future."

Refusing to release his eyes from her gaze, Kaede whispered, "This cannot be the will of the Fortunes."

"No, Kaede. It is not the Fortunes who set this path before us." Toryu let his hand fall away, stepping back. "It is the will of mortal man." Before Kaede could protest, Toryu said in a shaking voice, "Quickly, Sezaru-sama. Before the madness returns."

Over Kaede's shoulder, Sezaru held aloft the Obsidian Mirror. Raising his eyes over Kaede's shoulder, Toryu cast his eyes into the mirror's black depths, his face unafraid. In the passing of a single, fragile moment, he was gone.

"Why, Toryu?" Kaede fell to her knees, the Dark Oracle's sacrifice too great to bear.

Sezaru lowered the mirror. "For the same reason that all honorable samurai give their lives: To prove that the Empire is more than a single man." He held the mirror carefully, his eyes avoiding its depths. "I must return to Rokugan, Mother. The Empire is safe from this calamity, but the creature that spawned it is still free. He must be hunted down and destroyed. It would be far too dangerous for me to keep this upon my person, lest Daigotsu find it and unleash Toryu once more upon the world."

Kaede nodded, gently taking the silvered mirror into her hands. "He will rest with me, among the Heavens where he belongs." Reaching up into the starlight that surrounded them, she hung the silvered mirror upon the blackness of night. "Let the blackness of the mirror be forever turned from the world, and may the silver of its backing remind us always of the sacrifice that Tonbo Toryu has made."

The mirror sparked once, then faded, its silvered radiance igniting the heavens, a new star born against the backdrop of night.

"The star of Cherry Blossom," Kaede murmured, touching the faint light with the tip of her finger. "May it shine forever in memory of him."

The two stood beneath the stars for a moment, letting the silence fill their hearts.

Purpose. Sezaru's mind spun back to the Empire. "I must go back. Immediately. I am needed there."

Kaede's pale face was like porcelain against the dark sky surrounding them. "Sezaru, you must not—"

"Seize the throne?" he finished her sentence. With a wry smile, he shook his head. "No, Mother, that is not my intent. Rokugan will survive a bit longer without an Emperor. But it will not survive these constant games or the wrath of Daigotsu when he realizes his ploy has failed." At peace, he continued, "When the time is right, we will know the will of the Heavens. Until then, I will continue to fight to make certain that Rokugan is safe.

"The Empire before the Emperor?" Kaede asked softly.

Sezaru nodded. "So it must be." He took her hand for a moment, pressing it between his own. "Be safe, Mother. And do not fear. Daigotsu has manipulated everything from father's death to the imbalance of the heavens, but I am aware of him now. I will turn all the earth to stop him."

Kaede lifted the Dark and Light Covenants and turned to the dragon. "My son is wise. Will you grant me this wish that he might go home again?"

The dragon raised its massive head, yellow eyes spinning with the revolutions of burning suns. As the Void Dragon worked its magic, Sezaru felt a tremendous flow of power rush through him, intoxicating his soul.

The Void Dragon breathed gently on Sezaru, the soft wind rustling through his pale hair and Kaede's black fall, gently showering them both with starlight. The darkness gathered around Sezaru, and then began to merge with the void around them. As the celestial creature's golden eyes drifted into the foundation of the universe, Sezaru felt the world around him shift.

"Farewell, Sezaru," Kaede called to him. "Though this world may never bring us together again, know that I am forever proud of you."

As her voice faded, Sezaru found himself standing on barren plains.

22 SUN AND SHADOW

Hantei Naseru, a stern expression on his chiseled features, stood by the window of the throne room. Without the courtiers assembled to fill the room, it seemed sparse, empty of color and form. Here, within the hallways of Kyuden Miya, the long shadows of the evening stretched out like the fingers of a dead god. White walls painted with watercolor scenes paled without the vibrant kimonos of the assembly before them. The mahogany floor and beams looked over-dark, black painted lines against the white paper walls. Naseru's emerald robes were the only stain of color, a green jewel in the stark and empty room.

As Sezaru entered, Naseru looked away from the sunset. Both brothers paused, bowing fluidly in subtle gestures as the screens slid closed behind the shugenja. Between them, the chamber stretched, a long expanse of silence.

"Good travels, my brother?" inquired Naseru.

"My journey is my own," Sezaru replied. "But at its end, I find another beginning."

"So do we all, Sezaru-san," Naseru said smoothly, turning back on his view to face his brother.

"Why have you called us together, Naseru-san?"

"The others will be here soon, Sezaru. Have patience." Naseru looked out once more toward the sunset and smiled. "Ah. You see?"

Sezaru crossed the chamber, his soft footfalls echoing strangely in the peaceful silence. Reaching Naseru's side, he looked out at the fading sun and saw what had attracted the other man's attention.

Outside, in the courtyard, two strong steeds, one black and one red, galloped to a halt before the palace gates. The samurai upon them dismounted in sweeping gestures, hands gripping the hilt of their swords. One was tall and rugged, his face showing stubble of a week's growth; black armor covered in scars. The other was a tall, golden maiden, her black hair swinging gently in a fox-tail bound by golden cord. She spared not a glance for the man nearest her, looking instead up at the window where her brothers stood. Deep amber eyes spared no room for softness or mercy, her hard features both beautiful and relentless in their resolute demeanor.

They paced up the stairs into the castle together, hardly sparing a glance to the side. Golden and black, sun and shadow, they entered the palace in step. "Only a moment more, my brother," Naseru said softly to Sezaru, "and then we shall all speak together."

Toturi Tsudao and Akodo Kaneka entered the main chamber of Kyuden Miya in tandem, and Naseru smiled. "I thank you for your time, Tsudao-san, Kaneka-san."

"This had better be of importance, Hantei," Kaneka snarled, one hand rubbing the stubble on his face. "I have tasks elsewhere. Tasks of importance."

"I am certain that you do." Naseru smiled. "But I think you will also find this to be of importance. Unless, of course—" he turned away from the window, walking toward the raised dais at the end of the room— "you are no longer interested in avenging our father's death?"

At these words, all three of the other Winds started. Tsudao's eyes narrowed, her hand flexing about her sword's hilt. Sezaru raised an eyebrow.

"Vengeance is a way of life, Naseru," the rough Lion samurai growled. "We, who are born of the Emperor's blood, will never forget his death. Get on with it."

"What Kaneka is trying to say, I'm certain," said Sezaru, "is that we would be honored to hear of any new information you have on our father's killer. The dark priest Daigotsu is enemy to us all."

Sezaru watched Naseru's eyes flicker between the faces of his siblings, betraying nothing of his thoughts.

"Then you must agree with me. It is time we strike Daigotsu and end this for once and all."

"If we knew where to find him—how to strike him—then, yes." Tsudao's cool voice reflected the gathering darkness. "Show me where to strike, and I will end Daigotsu's power."

"Would you strike the gods themselves, my sister?" Naseru said. Gazing for a moment upon her face, he murmured an answer to his own question. "Yes . . . perhaps, in our father's memory, you would at that." Then, he raised his voice, addressing them all, "Well, it is what we shall have to do. To destroy Daigotsu, we shall also have to topple Fu Leng from his seat of power in the heavens. We cannot be content simply with destroying the priest. We must also tear down the god."

"Impossible." Kaneka grunted. "You speak madness. Gods and Dragons cannot be destroyed. They are eternal."

"Gods and Dragons can die, Kaneka," Sezaru whispered, still feeling the wounds of his battle within the Void. "Never assume that anything is forever." His words held a chill ring, and though he could see questions behind the faces of the other Winds, Sezaru said no more. The knowledge had cost him much. They were not ready to pay its price.

"On a certain night, not far from now, Daigotsu will be within his master's greatest shrine—the Temple of the Ninth Kami. On that night, Fu Leng will be watching him very closely, for as the Celestial Heavens pass on that night, prayers must be offered to all of the gods and demons of this world and beyond. That is the time when we must strike. Before their power grows."

"Dangerous." Kaneka rumbled disapproval. "To destroy a priest within view of his god? Will not Fu Leng lend aid to his priest?"

Sezaru laughed, a bitter sound in the vastness of the empty court chamber. "Fu Leng knows no mercy, nor compassion. Daigotsu must prove himself . . . or be destroyed."

Naseru nodded, in league with Sezaru. "It is so."

"But the Temple of the Ninth Kami is deep within the Shadowlands," said Tsudao. "Traveling there will taint us all—and any army we bring with us. To destroy him, we must venture into the darkness. By going there, we may damn ourselves as well as him. The Taint will blacken our souls. We will never again leave."

"Is this some kind of trick?" said Kaneka, stepping forward in sudden, flaring anger. His sword flicked an inch out of its scabbard. "To send us on some mad hunt into the Shadowlands—to taint and death—so that you may claim the throne?"

"Stand down, Akodo-san!" Sezaru opened his fan between the two men. Naseru stood, completely unmoving in the face of Kaneka's rage. "This is no place for your rage! If we are to have any chance of destroying Daigotsu, we must not fall to petty bickering!" Sezaru's too-pale eyes flashed, and glittering sparks danced along the metal edges of his outstretched fan.

"He is right, Kaneka," Tsudao was as cool as ever, though her hand was upon the hilt of her sword. "We must listen before we decide."

After a pause, Kaneka shoved his blade back into the sheath with a curse. "Blood stays together, neh?" he snarled. "I must trust you because they trust you . . . brother."

Naseru still did not move, nor did he respond to Kaneka's jibe. Tsudao and Sezaru exchanged a glance.

"How do you propose we reach the temple, Naseru?" asked Sezaru. "A thousand *li* of Shadowlands lie in our path—a thousand *li* filled with taint. Any army that marches through it will be destroyed long before they reach the temple."

"As will we." Kaneka grumbled, still unsatisfied.

"If you are so unsure," said Naseru, "and so unwilling, then remain. But I will go to the Temple of the Ninth Kami, and Sezaru will take us there. With your magic, brother, you can transport us to the site. I have enough information to give you a reasonable target—and a map to ensure that we can reach the location, with the help of the spirits." Naseru slid a rolled parchment from his sleeve and placed it in Sezaru's hand.

Sezaru unrolled the document, one eyebrow rising in amazement at the depth and detail it held. Many men must have died to acquire this information—deaths of taint and corruption in the heart of the Shadowlands. Looking at it, Sezaru was startled once more by his brother's ability to uncover information.

"It is a great distance," said Sezaru. "Nearly too far, and into those shadowed lands I can bring only a few—perhaps four. Certainly no army." Sezaru's eyes flicked up to focus on Naseru's face once more. "If we face Daigotsu and his onisu demons alone, we will be destroyed before we ever reach the Temple of the Ninth Kami. He has many minions in that dark land. They will surround the Temple and offer their lives to the dark god in order to protect the priest. We do not have the strength to face them all."

"Any army we bring will die in the attempt," Tsudao added. "These plans describe a location more than three months' march into the Shadowlands. Men cannot live that long in the taint. We do not have the jade supplies to protect their souls. Without jade, they will fall to the Shadowlands, and we will have done no more than to march a thousand souls into Fu Leng's jaws."

"Long ago, as you may already know," Naseru continued, "the Phoenix Master of Earth created a spell of great proportions, designed to protect his clan against the darkness when it rose. The spell gave life, gave breath, and gave movement to soldiers formed of clay, such as the Emperors of long ago used to stand within their hallways. But these soldiers were more than statuary created to glorify the past. With the power of his spell, the Master of Earth made them into an army."

"An army of clay?" Tsudao gasped.

Sezaru nodded. "I have read of such a thing in the Asako libraries." For a moment, the thought of those libraries pained him, his memories haunted by Sayuri's face. Pushing aside the image, he continued. "The Master of Earth was Isawa Tadaka, one of the most powerful shugenja in the Empire's history."

"And tainted," Kaneka added. "He died for his taint. Evil magic."

"He was a Thunder," Tsudao countered.

"More than that—" Naseru smiled— "he was a visionary. And his soldiers will walk into the Shadowlands with no fear of taint and no need of jade. You cannot corrupt inanimate beings, Kaneka. These clay soldiers will do our fighting for us. Once they have conquered the guardians at the gate, we four will sweep into the Temple of the Ninth Kami and shatter Daigotsu's power."

Sezaru pondered Naseru's plan. "But in order to enact your idea, my brother, we would have to convince the Phoenix to give us their soldiers."

"We are the children of the Emperor," Tsudao said, raising her chin in pride, "and I am general of the Imperial Armies. If we ask, the Phoenix will not refuse us."

Naseru nodded, a faint smile playing about his lips.

"It is already too late." Kaneka shook his head, fist clenching in impatience and frustration. "The night you speak of is only three days hence. God or no god, plan or no plan, we cannot march an army of clay soldiers that far into the Shadowlands in so short a time."

Sezaru shifted his attention to Naseru, regretfully agreeing with Kaneka's cynicism. "Kaneka is correct. My magic cannot transport an entire army that far into the Shadowlands. I do not believe any shugenja of the Empire could do this. Even a ritual designed to do so would take weeks to prepare. It would involve nearly a dozen shugenja trained to wield that much power. Three days? Impossible."

"I must concur with the others," said Tsudao, her amber eyes somber. "An army cannot march a thousand *li* in three days, no matter how tireless they may be. If this is our only chance, Naseru, then by the Sun we have no chance at all."

"You are all correct." Naseru's smile was that of the fox, free at last within a henhouse. "That is why I gained possession of the army before I summoned you. I have already sent them to the south . . . three months ago."

23 | FIGHT FOR TOMORROW

Deep within the Shadowlands, the heart of Daigotsu's strength, a battle for the Empire's future raged against the backdrop of graying mountains and twisted plains. Sezaru stood on a hillside overlooking the dark temple. It was the heart of Daigotsu's power, the core from which the monsters of the Shadowlands forged their betrayals. Battle raged on the plains below, surrounding the temple and its corrupted city with fire and shadow. Above, the Four Winds stood as a group, looking down at the fury below.

"The walls will soon break," said Toturi Tsudao, who knelt, one knee upon the ground and the other supporting her sword-arm. Her maiden's foxtail spun out like a cat's tail, long and black in the wind. Her golden armor shone in the low rays of the sunlight peeking through the cloud barrier, carrying the banner of the sun into the darkness of the shadow. Eagerness ran through every line of her crouch, like a great cat watching its prey struggling before the deathblow.

"When it does, we will be ready," said Sezaru. He stood at her side, his white hair standing out markedly against the black clouds overhead. He wore the robes of a priest, the robes given to him by his mother upon the day of his manhood. Winged flocks of white cranes spun out in patterns upon the deep red cloth, and the only sword at his side was the small blade of a samurai's honor. Magic swirled at his fingertips, waiting for his summons. "It is but a step from here to Daigotsu's side. With a word, we can be there. And he will be waiting."

"He will, indeed." Naseru's rich voice resounded from the rocky cliffside. "As he has been waiting since the moment he engineered our father's death and Otosan Uchi's fall." Naseru seemed neither impatient nor concerned, looking down on the battle and the dark temple with a steady, even eye. As usual, his hands were folded within the sleeves of his green robes, biding their time before the strike. But beneath the robes, he wore dark green armor that shone like leaves from the depths of the most secret forests.

The last of the Four Winds paced upon the stone of the cliffside, his hand clenching and unclenching the hilt of his katana. Akodo Kaneka snarled, his battered armor dull and covered with the grooves of many failed sword-blows. "I am tired of this darkness, tired of the waiting, and tired of these games. It is time to strike and finish this once and for all."

"Are you so certain we will win, Kaneka-san?" Tsudao said, never lifting her eyes from the battle below. "Daigotsu is more powerful than we guessed. Even now, there is no certainty that we will be able to crush his defenses."

"Give me ten minutes with him, Tsudao, and I will show you the limits of his power." The black-handled sword twisted in his hands in anticipation of the combat.

"Ten minutes?" Tsudao smiled, her full lips curving without humor. Kaneka spat upon the ground, snarling, and Tsudao continued quietly, "I pray the Fortunes for just one strike. With that alone, I will change the world."

"Our soldiers are breaching the last gate," said Sezaru, white hair coiling against his chiseled marble features. "It is time to ride the wind." He raised a white mask from his belt and covered his features with it. The mask, a gift from his mother, would serve as a focus for his spell—and for his revenge. The time had come, at last, to give his father's spirit peace.

He lifted his hands, calling with chants to the air spirits. As he did, the earth trembled, and a great wind swept across the mountain pass. It roared down from above, sweeping dust and leaves before it and carrying the smoke of a funeral pyre upon its laden breath. It raced through the fields, across the twisted plain, and swept against the cliffside where the four children of the Emperor stood.

Within a moment of its passing, they were gone.

* * * * *

Steel clashed on steel. The cries of the injured mixed with the occasional roar of a shugenja's spell. Within the Temple of the Ninth God, a place sacred to darkness and the horrors of the Shadowlands, Daigotsu drew his sword and rose from his throne. He was a tall man, his face marked with cunning and ambition; the perfection of the mask he wore reflecting all around him within its obsidian sheen, yet his body shone with the Taint of the Shadowlands.

He fell into a slow, graceful kata, waiting for his enemies to arrive. Each movement, while perfect, was a mockery of the ancient way of the sword. There was little honor in his poses, only precision—and death at any cost. Darkness and pain lived within his movements. Daigotsu swept the ground with perfect finesse, his blade chasing shadows from the corners of the room, reflecting the too-pale firelight like a mockery of the sun. This temple was his and his alone. Here he would make his stand, beneath the eyes of his dark god, Fu Leng.

Outside, legions of clay soldiers battled his army. Clay and steel shattered themselves against the greatest minions of the Shadowlands. They followed him, these lost souls, and they would die without thought for his goals.

Yet the armies of the Empire were strong—and equally unafraid. Created decades ago by the Phoenix Thunder Isawa Tadaka, the soldiers were a potent weapon against the Shadowlands. The Dark Lord had received reports of the clay soldiers

REE SOESBEE

growing in strength as they battled the Lost, but even that would not help them. They were too few, and the armies of the Lost were too many. No, the clay soldiers were merely a distraction, annoying the Dark Lord's armies while the Four Winds sought out their true enemy. They would arrive. He had no doubt of that.

As if on cue, the doors of the Temple were wracked by a tremendous explosion. A great wind swept through the hall, and one of the doors collapsed entirely. The other hung from its hinges at a strange angle, creaking as the metal bent under its own weight. Smoke and dust poured through the threshold, parting as a tall figure stepped into view. Standing out against the darkness, Daigotsu saw the figure wore a white mask, pale and perfect save for one brilliant touch of red—the forehead marked with the symbol of the rising sun. The figure's red robes billowed in the wind. He seemed a featureless specter behind the mask, stripped of emotion.

"The Wolf," Daigotsu said, saluting with his blade as paused before his throne. "We meet at last."

Toturi Sezaru said nothing, only clapped his hands together and unleashed a plume of brilliant white fire toward the priest of the Dark Lord. Daigotsu swung his no-dachi in a graceful arc, summoning a plume of black flame that served as a shield against Sezaru's spell. He spoke a word of magic and stomped the floor with one foot. As he did, a massive ripple shook through the floor toward Sezaru, floor tiles exploding upward in the shape of grasping claws.

Sezaru folded his fingers into a symbol against evil and shouted a loud *kiai*. The stone shattered harmlessly around him. For a moment, the two stared at one another in silence. Tense lines of spellcraft tightened like a noose between them, each unable to conquer the other's will.

Daigotsu eyed Sezaru carefully, a glimmer of respect in his dark eyes.

Sezaru nodded. "So we would stand in stalemate forever, Daigotsu, neither able to break the other. But you see, I foresaw this. My adventures with the Oracles taught me much of will—and of alliance. I should thank you for that, I suppose."

A faint smile curled Daigotsu's lips. "A lesson you failed, Wolf."

"Failed?" Sezaru smiled. "Because I survived?"

"Because you did not learn the basic principal: that power creates its own right. Power that you have within you, which you fear."

"I fear nothing," Sezaru whispered, his voice carrying without effort. "Least of all myself."

"Then come with me into darkness and prove your bravery. Your magic is as strong as mine. Together, we would be unstoppable."

Sezaru shook his head as if berating a child. "That is no choice at all, Daigotsu. I have spent my life unifying my soul, and I have stepped beyond the heavens to find its strength. I, like my mother, have walked between the stars into the Void. I can never return."

Daigotsu roared in anger at Sezaru's refusal, raising the no-dachi above his head. His anger was palpable, rocking the temple in ripples of white-hot rage—a fury that could only be answered with death and blood.

Before he could strike, another figure stepped from the smoke behind Sezaru. Kaneka strode through the smoke, his blade the only light against his dark armor and demeanor. "You seem evenly matched with the Dark Lord, Sezaru," Akodo Kaneka said, holding his katana in low to his hip with both hands. "Pity for him that you are not alone."

Toturi Tsudao entered behind her brother, her golden armor shining brilliantly in contrast with Kaneka's darkness. As if the Sun itself walked with her, Tsudao shone radiantly, her face peaceful and intent, her golden sword prepared for the future and all that war and battle could bring. "We are never alone, Kaneka-san," she whispered, her amber eyes shining like twin stars. "We are only parted by time and space, but never in truth apart. This is what you never understood, Daigotsu. This is what you will never be able to sunder."

Together, the Winds advanced toward Daigotsu.

Daigotsu sighed. "Children of Toturi," he said, "did you think that this would be your Day of Thunder? All of you together fighting the Dark Lord alone?"

He smiled and spoke a quick spell. Around him, four demonic creatures blurred into existence—Kyofu, Yokubo, Hakai, Muchitsujo, the most deadly of his onisu. They were creatures of nightmare, spirits of evil, blessed by the dark god himself. Behind the shield of their strength, Daigotsu laughed, a vicious, horrible sound.

"Show no fear," Sezaru called to his siblings, raising his hands in a gesture of prayer and summoning forth the spirits once more. "These onisu are his servants, the creatures of the Shadowlands. They feed from darkness, from vice, dishonor, and betrayal." As the powers at his command spread Tsudao's golden light equally among them, Sezaru smiled and faced Daigotsu once more. "They will fail, Daigotsu, as you are destined to fail. We are the sons and daughter of the Splendid Emperor. We bear no such burdens."

"You are wrong, Sezaru," replied the dark priest. "The Empire may have once been a bastion of such things, but the Four Winds have torn it apart. It seems the Celestial Heavens have forgotten Rokugan entirely, and it falls into shadow. *My* shadow. For that—" he laughed again— "I have only the four of you to thank. You have fed my creations well."

Unused to such taunts, Kaneka shouted a *kiai* scream and raised his sword to a strike. "Enough talk!" he shouted, charging forward.

His attack was swift, but crude in its forcefulness. Even as Sezaru watched his half-brother leap into the fray, he heard the whisper of his own soul.

Emotion is the enemy of a samurai. If it is allowed to conquer his will, it will lead him into darkness.

Daigotsu dodged to one side, deftly avoiding the enraged blow. Kaneka's sword buried itself instead in the dark lord's throne, shattering the blade in two. The samurai did not pause, but cast aside the broken sword and drew another. The second sword was much shorter and smaller than the first, but equally deadly. Without pause, Kaneka slashed out again, but once more, Daigotsu moved swiftly away. It seemed as if every strike moved through water, parting only the breeze as Daigotsu moved fluidly beyond its reach. Sezaru saw Daigotsu lift one hand from the hilt of his own blade and gesture the beasts forward into battle.

The onisu charged. The first, Kyofu, swung his tetsubo with a savage roar. Muchitsujo, smaller and more devious, scuttled forward on metallic claws as his brother Yokubo took to the air. The fourth and last, a monstrous demon named Hakai, remained at Daigotsu's side. Instead of attacking with weapons or claws, the demon chanted in a blasphemous tongue, lifting one hand to the sky and unleashing a bolt of unholy flame at Sezaru.

Sezaru smiled beneath his mask. Forget steel and shields—or armor and trappings. *This* was a battle on his territory, a battle he knew he could win. There was no hesitation, only the slow movements of someone perfectly at home with their actions and perfectly in tune with his soul. Sezaru felt the rush of power in his soul, and he drew upon it with both halves of his being. Dark and light, in unison, combined to turn aside the demon's assault. The Wolf summoned a shield of air to protect himself, turning aside the flame. Even with his tremendous power, the bolt struck the flame with a ferocious impact, forcing Sezaru to stagger back from its blow. The fire licked around the edges of the shield, burning away pieces of Sezaru's robes and singing him even through the massive shield. Any other shugenja would have died from the force of it. The wind knocked out of his lungs, Sezaru staggered back. With a shuddering breath, he ignored the terrible burns along his arm and chanted once more.

Power surged between Sezaru, Daigotsu, and Hakai. The room filled with swirling smoke and fire as the battle raged around them and the spirits themselves entered the combat at their command. Hakai advanced upon Sezaru while Daigotsu retreated, standing in the shadow of Fu Leng's statue.

Sensing movement to one side, Sezaru turned to watch his other brother. Alone and nearly forgotten in the fray, Naseru walked across the polished floor of the temple, avoiding both the demons and the magical fire until he reached the dark priest's bastion. Daigotsu turned quickly, holding his sword ready and facing the son of Toturi. Naseru seemed out of place, a thin man in dark green armor approaching without fear, his arms raised in parlay.

Daigotsu chuckled when he recognized him. "Hantei Naseru," he said, eyeing the courtier cautiously. "The Anvil. You do not fight alongside your brethren?"

"I am no warrior, Daigotsu," Naseru said. "I merely came to show them the way."

"You should have remained in Ryoko Owari," Daigotsu said. "Your battle is already lost. Even should I die here, I will become a martyr to the Lost. Their faith in Fu Leng will increase a thousand fold, and his conquest will be assured."

"Their faith in Fu Leng?" Naseru replied mildly. "I see no such thing. Your people do not believe in Fu Leng. They believe in you. You, in turn, believe in him. You are the focus of Fu Leng's power." Naseru looked up at the statue of the fallen kami. "I wonder what will become of you once Fu Leng realizes that he relies so heavily upon you." Naseru's voice was a coiled snake, poised for a devastating strike. "I hope he is a trusting god."

Daigotsu's eyes widened. He felt a sudden shift in the elements, a powerful attention upon his presence. He scowled at Naseru. "My faith in the dark god is absolute!" He hissed. "I shall prove it by destroying you in his name." Daigotsu advanced.

"By all means, slay the man who speaks of your faults beneath the eyes of your god," Naseru said, quickly moving backward like an asp rearing to strike. "I'm quite certain you would not wish for the dark kami to realize that your true plan is to supplant his place in the Celestial Order! After all, Daigotsu, were you not a Bloodspeaker before you were his priest? Did you not give your allegiance then as one of those who will always defy Fu Leng's will? If I were the dark god, I do not think I would rely so heavily on someone who could pose such a threat to me."

Naseru looked at the eyes of Fu Leng's statue. They seemed to gaze back down at Daigotsu in thoughtful disapproval.

"Enough!" Daigotsu shouted. He swung his sword at Naseru, but it was deflected by a metallic clang and flash of brilliant gold.

Toturi Tsudao stood between the dark lord and her brother. Her brilliant amber eyes, lit with the full fire of the sun, glared into Daigotsu's. Golden armor shone brilliantly in the gloom, and she was a shield against even the dark god's wrath. Her face was set in a firm scowl, her sword poised between them like a thin line of impenetrable fire. "You have feasted on enough murder, Daigotsu," she said with a sneer. "Stay away from my brother."

With her words came the wrath of the Heavens, transformed upon the earth. A tremor shook the temple as though the earth trembled beneath the weight of a terrible burden. Daigotsu and Tsudao fell away from each other and stood apart in martial stances.

Magic shifted within the temple, its boundaries and strengths torn asunder like a broken man's tendons. Sezaru stared in horror as spirits died, screaming, their incarnate vessels shattered by the spiritual upheaval. Something was terribly wrong, something beyond this world, created of the anger of a greater spirit.

The wrath of the Celestial Heavens roared like a flight of dragons through the Shadowlands. Screaming and writhing, three of the demons that stood by Daigotsu's side suddenly faded into nothing. Their ethereal shrieks continued long after their bodies had dissipated, filling the temple with a cacophony of pain. Reeling from the sudden shock, Daigotsu stared in terror at the statue of his god.

"What has happened?" Tsudao called out to her brothers, standing between them as they gathered together once more. "Where did they go?"

"They are no more," Sezaru said grimly. Of them all, he was the only one who understood. His brothers and sisters were warriors, not spiritualists. They did not have the temperament or the wisdom to see what lay before them. Only Sezaru, listening to the fading screams of the demons, could see clearly the cause. "Daigotsu serves his dark god faithfully. That, in the end, is his undoing—because his god is no more."

"What do you mean, priest?" Kaneka said, lowering his sword only a few inches. "Gods and dragons cannot die."

Sezaru's mind once more filled with the image of the wound in the Void Dragon's chest. Again he felt the ivory dagger in his hand. "You are a fool, my brother. All things can die." Toturi Sezaru looked up, cradling his burned and injured arm. "Fu Leng has been cast from the heavens." Sezaru felt his mother's presence speaking as if she were beside him, whispering truths into his mind, and he repeated them aloud. "He is no more."

"Impossible!" Daigotsu retorted.

"Your faith in your master was absolute, Daigotsu," Akodo Kaneka said, sharing a wry smile with Naseru. "A pity that your master did not have such faith in you. What happens to a god who draws all his power from your faith? What happens to a priest when his god no longer needs him?"

"No!" Daigotsu roared. He drew a short blade from his waist and slashed it across his arm, spilling his own blood. Blood, Sezaru knew, that powered dark magic. Blood that would fuel the most powerful spell of all. Fu Leng may have turned away from Daigotsu, but he still had his spells. "You may have defeated me, shamed me, and torn me away from my god, but I will do worse still to you. I will destroy the very thing you fought for. I no longer have need for the Empire. Now . . . none will survive."

As Daigotsu's spell took effect, an aura of black fire erupted from his body. The priest of darkness stood laughing within the flames as all around him were scorched by unholy fire. The power boiled outward, consuming everything in its path. Even Sezaru staggered, his magical shields buckling before the onslaught. The dark lord no longer reserved any thought of his own safety. Everything that he was now became focused on destruction alone. The fire would spread outward from this temple, burning all to ash. It would sweep across the Empire and leave nothing—man, woman, or child—alive in its wake. Nothing could survive its touch.

So it was that when Toturi Tsudao charged through the fire, Daigotsu was completely unprepared. Her once-golden armor sagged and melted in the flame's intense heat, unable to withstand the fury of its power. Her skin blistered and burned away, and her long black hair charred into ruin. Still, she kept walking, forcing herself through pain and anguish toward her opponent. Her eyes, amber and glowing with strength, were the only thing that could be recognized in the pounding wave of flame.

"Tsudao!" Sezaru whispered, tensing himself to leap after her. His magic could perhaps protect her, help her, stop her . . .

"No, my brother." Naseru's hand upon his sleeve drew him back to his senses with a cold and final touch. "This is her destiny."

Tsudao did not pause, nor did she move her eyes from anything save Daigotsu's terrified face. Through it all, her gold sun amulet burned brightly, outshining even the flames that surrounded them both.

"For my father," she whispered through lips as black as coal. Summoning the strength for one final blow, she struck Daigotsu down.

The dark lord fell, cleaved through the chest by Tsudao's blade. His black mask shattered and fell away, revealing his true face. Once-handsome Hantei features, now twisted in a bitter scowl, screamed into darkness as the flames consumed both he and his enemy. Without his will to control the fire, it ricocheted back upon him, wrapping them both in a tower of blazing fire before it hissed out into ash.

All that remained of Toturi Tsudao was her golden amulet, now shining on the temple floor within a cloud of black soot and empty stone.

Sezaru, Naseru, and Kaneka stood in silence as they looked upon the aftermath of the battle. All were too greatly shocked to speak, too stunned by their sister's sacrifice.

Sezaru reached up with one shaking hand and removed his mask. Tears streamed down his face as he stumbled forward, falling to his knees beside Daigotsu's charred corpse. He reached down, picked up his sister's amulet, and wrapped his sleeve around his hand to protect it from the heat that still radiated from the golden sigil.

"Why?" was all he could whisper. "Of all of us, why? She was the only one who truly deserved the throne."

"Perhaps that is why she was taken from us," Naseru said in a soft voice. "Perhaps the Empire does not deserve heroes such as the Sword. We must endeavor to better ourselves, to live up to her example, lest her sacrifice be wasted."

"Hm," Kaneka grunted, sheathing his wakizashi. "Lovely words, Naseru, but Tsudao favored actions. Prove your words true if you want to honor her."

Naseru nodded but said nothing.

"Tsudao," Sezaru whispered, clutching her amulet to his chest and sobbing quietly.

Naseru looked away, leaving his brother to his grief, but Kaneka stepped forward. Outside, the sounds of battle grew closer. "Sezaru, we are done here," he said, resting one hand on his half-brother's chest. "We must escape. Is your magic strong enough to take us from this place?"

Sezaru looked up at Kaneka with a glazed, unfocused expression. His mind sought answers, but his spirit sought truth.

Kaneka frowned and shook the Wolf by his shoulder. "Sezaru! Tsudao would not want us to die like this. We must escape before the Lost return to the temple and destroy us all."

Sezaru blinked. "Yes," he said, nodding quickly. "Yes, I can take us from here. I can take us back home, but it is best we flee the temple first. Fu Leng's power is too strong here to risk such powerful magic."

"Then let us hurry," said Naseru. "The Empire awaits us."

24 NEW EMPEROR

The Imperial Court waited in silence.

Light pooled upon the hardwood floors as the rising sun cut through the morning fog. The courtiers of the Empire knelt in rows upon the floor of the chamber, watching the dais with eager, expectant eyes. Their robes shone like pale flowers in the dawning light—purple, blue, yellow, and all the colors of the rainbow. Yet even their brilliant petals could not lighten the mood within the chamber of the Empress.

The world was forever changed.

For the last time, Toturi Kaede entered the royal throne room of Rokugan, her immortal eyes filled with the stars of her position. Within her movements, the coils of the Dragon of the Void flexed and relaxed in perfect rhythm. Her long hair flowed, unbound, like a river of molten night. Over the black and orange robes of the Oracle of Void, she wore the brilliant golden surcoat of the royal house, emblazoned with magnificent chrysanthemums and cherry blossoms. As she walked, it moved against the floor like a burden, cascading from her shoulders. It was the last time she would bear its weight.

The courtiers bowed as she passed them, touching their heads to the floor in utter reverence. Despite their courteous, passive faces, tears shone like newborn stars in many eyes as the Empress passed them by.

Kaede settled herself upon the Steel Throne, her golden robes cascading upon the sterling arms of the tremendous chair. In the far south, the city of the Ninth Temple was besieged; the Winds went to battle against Fu Leng and his dark priest, and the future was made certain. The sun inched across the horizon as Toturi Kaede stared into the Void.

As Daigotsu summoned the final flame, she closed her eyes. When Tsudao sacrificed herself to stop him, Kaede opened them again.

"It is done," she whispered. As one, the courtiers bowed, and a sigh like a summer breeze rustled through the room.

The Empress did not move upon her throne, her once strong presence now suddenly alone and somehow frail. Though the power of the Dragon still moved within her, Kaede's presence upon this realm grew more tenuous with each passing moment. The assembled courtiers watched her with fearful eyes. None doubted that Kaede would not remain in this world for long. She would exist in silence upon the throne until the Winds returned—*if* the Winds returned.

No longer.

The doors of the throne room opened, and the court turned their heads as one. Miya Shoin, Imperial Herald, stepped through the threshold and bowed to the Empress. His usual practiced courtier's countenance was grave as he rose once more.

"Empress," he announced, "the Winds have arrived."

Even as he spoke, the sound of heavy footfalls echoed beside Shoin. Toturi Sezaru swept into the throne room. His long robes were scorched and tattered. Walking into the room behind him, Akodo Kaneka wore dented armor and had a deep gash along one side of his face. Naseru entered last, now dressed in simple robes, the armor he had worn during his journey discarded.

"We have returned, Mother," Sezaru said, bowing tersely. "Daigotsu has been defeated, as you wished."

"Tell them of Tsudao." Kaede whispered, her coal black eyes solemn as she studied her son. "My visions . . . were unclear."

"She perished fighting Daigotsu," replied Naseru, stepping forward and addressing the assembly as well as his mother. "She died a hero, as her father did."

Several of the assembled courtiers gasped, and yet more bowed in sorrow and in honor at the Sword's passage. The story would spread quickly.

"There is more," Hantei Naseru continued. "Fu Leng no longer threatens the Celestial Heavens. He is returned to Jigoku, land of the dead, where he belongs."

Kaede's eyes widened, for that news surprised her. A hushed murmur echoed through the court, surprise not only that Fu Leng's threat was removed, but also that the Oracle had not foreseen it.

"So what becomes of the Empire?" Kaneka asked in a gruff voice. "Who shall take the throne?"

Kaede did not reply, as if the effort to speak were too great. All remembered the last time Kaede had been forced to choose and was stripped from this world as a result. The courtroom paused in tense silence. There was no movement, and even the soft breeze from the courtyard fell to stillness.

Sezaru stood a pace apart from his siblings, his burned hand still clutching Tsudao's medallion. Though his eyes were dry, his shoulders were bowed. He opened his palm, staring down at the golden sun emblazoned upon it.

You could be Emperor, the dark voice whispered in his soul. It seemed frail, distant, as though speaking down a corridor through a watery grave. *You would lead them in strength, in power, and in wisdom. Who better than you to sit upon the throne?*

I am the eldest of the legitimate heirs, Sezaru suddenly realized. Kaneka was illegitimate, and Naseru was the younger brother. Without Tsudao's claim, the throne could be his for the taking.

Sezaru lifted his head, the torn and burned red robes upon his frail body flowing in broken waves. White hair paused upon his shoulders before falling loosely in mimicry of his mother's dark wave, and his eyes lifted from the wooden floor. But before he could speak, his gaze touched upon a kneeling shadow in the corner of the room.

In the corner, Miya Gensaiken knelt, his body robed in humble garb. His once-magnificent presence seemed dimmed by tremendous guilt and pain. The Empress did not spare him a glance, and he did not lift his head even after she was seated upon the dais. Despite his freedom from the Taint, his soul would never be free of the torment of his past. It was Sezaru's gift and final curse that Gensaiken would forever remember what the Taint had forced him to do, and he was destined to spend his life in penance for those crimes.

Gensaiken, when the Taint held him, would have done anything to place Sezaru upon the throne—including risking his own life and the lives of his masters. For some reason, placing the Wolf upon the throne was integral to the Shadowlands' power, a step toward some distant future where the world would bow to the power of their Taint.

Sezaru paused, and his hand reached into his sleeve. There lay Sayuri's final gift, the last shard of the Obsidian Mirror, its black glass cold against his skin. As his fingers brushed against the surface of the mirror, his mind filled with a sudden, horrible vision.

The city of Otosan Uchi, reborn in black marble, with high towers surrounded by crows . . .

The Steel Throne, tinged red with blood, blazing with the stolen power of the sun . . .

A laughing voice, his own, reveling in the release of power beyond mortal understanding . . .

Sezaru's eyes widened as his mind fought the vision, but in his heart he knew it to be true. All his life he had fought the dark voice within his mind, struggled to control and understand it. If he became Emperor, fueled by the political games and the power he would wield, the temptation would overwhelm him. The Steel Throne was no gift to him. It was a trap. The Shadowlands had known this and counted upon it. He would not hand them victory now.

As he made his decision, a serene, beautiful smile passed against his thoughts, her soft eyes and keen intelligence beckoning him even from the distant Phoenix Mountains. Yes. He knew his place, and he understood his purpose. At last. His quest, after all, had never been for the throne. It had always been for truth.

Sezaru stepped forward with a precise bow. "If it makes your decision easier, Mother, I have no desire for the throne. I have my own concerns, and they do not allow time to rule an Empire. I hereby abdicate my claim upon the throne of Rokugan."

Kaede nodded, a look of relief crossing her face, as if the pain of the decision had lessened. She turned to Kaneka and Naseru.

Akodo Kaneka frowned and turned to Naseru, then looked back at Kaede upon the throne. Sezaru whispered a soft prayer under his breath as he watched the two half-brothers eye one another like tigers in a too-small cage. In this moment, the Empire stood poised between peace and civil war.

"It seems to me," Kaneka said at last, scratching the back of his neck, "that the life of an Emperor involves too much politics. The power it offers is an illusion. I prefer my role as Shogun. If you can keep your bargains, Anvil, and allow me to retain my title, I will relieve your mother of this difficult decision and abdicate as well."

"So be it," Naseru said. "So long as I am Emperor, Kaneka, you and your successors will remain Shogun."

A small smile spread across Kaede's face, and she nodded. "So be it then," she said with a small sigh.

Sezaru watched as the courtiers bowed again, as if a great wind pressed the flowers, one and all, to the ground.

"All hail Hantei Naseru," said Kaede, her voice strong and sure, "Emperor of Rokugan, the Righteous Emperor! Let the heralds spread the word across the Empire. On this day, Rokugan finds peace at last. On this day, the Empire recognizes a new Emperor."

Kaede lifted her hands to the heavens, rising and stepping forth from her seat upon the Steel Throne. The golden robe fell from her shoulders, surrounding the steel in shining sunlight as she was released from her final task. The light around her grew brighter and brighter, filling the room with the blessings of the Celestial Heavens.

Sezaru smiled as his mother was freed of the last of her burdens, returned at last to the place where she belonged, beside her Dragon, within the darkness of the Void.

"Farewell, Mother," he whispered, knowing that she would hear him. "May you find your peace at last." Later, Sezaru would swear that within the light, he saw her smile faintly.

In an instant, she was gone. The Steel Throne stood alone on the dais, covered in the gold of her fallen chrysanthemum robe.

The court looked at one another in confusion, but Sezaru only smiled.

"Where . . . ?" whispered a white-haired Crane courtier as the light died. As her voice carried across the suddenly silent room, her face blossomed like a pink sunrise. She all but dived behind her fan in an imitation of a frightened dove.

"My mother has returned to the Celestial Heavens to be reunited with the Dragon of the Void," Sezaru said. "The time of the Oracles is finished, for now."

"What are you waiting for, Miya Shoin?" Kaneka demanded roughly, raising his voice to rumble like thunder in the throne room. "You are the Herald of the Empire! You have news to deliver."

Shoin nodded vigorously and turned to run for the door, but Naseru held forth a restraining hand. The herald ceased his motion as Naseru stepped toward the throne. Naseru lifted his mother's golden robe in gentle hands, folding the silk delicately as he prepared his words. Uncertain, Shoin paused, bowing deeply before the newly named Emperor. "Your will, my Emperor?" he asked.

"Shoin, I do not wish to keep you from informing the Empire of this news, but I have something to add," Naseru said. "For ten years I have worn the name of a villain, for so was the wish of my father, the Emperor. Though the Steel Chrysanthemum and my father are both dead, it was never my right or my wish to defy the will of an Emperor . . . until today."

Sezaru smiled, understanding. Hantei Naseru, brother by birth but given to the Steel Chrysanthemum to be raised, was at last reclaiming his birthright. Their father would be proud.

"From this day forth," Naseru continued, "let me be known as Toturi Naseru, Toturi III."

Sezaru glanced out over the courtiers, reveling in their responses. Some in the court gasped in shock. Some could not keep themselves from grinning in sheer joy. No member of the court, no matter how practiced they were in concealing their emotions, was unaffected. Naseru would be pleased. He could read their loyalty as clearly as the day.

"Why not Toturi II?" asked a Scorpion courtier. Sezaru recognized the man as Bayushi Kaukatsu.

"Toturi III," Naseru's voice rang with firm conviction. "Toturi II was my sister, known henceforth as the Glorious Empress. May all the records of the Empire remember her, and may they praise her name."

"But she was not officially the Empress," said Shosuro Higatsuku. "Her reign was unrecognized—"

Naseru fixed him with an icy glare. "You would dispute the word of the Emperor, and the honor he wishes to bestow upon his sister, who sacrificed all for the Empire?"

None present dared to say a word.

Sezaru watched as his brother's fiery gaze stare out over the gathered assembly, seeming to catch the eyes of each and every courtier that knelt before him. Naseru seemed to radiate their father's awesome presence upon the dais, commanding both attention and respect without a motion or a word. His simple existence drew their gaze, their fear, and now, at last, their trust.

Naseru seated himself upon the Steel Throne. He folded the golden chrysanthemum robe across his lap, letting the magnificent fabric shine in sunlit waves about his feet. He needed no other symbol of office. No markings upon his brow or his hands could capture the regal motion of his eyes. A faint pang went through Sezaru's heart at the sight as he thought for an instant of his sister Tsudao. It could have been her upon that throne, but Naseru would rule as she would have ruled. In their father's name, and with their mother's grace, Rokugan was in good hands.

"With the aid of this noble court," Naseru continued, "and the blessings of the eternal Kami and Fortunes, may my rule be as glorious as my father's."

"Let me be first to bow before you, Naseru-sama," Sezaru said, kneeling before the throne. "If there is anything you wish of me, only speak and it will be done."

"Then from this day forth, you will serve as my Voice, mighty Sezaru," replied Naseru. "It shall be your duty to bring peace between the clans, to insure that arrogance and pride never threaten us again."

"And what of our bargain?" Kaneka demanded, arms folded across his chest. "Shall I remain Shogun as you promised?"

"Of course," Naseru said. "However, you cannot serve me if you are my equal." Naseru's fingers drummed upon the arm of the throne as he considered his options. "Kaneka, you must release those who have sworn personal fealty to you and renounce your ties to the Lion Clan immediately. The Shogun's armies will be built anew, to serve me."

Kaneka's eyes narrowed. "You would make me a wave man? A ronin, sworn to no man?"

"Certainly not!" Naseru frowned. "I have no doubt that any Clan Champion would be honored to offer you fealty . . . brother."

Sezaru nodded. It was the first time Naseru had openly recognized his blood ties to Kaneka. The gesture offered Kaneka full legitimacy within the eyes of the Empire. Kaneka's place would forever be secure. His children and his lineage would be forever tied with the Steel Throne.

With that, Doji Akiko, Master of Water from the Elemental Council, stepped forward. "If the Shogun would learn the ways of peace, then what better clan than the Phoenix? We would be pleased to have the Shogun among our number."

Naseru looked at Kaneka. "Is this acceptable?"

Kaneka scowled. "Very well then, brother. If Akiko will have it, I shall swear fealty to the Shiba. Within a year my armies will be even greater than before—all for your glory, of course. My brother."

"Indeed. Brother."

Kaneka bowed before his Emperor.

"And you, Sezaru?" Naseru asked, looking at the Wolf. "If you are to serve, you must find your place among a clan as well."

"Then let that clan be my mother's." Sezaru smiled with the memory of a far away mountain in his mind. "I will also join the Clan of the Phoenix. I have much to do there—and, I think, a debt to repay." He turned to Isawa Nakamuro, the Master of Air. "Is this acceptable?"

"Of course, Sezaru-sama," Nakamuro said with pride.

"We have an Emperor at last," Doji Tanitsu said with a sad smile. "This is a new day for the Empire!"

"To say the least," Naseru replied with a firm nod. "Now gather around, my court. We have much work yet to do. . . ."

* * * * *

Sezaru slipped out of the throne room, unnoticed in the press of issues and gladness that radiated from the assembly. His absence would not be noticed for some time, if at all. He walked through the Imperial Gardens, the white path crunching beneath his footfalls. Red robes swirled about his legs, their tattered edges brushing soft patterns in the sand.

Behind him, the Empire rose to greet the morning sun.

Before him . . . the unknown.

It gave Sezaru a strange sense of uncertainty. Since his father's death, he had turned his every action toward unraveling mysteries—finding his mother, avenging his father, seeing that his brothers and sisters opened their eyes to the truth. Now that the war was won, the battle finished . . . what was the Wolf to do?

"My master?" a soft voice behind him called.

Sezaru turned and saw Angai and Koshei kneeling upon the garden path, their dark heads bowed in reverence.

"Yes?" Sezaru's lips curled in a faint smile, his white hair rippling against his shoulders.

"The horses are ready to leave at your will, or they can be stabled, as you prefer." Angai said, her tone implying the question she left unasked: What will we do now?

Sezaru lifted his face to the wind. He remembered his father's words: *Remember, Sezaru-san. Nothing is more important to a leader than knowing what to take and what to leave aside.*

"Ready the horses to ride north—to the Phoenix lands," Sezaru replied. "As the world is reborn, so too are its puzzles. There are many things we do not yet know. My brother, the Emperor, cannot rule without allies. He will need us, and he will need our answers. We will do as we have always done, my friends. We will ask questions . . . and we will find the truth."

EPILOGUE

Black whispers threaded through pale, forgotten stars, shimmering like hidden lanterns behind the veil of night. Images flashed, almost too quickly to comprehend. Here there were no soft bedchambers, no quiet murmurs of a beloved to his dream. The stars were harsh and cold, colored with forgotten regret and the anger of a god denied.

This was the darkness at the heart of it, where no true star dared shine its light and all things fell to pieces. Broken, shattered, denied, but not dead. Never allowed the peace of death, or the silence that such would bring. Instead, fleeting images of denied joy, ruptured bodies and broken souls shattered by dishonor and hatred. These were the things that the mirror carried in its black, cold heart.

Somewhere in the darkness, a silent scream torn from madness haunted the images in their careless paths. It split through their peaceful recollection, reflecting from movements repeated time and again through immaterial immortality. The memories did not notice, reoccurring in their dubious patterns without regard to their prisoner.

This was not the Void, not emptiness and peace. This was eternal suffering, damnation, and indomitable madness. A place where fingers could not touch, nor lungs breathe, nor voice avail. Only images that would not change, repeating endlessly their cycle of betrayal, loss, greed and pain . . .

The darkness and the evil within it educated him. His eyes were ripped open, forcing him to watch each inflicted pain, each treachery. He learned, the madness in his soul drinking it in. It was nourishment to his tattered soul, giving it purpose where there was only emptiness. He clung to it, learning to revel in the torment—both his own and those of others, ceaselessly spinning in a spiral of anguish and despair. He watched the passion plays before him, learning from each expression—repeated endless times—and each movement. Soon, he came to know them as his own

Slowly, over time, the screaming turned to silence, the silence to mockery, and in the end the mockery became laughter. He knew what they did not, remembered the myth that never touched their hearing.

One day, when the mirror shattered again, he would be released.

The Hunter's Blades Trilogy

New York Times best-selling author
R.A. SALVATORE
takes fans behind enemy lines in this
new trilogy about one of the most popular
fantasy characters ever created.

THE LONE DROW
Book II

Chaos reigns in the Spine of the World. The city of Mirabar
braces for invasion from without and civil war within. An orc king
tests the limits of his power. And *The Lone Drow* fights
for his life as this epic trilogy continues.

Now available in paperback!

THE THOUSAND ORCS
Book I

A horde of savage orcs, led by a mysterious cabal of power-hungry
warlords, floods across the North. When Drizzt Do'Urden and
his companions are caught in the bloody tide, the dark elf ranger
finds himself standing alone against *The Thousand Orcs*.

R.A. Salvatore's
War of the Spider Queen

Chaos has come to the Underdark
like never before.

New York Times best-seller!

CONDEMNATION, *Book III*
Richard Baker

The search for answers to Lolth's silence uncovers only more complex
questions. Doubt and frustration test the boundaries of already tenuous
relationships as members of the drow expedition begin to turn on each other.
Sensing the holes in the armor of Menzoberranzan, a new, dangerous threat
steps in to test the resolve of the Jewel of the Underdark, and finds it lacking.

Now in paperback!

DISSOLUTION, *Book I*
Richard Lee Byers

When the Queen of the Demonweb Pits stops answering the prayers of her
faithful, the delicate balance of power that sustains drow civilization crumbles. As
the great Houses scramble for answers, Menzoberranzan herself begins to burn.

INSURRECTION, *Book II*
Thomas M. Reid

The effects of Lolth's silence ripple through the Underdark and shake the drow
city of Ched Nasad to its very foundations. Trapped in a city on the edge of
oblivion, a small group of drow finds unlikely allies and a thousand new enemies.

Starlight & Shadows

New York Times best-selling author Elaine Cunningham finally completes this stirring trilogy of dark elf Liriel Baenre's travels across Faerûn! All three titles feature stunning art from award-winning fantasy artist Todd Lockwood.

New paperback editions!

DAUGHTER OF THE DROW
Book 1

Liriel Baenre, a free-spirited drow princess, ventures beyond the dark halls of Menzoberranzan into the upper world. There, in the world of light, she finds friendship, magic, and battles that will test her body and soul.

TANGLED WEBS
Book 2

Liriel and Fyodor, her barbarian companion, walk the twisting streets of Skullport in search of adventure. But the dark hands of Liriel's past still reach out to clutch her and drag her back to the Underdark.

New in hardcover – the long-awaited finale!

WINDWALKER
Book 3

Their quest complete, Liriel and Fyodor set out for the barbarian's homeland to return the magical Windwalker amulet. Amid the witches of Rashemen, Liriel learns of new magic and love and finds danger everywhere.

The foremost tales of the FORGOTTEN REALMS® series, brought together in these two great collections!

LEGACY OF THE DROW COLLECTOR'S EDITION
R.A. Salvatore

Here are the four books that solidified both the reputation of *New York Times* best-selling author R.A. Salvatore as a master of fantasy, and his greatest creation Drizzt as one of the genre's most beloved characters. Spanning the depths of the Underdark and the sweeping vistas of Icewind Dale, Legacy of the Drow is epic fantasy at its best.

THE BEST OF THE REALMS
A FORGOTTEN REALMS *anthology*

Chosen from the pages of nine FORGOTTEN REALMS anthologies by readers like you, *The Best of the Realms* collects your favorite stories from the past decade. *New York Times* best-selling author R.A. Salvatore leads off the collection with an all-new story that will surely be among the best of the Realms!

November 2003